The Women *Who* Stand Between

JEANNÉE SACKEN

www.ten16press.com - Wauwatosa, WI

Published by Ten16 Press, an imprint of Orange Hat Publishing

www.orangehatpublishing.com
Wauwatosa, WI

Cover design by Kaeley Dunteman
Editing and interior design by Lauren Blue
Author photo © Agnieszka Tropiło

A vivid, multi-layered story that enthralled me from start to finish. Jeannée Sacken's love and knowledge of Zimbabwe and its wildlife and people shine in this gripping and inspiring novel. It's a page-turning adventure story with feminist heart and depth that swept me away and had me applauding Julia and the Mambas.

—Penny Haw, award-winning author of *Follow Me to Africa* and *The Invincible Miss Cust*

Jeannée Sacken's *The Women Who Stand Between* is a deeply moving and timely novel that gives voice to both the beauty and complexity of Zimbabwe. Set within the vast, vulnerable landscapes of Hwange National Park, this story powerfully illuminates the human cost of conservation and the silent battles women face behind the lens and beyond.

As a Zimbabwean, I felt seen and respected in these pages. Sacken writes with careful sensitivity, highlighting the strength of our local communities and the often-overlooked heroines—like the Mambas, Zimbabwe's real-life female anti-poaching unit—who are reclaiming their place in history. This is not a tale of Western saviourism. It's a story of solidarity, resilience, and sisterhood told with grit, grace, and empathy.

The Women Who Stand Between is a love letter to the wild and a rallying cry for justice. It stands as a shining example of how fiction can honour real stories, stir global consciousness, and elevate the voices of African women in our ongoing fight to protect what matters most.

—Thembelihle Moyo, Zimbabwean playwright and cultural storyteller

I couldn't put down this suspenseful and moving story of a cinematographer reclaiming her creative passion in solidarity with a group of all-women wildlife rangers in Zimbabwe.

As Julia Wilde makes a film about the Mambas—an impressive

female anti-poaching unit—she uncovers painful realities, from ruthless poaching rings to professional betrayals, all of which ultimately drive her to step into her own power. In the atmospheric Zimbabwean setting, elements of mystery, suspense, love, and friendship come together in Julia's gripping journey, bringing her face-to-face with the most brutal predators of all—entitled men. The jaw-dropping landscape, wild animals, and local communities come to life, thrumming with authenticity through the sensitive lens of author Jeannée Sacken, whose photography experience in the region shines through.

I devoured this captivating mystery-thriller while gaining insights into urgent issues that span the conservation of endangered species to female empowerment, all the way from Hollywood to Zimbabwe. *The Women Who Stand Between* is armchair travel at its most compelling—it will leave you breathless, transported, and enlightened.

—Laura Resau, author of *The Alchemy of Flowers*

I'm, admittedly, a big fan of Jeannée Sacken's Annie Hawkins series, so I was eager to get my hands on her newest—*The Women Who Stand Between*. Sacken's novels all contain exciting plots, rich characters, and outstanding writing—the things that make books memorable and a joy to read. But the thing that sets her stories apart is her cinematic writing. Like a movie, she has the ability to transport readers to a different land and immerse them in its culture.

The danger that dogs the heels of the documentary makers is omnipresent, palpable, and comes from all sides—humans, animals, the terrain, and the weather. The visual and sensual descriptions make the landscape, the people, and most importantly, the wildlife come alive in the reader's imagination. It will not be surprising to learn that Jeannée Sacken has traveled to Africa many times to photograph elephants and lions, among many other of its denizens. Take a look at her website, and you'll know what I mean! And the Black Mambas are not fictional. Check them out. They are awesome. Without hesitation: five stars.

—Jennifer Trethewey, author of the Highlanders of Balforss Series

Absolutely riveting! Jeannée Sacken proves herself a master storyteller on every level. Her writing immerses you in a vivid, intricately detailed setting that feels so real—I swear I could feel the hot, dusty air on my skin. The characters are raw, authentic, and emotionally layered, guided by the sure hand of a truly skilled novelist. The suspense builds beautifully, with a pace so expertly managed I was practically holding my breath as I raced through the pages. Most importantly, what I love about this novel and Sacken's other stories is how she weaves compelling fiction from real-world situations, opening a window into places and issues we might never otherwise encounter.

Smart, gripping, thought-provoking, and deeply satisfying—this is storytelling at its finest.

—Valerie Biel, award-winning author of *Circle of Nine: Mercy in the Mist*

As she did so masterfully with Afghanistan in her Annie Hawkins novels, author Jeannée Sacken once again transports readers—this time to the wilds of Zimbabwe—with vivid detail, emotional depth, and a deep respect for the land, its wildlife, and its people.

Jeannée Sacken has crafted a compelling, multi-layered narrative that explores resilience, betrayal, conservation, and justice. With heart-pounding suspense, richly drawn characters, and a stunning African backdrop, this novel is a gripping thriller, a testament to strong women and their choices, and a powerful tribute to those fighting for what's wild and worth saving.

—Patricia Sands, bestselling author of the Love in Provence series

Pitch-perfect from the first chapter to the very last page, Sacken bares her soul amidst the breathtaking beauty of Africa, where both man and beast prove treacherous. *The Women Who Stand Between* is fraught with tension and danger and a passion so strong it transcends continents. A must-read.

—Barbara Conrey, *USA Today* bestselling author of *Nowhere Near Goodbye*

Also by Jeannée Sacken

Behind the Lens
Double Exposure
The Rule of Thirds
Depth of Field

For

Jamie and Jennifer
Kili and Cody

and

the women of the Black Mambas and the Cheetahs and
the men of the Cobras who every day risk their lives to
protect endangered species

One

Zimbabwe – early August 2017

The lions arrive at the water hole late in the afternoon, the moment the western sky blazes red with the setting African sun. There are five of them, all males, possibly brothers. From where I'm standing on top of the steel shipping container partially buried in the Kalahari sand, they look to be fairly young, their golden manes still just fringes around their heads. I'm guessing they've only recently been kicked out of their natal pride and sent off to fend for themselves until they're strong enough to take over a pride of their own. The heat of the dry season has left them thirsty. From the looks of their sunken flanks, they're probably also hungry. Very hungry.

A go-away bird screeches its warning to the rest of the animals. The zebras, their black-and-white striped coats glimmering in the rosy light, paw the sand into clouds of dust to conceal their retreat. Already skittish, the large kudu backs away from the water's edge. He ducks his whirled horns, then sprints into the nearby mopane woods—his harem in close pursuit. I look at the fifty-some elephants knee-deep in the water. Mothers trumpet to their frolicking calves, gathering them close and draping their trunks across the babies' backs. Safe for now.

But hungry lions can wait them out. There's no way the cats will just have a drink and leave. The prospects for a meal are too good.

Completely exposed, I wonder if maybe my crew and I should retreat down inside the hide. Next to me, his legs dangling over the edge, our intrepid guide, Tonderai, doesn't seem at all worried. He can read animals better than anyone I've ever worked with. Of course, he's also got a .375 Winchester hunting rifle—a gun that packs a wallop of a kick and can bring down an elephant with a single shot. He's also got a belt of seriously big cartridges buckled around his waist. Unlike me. I'm operating cine camera number one and am positioned directly in front of the water, the best possible place to record this segment of the great elephant migration across Zimbabwe's Hwange National Park. Standing behind me—one of the sound guys with his boom and a guy from lighting who's keeping a close eye on his tungsten panels.

I look down the length of the water hole to the solar-powered pumping station—the second-best place from which to film—and wave at the rest of the crew. Two more guys on lighting and sound. Kyle on camera two is intently filming the lions. He's a great guy to partner with—anything I miss, he's sure to get. Next to him, our director Hal DeBeers, raises his hand in return. Hal is one of the best wildlife documentary directors around. I'm beyond lucky to be working with him.

My camera secure on its tripod, I get back to filming. And hope for some action.

The lions finish drinking and lift their heads, eying the elies. One by one, they push themselves to their feet and amble casually along the edge of the water until there are lions stationed equidistance all the way around the water hole. And around the elephants. I zoom in on a couple of the lions until I can see their muscles tensing. They mean business. Their strategy is obvious. With no hope of bringing down one of the mothers, they're aiming to create enough fear so the elephants will eventually charge out of the water. In the resulting chaos, they'll pick off a youngster.

Trapped, the elephants watch. Besides an occasional flap of the ears, they seem calm—deceptively calm. I'm shifting my focus to the elephant who looks to be the matriarch when, in the blink of an eye, she lifts her trunk and bellows. The mothers splash their enormous gray bodies through the water, forming a protective ring around the youngsters.

Next to me, my producer and boss Alex Silver rests his hand on my shoulder. "This is great stuff, Julia, but it's getting kind of dark. You sure you're getting it all?"

Damn it! He knows the number one rule of the game: no talking. Then, his hand trails slowly down my back, lingering at my waist. Way too close to a caress. And not for the first time.

Take your fucking hand off me! Not that I can risk my job by saying it out loud. All I can do is step sideways away from his proprietary grasp and trust editing to take care of his talking in post-production. Please let him start hanging out with Kyle instead of me.

Another trumpeting bellow, this one much louder than the matriarch's. And a lot closer. I ease the camera around and focus on the huge bull elie just now rounding the front corner of the hide—maybe fifteen feet from where I'm standing. His enormous tusks reach nearly to the ground—a super tusker. There's a bit of a swagger to his step, and now he's raising his trunk high above his head, all the better to sniff out the tense situation in front of him. And, of course, the humans atop the hide. Trailing behind him: three other large males. Put them together, and they probably weigh close to fifty thousand pounds.

I spot the tell-tale hormonal secretions running down the lead elephant's temple. This guy's in musth, which means he's got sixty times the normal level of testosterone coursing through him, making him totally unpredictable. Not to mention, ready to go on a rampage at a moment's notice. From the corner of my eye, I see Tonderai scramble to his feet and clasp his rifle, poised to lift it into position and fire. Probably just a warning shot. The last thing any of us wants to do is kill an elephant.

The elie stops right in front of me. Before I have a chance to react, to maybe dive to the roof of the shipping container, he swings his head toward us. As his trunk arcs over my camera, I absolutely freeze. Which is exactly the wrong thing to do.

He misses me but comes close enough to my head that he's able to snag my New York Mets baseball cap. He also takes out one of the lighting panels, sending it crashing to the ground. Somehow, though, he spares my camera and doesn't touch me, but it's a close call. If he'd hit me, I'd be dead. Or even worse, seriously mangled. Now I smell him—musky. There's an acidic odor, too—urine I bet. Like most elephants in musth, he's probably dribbling.

Even though my hands are shaking like crazy, and I'm having one hell of a hard time breathing, I somehow manage to keep filming. Through the viewfinder, I watch him take one more look at us, disinterested at best, then, still clutching my cap with the two fingers at the end of his trunk, he moves on toward the water hole, picking up his pace with each step until he's running. A full-out charge toward the lions.

Standing next to me, Tonderai doesn't break the rule of silence everyone but Alex recognizes. Instead, he rests his hand lightly on my forearm and catches my eye. *You're okay?* Oh, and where is Alex anyway? Why isn't he making sure I'm all right?

Nodding, I'm immediately back to the lions, who aren't waiting around. They recognize the danger they're in—even if I didn't—and scatter into the bush at warp speed.

Against all odds, I get it on film.

"Did you get that last bit?" Alex's voice sounds strange, pitched high and almost strangled. Once again, his hand is at my waist.

When is he going to stop asking me that?

Adrenaline pumping, I shut off the camera and turn to face him, wishing I could tell him off. The last remnants of the setting sun show me how pale he looks. And frightened. It occurs to me that he wasn't scared for me but for himself. What a prick! I'd like nothing more than to knee him in the balls. And that's when I look down at his crotch. Even in the dimming light, I can see the dark splotch. So, it wasn't the bull elephant I smelled.

"Yeah," I say, "I got it."

I zip my puffer jacket against the cold night air and scoot my lawn chair closer to the campfire. Despite wearing only light-weight windbreakers and shorts, the rest of the guys stay where they are, but eventually, even they stretch out their legs toward the fire. Each time I come to southern Africa in the dry season, I'm surprised by how quickly the temperature plummets once the sun sets and the heat of the day fades away. Especially here at the edge of the Kalahari Desert. But at least I read the packing details in the memo *National Geo* sent us. Apparently, the rest of the crew didn't bother. Or they're manning up. Our pilot Brent's also clad in khaki shorts, but he's a Zimbo—a white Zimbabwean born and bred—and presumably knows what the nights can be like in Hwange.

On the other side of the fire, Tonderai is bundled in a padded khaki Wildlife Safari jacket, his closely shaved head covered by a knitted ski cap. "I think maybe the tusker this afternoon was attracted to you." He smiles broadly to let me know he's teasing. "I am thinking he liked your red hair."

So maybe he's not teasing. Damn, I let it hang loose today. "I guess I should go back to my ponytail."

"Sometimes the color red excites animals . . . but your hat, it could have caught on your ponytail, and if the elephant had pulled. . ." He doesn't need to spell it out. A moment later, he's on to a different subject. "It was a surprise to see the baggage handlers this evening."

Kyle takes a long pull from his bottle of Zambezi lager then eases back in his chair and crosses his ankles. "Baggage handlers?"

"The five lions we saw at the end of the day, we call them the baggage handlers. Usually, they stay near Marula Camp. I have never seen them come down here to Jozibanini."

"Wait!" I laugh. "What's with the name?"

"Ah." Tonderai's smile reaches me through the sparking flames. "That is a good story. There was a kitchen worker at one of the camps on the Ngamo Plains. When his leave to visit home came, he wrapped up a great deal of the camp's meat in aluminum foil. Then, he packed it in his duffel, hiding it at the very bottom." He takes a sip of the full-bodied South African Pinotage our camp staff is serving tonight. "I drove him to the airstrip. When the plane landed, he left his duffel for the pilot to put in the cargo hold and started to climb aboard. But before the pilot could load the bag, there came the five lions we saw today, running toward the plane. They went straight for the duffel and ripped it apart—"

"Ha! Good one. That's why you call them the baggage handlers! Because they helped themselves to the baggage. Funny how you guys come up with names!" Alex slaps his thigh and finishes off his Zambezi. His beer bottle clinks against the three empties in the sand next to his chair.

"*Yebo.*"

Am I imagining things, or does Tonderai sound slightly deflated? I'm sure he would've liked to finish his story.

"More wine, Mrs. Julia?" One of the staff members hovers with the bottle over my raised glass.

For a moment I consider saying, "It's Julia. Or Ms. Wilde." But I don't. I've given up trying to correct the staff because I've come to realize "Mrs." is a sort of honorific—for white women. "Please. It's delicious." And it is, with lovely hints of red berries.

"What say we spend these few minutes before dinner talking about tomorrow?" Hal really has a great way of making Kyle and me feel like we've got a voice in the shooting schedule. The rest of the guys on the crew like him, too. He's a great manager.

Alex raises his new bottle of beer and leans forward—as if to take over—but Hal gives him a look that shuts him down.

"Let's have Brent take Julia and me up in the morning." Hal sounds excited. "I'd like to get some aerial footage of elephants moving through the bush. Maybe eating and heading toward the next water hole. It'd be great to find a big herd."

"Love it!" says Kyle, toasting me with his Zambezi. He knows that as camera one, I'll be the photog on the plane.

"Brilliant! I'm in." Brent rubs his jawline. "About time I did some work on this project instead of sitting around watching you lot have all the fun. Let's make it early, though. We go up any later than, say, ten, the thermals will make the air too choppy to film."

Hal grins. "Tonderai, could you follow in the jeep with Kyle and Alex?" He looks at the rest of the crew. "You lucky dogs can all sleep in. Just be ready to go when we get back."

Across from me, Alex glowers. "I think maybe I—"

"I'll need you on the ground, Alex." For all his equanimity, Hal sounds decided. Then, with a clap of his hands, he pushes himself to his feet. "Okay, everyone. We've got a plan. Just in time for dinner."

Jozibanini Camp is remote, but the chef doesn't skimp on meals. We've scarfed down bowls of acorn squash soup, homemade rolls, more wine and beer, and are waiting for our steaks that are sizzling on the nearby grill. Feeling comfortably warm, thanks to my jacket and the wine, I lean back in my chair and look at the sky. Above me, the firmament is alive with billions of stars. So vivid—especially with no light pollution down here to rob them of their grandeur. I locate the Southern Cross and am feeling inordinately proud of myself, ready to point it out to the guys, when I hear sharp cracks explode in the distance.

Glancing around the table until my eyes meet Tonderai's, I see that he knows exactly what we've all just heard.

Gunshots.

"What the hell?" This is from Alex.

"Most likely it is poachers." Tonderai's voice is grim but matter-of-fact. "It is a problem, still. They want the tusks."

"But CITES has a ban on selling," I say before thinking it through.

"Zimbabwe and a few other countries lobbied for permission to sell their stockpiles," Tonderai explains. "We need the money those sales could bring in. CITES denied their applications, but that doesn't mean the poaching has stopped. The ring leaders hire poor villagers to do the dirty work, then they smuggle the ivory out and sell it on the black market— mostly to China."

"So, the poachers are still making a fortune." I curl my fingers into fists.

Tonderai holds up his index finger to correct me. "Only the leaders make much money. Not the men in the villages who do this work because they are desperate to feed their families."

Alex rams his elbows on the table. "Sounds like you think poaching is okay."

Tonderai smiles. The total professional, he's not about to let Alex's belligerence draw him into an argument. "What I think is that it is never right to kill an animal for profit, especially one that is endangered. But in Zimbabwe, as in Zambia and Mozambique, it is a complicated situation."

"A lot of corruption." Alex isn't giving any ground.

"Yes." Tonderai nods.

I try to steer the conversation away from politics. "Those gunshots sounded close. Do you think we're safe here?"

"There is no need to worry. Those poachers are after elephants, not Americans."

After dinner, the guys decide to keep drinking. They're quick to invite me to join them, but I opt to give them some time without me around and ask Tonderai to walk me to my tent. It's a long walk. For some reason, I ended up in the tent farthest from the center of camp. Not that I wander around in the dark, but I would've thought that the only woman on the crew might have drawn the long straw and been a bit closer in. Still, with my tent pitched on a platform a good ten feet off the ground, I'm sure to be safe for the night. Tonderai must see me counting the steps as I climb. "The lions will leave you alone. But the elephant highway is right next to your tent. You may hear them eating mopane leaves."

"Thanks for escorting me."

"It is my pleasure. Please, I hope you enjoy your evening."

There are no more gunshots, and the night is quiet, except for the distant conversation around the campfire. To my delight, the elephants are quick to make their presence known, shaking tree branches and munching on butterfly-shaped mopane leaves next to my tent, offering the occasional deep rumble. After I wash my face and brush my teeth in the bathroom out on the back deck, I climb on the toilet to peer over the canvas walls in hopes of seeing some elies. But they're gray, and the night is dark, especially here under the canopy of trees. No matter how long I stare, I can't see them. Back inside my tent, the screens and flaps securely zipped shut, flashlight at the ready in case I need to make a midnight run out to the bathroom, I crawl into the double bed. Then, snuggling under the thick woolen blankets, I let the elephants' gentle noises lull me to sleep.

Sometime later, I wake to the sound of scrabbling on the canvas at the front of my tent. A poacher? Or maybe an animal? Could a lion possibly have climbed the steps to the platform? Grabbing my flashlight, I whisper, "Tonderai? Hal?"

"For God's sake, Julia, let me in!" the man says way too loudly.

Alex? Seriously?

"Julia? Fuck, I know you're in there." He's talking loudly enough that everyone in camp must be able to hear him. And, oh God, they're all going to think we arranged for him to come to my tent.

I cross over to the front flap and do my best to keep my voice low and firm. "Alex, go away! Go back to your tent."

"Let me in!" he yells.

More than anything, I want to shut him up. I sure don't want the rest of the guys thinking I've had any part in this. *Please,* I want to shout across to the other tents, *some help here!* But no matter how hard I listen, hoping to hear footsteps pounding on the path, all I can hear is Alex's heavy breathing. No one is coming to bail me out.

Finally, before he yells again, I do what I know is absolutely the wrong thing and unzip the screen, then the flap. Alex is right there and pushing his way inside. How well I know if he gets any further into my tent, there'll be no getting him out. I try to stop him, but he's in, then halfway to my bed, practically dragging me after him. Moving his hands to either side of my face, he pulls me against his chest and lowers his lips to mine. He opens his mouth, and oh, God, he reeks of booze.

I push him back. "You're totally wasted!"

He laughs and grabs my wrists. "Not totally. I still know how to give you a good time."

"No. Not interested."

"Oh, I think you are."

"I said 'no.'"

"You know you want me."

"No! I don't."

He tightens his hold. Even drunk, he's strong. After several futile attempts to pry his hands off my wrists, it's clear I need a different strategy. I probably have only one shot at this, but his crotch is at the perfect height. Leaning in close, I whip up my right knee. And connect.

He all but crumples to the floor. Barely able to move. Which is actually a very bad thing, because I want him out of my tent. Somewhere in the deep recesses of his saturated and atomized brain, he seems to realize he should retreat. He staggers to the front of the tent and then trips over the tent flap to the deck, where he finally collapses into a fetal position. Complete with moans. The elephants aren't happy with him being there, though, and after a chorus of their angry bellows, I hear him stumble down the steps and shuffle off to his own tent.

A half hour later, when I'm confident he won't come back, I climb back under my blankets and wonder if I should tell Liam about what happened. My husband's in the business— on the other side of the camera. An actor. The first couple years we were together, he was struggling to get any role he could, but now he's landing some guest appearances on TV shows like *Law & Order* and *NCIS*. And just last year, he had a lead actress come on to him. So, he knows how rampant sexual predation is on and off the set. And how wrong it is. He'd empathize. And it'd piss him off, maybe to the point of saying something to Alex, telling him to leave me alone.

Wouldn't he?

But this is Alex Silver—one of the biggest names in Hollywood. Lest I forget, Liam made me promise to get in good with Alex to help get him a shot at a role in an upcoming film. Honestly, telling Liam could go either way. Not that I can tell him anything until the job is over and I get to Johannesburg. Here in Hwange, we're about as off the grid as you can be.

I twist under the covers until the sheet is curled tight around my legs. It's probably best not to buy trouble with Liam. What's the point? He's not a big-enough name to take on the likes of Alex.

Instead, I listen to the elephants once again rustling among the leaves. Except sleep is impossible. My thoughts keep drifting to Alex. How much will he remember in the morning? And how will he spin it?

Two

Still yawning from lack of sleep, I'm the last to arrive at breakfast, my Pelican case with my camera in hand. The guys are chowing down on the full English of eggs and sausage, bacon and mushrooms, tomato and baked beans. And they're all staring at their plates, avoiding eye contact with me. Clearly, they heard Alex and me last night. Can they honestly believe I led him on?

"Something to drink?" At least Tonderai is speaking to me.

"Just coffee, please." No way am I eating a huge meal before going up in the light wing Cessna. Even though Brent promised a smooth flight, I can already feel the day heating up and well know the turbulence those thermals create, especially at one thousand to fifteen hundred feet.

I haven't taken more than a sip, when Hal waves me over. "A word?" He walks me away from the table where Kyle and Alex and Brent are still focused on their plates.

Something's going on.

Hal smiles—sympathetically, it seems to me. "A change of plans. Alex and Kyle are flying with Brent this morning. You and I will ride with Tonderai in the jeep."

I tighten my hold on my mug, but not in time to stop hot

coffee from sloshing over onto my hand. So, this is how Alex is getting back at me. Not what I was expecting, and I'm not sure how to respond without making things worse. Which means I should probably keep my mouth shut, but I don't. "Sorry, I don't understand. I'm camera one. I do the overhead shots. It's in my contract." Of course, Hal already knows this.

Hal strokes his chin—a clear sign he knows more than he's telling me. But what he says next is my second surprise of the day. "Alex got a look at your reaction when that elephant took a swing at you yesterday. Said you were pretty shaken. I need steady hands up there, especially if there are any thermals."

"I wasn't the one who peed my pants," I say softly, hoping he hears me. Then hoping he doesn't.

"What's that?" He cups a hand around his ear, but his grin tells me he heard. Leaning in close, he adds, "He's the boss, Julia. Not to mention the money man, which means once in a while I've got to listen to him."

Even though we both know he's lying? That the real reason is because I wouldn't let him fuck me last night? I should tell Hal what's really going on.

Hold on! You think he doesn't know? Alex was loud enough last night that everyone heard. You say something now, it could cost you your job.

But this is Hal DeBeers. He's got balls. He's gone up against Hollywood in the past. He'll stand up to Alex. I take a deep breath. "Hal . . ."

"Julia?"

I kick the toe of my lug-soled boot into the sand. "When I went to my tent last night, we agreed I'd be going up. What happened?"

"Alex spoke to me first thing this morning." He looks at my half-empty mug. "Said your hands were trembling yesterday."

"Yeah, when the elephant grabbed my cap."

"Ah."

"But let me get this straight: you changed your mind *after* he tried to force himself on me last night." There's no missing the anger in my voice.

"He what?"

"You heard me. He frigging assaulted me." I tighten my hold on the mug. "And he wasn't quiet about it. You must've heard."

"Fuck!"

"That's precisely what he wanted to do."

Hal exhales sharply, then claps a hand on my shoulder. "Look, I'm sorry. We'd all been drinking, and by the time I got to my tent, I was out. My tent's the closest to yours, and I didn't hear a thing. Did he . . . hurt you?"

"He tried hard enough, but I fought him off." I grind my heel into the sand. "And being drunk isn't an excuse."

"Thank God you're okay. Look, if you want to pursue this, make a formal complaint . . ." Something in his voice warns me away from doing exactly that. His real message is clear. He didn't witness anything. Chances are, none of the guys did. And it happened in Zimbabwe. I'll be on my own. She said, he said. And I know which side the powers-that-be here will come down on. Not to mention the studio execs.

I throw up my hands in defeat. "Seems like I don't have a lot of options."

"Look," he says gently, "at least, you were able to fight him off."

"This time," I hiss angrily.

"Yeah." He takes a deep breath and lets it out slowly. "As for this morning, it wouldn't hurt to give Kyle a chance at some aerial. We can always reshoot if we have to."

Bottom line: Hal doesn't want to make waves as far as Alex is concerned. He's letting the man think he's getting his way, but he's not expecting much from Kyle. A nice guy and a solid cameraman, but he sometimes lacks imagination.

Message received. "Okay then. Well, since I won't be vomiting up my guts anytime soon, is there at least time for me to eat breakfast?"

He checks his watch. "Make it quick and meet us at the jeep in five."

Not twenty minutes later, our mini-convoy of two open-air jeeps arrives at the airstrip. We'll leave one vehicle here for when the guys fly back. Meanwhile, Hal, Tonderai, and I will follow the Cessna on the ground. We watch as Alex crams himself triumphantly into the back of the four-seater Sky-hawk. Kyle, his camera mounted on his shoulder, maneuvers his way into the front. Brent finishes checking over the plane, then climbs in. To show there are no hard feelings, at least between Kyle and me, I wave and give him a thumbs-up. He flashes a grin. A moment later, they taxi to the far end of the runway and then, barreling past us, lift off above the acacias and camelthorns.

As Tonderai brings our jeep to life, we pull up our Buff neck gaiters to protect mouths and noses from the dust that's sure to swirl, then head out toward the first of the coordinates Brent gave us. But my heart is in the plane. No matter what Hal said, I should be up there, and we both know it. Still, there's no point sulking about it. I won't feel any better, and Hal and Tonderai will end up miserable.

Despite Tonderai's best efforts to keep the plane in sight, it soon vanishes into the haze over the horizon. We feel every bit of the uncomfortably hard washboard dirt roads of the park, and when we occasionally hit deep sand, we end up sliding sideways and spinning our wheels. The first time we have to push the jeep back onto packed dirt, under the watchful eyes of a curious giraffe and a family of warthogs, Hal curses his frustration. Once we're back in the vehicle, Tonderai picks up speed. I'm holding on tight to the roll bar in front of me, but that doesn't prevent me from bouncing out of my seat and then pounding down hard every few seconds. There's absolutely no question of stopping to film anything even though we pass a spectacular sighting of elephants with a newborn covered in still-wet, wiry hair nursing from mom. But finally, we catch sight of the Cessna circling back in our direction.

"Have they spotted something?" Hal's voice borders on exuberant.

"Perhaps they have found the large herd that was in camp yesterday? There is a mopane forest a few kilometers ahead, and they may be browsing." Tonderai accelerates only to have us jounce even more painfully over a series of ruts.

"Could make for some great aerial footage." I'm doing my best to be charitable.

A moment later, we hit another patch of sand, deeper than before, which sends us sliding nearly off the road. Hal doesn't say anything this time. We just climb out and push. He probably figures we've got a good idea where to find the plane and the elephants. Which is really all that's important this morning.

We start driving again, and that's when the two-way radio crackles to life. "Come in, Tonderai." Brent's voice.

"Tonderai here." He pulls down his gaiter to make talking easier. "What do you see?"

"Elephants down."

I lean closer, not at all sure I'm hearing correctly.

"How many? Do you have a count?"

"Three. Maybe four. One very large. Looks to be male. Not sure of the others."

Oh, God, no! My stomach clutches, and I know I could be heaving up my breakfast sometime very soon.

"Damn! I see some men down there. Alex wants me to go lower to get a better look. See what we can get on film."

"No!" shouts Hal from the front seat. "Take the plane up!"

"They've got chain saws. Automatic weapons. Could be our poachers from last night back to take the tusks."

"Get the hell out of there!" Hal yells, the sideview of his face a disturbing shade of purple.

"Trying . . ." Brent's voice sounds strained. I can imagine him putting all his strength into a steep climb. *Please don't stall the plane!* The channel is still open—we can hear what sounds like the drone of the engine.

Finally, Tonderai, his voice cracking, yells into the radio, "Brent, Brent, come in! Are you there?"

"Can't get enough speed." Then static fills the line. "They're shooting at us. . . . Bloody hell! We're going down."

A minute later, even the static is dead.

Oh, God, please let them still be alive! I hang onto the roll bar as Tonderai speeds toward what we all assume is the crash site. With our jeep pounding over the washboard road, I can barely make out what Tonderai says into the radio. ". . . a few minutes ago . . . poaching."

Maybe fifteen minutes later, he again picks up the radio receiver, then slows to a stop and lets the jeep idle. This call clearly needs his full attention. "Yes, sir . . . No, sir . . . I haven't heard from them . . . But, sir, we should go there. What if they survived the crash? What if we could save them?" Shaking his head in obvious disgust, Tonderai slams the hand radio onto the dashboard, then sinks back against his seat.

Hal leans forward. "I take it we've been called off, told to wait for reinforcements?"

"*Yebo.* That was the deputy commissioner of the national police—Mr. Simon Gwanzura. He ordered us to stay away. He is worried we could be killed if we go any closer."

"And you don't believe him?" Hal has clearly heard the sarcasm in Tonderai's voice. I heard it, too.

"Let me say I have never been given an order like this before—not to help injured people? Or animals? It is unthinkable."

"Wait a minute!" I sit up straight. "Did I hear you right? The Deputy Commissioner called? How does he even know what just happened? And why the hell is he even involved?"

Tonderai shakes his head. "I have no idea. Perhaps because there are Americans on the plane?"

"But how does he know who's on the plane?" Hal looks troubled.

Tonderai takes off his sunhat and rubs his hand over his

shaved head. "Good question. Perhaps my boss called the police after he alerted the anti-poaching unit. But why would Gwanzura himself radio me? This does not make sense."

"So, what are we supposed to do? Just sit here?" The anger and frustration in my voice cut through the warming air.

"That is what he ordered me to do." Tonderai sounds equally frustrated.

After a count of sixty, Hal pounds his fist on the dashboard. "Not on. At the risk of sounding like an arrogant American, I say we push forward. Carefully. We'll stop well back, scout the area. In the meantime, is there anyone else you could call?"

Tonderai nods. "I have an idea. Have you heard of the Mambas? They are a women's anti-poaching unit operating in this area. I'm sure my boss has already called them, but I'll make sure." His smile climbs all the way to his eyes, and his thumb is already pressing the call button on the radio receiver. He relays our request with a strict caution to avoid involving the police. But I'm betting our ask will go from radio to radio, all on open frequencies. It'll be a miracle if the police, or people who want to curry favor with them, don't pick up on this.

Before he presses his foot on the gas, I ask, "The Mambas? Are they armed?"

"*Yebo.*"

We set off again, Tonderai driving as fast as he can until we come to a tree toppled across the road. By the looks of it, the tree only recently came down. An elephant having a snack? Or poachers barricading the road? Breaking gently, he eases the jeep off the dirt road, and then we're winding through a stand of mopane bushes. Stopping, Tonderai picks up his binocs to scope out what could be ahead. All I can see is a couple tall, mudded termite mounds and, next to them, four gray hillocks. It takes me a few seconds to realize the hillocks are elephants lying on their sides. Dead. Nauseated, I turn away, but not before I see a mutilated face, sawed off to harvest their ivory tusks—a sight I'll never be able to forget.

Then, squinting against the brightening sunlight, my eyes land on the Cessna. It looked small before at the airstrip, when it was intact. But now, crumpled with steam rising from the wreckage, I can't imagine how it ever soared through the air.

"I don't see any poachers." Rifle in hand, Tonderai climbs from the jeep and motions us to follow. "Please, stay close. I think the poachers have left, but who knows—they could still be hiding somewhere nearby. Also, there will soon be hyena and jackals coming to scavenge the elephants. Maybe even a lion or leopard."

Three of us and only one gun. I don't feel so great about those odds. And I really don't like the silence surrounding us, uncanny at best, as if all the wildlife is holding its collective breath, waiting to see what happens next.

We don't stop to check out the elephants—that can wait— but veer around their bodies, tramping through waist-high dried grass and skirting the partially eaten mopane bushes toward the crushed fuselage. One wing has been sheared off. I scan the surroundings and finally spot it lying a good fifty feet away near an acacia tree. The other wing is pitched straight out from the plane, then folded back on itself. *Oh, God! The terror the guys must have felt as they went down.*

A sudden flapping of wings causes me to glance up. What look to be marabou storks and white-headed vultures are swooping in to feed on the elies. Some perch atop trees, filling the bare branches. Others land on the elephant car-casses and set to work, gobbling what they can before the larger predators arrive.

"Nature's garbage collectors." Tonderai nods as the massive recycling project begins.

The crack of a gunshot catches us unaware. "Stop where you are!" A woman's voice. "Put down your weapon!"

In an instant, we're surrounded by women—I count ten of them—clad in camo khakis, their semi-automatic rifles at the ready. From beneath the brims of their caps, they glare at us with hate-filled eyes.

My hands in the air above my shoulders, I want to tell them we had nothing to do with this. We didn't slaughter the elephants or shoot down the plane. We're here to try to save our colleagues. But Hal meets my gaze and gives a quick warning shake of the head. *Let Tonderai handle this!*

Tonderai's single-shot ranger's rifle is no match for so many guns. He pulls down his neck gaiter, then raises his hand in front of him in a sign of peace. "Margaret." I can hear the relief in his voice.

Neck gaiters. Yeah, masking the lower half of our faces makes us look real innocent. I pull down my Buff and note the coiled snake—a black mamba—embroidered in olive thread on the chest of Margaret's shirt. The Mambas. Oh, thank God. For the first time in an hour, I feel like I can breathe.

Margaret adjusts the safety on her gun, moves it to her side, then offers a small, tight smile. "Tonderai. You called in this mess?"

"*Yebo.*"

She looks over her shoulder toward the plane. "These are your people?"

Tonderai nods toward Hal and me. "Part of their film crew. We've been following the elephants on their migration."

I look from Margaret to each of the other women in turn as their eyes soften in sorrow.

"Why were they right here? Flying so low?"

Tonderai lets Hal answer. "Our cameraman was filming an overhead of elephants on the move toward water. The pilot let us know they found the poachers, and our producer told him to fly lower for a better look." He sighs heavily. "And presumably to film the poachers."

I've got a question of my own. "Tonderai called this in maybe an hour ago. How did you get here so fast?"

Another grin from Margaret. "Ah, you are the smart one. We were called last night about gunfire and possible poachers. First thing this morning, before sunrise, we started looking for them. It was too late to save the elephants, but we hoped to catch the poachers collecting the tusks—"

"And we might have caught them." A Mamba on the other side of the circle interrupts. "Except your plane found them first. The poachers, they got worried. They grabbed their bounty and ran."

Margaret nods toward the woman who spoke. "Mercy is right. I do not think we will catch these poachers today."

"I'd like to get a better look at the plane. And our colleagues." Hal wants to move past the accusations that we ruined the Mambas' chances of nabbing the poachers.

"Of course." Margaret turns toward the wreckage. "But I am afraid both of the men are dead."

"Both?" My voice is sharper than it should be. "Do you mean there are only two men?"

"Yes, as I said."

I grab at Hal's arm, and together we run, our feet sliding through sand, dry grass whipping at our jacketed arms. Tonderai is right with us, and from the sound of pounding boots, the Mambas are close behind. Margaret's right. Looking through the cracked windshield, we see Brent's head lolling at an unnatural angle against the crushed door. Kneeling in the sand next to the open door, Hal starts to crawl into the wreckage, only to have Tonderai stop him with a hand on his shoulder.

"No! It is far too dangerous."

Hal shrugs off Tonderai's hand and maneuvers forward another foot, then stops. He takes a full minute, studying Alex's body in the back seat, then slowly inches out of the wreckage. Pushing himself to his feet, he turns to me, his face drawn. "I had to see for myself. So I can tell Leslie." Looking at the others, he clarifies: "Alex's wife." He barely manages to choke out the words before he has to wipe the tears from his eyes.

"As you see"—Margaret points toward the open door—"there are only the two men. No more."

"But where's Kyle?" He was absolutely on this plane. We saw him in the now-vacant front passenger seat, waved to him. It was supposed to be me in that seat. My gut is back to roiling, and my wobbly knees are threatening to sink me into the sand, but I can't give in. I owe it to Kyle to find him. He could be out here somewhere, still alive.

Think! What would I have done if I'd been in that seat instead of Kyle? If we'd crash-landed, and I'd survived?

With Brent and Alex clearly dead, no saving them, I'd have climbed out and run to safety. Tried to hide somewhere.

But wait! Where's his camera? I picture him maneuvering it into the confined passenger seat. It sure as hell isn't there now. Did he take it with him, or did the poachers help themselves to it? What if Kyle was hurt but still able to carry it? He would've filmed the poachers. That's exactly what he would have done. Even if he knew it could cost him his life. He absolutely would've wanted to leave some evidence. So, where would he have hidden?

"What are you thinking?" Tonderai's voice is gentle.

"Where's the highest spot around here? Someplace he could hide but also film."

"The *kopje!*" Margaret and Mercy are already running toward the pile of boulders with tall waving grass, an acacia growing from among the rocks, and lots of little caverns—maybe a hundred yards past the wreckage.

I'm right with them.

"Be careful," Mercy cautions when we reach the rocks. "Black mambas—the snakes—love to sun on these rocks. They can be aggressive."

I stop dead in my tracks. Meet up with a black mamba and the neurotoxin in its wet bite will leave you dead in a quarter hour.

"Lions like this *kopje,* too." Tonderai scrambles past me with Hal right behind him.

I look around, and as far as I can tell, we're safe from predators—no snakes, no big cats. *Let's keep it that way, please!*

But Kyle wasn't so lucky. We find him lying face down in the dry grass. No sign of his camera.

My knees give way, and I sink down next to him. *Who did this to you?* But he's way past answering.

I catch sight of a bright flash—something metallic in the tall grass a few feet from his body—right by Mercy's feet. She must see it, too, because a moment later, her back to us, she kneels down and rummages along the ground. For a brief moment, she seems to freeze, then stands again. Whatever was causing the glint is gone.

From her position next to Kyle's body, Margaret glances at Mercy. "Did you find something?"

"No. I thought maybe, but there is nothing."

But there was something. I saw it, too. Then again, maybe it was just a bit of pyrite or some other shiny stone, or even a metal shell casing that was catching the morning sun in exactly the right way.

"This, this is not good." Margaret's grim voice calls our attention back to Kyle. She points to the still-wet blood at the back of his head that is smeared down his neck, staining the collar of his shirt bright red. "This wound, it is not from the plane crash. It is from a bullet."

Three

Williamsburg, Brooklyn

National Geo halts production on the film. At least for now. They'll reconsider after the funerals for Alex and Kyle and Brent—and a decent interval. Of course, we understand. I text Liam from Jo'burg to let him know what happened and that I'll be home way sooner than expected, but I don't hear back.

Hal and I share a flight into Kennedy. He continues on to LA.

I text Liam again—still no answer—then get an Uber and head home to our one-bedroom apartment—an entire floor in a brownstone. Williamsburg may not be the safest neighborhood in Brooklyn, but I love the art scene here. A lot of creatives, off-Broadway venues. Plus, there are television shows filming here and just over the East River in Manhattan—perfect for Liam. He's able to wait tables and be close to the auditions every struggling actor scrambles after. For the time being, it's mostly my camera work that keeps us afloat.

Romantic that I am, I was kind of hoping to catch Liam at the apartment—a chance to celebrate my early homecoming in bed. But he's not here. I try his cell, but he's not answering.

There's no point in leaving a voice message; unless it's from his agent, he never listens to them. I text him yet again, this time a proposal for Chinese takeout, hoping for a fast response. Which doesn't come.

Unpacking my duffel, I make a pile of clothes needing to go to the washer and dryer in the basement. Finally, I plug my cell into the charger on my bedside table, and that's when I find the pair of gold hoop earrings. Not mine. I never wear hoops because they either get caught in my long hair or snag on my camera. Not a particularly pleasant sensation. In fact, I don't wear earrings at all—too easy to lose one on the job.

My legs wobbling, I sit down hard on my side of the bed. And even though I don't want to look for any other incriminating evidence, that's exactly what I do. Pulling back the duvet, I find the one thing I don't want to see. A condom packet. Torn open. Empty. No way this is from our farewell several weeks ago because I've got an implant. My chest tightens, and I try desperately to get enough air in my lungs so I can actually breathe.

That's the moment Liam chooses to arrive home. I hear the front door open and close. Then the door to the fridge. The clink of a metal bottle cap landing on the counter. Then footsteps heading toward the bedroom. I'm pretty sure there's only one pair of shoes slapping across the squeaky hardwood floors.

He stops in the doorway. God, he's handsome—an absolute hunk. And until a few minutes ago, I reveled in the belief that he was all mine. Something he told me all the time. *No need to worry, babe—ever.* His eyes meet mine and widen. A smile crosses his face, but given the circumstances, I'm thinking it's a smile of relief that he didn't bring her home with him today.

"Babe! I thought you were still in Africa. When did you get in?"

How can I possibly answer? But I do. "Maybe an hour ago." The words sound wooden.

"Why didn't you text me?"

"I did."

Furrowing his brow, he pulls his cell from his messenger bag. What? He doesn't believe me? He flips through his texts, where he lingers over one in particular, a smile toying at his lips. Something tells me it's not the one I sent. He takes a moment to type an answer—confirming it's not mine.

"Sorry. Sorry. I guess I missed it." Turning off his phone, he shrugs an apology and grins, confident that I'll believe he hasn't been screwing someone else. "Whaddaya say we order in? "Egg rolls? Lemon chicken? Pepper shrimp and squid?"

My heart sinks. Although we both love Chinese food, we have never, not once, ordered any of those things. I can only guess that's the menu he orders for whoever's earrings are sitting on my bedside table. It hurts even more knowing he can't keep us straight.

Instead of answering, I pick up the hoop earrings and hold them between my thumb and index finger, swinging them back and forth.

Actor that he is, Liam makes a valiant effort to hide his dismay. He almost succeeds. Except that he takes a couple seconds too long to slip into his role of the innocent husband. Finally, crossing the room, he joins me on the bed. "Aw, jeez. I meant to wrap them. A welcome-home present." His hand massages my thigh.

I could avoid the confrontation-to-come and say thank you. But I don't. "You know I don't wear earrings." Somehow,

I manage to keep my voice cool and calm. But inside, I'm raging.

"You should. They'd look great on you." Damn, he's good; there's even a little bit of hurt creeping into his voice. Like I'm not fully appreciating that he thought of me, that he bought me a present.

I take a closer look. They're nice earrings—a beautiful, warm gold. Probably eighteen-karat. "Did you buy them for her? Or did she forget them here?" My voice doesn't sound nearly as calm anymore.

"Babe." His hand moves up my thigh. "They really are for you. Like I've told you before, there's no one else."

This is the moment when I should fling the condom wrapper in his face. But I'm still way too upset over everything that happened in Zimbabwe—the plane crash, the film being put on hiatus—maybe scrapped. I can't possibly deal with the likely end of my marriage. Not today. So, I make a snap decision to let it go. For now. And promptly kick myself as he stretches out invitingly on the bed.

You're letting him get away with cheating on you? Coward!

Not so fast. What if he's actually telling the truth? What if I'm still the only one?

You don't believe that. How do you explain the condom wrapper?

Maybe it was a one-off. Or maybe, since I'm home, he won't see her again.

Easing me back toward him, he lifts himself up and kisses me. Nice, but not particularly passionate. "So, why're you back?"

Seriously? He doesn't know what happened? Didn't he see the story on CNN? Hal and I were both interviewed, and then we watched it on television at the airport in Johannesburg.

But as I should know by now, Liam is very selective in the news he follows. He's so focused on his career that he doesn't want to stress out by reading or watching anything upsetting. In the past, I thought his single-mindedness was kind of charming, something to be admired. Now, I wonder what the hell I was thinking.

I give it to him straight, as horrific as I can make it. "Some of the guys on our film crew were killed in a plane crash."

He pushes back from me. "What're you talking about?"

"Poachers were killing elephants, taking their tusks. The pilot and Kyle and Alex flew low overhead and got shot down."

"Alex . . . is dead?" Liam's voice cracks—a clear sign of how upset he is that he won't be getting an audition for Alex's upcoming film. I almost gag as I remember that Alex was most definitely up for an audition—with me.

Liam's betrayal hurts like hell, and I know I should kick him to the curb. But I'm too strung out to do it today. Or even tomorrow.

Soon, I promise myself. After I find a good lawyer.

Four

Barely a week later, Liam finds me in the kitchen scrounging a yogurt from the nearly empty refrigerator. "Hey, babe, you've got mail." He drops the envelope on the worn, knife-gouged butcher block counter.

I immediately recognize the logo in the return address—three black squares with a bold white letter in each—and for some inexplicable reason, dread washes over me. It's hard to make sense of the legalese in the brief letter except for a few words at the end of the first paragraph: *Your services are no longer needed.* Even though I signed the contract a few months ago, my BBC job to work on a film in Sri Lanka is gone.

"No worries." Liam is playing the role of a supportive husband. "So, you'll take a couple weeks off. You deserve it. Besides, you've got other jobs coming up."

But another week goes by, and two other jobs—with Disney and Africa Geographic— go south. This time, Liam isn't as supportive. "What's going on? Maybe you should call around, see if you can line something up. It's not like we've got a ton of savings."

What's going on is that no one wants to work with me. But why? It's not because I'm a woman. Okay, so there aren't many of us out there. Me, Cate Darlington, and a few others. But I've proven myself as a cinematographer and as a camera operator. Everyone knows I'm as good as any of the men out there. Better than many. The women in the business—we're willing to take risks that some of the guys aren't. Clearly, this started after the Zimbabwe shoot. When Alex Silver came on to me. But I find it hard to believe that I'm losing jobs because I wouldn't sleep with him. I mean, who even knows that happened? Except for the guys on the shoot in Zimbabwe. So, what *is* going on?

I get in touch with each of the companies, but don't get to speak to any of the powers-that-be. And no one who does talk with me can tell me anything. It's like bashing my camera against a concrete wall.

In desperation, I call Hal DeBeers. We worked well together. He'll be straight with me. Maybe he can even help.

"Julia. You doing okay?" His voice hasn't changed one bit, still warm and welcoming.

"Still a bit unnerved. You?"

"What went down in Zimbabwe was bad. God, I hope never to go through something like that again. Telling Leslie what happened to Alex was one of the worst moments of my life. But we've got to carry on. There are films waiting to be made."

"Speaking of which, I'm finding myself in kind of a strange situation."

"What do you mean?" He sounds wary now.

"I've lost three jobs in the last couple weeks."

"You had signed contracts?"

"Absolutely. But they sent letters saying my services were no longer needed."

He's quiet for a moment. "Maybe the projects were

canceled? Or there were cutbacks? What did they say when you called?"

"Nothing. As in, no one's taking my calls."

Another pause, this time longer. "Julia, I don't know what to say. You're one of the best out there. This doesn't make sense. Look, if I hear anything, I'll let you know. With any luck, you just got caught up in some crazy funding fluke and you'll be back working soon."

So, here I sit, my career going down in flames at the same time that Liam's could be taking off. He's filmed a couple guest roles in television shows—not that those gigs are all that highly paid. But he's also auditioned for the lead role in a Netflix series. He was even called back for a chemistry read. And that could pay a lot better. All of which means he's not often home. I'm trying not to imagine him spending time with the woman whose earrings are still on my dresser.

We're home watching *Killing Eve* when Liam's agent calls. I mute the sound while Liam hunches over his iPhone, the faint lines around his eyes crinkling with excitement, a smile of utter joy spreading across his face. Why does he have to be so damn good-looking? Women lose control around him. From what I've heard, some men do, too.

Ending the call, he tosses his cell onto the sofa and pumps both fists in the air. "Time to celebrate!"

He pulls me to my feet for a celebratory kiss—not nearly as deep or passionate as in the past. Then, taking a step back, eyes closed in sheer bliss, he wraps his arms around himself.

"Tell me."

"The role in the Netflix series—"

"Oh my God! You got it!" Clapping my hands, I twirl in a very happy circle. Even though I'm not over him cheating on me, he's a good actor and really deserves this. His success has me ready to forgive him and move on. So long as he keeps his pants zipped. But when I reach for his hand, hoping he'll gather me in his arms for another kiss, he jogs to the kitchen and pulls out the bottle of Veuve Clicquot that's always being chilled—for exactly this occasion. The cork explodes with a satisfying pop, and a moment later he's back with the bottle and two flutes.

"This is so great!" He pours champagne into one of the glasses and hands it to me. "We start shooting next month. And get this: we're shooting in New Mexico!"

Now I'm really excited. "Oh, God! Autumn is absolutely the perfect time to be there." My thoughts are spinning. "Hey, since I'm not working, I'll be able to visit. You know how much I love New Mexico."

"Sorry, babe."

My thoughts stop spinning. "Sorry? What?"

He looks away. "This is gonna be a rough schedule. As one of the leads, I probably won't have much free time."

"Seriously? You'll be working twenty-four seven?"

"I know it'll be long hours."

My stomach starts to churn. It's sounding a helluva lot like he doesn't want me there at all. "How long is the shoot?"

Still avoiding eye contact, he downs his champagne and pours himself another. "Hard to say. Four, five months. Maybe longer."

I watch the bubbles in my glass rise to the surface and burst. "So, you'll be back—"

"Julia . . . look . . . I might as well tell you, I'm thinking of relocating to the west coast after this. It'll be a lot easier to get TV jobs. And movie roles."

Call me innocent in the ways of men dumping women, but despite the cheating and the lying, I didn't see this coming. And instead of thanking the universe that he's soon to be out of my life, I frigging argue the point of his needing to be on the west coast. "Lots of actors live in Manhattan. And Brooklyn."

He doesn't respond, just sets down his empty glass, grabs his messenger bag, and heads toward the front door.

I think of the nameless woman whose gold hoops now reside on my dresser, right next to the locket from my brother, in the delicate antique dish my father gave me for my thirteenth birthday—not exactly the gift every teenage girl would want, but I love it, even though the dish is currently hosting the evidence of my husband's infidelity. I have an idle thought: if Liam's off to celebrate with his lover, maybe I should send along the earrings for him to give back to her.

Instead, I yell after him, "Liam! What the hell's going on?"

He yanks open the door, then turns back to look at me. "I just told you."

"You told me some crap about being in LA getting you more access to roles."

"It's the truth."

"Bullshit!" Then before I can consider the consequences, I follow up with what I've been wanting to say for weeks. "Don't bother coming back. Tonight. Or ever." I take a deep breath. "And for once in your life, why don't you tell me the truth!"

"You want the truth? Okay. I want a divorce. Happy now?" He crosses his gorgeous forearms over his muscled chest. Damn, he's going in for the kill—I've seen him make this exact move so many times on TV shows. "You want more truth?" He spits out the words.

I take a step back.

"You honestly think you can lose half a crew on a shoot and still get a job?"

"*Lose* them? I didn't fucking lose them. Look, damn it, I was supposed to be on that plane. Me! I would've been the one killed instead of Kyle. Hal DeBeers would've died instead of Alex Silver." I take a breath. "But Alex made sure I didn't go up that morning."

"Oh, so now you're blaming Alex?"

"It was payback! The night before, he came to my tent and tried to rape me. He assaulted me."

Liam stares at me, then curls his lip and claps his hands. "You're accusing him of sexual harassment? Un-fucking-believable."

"It's the truth!" I yell.

He shakes his head. "No way. Everyone in the industry is talking about how you were too scared to go up in that plane. Bottom line: you couldn't do your job, and people died. Even my agent told me. Face it: you're toxic. That's why all your jobs are bailing. No one's gonna hire you. And you seem to be the only person who doesn't realize that."

I open my mouth to tell him he's wrong. "No—"

"I'll tell you something else: I'm not about to let you drag me down." He flings open the door to the apartment. "Let me know when you're not gonna be here, and I'll come back for my stuff. My lawyer will be in touch." Slamming the door behind him, he stomps down the interior flight of stairs and out to the street.

"Fuck you!" I scream after him.

It's not until I'm pouring my champagne down the kitchen drain that I think about his last words. *My lawyer will be in touch.* His lawyer? He's already hired a lawyer? It's taken me weeks just to get appointments to interview a couple attorneys. How far into this separation and divorce is he?

I spend the rest of the night stuffing his clothes into black plastic garbage bags. Then, I debate carting them down to the sidewalk. Too much trouble, I decide, and stack them on the landing outside our apartment.

First thing the next morning, I call a locksmith. If Liam wants anything else, he can damn well have his lawyer call mine. When I hire one.

Five

Liam's been gone a week, and I'm nearly done with my pity party. We were together for five years, married for three, but it sure wasn't always a bed of roses. A big part of me is happy he's gone. No more lies. No more cheating. No more living mostly off my earnings, especially when I don't have any money coming in.

It's definitely time to make some serious decisions about my future before I run through what's left in my bank account. But cinematography is all I know how to do, and it's what I love doing. Not that anyone's willing to hire me right now. For the last few days, I've been toying with the idea of picking up a still camera again. I'll build a portfolio and see if that can get me some gigs as a wedding photographer.

I've almost convinced myself that's what I should do when my cell rings. The caller ID shows the name. Cate Darlington. As far as I'm concerned, she's the best camera operator working today. About twenty years older than me, hard talking, heavy drinking, straight shooting. She smokes three packs a day, Gitanes when she can get them. I had the incredible good luck to work with her on a couple films when I was first starting out, and she taught me a lot—including that it helps enormously if you've got thick skin. Now, she's one of the few people in the business who's still talking to me.

I swipe my finger across the phone. "Cate?"

"Glad you answered. I was worried you wouldn't." Her voice is as gravelly and gruff as it always was. I wish she'd stop smoking.

"What've you heard?"

She coughs. "That you're going through a rough patch."

I wonder if she's referring to the plane crash or Liam or both. "I've had better months."

"Yeah, losing part of your crew can take it out of you. Not that I've ever had to deal with losing more than one crew member, but I can imagine."

My stomach tightens. "What I can't understand is why everyone's blaming me—as if I did something wrong."

"From the way I hear it, Kyle wasn't supposed to be on that plane. You were."

So, Liam was right. That's what has everyone up in arms. "Yeah, I was. But Alex made sure I wasn't."

"You care to explain?"

"Cate, you know how it is in this business. People like Alex can be predators. He came on to me during the shoot. Showed up drunk in my tent."

"Damn. I knew he had a reputation, but he usually went after pretty, young actresses."

"I was the only woman there, so it was slim pickings."

"What happened?" Her voice is tight—the anger coming through loud and clear.

"Nothing. He tried to rape me. I kneed him in the balls and kicked him out. Next thing I knew, Hal decided Kyle was going up—instead of me. He swore that Alex insisted on it."

She coughs. "Hal DeBeers, huh? Well, that explains a lot."

"Oh, God. Tell me."

"Hal's a huge gossip. He was also pretty tight with Alex. I'd bet anything he's the one spreading this shit about you."

I'm stunned. "But I talked to him a couple weeks ago. He said he had no idea what was going on. Damn. And here I thought he was on my side." Pausing a moment, I let Hal's betrayal swirl around my brain. "So, he's a creep—just like Alex. Any idea how I can shut him down?"

"Just don't go screaming about how misogynistic the industry is."

"Even if it's true?" I say tightly.

"Especially if it is. And don't go public about Alex Silver. No one's going to look favorably on you accusing a dead man. And you're too good a cinematographer *and* camera operator to get tossed out."

I snort a laugh. "Then why has every job been canceled out from under me? And let's remember, I wasn't in charge of that shoot. Hal DeBeers was. As far as I know, no one's canceling his jobs."

"Hey, I'm on your side. What's happening to you is stupid and outrageous. Give it some time to settle. People will forget—eventually. You're still young. What, thirty?"

"Thirty-one."

"Look, I'll do what I can to help." She coughs again, and seems to have a hard time catching her breath. I wonder if I should ask what's wrong, but knowing her, she either won't answer or she'll get pissed. "Which brings me to the reason why I'm calling. I may have a job for you—"

"Seriously?"

"Hear me out. It's not what you think." She pauses as if

she's expecting me to interrupt again. "The film department at the University of Wisconsin in Milwaukee called me. A top-notch program. Their guy who teaches cinematography left with the semester starting in two weeks to take a gig on a film. I'm booked solid for the next year and a half, but I thought of you. Interested?"

It takes me half a minute to make the transition from the expectation of working on a film to the reality of an offer to teach. "Thanks for thinking of me, Cate, but I've never taught before. Well, other than as an assistant while I was getting my MFA."

"Let me be clear: they need someone now. And I know you can do this. Plus, it's short-term—until next May."

"Cate, thanks, but—"

"Don't 'but' me. This is a paying job and will show the assholes who are screwing you over that they can't get you down. Hell, girl, you might even end up liking the academic life. It's been known to happen."

"I sure don't have anything else lined up."

"And I bet you could use the money, especially after that useless son of a bitch Liam Shepard walked out on you. I hope you've come to your senses as far as he's concerned."

"How did you know?" Now I'm coughing, mostly to hide the catch in my throat—a sure sign I'm close to tears.

"The news is getting around. Someone as hunky as Liam doesn't stay single for long."

"Really . . . I—"

"Word is he's hooked up with his co-star on the Netflix series. Natalie Powers."

"Fuck." I gulp and wonder if she's the reason he was so excited to get cast in the show. And leave me behind.

"Don't go all weepy on me. Take the call from Shan—he's the chair of the department—last name is Nielsen. Not sure if he's a PhD or not. I expect he'll call you tonight. Tomorrow at the latest. Hear him out, then take the damn job. You can thank me later."

How well I know from our time together in the field that the thanks she wants is a bottle of bourbon. Blanton's.

"Oh." She always wants the last word. "Just so you know, my coughing has nothing to do with me smoking. I've got bronchitis. And you can keep that to yourself."

Ten minutes after Cate hangs up, Shan Nielsen calls. He explains the job in terms so succinct he's got my head spinning. Three courses a semester for fall and spring. Advise majors. Starting two weeks from next Monday. For this, he'll pay me seventy thousand.

Dollars? I almost squeak but somehow manage to maintain my dignity. "Don't you want to interview me?"

"I just did. Besides, Cate assured me you'll be great. And I looked at one of your films. She's right."

Oh God, Cate. Thanks for saving my life, but did you have to build me up quite this much? "Cate was a good mentor."

"So, you'll take the job?"

Oh yeah.

I manage to load a PODS container with the stuff I want to move to Milwaukee, let Liam know he's got till the end of the month to take whatever he wants—including his girlfriend's gold hoop earrings—then leave the key with the super.

Six

It turns out I'm a natural at teaching. Well, maybe not at first. I'm sure Shan is fielding a file cabinet's worth of complaints about all the mistakes I make in the first month. But by mid-semester, I've got a pretty good idea what I need to be doing. And my students—undergraduate and graduate—are incredibly forgiving. They even say they're learning a lot.

When the professor I'm replacing fails to return, my visiting position becomes tenure track. I settle into a cozy navy-blue bungalow in the village of Shorewood—within walking distance of the university.

Fast-forward a few years, and at my pre-tenure review, Shan tells me that I'll need to pull together a portfolio for the faculty to vote on granting me tenure. "New work," he says.

Wait. *What?* "I thought you said I could use my films from before." I could swear he told me that way back when I started.

He shakes his head. "It's good work. But we want to see what you've been doing here at the university."

I gape in disbelief. What does he think I've been doing? Making films in my half hour of spare time each weekend? There's a reason why the students love me and learn a lot in my classes. Prep, teach, mentor—it's all I do.

"It doesn't have to be a major motion picture. It doesn't even have to be feature-length. A short indie film would be acceptable. Maybe an article or two." He also lets me know the committee will be very impressed if I could somehow secure funding for an internship so a grad student could work on this film he's sure I'm going to make. As in, find the money from somewhere other than the department's coffers.

This is my catch-22: I'm teaching because no one in the business will touch me—even five long years after that horrible day in Zimbabwe. But to be able to continue teaching, I've got to get someone to hire me to shoot a film.

Or make my own.

How the hell do I make a movie? On my own? During my non-existent free time each weekend? I pace a circle around my small living room and fail to come up with any answers. Fuck it! I throw my notebook onto the coffee table, plant myself on the sofa, and stare dejectedly out the front windows to the street where kids are playing soccer.

How many kids have I seen play soccer when I've been in the field shooting a film? Flashing back to Zimbabwe, I remember the day a few crew members and I visited a school—on the Ngamo Plains. The boys, some of them barefoot, were kicking around a well-worn soccer ball—football, they called it. They were so into it, and I just loved watching them. I filmed them for a bit, and they pumped their fists in excitement when I showed them the footage. The next day, the crew went on to Jozibanini, and then . . .

The poachers shot down the Cessna.

And the Mambas nearly shot us.

The Mambas. Those fierce women who risk their lives every day to keep animals alive, to keep them from being hunted to extinction.

Who make sure there will be elephants and lions for generations to come.

Who run toward dangerous poachers—to stop them from killing.

Yes! This is the story I want to tell.

The Mambas.

Could I possibly make a short film—a documentary—about them? Where they came from. Why they joined up. I grab my notebook and pen and start jotting notes. How do they train? What are their lives like? Who did they leave behind?

I chew the end of the pen. This might just work.

Wait a sec. I could shoot this film, but I need someone to direct. And someone to write a screenplay. Sound people. Lighting people. I don't have a clue how to do any of that. And another camera operator. Not to mention money. Lots of money. Even if I empty out my savings account, I won't have nearly enough.

Unless I wrangle some of the friends I still have in the industry.

I call Cate.

"Hey, girl, it's been a while." She coughs. I'm sure she's still smoking those Gitanes.

"Good to hear your voice." And your cough. "You have a minute?"

"Five minutes and then I'm back behind the camera."

I talk fast. "I need a favor. Big-time. I've got to make a film for tenure, and I'm thinking of going to Zimbabwe to make a short documentary about the Mambas. The anti-poaching women. Interested?"

"Keep talking. You've got four minutes."

"You'd need three to four weeks next summer. August maybe? It'll be a miniscule budget."

"I take it the pay will be non-existent." It's not a question.

"In a word. I can offer you a percentage."

"Right." She coughs again. "Count me in. I'm guessing you'll need a director. Call Matt Monahan. He's a great guy with some good connections for editing and distribution."

Damn, I hadn't even thought that far.

"And I happen to know he'll have time next summer."

"You're an angel."

"An angel who wants you back out here. Too much work for me. Ah, they're signaling me. Gotta go!"

I sit up straighter and wish Cate would see someone about her cough. And stop smoking.

Matt Monahan. I'm back to chewing my pen. Would he even consider doing this? It's been a few years since Cate and I worked with him. Cate's right: he was great on set, always listening to our ideas, making us feel like we were part of the team, really getting us engaged in making the films. I lean back and curl my feet under me. But he's also a bit old-school, shooting scene by scene—not really a documentary filmmaker. He's made a name for himself in Hollywood, though; was even nominated for an Academy Award. What are the chances he'll remember me? And that he'll say yes?

And what are the chances that I've still got his phone number?

Half an hour later, my cell phone vibrates across the

coffee table. I don't recognize the number and almost don't answer. "Hello?"

"Hey, Julia. Matt Monahan here. Cate told me you'd call, but we've got a lunch break now, so I thought I'd try you."

He remembers me. "Matt."

"What can you tell me about this movie you want to make?"

I pitch him the idea. Bare bones. It's all I've got.

"Cate said I'd like it, and she's right. And I'd do anything to work with you again."

"Why?" I can't help it.

He laughs. "Because you're one of the best. And, if I'm being honest, I feel guilty as hell that I didn't stand up for you more when Hal DeBeers spouted all that crap about you. I didn't believe it, and Cate disabused me of any doubts I might have had. I know this doesn't make up for it, but please count me in. It'd be an honor and a pleasure to work with you. Even without pay. A percentage is fine with me. But I'm not sure I'll be able to get you editing for free. Might have to cough up for that."

I can hardly get my thanks out. I can hardly say anything. But I pinch myself and go for it. "I've got some savings, and I'm applying for a grant." Well, I will apply for a grant. "But we may have to improvise on sound and lighting."

"We'll make it work. I take it you're writing the screen-play yourself?"

I guess I am—unless I can talk Cate and Matt into help-ing. "I'll draft something and send it to both you and Cate. And I'll run it by the Mambas."

"I like that. Working as a team. Haven't done that in a long time. One last question: when do you want to go to Zim-babwe to shoot this?"

"Does August work for you?" I hold my breath.

"As it happens, yes. Oh, and I may have an idea for a voice-over narrator. A big-name actress. I'll keep you posted."

Seven

Atlanta, Georgia – August 2023

The airline announces one delay after another as thunderstorms light the skies over Atlanta's Hartsfield-Jackson Airport. Sitting next to me at the crowded departure gate, Amie Raffelock, one of my grad students and my intern for the next month, swings her foot rhythmically back and forth, back and forth. She catches me watching. "I hate flying." Her voice is tight. She tries to smile but ends up gnawing her lower lip.

To be honest, I'm not very fond of flying myself, after what happened six years ago. But I suck it up and go. Amie, though, she's looking way too pale. And now I see her hand pressing against her stomach, as if she's holding herself together. She looks downright scared.

I try my best to come up with something calming to say. "It's safer than driving. Really." Oh, God, how lame can I get?

She practically rolls her eyes. "I know. Everyone tells me that."

I'll admit I'm confused. "If flying bothers you so much, why . . ."

Another attempt at a smile. "You mean why did I apply for the internship?"

"Well, yeah. I mean, it's a lot of flying time to get to Zimbabwe. And when we're in Hwange, there might be some small Cessnas—if the drone doesn't capture the footage we need. I thought I briefed you on all this."

"You did. Really. It's just that I wanted this internship so badly—it could open so many doors for me. And I was kind of hoping . . . maybe I could skip the small planes? I could do other things—anything you want."

I let her request sit in the air between us. Damn, I was hoping *I* could skip the light-wing planes. But here we are, and it's not like I can send her home. Thank God I brought a drone, although getting the license needed to use it in the park was a huge process that caused me no end of headaches. And who knows? We might still need a Cessna. "Tell you what. Let's play it by ear." I seriously hope I don't have to give pep talks before every flight.

"Thanks." She smiles, but her hand is still on her stomach.

Finally, the storm moves on, and we board the 777 for the fourteen-hour flight to Johannesburg. Most of our gear is checked—fingers crossed it all survives the trip intact. After stowing our backpacks and one Pelican case of camera gear each in the overhead compartment, we settle into our economy plus seats. Ah, luxury! Both of us are tall, and trading in my many frequent flyer miles that were about to expire got us the upgrade we'll need if we want to get any sleep. Amie, though, still looks seriously nervous. I bet she won't be able to relax enough to close her eyes, much less sleep.

An hour after take-off, the attendants serve dinner, and Amie unclaws her hands from the armrests. I hear the man in the row in front of us order the beef burgundy. His voice is rich with a Zulu accent—not Ndebele, but close—almost as if I were hearing Tonderai speak. Then there's the choice of wine—a glass of South African Pinotage—which takes me back to Jozibanini Camp the night before everything went to hell.

Funny that Amie chooses this very moment to ask me about the last time I was in Zimbabwe. "I read your article, the one in *American Cinematography*, and I was wondering . . ."

I don't want to talk about what happened, which is why I published the article—that, and to have something on my CV for tenure. I figured if I put it all out there, people would stop asking me. But I also don't want to shut Amie down. We'll be together for the next few weeks and have to trust each other. Besides, I'm her teacher, her advisor, and also her sometime confidante. A sip of the rich and full-bodied red wine, and I say as encouragingly as I can, "What do you want to know?"

She takes a deep breath. "Everything. Not about the ethical decision to leave off filming and shelve the project. That's all in the article. I want to know what it was really like that day."

Another sip and I'm back in Zimbabwe's Hwange National Park. In a jeep with Tonderai at the wheel and Hal in the front seat, going as fast as we can to reach the crash site. Hoping against hope the guys are still alive.

I tell her what really happened. "It was actually kind of strange. There we were racing across the savannah, wondering if we'd get there in time to save the crew, and Tonderai got a radio transmission from the deputy commissioner of the national police ordering him to stand down."

Amie stares at me, her dinner forgotten. "Why would he do that?"

"The best we could figure out is he didn't want us in danger from the poachers. But it didn't really make sense." And it still doesn't. Something about that radio call doesn't ring true.

"But the poachers were gone by the time you got there, right?"

"Yeah. Or hiding."

"And that's where you first met the Mambas."

I grimace at the memory. "They were there before we got to the crash site. They opened fire on us. At least, they shot over our heads."

"Oh my God! You didn't put that in your article. Why'd they shoot at you?"

"Probably because they didn't know who we were. And with our Buffs on, we looked kind of suspicious. They finally recognized Tonderai, though. It turned out they knew him fairly well. Which probably saved our asses." I nod toward her tray of food. "You should eat. I've been on this flight before, and I know it'll be hours until the next meal."

She studies me for a long ten seconds, probably wondering what the hell she's gotten herself into, then forks some beef burgundy into her mouth. "So, all three of the men on the plane died."

Looking past her, I lock my eyes on the darkness outside the cabin window. At this point, we're somewhere over the Atlantic. Sheer nothingness all around us. It's not really a question, but I answer anyway. "Yeah, they all died."

"Such a waste." She takes another bite.

"Not a waste. A crime. That went uninvestigated."

She gulps hard. "What do you mean?"

"The poachers shot down the plane. The pilot—Brent—and Alex, both of them probably died instantly. But Kyle . . ."

I close my eyes, willing myself not to cry. "We think he was injured—seriously. Still, he managed to get out of the plane, then hide in the bush."

She pushes her plate to the other side of her tray. "But all the news coverage said he died in the crash."

"He didn't."

"Oh, my God. The poachers killed him?" Amie looks suddenly green.

"Yeah. And they took his camera. At least, I think they did. We couldn't find it anywhere." Okay, it probably wasn't my brightest idea to tell this story to a fearful flyer on a long-distance flight. I dig through the pocket on the back of the seat in front of me for a vomit bag, but Amie waves it away. A few deep breaths, and her face isn't quite so green.

Certainly, she's done with eating. She hands off her dinner tray to the steward and shakes her head at the offer of dessert. A moment later, she digs her iPhone out of her jacket pocket, attaches her earbuds, and curls up in her seat. But a few minutes later, she pulls off the earbuds, letting me hear Billy Joel crank out "The Longest Time"—not something I would've expected to be on her playlist. I figured her for more current music, Billie Eilish or maybe Pink.

"Can I ask you a question?" She sounds hesitant.

"Go for it."

"I know you didn't finish the documentary. You talk about that in the article. But did you ever go back to Zimbabwe?"

I take a deep breath and let it out slowly, wondering why the hell I told her so much about what happened. Although I don't want to keep her at arm's length, I do need to remember there are boundaries between professors and students. With tenure on the line, I can't afford to share so much personal information. I trust Amie, but who knows what she could inadvertently tell another student. Or, God help me, another faculty member. "Nope. This is my first time back." And that isn't in the least personal.

"Yeah, that makes sense. You went through some really heavy stuff. But it's good you're going back now—ready to confront what happened—and make this new documentary." She smiles. Her first really happy smile of the trip. "This film is gonna absolutely rock! I'm so glad we're telling the story of an anti-poaching unit of women. Finally, some glory for them instead of always for men." Then, earbuds back in place, she closes her eyes and damn if she doesn't drift off to sleep.

Meanwhile, I'm wide awake, the mental video of what happened on my last trip to Zimbabwe playing on an endless loop. I've told Amie a lot tonight, but not everything.

Eight

Johannesburg, South Africa

Thanks to the delays in Atlanta, our flight arrives so late that it's nearly 10:00 p.m. by the time we make it through immigration and collect our duffels and all our gear. We cross the street to the InterContinental—my hotel of choice when I'm flying through this part of the world. A super convenient fifty yards from the terminal, it's got a lovely spa and great food. Once again, I cashed in my loyalty points to get us a room for the night. Checking in, we hear the scrape of forks against plates and a lot of laughter spilling out of the restaurant at the other end of the lobby. At this hour, neither of us wants dinner, but we agree that a drink could go a long way toward relaxing us. One drink. We've got a morning flight to Victoria Falls, and I for one want to get some sleep.

A quick trip to our shared room to secure our gear, and we're back downstairs in Quills bar—so named for the incredible installation of African porcupine quills hanging from the ceiling. A Castle Lager for Amie. I go for a G&T with Bayab gin.

"Gin made from baobab trees?" Amie sounds dubious.

I clink my glass against hers. "The botanicals are great. Besides, elephants love baobabs."

"If you say so."

Another sip of my drink, and I cross my fingers that she'll loosen up a bit and go with the flow of Africa. Otherwise, it could be a very long, very tedious shoot.

Pushing the bowl of roasted cashews toward her before I eat them all, I see something or someone has caught her attention. I follow her gaze to the round table at the far side of the bar. Six men who look to be in their forties, all of them sporting two-hundred-dollar haircuts with an occasional white hair. I notice gold bands on most of the ring fingers. My guess: this is a guys-only trip, spouses left at home or maybe traveling with girlfriends to Paris or the Riviera. With no evidence to suggest it, I suddenly realize these guys are probably trophy hunters. They're definitely dressed for the part: khaki shirts and slacks so new they still have the telltale fresh-out-of-the-package shininess. My stomach twists at the thought of a large bull elephant or an aging lion being baited for these men to shoot and kill, its head stuffed and eventually mounted on the wall of a McMansion in Texas or Palm Beach.

On closer inspection, one of the men has hair longer than the others. No fancy haircut for him. Tall and lean and oh-so hunky, he's got blue eyes that could pierce body armor. His well-worn khaki shirt and slacks look as though he was born in them. Rolled-up sleeves show off muscular and well-tanned arms, clearly from a lifetime spent working in the sun. Not one of the hunters, but their guide, here to meet them and take them out on safari.

The hunters are pushing back their chairs now. Like us, they probably arrived after long flights and are ready to head to their rooms for the night. The guide, though, I'm betting he'll spend more time in the bar, decompressing with another drink or two.

I'm about to turn back to the cashews when he locks eyes with me, then Amie, and holds up his glass. Dang, we've been caught staring. Whether he's saluting Amie or me or both of us isn't clear. But I'm pretty sure he's just issued an invitation to help him "relax."

A few minutes later, Amie sets down her empty glass as I swallow the last of my drink. The bartender is instantly in front of us, placing another lager and a G&T on the bar top.

"No thanks." I shake my head. "Just the bill, please."

"From the gentleman." He nods toward the guide now alone at his round table.

He really is good-looking, and that smile is something else. Honestly, I could be tempted—a fun diversion for the night. It's been a long dry spell. I reel in my imagination. Not tonight. I've got a flight tomorrow and a film to make. "As I said, no thanks."

Amie clears her throat. "Do you mind? I'd like the drink. I mean, why waste it." She closes her fingers around the glass and lifts it to her lips.

Oh. He did look at both of us. Maybe he's really interested in Amie. Not me. Should I say something? But she's twenty-three, and what can I say without sounding like her mother? I finally settle for, "Are you sure?"

She takes another sip. "It's only a drink."

I glance over at the guide. He's likely slept his way through scores of women. "I think he might want something more."

"Okay, so a drink with benefits."

"It's your call." I shrug. "Remember we've got a flight in the morning."

Lying awake in bed, my mind races with worry over a middle-aged big-game hunting guide taking advantage of Amie. She's my intern. Even though she's a grad student, I'm sure the university—not to mention her parents—think I'm the responsible party. I should go back down to the bar. If they're not there, I'll go to the front desk, explain the situation, and demand his room number. And what if he's not staying at the InterCon? That's often the case: guides stay in way less pricey accommodations. So, what the hell can I do?

Stop! She knows what she's getting into. Just because you're not up for spending a night with a complete stranger doesn't mean it's wrong for her. In fact, has it ever occurred to you that maybe sex with a stranger could be a good way to help you get over Liam?

I'm over him.

You're over him? Really? You still seem pretty rattled. And bitter.

He hurt me. Big-time.

All true. Now get over it.

I finally shut down my inner argument and am drifting off to sleep when the slow creak of the door has me wide awake. "Amie?"

"I'm sorry, I'm sorry! I was trying to be quiet."

"It's okay. I'm still awake. You're back sooner than I expected. Is everything okay?"

"Nothing happened." She snorts her frustration. "At least I got a beer out of it. But as soon as I sat down, it was clear he wasn't interested."

"Then why did he buy you a drink?"

"Us. He bought *us* drinks, and I'm pretty sure Gus—that's his name, Gus Sinclair—was hoping to hook up with you."

"What?" I flip on the light so I can see her. And she looks totally fine. Her shirt is right side out, and the snaps are all in place. Which confirms there wasn't a quick fuck, after which he kicked her out of bed. I study her more closely.

"It was just a feeling I got. I mean, he was friendly enough, but he sure didn't put any moves on me. We chatted for a while until he said he was tired. I actually thought he was hinting about us going up to his room, and I was up for it, but . . ." She sinks down onto the side of her double bed.

I sit up and dangle my legs over the side of my bed. "You're probably lucky you didn't go to his room."

She looks up at me. "What do you mean?"

"Some of these guides can be . . . you know . . . And you never know who their last ten partners were."

"Yeah, whatever." She rolls her eyes. "It was just a drink and conversation. He was nice. And just so you know, I didn't tell him all that much about you."

"He wanted to know about me? What did you say?" I ask warily.

"Well . . ." Her cheeks redden. "Your name, obviously, and that you're here to make a movie about the Mambas. He actually asked if you'd been to Zimbabwe before, and I told him about your last film. He seemed . . . really intrigued, like he wanted to hear more. That's when I finally caught on he wasn't interested in me—only you. A little while after that, he left."

"Weird." I rub the goose bumps off my arms, not at all sure I like him pumping Amie for information about me—no matter how good-looking and nice he is. "Did you find out anything about him?"

"Not much. Oh, but get this, those guys he was with? They're all heading to Zimbabwe tomorrow morning to go big-game hunting. Even if I'd liked him, knowing he's into hunting was a total turnoff."

"They're flying tomorrow?" I groan.

"No worries." She grins. "They're on an earlier flight. With any luck, we'll never see them again."

Nine

Back at the airport's international terminal, I stare at the maze of check-in counters, each with a long line snaking back and forth. The Fastjet counter is nowhere to be seen. An agent takes pity on me and points me toward Terminal B. Pushing luggage carts mounded with duffels and Pelican cases full of gear, we head to the next terminal only to be stopped by a young man wrapping suitcases with plastic. "This is the way to keep your belongings safe."

Amie stops in her tracks. "Should we?"

"I don't bother. The TSA locks should be good enough." I resume pushing my cart up the ramp toward the next terminal where, we discover, the lines are even worse. Amie spots the Fastjet counter. Yes, the agent nods, she's checking in passengers for the 11:10 flight to Vic Falls.

"Are you sure?" Amie points to the sign that reads Maun, Botswana.

The agent shrugs. "I guess no one changed it."

We get on the end of the line, and an hour later, the agent slaps more FRAGILE labels on the cases and hands us each a boarding pass—for seats nowhere close to each other. Amie looks seriously unhappy, but she doesn't say a word. Then, earbuds in place, she turns on her easy-listening music from the seventies and tunes out the world.

Except for one seat next to me, the flight is full. I figure I'll have Amie move forward from the back row once the attendants close the doors. But at the last minute, an elderly white-haired man who looks to be Ndebele walks down the aisle and stops next to me. His black suit is so old it's worn to a shine, and his wristwatch—the gilding rubbed off to reveal the base metal underneath—hangs partway over his hand. I stand to let him hobble past but then think better of it—unless he really wants to sit by the window. "Sir, would you rather sit on the aisle?"

"Thank you, young lady. You are most kind." His voice is soft and gentle, each word enunciated with great care. After I scoot over to the window, he settles into my vacated seat and stows his battered leather briefcase in front of him.

Once we're airborne, the attendants quickly serve cans of Mazoe Orange Crush and a snack. I nearly laugh when I open the box and see potato chips, biltong, and a chocolate bar. Closing the box, I see my seatmate slipping his snacks into his open briefcase. A moment later, he looks toward me.

"You caught me!" He smiles. "These will make nice treats for my great-grandchildren."

"Do you think they might like mine as well?"

"You are not fond of biltong?" He chuckles, his face crinkling as he laughs.

"Not before five p.m. and not without a beer to drown the taste."

"Then I thank you. And the children thank you."

I offer my hand. "Julia Wilde." Too late, I remember hand-shaking isn't so common in southern Africa.

He softly palms his hand to mine. "I believe I have heard your name before."

"Really?" Staring at him in disbelief, I can feel the confusion inching its way across my face. "I can't imagine . . ."

"You have been to Zimbabwe before, I think. A few years ago. You worked on a film with my grandson Tonderai."

"Yes, Tonderai, of course. He's a wonderful guide. I'm looking forward to working with him again."

He smiles broadly. "He is a good grandson. I am Solomon Mkhwananzi." His last name has a click of the tongue, a sound I couldn't possibly make, but one I remember from when Tonderai introduced himself. "It is good that you have returned."

I lean back in my seat, amazed by this coincidence. Of all the people who could've sat next to me. "I assume Tonderai told you what happened—that we never finished the film."

"Yes, he told me that, too." He nods. "This new film you are making will go better, I am certain."

God, I hope so.

Solomon closes his eyes, and a few minutes later, his chin falls forward onto his chest. I'm left staring out the window to the desert below. Sand, sand, and more sand. At thirty-five thousand feet, I can't see any of the wildlife I know is down there. Instead, I focus on the real reason I'm returning to Zimbabwe. Much as I'd like to think I'm making a documentary to celebrate the Mambas, the bottom line is that this film is my one and only shot at tenure. No film, no job.

Ten

Zimbabwe

Two hours later, we attempt our first landing in Vic Falls. But as our jet lowers to meet the runway, the pilots suddenly lift off again—climbing fast and steep. I swallow hard. Around me, people murmur uneasily. An attendant explains over the PA: "Folks, sometimes this happens. A large bull elephant is on the runway. The captain says we'll try again in a few minutes." My stomach churns as I think of what could've happened. And what poor Amie must be feeling right now. Turning as best I can, I spot her all the way at the back, eyes squeezed shut, face devoid of any color.

Fifteen minutes later, we touch down—a landing so gentle it's as if we kiss the runway—to loud applause from the passengers.

I deplane right after Solomon, and Amie catches up to us on the tarmac walkway to the terminal, where I take a moment to introduce her to Tonderai's grandfather. We stay right by his side, matching our pace to his. Much as I'd like to power walk to customs and immigration so we can get to the head of the lines, I want to make sure this man is okay.

He waves us on. "Don't you worry about me. You just go about your business. It takes me a little longer, but I will be fine."

I shake my head. "Is someone meeting you?"

"Oh, yes. I believe my granddaughter will be waiting for me. You do not need to worry."

By the time we have our COVID vaccination cards approved and get to the row of immigration booths, we three are at the end of a very long line. We wait and wait, shifting restlessly from one foot to the other. Passengers from a second, newly arrived plane take their places behind us. And we all wait.

Finally, it's our turn. I encourage Solomon to go first—he must be exhausted, ready to go home. But he seems to sense Amie's nervousness and insists she go first. She passes through in less than a minute. I'm next.

"Your name?" The uniformed man behind the plexiglass window scrutinizes my passport and entry form. Back and forth he looks from one to the other.

"Julia Wilde."

"American?"

"Yes." I smile, calm and relaxed, but the khaki-green-clad soldier standing a few feet away has my attention. He's watching me closely, his index finger flexing the trigger on his AK-47. Soon enough, we both realize something's wrong with my passport, although I can't imagine what.

"No. This is a problem." The immigration man points to the "profession" and "purpose of visit" lines on my entry form, then to the visa pasted in my passport.

"I'm sorry? I don't understand."

"It says here you will be working on a film in Zimbabwe."

"Yes." Damn it, I know my paperwork is in perfect order.

I dealt with the Zimbabwean consulate myself. But I keep my answers short and don't volunteer more information than is strictly necessary. Saying too much could get me in a lot of trouble.

"That is too bad for you. We are not allowing any filming in Zimbabwe at this time." His eyes harden. His voice is stern, accusing, almost as if he suspects me of trying to enter illegally. I'm guessing the soldier has picked up on the change in demeanor because his gun is now at the ready. And pointed. At me. A few feet beyond him, I see Amie waiting anxiously.

I take another look at the visa, authorizing me to stay for twelve weeks—even though I'll be leaving a lot sooner. Signed and stamped by the consul. Turning my passport back to him, I point to the key words.

"Except for journalists, photographers, and filmmakers." He stabs my visa with his index finger for emphasis. "They are disallowed."

Disallowed? What the hell does that mean? And wouldn't the consulate have known about this? I glance again at the visa: there's nothing about certain jobs being disqualified. "Excuse me, but I don't understand. I got this visa from your country's embassy a few weeks ago."

When he next looks at me, I nearly take a step back. He's scowling, eyes cold. "The law has changed. You will have to go to Harare, to the government ministry in charge."

This time, I do take a step back. Seriously? This is his solution? He won't let me in the country here, so I'm supposed to somehow go to the capital and see what happens? And here I've always heard that getting in-country at Vic Falls is a whole lot easier than in Harare. Hands trembling, I take a deep breath. "So, what can I do?"

"You cannot enter Zimbabwe with this visa." His voice is loud enough to attract the attention of everyone in the room.

Yeah, that message is clear. "What visa do I need?" All of a sudden, I'm pretty sure I know where this is going, and it really pisses me off.

He looks to either side of him—stealthily, as if to see whether any of the other agents are listening. The soldier is definitely paying attention, as are the people behind me. Motioning me closer to his window, he lowers his voice. "This is generally not allowed, but I could issue you a special, single-entry visa for filmmakers. But if you depart the country, you will not be able to return."

Exactly what I thought. A bribe. He's all but spelled it out. "And how do I get this visa?"

He lowers his voice. "You pay five hundred dollars. US cash. Now."

Outrageous! Somehow, I manage to swallow that thought and keep my jaw from dropping. I've paid bribes before, but never this much. I'm about to counter at a hundred dollars, but his eyes aren't very encouraging. Then, a hand is on my forearm. A gentle hold, but unexpected, making me jump. Solomon's hand, dark-brown skin stretched taut over his protruding arthritic knuckles.

Steady! his hand seems to say. Then, he slides his open passport through the hole in the plexiglass panel.

The immigration man looks down, and the transformation is startling. He abruptly stands straighter, shoulders back, much like a soldier drawing to attention in front of a general. *"Baba mkhulu. Sawubona."* Then, to my amazement, he bows from the waist, somewhat stiffly, but it's clear he's showing deference.

Next to me, Solomon Mkhwananzi smiles. "*Sawubona.* I see you have met my granddaughter."

The immigration man gapes. "Your grand . . . daughter?" He stumbles over the word, his disbelieving eyes shifting back and forth between us. It's pretty damn clear he's thinking, *What the heck?* I can understand why. Solomon's skin is brown—dark and rich. Mine is as white as can be. Nearly translucent, which explains the blush that at this very moment is climbing up my neck to my cheeks. Then, there's my hair—long and straight and naturally red. Not to mention I'm almost a head taller than my new grandfather. There's no way on earth this ploy is going to work.

I smile as sweetly and innocently as I can. *The resemblance is clear, don't you think, Mr. Immigration? Well, maybe not physically. Perhaps we should call it spiritually simpatico?*

"*Yebo.*" Solomon's voice is firm. "My granddaughter."

Now, the man behind the plexiglass is totally flustered, his nostrils flaring, his eyes wide with disbelief. And there's something more I can't quite read. Embarrassment? No. It's fear. A sidelong glance at the soldier tells me he's scared, too. But thankfully, his gun is now pointed toward the floor. Neither man is about to state the obvious: there's no way this woman is related to you, Mr. Mkhwananzi.

For the first time, I have to wonder who exactly Solomon Mkhwananzi is. Other than Tonderai's grandfather. Old and somewhat frail, slow on his feet and most clearly a very powerful man.

Mr. Immigration bows again, this time in contrition. "I am sorry, *Baba mkhulu.* I did not know." Bending over, his face close to the passports, he writes a few indecipherable letters on my visa. He then stamps both passports and pushes them back to us. "*Siyabonga. Sahle kahle.*"

"*Hamba kahle.*" Solomon hands me my passport and, taking my arm, heads toward the exit. After we're clear of immigration and have Amie back in tow, he points us toward baggage claim. "Thank you, my granddaughter. The spirits willing, I hope to see you again soon."

"I hope so, too. You saved me back there, and I truly appreciate it." I also make a mental note to learn some Ndebele as soon as possible.

He smiles gently and, turning, strides like a much younger man toward the door. I nearly laugh out loud. So, who was helping whom all this time? He passes by the customs desk without stopping, then just as he's about to round the corner and move out of view, a young Ndebele woman steps forward. His granddaughter, I assume. His real granddaughter.

On to collect our gear. Pelican cases full of camera equipment and lighting panels, and our duffels—all accounted for, even after sitting all this time unattended next to the conveyor belt. I heave a major sigh of relief. If anyone had known there's tens of thousands of dollars' worth of cameras and lenses in these cases, they'd have disappeared in a flash. In a country this poor, gear like we're carrying could make a huge difference between life and starvation. We need to remember to keep them out of sight except when we're on the job.

We're each pushing a loaded cart toward customs when Amie stops short and points to what looks like a small flat tablet, maybe one by three inches, on the floor. "What do you think that is?" I'm ready to walk on, but she toes it with her shoe, then kneels next to it. "It kinda looks like a bone."

Squatting next to her, I pick it up. Bleached and polished.

I run my index finger along the finely wrought carvings—intricate lines and patterns. "Definitely a bone. It's beautiful, don't you think?"

"Well, um, I actually prefer bones to be inside people . . . and animals."

Closing my fingers around the bone, liking the feel of it in my hand, I push myself to my feet. And there, a few feet farther on, I notice another one. Reaching for it, I lay the second one on my palm next to the first. "This one's shaped a little different, and it's a bit bigger with even more elaborate carvings."

"What do you think they're for?"

I study the two bones. "They aren't souvenirs for tourists, that's for sure. I'm guessing they're important to someone—very important. And I just bet that person is Solomon." The more I think about it, the more certain I am these belong to him. I'm about to tell Amie to run after him, but we've still got to pass through customs, and I seriously don't want to get into any more trouble.

We hand our passports and paperwork to the customs official, and I show him the two bones, letting them slide back and forth on my palm so he can get a good look.

His eyes widen in fear. "Where? Where did you get these?" he sputters.

We're both taken aback. "On the floor—" Amie begins.

I take over. "I'm fairly sure—"

He doesn't let me finish but barks a series of commands into the radio on his lapel—not in a language I understand. Given the clicks I'm hearing, it could be Ndebele. Finally, I hear two words I can make out: Solomon Mkhwananzi.

From various places around the large room, soldiers charge toward us, guns drawn. Shit! Cowering, Amie raises her hands over her head and looks ready to break down in tears. I'm sure I look the same. At the last possible moment, they veer around us and out the door. I assume they're running after Solomon, but shouldn't we follow them? It'd be so much easier than dragging him all the way back inside. I tuck the bones inside my cargo pants pocket and start to push the cart, but the agent jumps in front.

"You will not move!" His eyes are still filled with fear, but the gun he's pointing at me is what stops me dead. Then he waves his weapon at Amie, motioning her to stand next to me. She looks as confused as I feel. Does he want her to stand still or to move?

"Sorry, but we need to get going. Our driver is waiting for us." At least I hope he's still out there. After all this time, he may well have left. "Maybe you could give these to Mr. Mkhwananzi?" Taking the bones back out of my pocket, I try to hand them over. He backs quickly away—a good ten feet, but still close enough that he won't miss if he decides to shoot his damn gun.

Okay, we get it. These bones are important. And obviously powerful.

Finally, one of the soldiers returns, his gun pointed at us as well. Damn! Give men guns, and the power goes straight to their heads.

"Come!" The soldier uses his automatic to direct us and our carts toward the exit. "Solomon Mkhwananzi, he is waiting for you outside."

Well, thank God they're not dragging the man all the way back inside. I lean into the cart and get it rolling. Amie sticks close to me. Shoulder to shoulder. Out the door and across the meet-and-greet hall where I glance around at the drivers holding placards with the names of arriving passengers. Not a single one has our names. Which I guess means our driver has vanished. We trundle our carts through the exit to the great outdoors. All under the watchful glare of the Zimbabwean armed forces.

"There!" He points toward an aging Toyota Corolla parked at the curb.

Surrounded by soldiers, we make our way to the car and to Solomon sitting in the front seat.

"We meet again." He smiles warmly. "I did not expect it to be this soon. These soldiers say you have something that belongs to me?"

"I'm so sorry to delay you." I kneel next to the open car door. "We found these bones inside, and I thought they might belong to you?"

Solomon looks at me sharply, then at the bones cupped in my hands. Reaching into his jacket pocket, he pulls out a small, nearly threadbare cloth bag, neatly tied and very decidedly closed. I can't imagine how the bones could've made their way out of the bag and out of his pocket. But he tugs at the string, opens the bag, and gently pulls out a rolled cloth, which he unfurls to reveal two bones almost identical to the ones in my hands.

"How very curious." He nods. "Yes, these are my bones. Thank you for finding them, Julia." He takes a moment to study my face. "Or perhaps they found you." He lifts his hand above mine as if he's going to pick up the bones, but then he doesn't. Instead, he says a few words, I guess in Ndebele, and once again, I don't have a clue what they mean.

Finally, he cups his hands beneath mine to catch the bones as I let them slide. But he's not finished yet. He looks carefully at the rough T the bones have formed on his palms.

No one says a word. The soldiers move in closer and seem to be holding their breath.

Everyone waits for the old man to say something. Me most of all. But he doesn't. Not a word about what the T means.

Finally, his eyes lock on mine. I'm pretty sure I see a flash of concern, but it's so brief that maybe it wasn't even there. At any rate, his next words are calming. "Thank you, Julia. You have done me a very great service."

"I'm glad we were able to catch you."

After a good ten seconds, he shifts his gaze to Amie's face. "Something is worrying you?"

"The guns." Her voice is barely a whisper. "I wasn't expecting so many guns."

"They're a bit much," I add by way of support.

"Do not let the guns worry you. Once you leave the airport and are in the bush, you will leave the guns behind."

I nearly scoff. How I wish Solomon were right, but I remember all too well the sound of gunfire from my last time in the bush. Still, I opt not to correct him. He seems to know Amie needs reassurance right now, not a warning.

Finally, with the utmost care, he rolls all four carved bones into the cloth and returns them to their bag, and the bag to his pocket. Again, he smiles. "Julia. Amie. Please open your hearts to my country, and you will find the answers you seek." He pulls his car door shut and waves. "Take care."

His final words stop me. Not so much the words, but the tone. He sounds worried, troubled—as if something isn't quite right. Or maybe that something could go wrong. With the film? Is that what he saw in the bones? Oh, God, just what I don't need.

Eleven

The soldiers amble back to the terminal where they slouch against the outside concrete wall and light cigarettes. They look completely innocuous until I notice them staring intently at us and flexing their index fingers against the triggers of their guns. As if we're an imminent threat. Nearby, the costumed Ndebele dancers sip Cokes and take a rest between performances for arriving tourists.

"Hey!" I nudge Amie. "Are you okay?"

"I don't know." Her voice sounds wobbly and a bit scared. "This isn't anything like I thought it would be."

"Yeah, well, it's not always like this. Why don't you give it a little longer, a few days at least, and we'll see how you feel."

She nods. "Okay. That'd be good."

And what exactly I'd do without Amie at camera three, I have no idea. I'm trying to come up with plan B when I hear a familiar voice. "Julia Wilde!"

Tonderai Mkhwananzi, clad in his familiar khaki uniform, strides toward me, his hand extended. A firm shake. Very different from Solomon's on the plane. His hand palms mine, our thumbs curl around each other, then our hands slide back to complete the greeting. My hand knows the routine from the last time I was here. Then, he pulls me into a hug. "*Sawubono!* It is very good to see you again." He smiles broadly. "*Linjani?* You are well?"

"Now that we're here and with you, yes"—I nod toward Amie—"all is well. And you?"

"I am also very well." He points toward the car at the parking toll kiosk. "I see you met my grandfather."

"I sat next to him on the plane, and he helped me with a little glitch at immigration. A lovely man."

"Yes, he is a good grandfather, and a good headman for our village." He turns to Amie and holds out his hand. "You must be Amie." He pronounces her name with a long 'a.'

"Ah-mie," she says with a smile, reaching forward to shake his hand. "Hi, I'm Julia's intern. We actually found two of your grandfather's bones. That's what took us so long—we were returning them."

Tonderai furrows his brow, then laughs. "Ah, you mean his divining bones!"

"Divining bones?" Now it's my turn to look puzzled.

"My grandfather is a *sangoma*—a healer. And a seer. I should be clear: he's a good *sangoma*, not an evil one."

I shrug. "Sorry, I don't know what a *sangoma* is. Or does."

He grins. "My grandfather, he helps people with their problems—health, marriage, troublesome neighbors."

"Kind of like a witch doctor?" The moment the words are out of Amie's mouth, she gets a stricken look on her face. "Oh jeez, I'm sorry, I—"

Tonderai holds up his index finger. "Some *sangomas*, those who place curses on people, could be called witches, but not my grandfather. He's also not a doctor, at least not the kind of doctor you have in the West. Here in Zimbabwe, we believe in traditional as well as modern medicine. My grandfather is a traditional seer and healer. He's able to treat some minor ailments, but he knows when he must insist people go to a medical doctor. His bones are very important to him. He throws them to help diagnose and heal problems. Without them, he couldn't do his work."

"I'm glad we found them—and that he was still there."

"Did my grandfather say anything? Give you a reading?"

I remember holding the bones, liking their feel against my skin, then letting them slide onto Solomon's open hands. "Not really. But . . . well, the two bones formed a shape kind of like a 'T,' and he studied it for a minute. But no, he didn't tell me what it means. Do you have any idea?"

He frowns for a moment, as if he's debating whether or not to say anything. "Probably nothing. You held only two bones—not all of them. Besides, a divination depends on many things—your ancestors, the problem you present to my grandfather." He rests his hand gently on my shoulder. "And you must believe in what the bones have to say. You are not Ndebele, so I think the bones have no power for you. Nothing for you to worry about."

Worry? An interesting choice of words given Solomon's reaction. Is there something I should be worried about? Besides all those men with guns.

No, stop! I absolutely cannot allow myself to worry. I've got a film to make. "Hey, by any chance are Matt and Cate here yet? I wasn't sure if they'd be on our plane or not."

He raises an eyebrow. "They flew in yesterday and are waiting for us at the River Lodge. If I may suggest, it is getting late. I think we should go to the lodge for sundowners and dinner. Tomorrow we will drive down to the Ngamo Plains."

"Sundowners?" This is from Amie.

I grin. "You'll see."

Tonderai takes over pushing Amie's luggage cart across the parking lot to the Ford Explorer with Zambezi River Lodge painted on the driver's door. I follow with the second cart. As he stows our gear, I grab the Pelican case with my camera and some lenses and load it onto the back seat. My motto on a shoot: be prepared. You never know when you might come across something that needs to be filmed.

Amie's in the front passenger seat, earbuds nowhere to be seen, chatting with Tonderai. From the little I can hear, he's telling her about the young male leopard that was seen in camp last night. She doesn't seem scared or nervous. In fact, quite the opposite. For the first time on this trip, she seems relaxed and happy—even excited. Leave it to Tonderai to work his magic on her. Maybe she'll make it after all.

We're about ten minutes from the airport, heading into Vic Falls, when I spot women in long white dresses and white veils, many of them barefoot, walking single file along the side of the road. Up ahead, more women in white head into the woods. Peering through the trees, I see other women sitting in an open field. Facing them, a small group of men, also in white.

I point to the women walking, then to the people sitting on grass. "Tonderai? Sorry to interrupt, but those women on the side of the road, what can you tell me about them?"

He slows the vehicle and pulls to a stop on the verge. "They are members of the White Garment Church. That is what we call them. Officially, they are called Vapositori."

I repeat the word. "Vapositori? There are so many more women. And girls." I don't add that many of the young girls are pregnant.

"Yes. They are polygamous." He stresses the third syllable. "You would like to film them?"

I roll down my window and, looking back at the parade, pull out my cell phone, aim it as unobtrusively as possible, and snap off a number of shots. Damn! Some of them are young girls, maybe thirteen or fourteen. And visibly pregnant under their virginal white. Stuffing my cell into my pack, I slide back across the seat. "Thanks, but no." Something tells me, though, that there's the potential for a documentary here—if I'm able to talk my way into their community.

Tonderai pulls back onto the road. Another fifteen minutes and he turns off the pavement onto a narrow dirt road. He takes it slow, trying to keep the dust to a minimum. Even so, the trees along the verge are sporting dusty red leaves. He avoids the rock-hard ruts as best as he can, easing down into gullies and back out again. "When the rains come, these will fill, sometimes to overflowing. It becomes very muddy and is very easy to get stuck."

I look at the tall green grass lining the road. "There was rain this past year?"

"Yes! A lot of rain. Even in April, which is late for us. Usually by now, the grass would be brown and dry, but as you see, it continues to grow."

A few more bends in the road, and Tonderai stops next to a white pickup. Zimbabwe National Veterinary Service is printed on the driver's door. *"Yebo!"* he calls to the man in a khaki shirt and shorts lifting large yellow plastic jerry cans out of the flatbed. A brief back and forth in Ndebele, then Tonderai looks at me in the backseat. "There's a bull elephant that has been snared. Probably by Zambians." He sounds angry.

I lean forward. "How do you know it's the Zambians?"

"We've caught a couple. They sneak across the river at night to set the snares, then come back to harvest the tusks. The bull is still alive, but it's serious. The vet needs to operate. Want to go see?"

I'm already unpacking my camera. "Count me in!" In a matter of seconds, I've got a short lens threaded on, the tripod screwed in place, and one leg out of the vehicle.

"We're walking? Into the woods?" Amie doesn't sound nearly as excited as I'm feeling. I bet she's remembering Tonderai's story of the leopard.

"Don't worry." Tonderai's voice is reassuring. "Any leopard or lion will smell the elephant and us. They will not want to come anywhere close by. And I will have my rifle." He buckles on his belt of cartridges and lifts his .375 Winchester off the dashboard.

Amie takes a deep breath, manages a small smile, then joins me in the middle of the road. I notice she doesn't make a move to take her camera, which is probably for the best. Let her get used to walking in the bush first. But she's also got to practice filming in the bush, which is much different than any other cinematography she's done.

Tonderai holds up his hand. "First, I must call the lodge and let the others know."

The conversation is one-sided, and I can't quite figure out what the rest of the team wants to do.

"Are they coming?" Amie asks before I get the chance. It occurs to me that she's hoping for as many people as possible—safety in numbers.

Tonderai shrugs. "I spoke with Matt. He told me to wait until he and Cate get here."

The man with the water-filled jerry cans shakes his head emphatically. "They coming all the way from the lodge? No, man. The doctor, he won't want to wait. This bull is in pain. We need to take care of him now."

"I agree." And, tripod propped against my shoulder, I follow the vet's assistant with his two containers of water into the woods. The sound of footsteps shuffling through fallen leaves tells me Amie and Tonderai are bringing up the rear.

It's a hike. We're walking deep into the bush. The canopy overhead is thick, making the air cooler, but also buggier. I slap at a mosquito just as he bites my arm. Damn! I should've put on repellant.

Finally, the man in front of me slows, lowers one of the jerry cans to the ground, then looks back, his index finger in front of his lips. I stop in my tracks, and suddenly all is silent. No crackling of dried leaves or snapping of twigs underfoot. Elephant ahead. We're downwind. I can't see him yet, but I can sure smell him. Maybe ten yards ahead of us, the vet stands motionless, rifle in hand. Over his shoulder, he stage-whispers what's happening. "The tranquilizer dart bounced off his thick skull. I'm giving him a minute to calm down, then will try again."

Now I see the elie. He's young, but his tusks are already large, probably weighing fifty pounds each. No wonder the Zambians are trying to poach these guys. He lifts his trunk in the air, letting it hover above his head, sniffing, trying to find smells that will explain the sounds he's hearing. Sweat pours down the sides of his massive head. Is he in musth? Or is it the pain from the snare that's stressing him out?

In a matter of moments, I've got the tripod on the ground, the camera on, and I'm filming as Tonderai skirts around Amie and me and moves silently through leaves that a moment ago were a chorus of noise. From somewhere nearby, a grey laurie calls out, "Go away! Go away!" Is he warning the elephant, the Zambians, or us? A single word to the vet, and Tonderai takes the tranquilizer gun. Moving off a little farther into the trees, he brings the rifle to his shoulder, aims, and fires another dart into the rump. This shot doesn't miss.

In an instant, the elephant is bellowing his outrage and swooshing his head back and forth, his trunk flying through the air. Another rifle exchange, and Tonderai takes his position next to Amie. A quick glance tells me she's wary but transfixed by what's happening.

Get used to it, I want to tell her. *Something like this is always happening out in the bush, often with not more than a moment's notice.*

The vet motions for everyone to move back. "It takes about eight minutes for the tranquillizer to take effect. We never know how these young bulls will react."

Still thrashing and bellowing, the elephant moves deeper into the woods. We follow at a distance, the vet keeping a close eye on the elie. "The sedative is safe, but if we use too much, he might not come out of it. We try to use the least we can. It's something of a guessing game."

Six minutes. The bull is woozy, swaying, then collapsing down onto his knees.

Eight minutes. He rolls onto his right side.

"Brilliant." The vet grins. "The snare's on his left front leg. He's in the perfect position. Let's get to work."

The team knows exactly what to do. One slowly pours water from the plastic can onto the elephant's head.

"Can't have him overheating," Tonderai explains.

Another assistant readies the surgical tools while the vet examines the wound. "Looks like the snare has cut all the way to the bone."

Hoping for a better view, I move my camera and tripod to the side, close to the elephant's head, trusting the sedative will keep him quiet. Shooting in the dim light of the shade, though, is a serious challenge. Plus, I've got a dark-gray mass of an animal. This is so different from filming out on the veld. Finally, the vet gets to work, digging down into the white flesh of the elie's lower leg.

"Bloody hell!" The vet spews his fury. "They used thick-gauge barbed wire. Someone wanted to make sure this guy would suffer first. It's ripped the tissue every which way. This must've been driving the poor beast mad."

I pan the camera slowly so I get the vet in the frame, head-on. His arm and shoulder muscles tense visibly as he tries and fails to cut the wire. One of the assistants wipes the vet's forehead, and then out of the corner of my eye, I see Amie lifting one of the jerry cans and gently pouring a stream of water onto the elie's ear. Glancing over at her, the assistant smiles and nods his approval.

Finally, the vet calls out, "Tonderai! I need your muscles here!"

The vet and Tonderai and one of the assistants cluster around the great gray leg. I film three pairs of hands. After some fumbling, two of them grip the thick wire, pulling it clear of flesh and skin. Tonderai bears down and cuts the double ring free.

"Let's get moving!" The vet works fast and with no wasted motions. His assistant hands him an antiseptic to clean the wound, which on film looks like a gaping hole. There's a hell of a lot of tissue that's been lacerated.

Next, he packs on a white powder, then purple. "To keep out debris." Finally, a heavy dousing of antibiotics. I document it all.

"Aren't you going to stitch him up?" Amie asks as she continues to dribble water on the animal's head and ear.

The vet rocks back on his heels. "No way he'd stand for it. Besides, I've already spent enough time on this beast. I need to get him on his feet. If he's out any longer, he might not find his legs again. The bigger the bull, the harder it can be." He checks over his work, then nods. Satisfied. Reaching for the biggest hypodermic needle I've ever seen, he plugs it into a vial and fills the syringe.

Amie pours the last of the water over the elephant. The vet grins at her. "You were a great help. Thanks for freeing up the guys so we could get the wire off."

The assistants repack the vet's surgical kit while Amie collects the jerry cans. I stop filming and, folding up the tripod, lift it to my shoulder. We're about to start our trek back to the road when we hear people tromping through the woods. Another moment, and they come into view: a guide in a khaki uniform, then Cate with a cine camera on her shoulder, and finally Matt, his lips pressed tightly together in a straight line, a sure sign he's seriously annoyed.

From where he's kneeling next to the elephant, the vet takes in the newcomers. "We're done here. I'm about to send everyone back to the road."

Cate frowns—first at the vet, then at Tonderai, finally staring pointedly at me.

Matt nods toward Tonderai. "I told him to wait for us."

"*Yebo.*" The vet pushes himself to his feet and walks over until he's nearly in Matt's face. "He told me. And I'll tell you. That elephant was in agony. I wasn't going to let him suffer a minute longer than necessary so you could get some film. Besides, she was here." He tips his head toward me. "And from what I could tell, she probably got some good footage." He holds up the syringe. "Now, you best clear out. Once I shoot this in him, we'll have about three minutes before he comes around. I daresay he'll make a bit of a fuss."

Guns in hand, Tonderai and the guide from the lodge corral Amie, Cate, and Matt. One by one, they silently follow the vet's two assistants through the trees to the road.

I should go, too, but I'm not done yet. Moving a little farther off, I position the tripod again, ready for the vet to bring the elie around. Zooming in tight, I film the vet easing the needle through the thick skin.

Injection complete, he massages the skin. "It looks thick, but make no mistake, elephants suffer from sunburn and mosquitos. Drives them to distraction."

I zoom out, waiting for the elie to regain consciousness. "Is he going to be okay?"

"Don't you worry about this boy. He's got a lot of years left in him." He pushes himself to his feet and studies me. "We've got two minutes. You ready to run?"

"I can cover a lot of ground in two minutes." But I don't move.

"I've got to be here to make sure he gets up. I don't want to put you at risk, though. Could I convince you to move farther back? A lot farther back. When this guy comes to, he could well charge. Even with his wonky leg, he can run a lot faster than either of us."

I move back a few more yards. "How's this?"

"Hardly." He paces off another thirty feet, clearly expecting me to follow his lead. "Look, I don't want to fight you on this."

I carry the tripod and camera and move back to stand next to him. And not a second too soon. The massive beast rolls onto his belly, then, pulling his legs under him, he pushes what has to be six tons off the ground. Swinging his giant head back and forth and flapping his ears, he raises his trunk and trumpets. I get it all on film.

The vet grabs my arm, and now we're moving stealthily backward, around trees, until he judges us to be safe. "I want you back at the road. Now. I'll be a minute or two behind you, but first I've got to see him walk on that leg."

I head out of the woods as quickly and as quietly as I can. Back at the road, Matt and Cate are in what sounds like a pretty heated conversation with Tonderai. I can only imagine what they're saying. Before I can join them and defend Tonderai, the vet emerges from the woods, the bloody snare in his hand. He catches me looking. "Evidence. In case we catch these criminals," he says, loud enough for everyone to hear.

Matt quiets down and joins me to study the jagged barbs trimmed with bits of elephant flesh. "You ever make any arrests?" he asks.

Tonderai shakes his head. "Not enough."

The vet looks grim. "It's a serious problem and getting worse. Even in the parks where the Mambas are on patrol." He hands off the snare to one of his assistants, then grins. "At least this boy will be fine. He's on his feet and mad as all get-out. A great sign!" After washing his hands in a stream of water from the tank under his pickup, he turns to Tonderai and Amie and shakes their hands.

"Thanks for letting us help." Amie is literally vibrating—in a good way.

"And many thanks to both of you! Couldn't have done it without you." Next, he offers his hand to Matt, then Cate. "No hard feelings, I hope. The animal comes first. Always." Finally he turns to me. "Happy days! Hope you got some usable footage back there."

I show him my crossed fingers. "We'll see once I upload it."

"Your group heading down to Hwange?" He seems to be directing his question to Matt, perhaps to make amends for their earlier disagreement.

"Tomorrow." Matt crosses his arms and nods. "We start filming the day after."

"It's a documentary on the Mambas," I say as I stow my tripod and camera in the back of the Explorer. "The anti-poaching group, not the snake."

"Good deal. A group of very brave women. A real credit to the anti-poaching effort in this part of Africa. Hope you don't run across anymore snared elephants while you're down there. But you know where to find me if you do." He salutes our group and climbs into the cab of his truck.

Matt catches my eye as he heads toward the three-tiered safari land cruiser the guide drove down from the lodge. "See you three in another hour or so. We'll sort all this out over sundowners. It's clear we need to set some parameters if we're going to work together." Then, he climbs into their vehicle, and they're off.

Twelve

Camera and tripod perched on my shoulder, I make my way out to the deck behind the main lodge ready to enjoy a sundowner with the crew. But no one from my group is here. Readying a gin and tonic, the bartender tells me they're out on the river, enjoying a cruise. "They waited a few minutes then went on. Shall I radio them to come back for you?"

Okay, so I was a little late, but I was coated in dust and sweat and needed a shower. "Thanks, but no." I don't want to imagine how Matt and Cate would respond to having to turn the boat around.

I gravitate to a comfy chair and a low table in the far corner—a good distance away from any other seating. Facing west, this is the perfect spot to watch the sun set over the Zambezi River. To be honest, I'm pleased to have the next couple hours to myself before having to deal with Matt and Cate and sorting everything out. And here I thought we already had everything sorted weeks ago.

A moment later, the bartender gently taps my shoulder. I look up, and he points across the inlet a few yards to my right. Just beyond, there's a narrow spit of land and a small, sandy island. Boulders upon boulders. But I doubt that's what he wants me to see. Then I hear them. Deep, echoing rumbles. A few squeaks, then a trumpeting of anger. The splash of a massive body plunging into the water. Another splash, bigger than the first. Water roiling.

Pushing myself off the chair, I move soundlessly to the nearby railing, set up the tripod on the deck, turn on the camera, and aim in the direction of the splashing. Now, I see them—coming out of the water onto the sandy island. Maybe ten yards away. Two elephants. A large bull and, in front of him, a much smaller female. There's still enough light for me to see the dark staining on his temples, meaning he's in musth and horny as hell. The female is much smaller and very young, maybe nine or ten. This is probably her first time in estrus and her first time mating.

With a loud rumble, he suddenly mounts her from the rear. Trunk raised above her head, she bellows—more of a scream, it sounds to me—and tries to lunge. But with his enormous weight pressing down on her, she can't move. Across the inlet, the other females in the herd gather to watch. If he hurts this young cow, I have no doubt the matriarch will chase him off.

I keep filming even though the light is fading fast. Damn, my tungsten panels are back in the tent, and I hesitate to use my on-camera LED. Although it's powerful enough to illuminate the action, it might disturb this pair. However much I might want to stop what feels more like a rape, the number one rule of wildlife cinematography calls for me not to interfere. Right. I nearly laugh. As if this giant male with all that testosterone coursing through him would even notice.

Another roar of protest, and then finally the cow squirms out from under the bull. Bellowing her fury, she plunges into the narrow waterway and swims back across to the spit of land. I follow the young female's safe return to her family, and then zoom in on members of the herd draping their trunks across her face. I capture an older female inserting the tip of her trunk into the still frightened female's mouth. Comfort.

Back to the bull on the island. He looks like he wants to cross the channel and have at her again. Taking a few steps, he wades into the water. He's bigger than any of the cows, but if he were to go after the young female again, they could do some serious damage.

Panning my camera back to the herd, I see the older and larger females surround the young elie. They're guarding her now—as if she were a calf. Wishing I had Amie or Cate here with a second camera, I cut back again to the male. He comes ashore on the spit but a good distance away from the herd. Here, he finds the perfect place from which to stop any other bulls. Lifting his trunk above his head, he bellows what I can only imagine is his claim. "She's mine!"

Turning off the camera and leaving it in place for now, I retrieve my G&T and walk to the front of the deck. Listening to the river lap against the poles beneath my feet, I watch the sun begin to set. One minute, there's a giant pink and golden orb hovering above the river, the sky an abstract painting of mauve and lilac streaks. The next, the sun dips below the horizon, and night is on us full force. The temperature drops just as suddenly, and I'm shivering. Back at my chair, I pull on my fleece, which helps a bit, but I'm still cold and wish I'd brought something heavier. I hate to admit it, but I'm also missing having an arm draped across my shoulders, holding me close, keeping me warm.

Liam's arm. It's been years since we split, but he still

appears unbidden in my thoughts—usually at the most unexpected moments. Could be the result of the lack of romance
in my life since he left. In the beginning, Cate told me more
than once to get myself back out there and have some fun. I
tried, but most of the time, it was one and done. Not a good
fit. Finally, I called a time-out on dating and decided to focus
on my career in academia.

"Julia?"

Oh, God. Now I'm even hearing him. No, not Liam with
his deep, resonant voice. This is Matt. The crew must be
back from their sundowner cruise, which means it's time to
sort things out. I take a big swallow of my drink and turn to
face him.

He's smiling—a good sign. "Do you really need a stiff
drink before we talk?" I'm pretty sure he's teasing, but he
landed on the truth.

"Yeah, well . . ."

His smile slides off his face. "Look, my apologies. I was
out of line earlier. It's just that I'm used to being in charge—
that's my job—unless there's a producer onsite, throwing
weight around. But we're not even working on the project
yet. I'm sorry."

"Thanks. I appreciate it."

"So, we're good?"

Another sip of my drink. "What about when we're onsite, actually at work?" Hell, I know we've already agreed we'd
each have an equal say—unorthodox, to say the least, but I
was all for it.

"That *is* the question." He waves over the rest of the crew,
and the five of us find two cushy sofas facing each other.
Then, forearms resting on his thighs, Matt takes a moment

to look at each of us in turn. "Julia has raised a pretty critical question: who's got the final say?"

Cate curls her legs under her and nods in my direction. "We already discussed this. You saying you want to renegotiate our agreement?"

Matt nods. "I think we have to. Let's look at this rationally. We've got four weeks max to make this film, which includes filming and getting it home for post-production. If the three of us each have an equal voice, we'll be arguing constantly. There's no way we'll finish."

Raising an eyebrow, Cate murmurs, "And we've all got other jobs starting."

Matt doesn't respond. Neither do I. We don't have to. Until Tonderai sets his glass of red wine on the low table and clears his throat. "I am thinking where the wildlife is concerned, I need to be in charge. That is the way in the bush."

"Agreed." Matt's voice is firm, emphatic, brooking no disagreement. And it's not as though any of the rest of us are going to protest. "And I think as far as the actual film production is concerned, I've got to call the shots."

A man in charge. Top-down. And here I thought Matt and Cate and I would be operating under a new paradigm. Showing the industry it could be done. More fool I.

As if he's able to read my mind, Matt palms the air between us—a peace offering. "I like to think I'm freeing up you and Cate to do what you do best. Neither of you really knows what all's involved in a shoot. I'm not saying I won't take your vision into account. Believe me, Julia, I'm well aware you're the driving force behind this project. I'm just saying that with the time crunch we're facing, let's each focus on our expertise."

Quite the power play, Matt, even if you're doing it in the nicest and most practical way possible. I look across the table at Cate, who's processing this change and now nodding. Next to her, Amie, though, is twirling her long braid. Somehow, I know what's on her mind. The first class she took with me last year was in documentary film production. An overview of the process into which I packed a lot of detailed information and tricks of the trade—everything I'd learned during my years in the field.

"Amie, you look like you've got something to say." Kudos to Matt for involving our intern, but I hope she doesn't bring up the course.

A quick glance at me, then she shakes her head. "No, I'm good."

Matt looks at me, waiting for my buy-in.

"Yeah." It sure hurts to give him so much power over my film, but I don't have a hell of a lot of choice.

"Okay, then. What say we have dinner." Matt claps his hands on his knees and pushes himself to his feet.

I look toward the one long table where waiters are lighting small brass Moroccan lanterns and other guests are claiming seats. At this lodge, we all eat together.

"One more thing." Cate's voice stops us. "Any word on locking down the voice-over narrator?" Something in her tone tells me she already knows the answer and is encouraging Matt to share the news.

He stands in front of us, looking like a kid who's been keeping secrets and is now caught out. "As a matter of fact, I've got good news on that score."

"Do tell!" I metaphorically cross my fingers. I remember months earlier when Matt let on he could probably land a big name to narrate. That alone could help us market the film. So, why's he holding back?

"I'm sure you've all heard the name Natalie Powers?"

I nearly gasp, and not in a positive way. Nothing against Natalie Powers; she's immensely talented, one of Hollywood's newest rising stars, and she's already won a couple prestigious acting awards. According to *People* and Cate, she also scored Liam Shepard, or more likely he scored her. I'm not exactly sure when they got together, but the way Cate tells it, awfully close to the time when Liam and I split up. Maybe even before. I'm so lost in my thoughts, I almost miss the rest of what Matt says.

"We were working together on a film, and I pitched the idea to her. She loves it. Apparently, she's an ardent conservationist."

"Seriously?" I sound skeptical at best. Bitter is probably more like it.

"You okay with this, Julia?" Cate sounds concerned, which has me puzzled for a moment until I realize there's more to this announcement.

"Strange that I've never heard her name in the same sentence with animal conservation. Has she ever even been to Africa?"

Matt jumps back in. "We talked about that. If you're both willing to sign off on this, I'll let her know. She's all set to get a feel for what we're doing. Maybe even contribute to production costs."

My eyes meet Matt's. He finally blinks—a sure sign there's still more to this. "What aren't you telling me?"

"She'll be bringing her boyfriend."

Liam Shepard. The last person I want lurking around while we film. It's my turn to blink. "And if we don't? Agree to her doing the voice-over, I mean."

It's Cate who finally answers. "She's agreed to do the narration free of charge, Julia."

I exhale. Having Natalie Powers' name on this documentary is huge. Not having to pay her is even bigger. Bottom line: I need this film made and distributed—if I have any hope of getting tenure. Her name will help make that happen. So, I nod. "Sounds like a deal." What else can I say?

"Great! We thought you'd agree." I can hear the victory in Matt's voice. "And Julia, no worries about having to deal with them. They'll mostly be going out on game drives."

"Wait a sec. They're coming here?"

Matt nods.

"Why? Voice-over narrators don't go on location."

"That's the way Natalie works. She goes all in on projects and wants to get a feel for Zimbabwe and Hwange."

Just when I thought the evening couldn't get any worse, I take one of the last seats at the table, directly across from the big-game hunter Amie and I ran into at the InterCon—Gus Sinclair. The golden light of the Moroccan lanterns accentuates how ruggedly handsome he is. He looks delighted to see me, but after the way he pumped Amie for information about me, I'm feeling a little wary.

Give the man a chance! My inner voice seems determined to get me hooked up with a man on this trip.

The attraction is there, but I don't know . . .

Sitting next to me, Tonderai unfurls his cloth napkin in his lap. "This woman. Natalie Powers. She is very famous?"

I'm not quick enough with my answer. Gus invites himself

into our conversation. "You don't know? Bloody hell, she's one of the biggest Hollywood stars around." His accent tells me he's a Zimbo—a white Zimbabwean. His family's probably been here for generations.

Tonderai shrugs. I'm not sure if he could care less or if he's sloughing off Gus. What I do know is he's curious why I'm upset about a very famous person coming to help with our little movie.

Shifting in my chair so my back is to Gus, I lower my voice and let him in on my secret. "It's kind of awkward. My ex-husband—"

"His name is Liam, I think? And he is an actor?"

"Yes to both. And he's now her boyfriend."

Tonderai purses his lips, clearly understanding my lack of enthusiasm about Natalie and Liam's impending visit. It suddenly dawns on me that the game drives Matt so casually proposed will fall on our guide's shoulders—which means Tonderai's shoulders. Might've been nice of Matt to ask instead of just adding to this man's workload.

Apparently, Gus's hearing is better than I thought. "So, you were once married to Liam Shepard?" His voice is loud enough to draw the attention of the people at our end of the table. Amie shoots an awestruck look in my direction. "Hard to imagine why you let him get away. Must be quite a story."

"Sorry to disappoint," I say as a waiter places a bowl of cream of mushroom soup in front of me. "No story at all. We simply went our separate ways."

Glancing over at Cate, I see her grin and mouth the word "liar." She's right, of course. I stayed with him a lot longer than I should have, and there was no 'simple' about any of those last few weeks together. Just a lot of pain.

I clink my spoon hard against my bowl, hoping Gus will see how focused I am. This is not the kind of conversation I want to have with him. But either he doesn't see or doesn't care.

"No fuss. No drama. My kind of woman." He points his spoon at me and looks ready to keep talking.

If he's so determined to talk, I'd rather my former marriage and divorce not be the focus of his observations. Casting around for something—anything—to say, I land on the first thing that comes to mind. "You're a hunter." Next to me, I feel Tonderai stiffen.

"*Yebo.* How'd you know?"

"A lucky guess." I try valiantly to concentrate on the velvet deliciousness of my soup.

He chuckles softly. "Here's my lucky guess: you don't hunt."

"Correct." I want to keep my part of the conversation as terse as possible, but this is one of those times when I just can't help myself. "Hunting is the last thing I'd ever do."

My soup done, the waiter removes the bowl, replacing it with a steak cooked to perfection—meaning rare.

And that's all Gus needs. "I take it you're one of those animal-lovers who believe meat comes wrapped in plastic from the grocery or butcher shop. You're willing to eat meat, but not shoot it." Although his words sting a bit, his smile is actually warm and friendly as if he really wants to engage me in a conversation.

Pausing for a moment with my fork and serrated knife ready to slice into my steak, I caution myself: *Don't ruin this meal for everyone! Just let him think he's right. Tomorrow we'll go to Hwange. He'll take his clients and their guns to some private reserve, and I'll never have to deal with him again.* I look him in the eye. "Guilty." I suppose I could add a little girlish laugh, but I chew a piece of brilliantly cooked beef instead.

"Have you ever hunted?" He sounds solicitous. Will he actually offer to take me out and show me the ropes?

"Nope." I try to infuse finality into my voice so we can just move on.

"Maybe you should give it a try." He's still going for friendly. "Just let me know, and I'll be happy to take you out."

Determined not to say anything, I shrug and signal the waiter for a refill of my wine.

"You might not believe me, but hunting actually helps the economy in this country. It's also an important part of animal conservation. Did you know that? Each of my guests pays good money. Just ask Tonderai; he'll back me up." Still the pleasant tone. Still flirting.

I glance at Tonderai, who focuses quietly on his steak, not offering any backup. It takes me a few more seconds to wonder how Gus and Tonderai know each other in the first place. I'm sure Tonderai will fill me in.

But really, 'hunting helps the economy'? I've heard others make Gus's argument before, and I'm sure he believes what he's saying. I wonder if his idea of 'hunting' involves trotting out old animals in what's little more than a canned hunt. Sometimes guys like Gus go in for gorgeous specimens. The guests demand an animal in his prime for bragging rights. As far as I'm concerned, these hunters are no better than legalized poachers. And I don't for one minute believe the money they pay to bag their trophies is all going to help the majority of the Zimbabweans who live close to the poverty line. My guess: it's lining the pockets of government officials and some wealthy private citizens. Not that I could ever prove it.

The awkward silence at this end of the table finally gets to me. It's way too uncomfortable here, so as soon as I finish my steak, I push back my chair.

A waiter is with me in an instant, carefully retrieving the napkin from my lap and refolding it to place next to my plate. "Madam Wilde, you would like the dessert?"

Wherever I go in southern Africa, it always amazes me how everyone in the camps—from the manager to the waiters to the housekeepers—knows my name. Impeccable service. "Thanks, but no. I think I'll call it a night."

Amie starts to stand, but I wave her back to her seat. "No need. Stay and enjoy yourself."

She smiles and nods.

Tonderai, though, is on his feet. "Come. I will walk you to your tent."

After I collect my camera and tripod, we stop at the bar for the key to the gun rack. Then, carrying his rifle, he walks me down the gravel road.

I know having an escort after dark is absolutely mandatory in Africa's national parks, but I've never seen or even heard anything other than a bird. "Is this really necessary? I hate taking you away from dessert."

"It is no bother. They will save my dessert."

"So tell me, what's the going rate for an elephant these days?"

He doesn't miss a beat. "From what I hear, it is seventy thousand U.S. to be able to export the head and tusks."

"Wow! I didn't know the permits are so pricey. What about for a lion?"

"I am thinking fifty-five thousand, but it can be as high as one hundred thousand for a male in his prime."

"And like Gus said, all the money goes to help poor families and to conserve endangered species. It's truly amazing." I hope Tonderai picks up on my sarcasm.

He coughs. "I hope you do not believe that."

"Not for a minute." A few steps later, I add, "I guess we've seen the last of Gus and his hunters."

"I worked with him some years ago at Mana Pools, and he was a very good guide. Honest and truly caring for the animals. But now . . . he operates a private reserve—Buffalothorn Camp. It is very close to the Hwange border, near where we will be on the Ngamo Plains. It is possible you may see him again."

"Where does he hunt?"

"On his reserve."

"He's got enough animals there for all his hunters?"

Tonderai presses his lips together. "As you may remember, there is no fence around the park. The animals cross back and forth. When they're not in the park, his guests can kill them legally and take home their trophies."

I tighten my hands around my tripod and look closely at Tonderai. What else isn't he telling me?

Thirteen

First thing after breakfast, Tonderai and another guide lash our gear onto the luggage rack atop one of the lodge's vans. We'll drive to the train depot at Dete and catch the one-car train called "The Elephant Express" for the three-hour trip straight down the boundary of the park to Marula Camp. Tonderai tells us chances are good we'll see a host of animals: elephants and giraffes, buffalos and lions crossing the tracks in and out of the park.

The engineer and conductor are waiting for us when we arrive and help us shift our gear onto the forest-green, open-air train. With a nod to Cate, I park the Pelican case with my camera and several lenses on one of the bench seats, then thread on the 100-500 mm. Across the aisle, Cate does the same, and Amie follows our lead. We've got both sides of the tracks covered.

Tonderai moves to the front of the train car next to the engineer. He'll be our wildlife spotter. Matt helps himself to the seat next to me, and Cate waves Amie onto the seat by her. She knows Matt and I need to talk.

We don't launch into our conversation right away. Almost as soon as we start to roll, Tonderai calls a halt. "Giraffe on the left." Cate and Amie's side of the car, so after the engineer turns off the engine—an absolute whenever we film to eliminate any vibration—I let them work undisturbed.

Watching Amie pick up the camera for the first time on the trip, I try to ignore the pronounced tremor in her hands. But I'm sure Cate doesn't miss it. After a few minutes of filming three giraffe cows and a youngster browsing on acacia leaves, Cate turns off her camera and signals to move on.

"Wait!" Amie keeps filming. I can tell she's watching the animals intently, and it's almost as though she's anticipating something's about to happen.

And then it does.

From out of nowhere, a large giraffe bull lopes into view. That's enough to startle the females and the calf into a sprint along the tracks. They then turn and gallop in the opposite direction, all the while the bull in eager pursuit. Another abrupt turn, and they race past us again. Some nice footage—if Amie's trembling hands don't ruin it.

From the corner of my eye, I see Cate tap her fingertips on the table-top, signaling her judgment. Clearly, she saw the tremor. It was kind of hard to miss. I've watched Amie film on any number of occasions and reviewed her projects but never seen any evidence of this before. Is she nervous about shooting under Cate's watchful gaze? Or is it something else?

Years ago, I saw Cate tap the same tattoo against her tripod. Certain it was in response to something I'd done wrong, I asked during the next break in filming. She let me know exactly where I'd gone astray—zooming in and out on the scene way too fast. "You'll make viewers dizzy." The mistake of a newbie, and I should've known better. Her criticism was harsh, and it stung. But I stayed awake most of the night, practicing over and over until I could zoom almost as smoothly as Cate. When I snuck back into the room we were sharing, she was awake. "You'll do." That was all she said, but it was enough, and it thrilled me.

When the train moves on, Matt leans in close and whispers. "You going to be able to handle this?"

"I assume you're talking about Liam and Natalie?"

"I am. Cate told me off last night after you went back to your tent. Called me a few choice names."

"Ouch!" I smile at the thought of Cate speaking her mind. It also feels good that she's always got my back.

Matt looks directly at me. "Yeah, well, I deserved it. But honestly, I didn't know you and Liam were once married. Contrary to what you said at dinner last night, I hear it was a messy split."

"He was pretty much a prick."

"Men often are."

I laugh out loud. "It all came apart right after the debacle six years ago. And yes, it was rough. I caught him cheating on me. Then, as he was walking out the door, he announced he was dumping me so I wouldn't drag down his career. Given that I'd just been basically blacklisted by Hollywood."

He draws back, all the better for me to see him cringe. "That was harsh."

"Tell me about it."

"Look, tell me what you want me to do. I can still call them off. Or tell Natalie to leave Liam behind. It's not like he's got any skin in this game."

I study the acacia bushes we're passing and see a family of warthogs look up as the train clatters past, then scamper into the woods. Oh, those huge warts on the male's temples and the curved tusks—a face only a mother could love. We cover mile after mile of track as I delve into my feelings. Hell yes, it'd be easier to make this film without having to deal with either Natalie or Liam. But there's Natalie's star power to consider. Her name alone could get us a debut at a festival.

Take the long view! I can almost hear Cate telling me from across the aisle. *All that matters is the film.*

Okay, so Natalie's one thing, but I seriously don't want to be around Liam again. Not in this lifetime. It would make things uncomfortable and awkward, and that could have a seriously negative impact on my work.

I turn back to Matt. "Do you think Natalie would come without him?"

He shrugs. "Don't know. I'd need to find out."

Suddenly, none of this makes sense. It takes time to get plane tickets—unless they've already bought them. It takes time to get from LA to Jo'burg, then to Vic Falls. Unless, of course, they're already on their way. I look Matt in the eye. "Where are they?"

He looks away and exhales. "Back at the lodge."

On the off-chance he's joking, I say sarcastically, "Guess I was so caught up talking with Gus Sinclair that I missed them at dinner last night."

"They're staying in one of the luxury villas on the island in the middle of the river and had dinner over there."

I gape. "Wait, you're serious, aren't you?" I'm ready to push myself to my feet and storm away, except I'm stuck on this train. "What the hell were you thinking?" I hiss. "That this would be a happy reunion?"

"Believe me, Cate disabused me of that notion very quickly. Didn't you see how pissed she was yesterday afternoon? I'd just finished telling her when Tonderai called."

"Well, yeah, but I thought that was because she'd hauled

her camera all the way through the woods only to discover the surgery was over."

He slips off his black Save the Rhino cap and runs his fingers through his hair, revealing a bit more gray and a larger bald spot than the last time we worked together. "Look, we can talk this out in a thousand different ways. But I need an answer. Does Natalie do the voice-over or not?"

I glance toward Cate, but she's intently studying the bush, looking for wildlife. The hunch of her back, though, reveals a lot. *You're a pro. Suck it up and act like it!*

Turning back to Matt and speaking loudly enough for Cate to hear, I give him my answer. "Yeah. It'll be good for the film. Might actually get it out there."

"And Liam?"

"Gotta keep the star power happy."

"I take it that's a 'yes.'"

I nod. "Just keep him away from me."

Grabbing my camera, I make my way to the front of the car. Tonderai gives me a sympathetic glance as well as his seat next to the engineer. Just as I thought: everyone heard Matt and me—at least the tail end of the conversation.

He leans in close. "I will do my best to keep them out on safari."

"Thanks, but we'll need you on set, too."

Instead of commiserating further, he taps my shoulder and points ahead through the front window. At the same time, the engineer slowly applies the brakes.

"What?" I squint but can't make out much of anything.

"Straight ahead, lying on the tracks. Can you see them?" Tonderai starts to open the front window, as slowly and as quietly as he can.

We inch forward until finally I realize that what I thought was a pile of sand on the tracks—stupid, of course—is really a lion. No, two lions. We pull closer, and I count again: six of them splayed on their backs across the tracks, sunning their distended bellies.

"They're huge!" I whisper.

"The Ponies." Tonderai's voice is full of admiration. "Their mother was the largest female anyone had ever seen, so we called her Horse. These are her daughters. They're pretty far from home, and from the looks of them, they've had a very good kill. Probably a buffalo."

An instant later, Cate is next to me, squeezing Tonderai into the corner. We both raise our cameras to our shoulders and start to film as the train creeps forward. The lion in front wakes and sleepily turns her head to watch the train coming closer. No worries on her part; she lifts her front legs and stretches hard, then eases back down against the rails.

Then, I see them. Cubs—maybe six months old and a few more who seem to be even younger—lifting their heads and peering over their mothers to get a look at what could well be their first train.

I zoom in on them, but the vibration of the train, however slight, is getting to me, and I'm sure it must be annoying Cate. Just as I'm about to signal the engineer to turn off the engine, Amie speaks from directly behind me where she's peering over my shoulder, "Please, don't go any closer!"

Next to me, Cate stiffens. I know there will be words later, and I don't blame her. No one speaks on a shoot, and I mean *no one*, unless it's a dire emergency—as in the lion jumps into the train and is about to eat one of us for lunch. And Amie knows this from filmmaking 101.

Still, it gets the job done. The engineer turns off the engine, and until the lions finally decide to clear off the track, we're in our element.

An hour later, the train slows and stops. Looking along my side of the tracks, I don't see any animals. Instead, parked on the verge of the dirt road, there are two open-air safari land cruisers each with three tiers of seats behind the cab. The drivers are both waving their welcome as they walk toward the train to help us unload. I pack up my camera, but Tonderai waves me aside when I start to lift the Pelican case. "It will go much faster if you let us take care of everything."

"Many thanks!" Grabbing my backpack, I leave my gear for the guys to carry. But a moment later, as I climb down the metal steps, I manage to snag my pack on the railing and miss the final step, pitching forward.

Two hands are there to catch me. "Hey, steady there! Won't do to twist your ankle before you even arrive in camp."

In front of me, the man in an olive khaki shirt with *Mambas* embroidered on the breast pocket gently sets me on the ground—close enough to breathe in his faint scent of lime. Unfortunately for him, my pack now unsnagged from the railing swings around and slams against his shoulder.

"Oof!"

"Oh, jeez! I'm so sorry. Are you okay?"

"No worries." He grins. "How's the ankle?" His British accent definitely catches my attention. So does his neatly trimmed brown hair, not to mention his smiling green eyes.

What a way to make a first impression. "It's fine. Really." I wriggle my foot back and forth to prove my point, then take a step, putting my full weight on it. Thank God I wasn't carrying my camera. Although the Pelican case is strong, with lots of interior padding, the last thing I'd want is for it to smack against the ground. No telling what that'd do to the camera or the lenses.

"Ground's a bit uneven here." He nods toward the hole I just stepped into. "You're all right then?"

"All good. I'm Julia Wilde by the way. Thanks for making such a great catch."

"Pleasure. Name's Colin. Colin Tremblay. I'm the director of the Mambas. Right next to you, this is Dabney."

A giant of an Ndebele man steps in front of me to help Cate negotiate the final step off the train, then turns to me. "Everyone calls me Dabs." His large hand envelops mine. "Why don't you two ladies walk over to the vehicles while we transfer the gear."

Eyes twinkling, Cate links her arm around mine and sets us walking to the vehicles. "Quite the flying leap you made back there. Lucky Colin was there to catch you."

"He's got good hands."

She nods approvingly. "Good everything, I imagine. It'll be nice to have some eye candy on this shoot. And between this guy and Gus—"

"Oh, please."

"Don't give me that. Unless you've been holding out on me, it's way past time you had some fun."

I glance back over my shoulder to see Colin watching me. Damn, I hate to be caught looking. Cate's right, though: he is handsome. And based on his accent, not a Zimbo. "Sorry to disappoint, but I'm officially off men. They're too much work.

Besides, I need to focus all my attention on this film. But if you're interested, have at him. With my blessings."

She laughs. "I play for the other team."

I try to hide my surprise. "I didn't know."

"I don't exactly advertise my sexuality." She looks past me toward Colin and the rest of the guys unloading our gear. "I'm not telling you to marry the man. But Colin could be exactly the diversion you need while Liam and Natalie are here."

I groan. "You had to remind me about Liam?" I hold up both hands in near surrender. "It'll be okay. Tonderai and Matt promised to keep them away from me—out on safari."

"Tonderai. Now, there's a good man. And I'm proud of you for being so professional about this."

"Thanks."

"Still doesn't mean you can't have some fun." Snorting a laugh, she walks us a few meters past the vehicles, stopping next to a clump of mopane trees—no elephants in sight. "We need to talk."

I close my eyes for a count of three. "Go ahead. Say what you need to say."

"Amie. She's not cinematographer material. I even question her camera-operating ability."

"You're basing this on what? A couple hours' work? I had her in class for a year, and I'm telling you she's got promise."

She shrugs. "So, maybe she'll make some entertaining home videos with friends, but I'm not seeing any natural ability."

"That's pretty harsh. Besides, she's just getting started. Cut her some slack. You sure let me get by with a lot of mistakes."

"I didn't let you get by with squat. And I could tell from the get-go you had something, not only promise—real talent."

"Thanks, but I think you're wrong about Amie. She'll get it together. She needs some time."

Cate studies the ground in front of her, then takes another few steps—careful to avoid a pile of fresh elephant dung—and turns to face me, her eyes sympathetic but decided. "Look, I'm all for supporting women. But I don't want to see her wasting her time, especially when I suspect she's in the wrong field. She needs to find what she's passionate about."

"You hardly know her." I'm baffled by this quick judgment. "Give her a chance."

Cate kicks a round of dried elephant dung. "Are you going to tell her? Or shall I?"

"Don't you dare breathe a word of this to her. If things don't improve, I'll talk to her—when we get home."

Fourteen

Once our gear is piled in the back of Dabs' safari vehicle, Tonderai and Amie join him and head out to the lodge. I start to climb into the back of the second vehicle, leaving the front seat next to Colin for Matt, when Cate stops me with a wry grin. "With your injured ankle, maybe you should sit in front."

"Absolutely!" Matt is quick to agree. "When did you get hurt?"

Cate is equally quick to answer. "Just now. She fell off the train."

"My ankle is fine, and you know it." Grinding my teeth, I all but slam myself onto the front seat.

Pressing his lips together to hide his amusement, Colin slips behind the steering wheel. "Glad to have you up front. Much better view from here."

I glance over at him and nod. "Duly noted. Thanks."

It's a quick drive across the savanna to Marula Camp—maybe fifteen minutes—and although Colin's not an official driver, he handles the vehicle well, easing it gently down into ruts and out again. He stops to point out a lilac-breasted roller. With its gorgeous aqua and tan, pink and purple feathers, this could be my favorite bird ever. Later, he stops again to let me watch a pair of red-beaked bateleur eagles performing acrobatics through the air. From their seats further back, I'm pleased to note, neither Matt nor Cate can see them.

"So graceful." Leaning my elbows on the dashboard, I prop my chin in my hands and follow their diving swoops and rolls. "I love watching them."

"Their mating ritual." Colin studies them through his binoculars. A moment later, he offers them to me. "Would you like to take a closer look?"

I train the binocs on the birds and smile. "They're incredible. I could watch them forever, but I guess we're expected at the lodge."

In front of us, the road narrows until it's nothing more than an animal trail. Grass brushes against the sides of the vehicle—tall and still green—some of it high enough to lash my upper arm. Impressive, especially when it should be brown and dried out by this time of year. "I know there were late rains up near Vic Falls, but it looks like you had some down here, too."

Colin nods. "We did. It lasted well into April, which is unusual for us."

Ahead, I can see the lodge rising out of the grass to greet us. Its thickly thatched roof and poles made of quirky twisted tree trunks lend a magical quality to the place. And there behind the main building, I can just make out the expansive water hole with elephants and a few impala already gathering. Half a dozen tents on platforms with wooden decks, maybe five feet off the ground, overlook the water. More tents on the other side of the water open onto patios. It's absolutely perfect. I can't help grinning.

"Charming, isn't it?" Colin stops next to the lodge and drapes his right arm across the top of the steering wheel.

"I love it. We stayed here a few nights last time before going on to Jozibanini . . ."

"Ah, yes." Only two syllables, but the sympathy is evident in his voice. Of course he knows what happened.

"Yeah." I appreciate the acknowledgement—and that he doesn't ask for details. Despite Cate's ridiculous attempt to throw us together, I'm starting to like him.

He's quick to move the conversation along. "Jozi's brilliant, although I haven't been able to spend nearly enough time there. Maybe one day." Turning in his seat, he takes in Matt and Cate. "Tell you what. How about you go on to your tents. The ladies are all in number one. Matt, you'll be in number two. We'll bring your gear. Take some time to sort yourselves, then meet me back in the lodge to discuss the project. Say, in an hour?"

"Sounds good." Matt swings his leg over the side of the vehicle and jumps to the ground.

Cate follows.

"Do you need a hand?" Colin asks me.

"I'm never going to live this down, am I?"

"I wouldn't want you to stress a wonky ankle." He's making a clear effort to swallow his laugh.

"Thanks, but no. I'm good." I shoulder open the passenger door and climb out, debating whether I should jump up and down to prove my ankle is fine. Then again, perhaps that would be a little too childish.

Our tent is spacious enough for two people, but there are three of us sharing, so it's a little crowded, especially given the tension threatening to erupt between Cate and Amie. At least there are three single beds. No dresser, though. Instead, there are luggage racks for our duffels—one next to each bed. Not a problem—I've lived out of my duffel many times before. A bonus: unlike at Jozi, the bathroom's inside. No need to unzip the tent flap in the middle of the night and go outside to pee. Plus, there's a real shower—not the overhead bucket. True luxury!

As soon as Dabs and Colin deliver our luggage, I take some time to check over my camera gear. One thing I pride myself on is making sure the lenses are crystal clean and everything's in good working order. Apparently, I'm the only of us who thinks this is important. Amie is the first to leave, heading back to the lodge to watch the elies at the water hole. She makes sure to take her cell phone with her for personal videos and pics. Cate leaves soon after. For a moment I worry she's following Amie to tell her she'll never be a cinematographer. No, Cate wouldn't go behind my back.

A few minutes later, she's back, hands on her hips, talking through the zippered screen. "I'll let you share the news with her. So long as you promise to do it."

"When we get home."

"What's the point in waiting?"

I counter. "What's the point in telling her now?"

She turns away from the screen. "I'll see you up at the lodge. Word is they'll be serving tea and cookies."

It's late afternoon by the time I make my way to the lodge, where I discover neither Amie nor Cate is anywhere to be found. Or Tonderai. Walking the back deck along the water hole, I find no one, not even staff. The dining room, the bar—both empty. I retrace my steps to the deck and claim a chair—all the better to enjoy the elies playing and drinking and bathing. They're even climbing down into the swimming pool not ten feet in front of me.

A few minutes later, Colin claims the chair next to mine. He's wearing an olive sweater that looks to be military issue, which has me wondering if the temperature is about to get colder. Of course it is. I wish I'd remembered before I left the tent. "They're fun to watch," he says, handing me one of the two glasses of iced tea he's carrying.

"Believe me, I could stay here forever."

"You don't think you'd get bored?"

"Never! Big cats, elephants, rhinos. They make my heart sing."

"What about wild dogs?"

"Them, too."

He laughs. "Not very discriminating."

"I prefer to think I'm inclusive."

"Touché."

I clink my glass against his. "To happy days! And thanks for the tea." One sip later, "God, this is lovely. And I mean it's really, really delicious."

"Glad you like it. My secret recipe."

Another sip and I set down my glass on the small table between our chairs. "You sharing the recipe?"

"Sorry. Then it wouldn't be secret." Unfortunately for me, he looks serious. Except then the corner of his lip curls up. Maybe I can wrangle the recipe out of him.

A moment later, he lays his hand on mine, barely touching me, then points to the other side of the swimming pool. An elephant calf maybe all of six weeks old and still covered in thick hair. Her trunk is way too short to reach the water, even if she knew how to use it, which at this age she doesn't. For her, water is something to play in. I'm suddenly afraid she might take a running leap into the pool and find herself in way over her head. Her mother and aunties wouldn't be able to get her out. Apparently, the adults must share my concern, because several long trunks are quickly on the baby's back, steering her away from the edge of the pool and over to the water hole. There she'll be able to stand in the water, playing to her heart's content, without risk of drowning.

"It always amazes me how smart elephant mothers are." My voice sounds almost wistful. Although wistful for what, I'm not sure.

"They are. It's one of the many great discoveries I've made since moving out here."

"Where was home?"

"England. Originally. But I spent so many years in the army—posted outside the country—that by the time I left the military, it didn't feel like home anymore."

He doesn't tell me where he was posted, and something tells me not to ask. "Does this feel like home?"

"Most definitely." He smiles. "I'm here for the duration. What about you? I realize you travel a lot for your work, but where do you call home?"

I stare in response and for a few long seconds realize I can't answer. "It's kind of hard to say. For the last few years, I haven't been traveling." He looks puzzled, but I decide not to explain, other than to say, "I've been living in Wisconsin. A small town near Milwaukee."

That's when Matt joins us, sinking onto the chair on the other side of me. He's got a plate of treats in hand. "So, here you both are. By the way, these peanut butter and chocolate things are great. The others ate theirs before they left on the evening game drive."

"Game drive? Shouldn't they be here for this? Certainly Cate should be."

Matt shrugs nonchalantly. "There was a drive about to start, and they wanted to go. I gave them my blessing." He takes a bite of a chocolate peanut butter bar and nearly purrs, then remembers to offer the plate to me.

One bite, and I'm converted. This is officially the best treat ever.

He takes his time eating, but finally he's ready to get down to business. "I think the three of us can handle the schedule." He tips his head toward Colin. "And anything else that might come up."

Yet again, I've got the feeling discussions are happening and plans are being made without my knowledge. Why did I ever think making this film with Matt directing would be a good idea?

Colin takes a long drink of his tea. "How early do you want to start tomorrow?"

"I'd love to get going by seven, if possible," says Matt. "I'll need time to brief the women—"

"Margaret, Zinhle, Pepsi, and Barbara," I say, wishing I didn't have to interrupt Matt, but these women have names. Both men stare at me. "Well, they sent me their stories, and I wrote their lines."

Colin continues. "The women and I talked about their reasons for joining the Mambas. It was a tough choice, but along with Margaret, these are the three who fit best with your screenplay."

"Great." Matt takes over. "I can run through their lines

with them, make sure they know the delivery and emphasis I'd like, and if we've still got some good light, we can start filming."

"Okay then. I'll let them know." Colin tips his glass of iced tea to both of us.

Matt suggests how he'd like to schedule the rest of the shoot—at least for this week—and when he'd like to work with each woman. He also asks for a day when the entire Mamba force could be available.

"Why is that?" Colin seems puzzled.

"I'd like to pan along the line of women to show the number of them who've been recruited for this work. Another day, when we've got nice weather and blue skies, I'd like to film three or four of the women out on patrol. Maybe even in action—if a poaching call comes in."

I have to hand it to Matt: from what he's sketched out so far, he's keeping to the narrative arc we planned.

"No worries. We should be able to handle all of that. Unfortunately, we've had a bit of an uptick in poaching this last month. As a result, we're getting calls every few days. Even if no call comes in, though, you could film the women on patrol. That's a big part of their job."

"Outstanding. What do you think, Julia?"

I smile my thanks for being included. "It all sounds good. I think you've got things well in hand." And he does. The more I listen to him, the more I'm reminded that he absolutely knows his craft. He can put a film together, get performances from the actors, set up the shots he needs. All I can really do is film those scenes. Which also takes real talent. But I've come to realize he was right to put himself in charge. I'd have made a hash of it.

"Then it sounds like we're ready to go." Matt slaps his hands on the armrests, ready to push himself to his feet and head to the bar.

Colin raises his hand. "Two more things, if you don't mind."

Matt settles back in his chair. "Shoot."

"Tonderai told me there are two more crew members arriving tomorrow?"

"Yes." Matt nods. "The actress Natalie Powers. She'll be doing the voice-over narration. And her partner Liam Shepard, although he's not really part of the crew."

"They'll need a tent?"

"Of course." Matt slaps his hand against his forehead. "Damn. I forgot to let you know. Sorry about that. Any chance there's one still available?"

"I checked with Dabs, and as it happens, yes. But there will be an additional charge."

Feeling suddenly nauseous, I close my eyes. Does Matt seriously think I'm going to pay for Natalie and Liam's stay in camp? Those two earn more on a single film than I'll make in ten years.

Matt brings his hand down on mine. "We'll work it out."

"You said there was something else?" I drink the rest of my tea. Oh, I definitely need to find out how to make this.

Colin sits up straighter, appearing like nothing less than the soldier he used to be. "There is. I need to know what kind of compensation you have in mind for the Mambas. Certainly for the four women whose stories you'll tell, but now it sounds like you want as many of them as possible to appear in scenes."

I sit straighter, too, but don't come close to matching Colin's erect posture. "Compensation?"

Matt leans forward. "Julia, let me handle this, please."

A moment later, Colin's out of his chair and leaning against the deck railing. Behind him, the sky is turning red and orange with the setting sun—the perfect backlighting for the animals clustered at the water hole. No stranger to power moves, Matt is also on his feet, his hand resting on the railing. Hating the optics of the woman sitting by while the men hash this out, I stand too. But there's no room for me to wedge myself between the two of them.

"I assumed there would be some sort of payment for the women, if not for the organization." Colin sounds determined. "Don't the people who work in the film industry get paid?"

"Of course they do." Matt sounds like he's ready to talk this out, man to man. "But documentaries are a bit different—"

"What do you mean?"

"Well, with documentaries, we don't pay people to tell their stories."

Colin furrows his brow. "You need to explain why that is."

"Paying would be akin to checkbook journalism. It compromises the integrity of the story." Matt keeps his voice even and rational. He really is a good negotiator—something I am not.

"Rather convenient, don't you think? You Hollywood people come in and tell these women they've got to work but can't be paid because that's the rule of documentary filmmaking?"

Matt palms the air between them. "No one's trying to take advantage of the women. This is just how we shoot documentaries."

"Maybe in Hollywood, but life is very different here."

Matt glances over at me. "You know, with the attention you'll get from this film, donations to the Mambas will likely increase—to a much higher level than anything we could offer."

Colin is quick to shake his head. "Sorry, that's a gamble the women can't afford to take."

I've had enough of sitting back and listening to these two. This involves me, and I'm not about to let them come to an agreement without my input. "Then why didn't you say something before now?" I pitch my voice to match Matt's.

"I did mention it." Colin sounds steady and firm. "But then the contract you sent didn't include anything."

Oh God, don't let this be happening. "Please understand that no one who's working on this film is getting paid." Okay, my voice is getting a little shrill. I need to rein it back down to a normal tone.

Colin makes a fist, then relaxes his hand. "It's one thing for all of you to opt to work for free. It's quite another to expect the Mambas to do the same. That's just not on."

"Maybe you don't understand. We're on a miniscule budget. We can't just suddenly change the contract—" My voice isn't anywhere back to normal.

"Julia." Matt's voice is a little harsher.

Colin leans forward and looks me in the eye. "To be honest, I'm not concerned about your budget, although I think you probably have a different definition of 'miniscule' than we do here in Zimbabwe. I'm here to make sure the Mambas get a fair deal." Damn if he isn't still speaking calmly. "And I haven't signed the contract yet. Nor have any of the women."

"You what?" Definitely not a normal tone.

"We'll sign the contract when the women get the respect and the compensation they deserve."

Matt clears his throat. "What about a percentage of any

profits going to the Mambas' organization? You could divide it among the women however you want." A sly offer on Matt's part. Something that wouldn't have occurred to me. Probably because we both know a short documentary is never going to turn a profit, unless by some miracle it's a blockbuster. But it's highly unlikely Colin knows the reality of the market.

Colin shakes his head. "Sorry, but no. These women need to be paid now. If not upfront, then by the time filming is complete. So much of their escape from abusive situations has depended on getting work and being paid. Didn't you read the stories they sent you before you wrote their lines?"

I feel my cheeks burning. "Of course I did."

"Then why is it so difficult for you to understand how important money is to them? They've been at the mercy of their husbands, their fathers, their brothers. They're the victims of domestic abuse. Joining the Mambas was the only way many of them could get the money they needed to leave these horrible situations. To take care of their children. To ensure their future."

"I know money's important! But I'm strapped, and this film is something I've got to make to get tenure at my university. Without it, I'm out on the street." I look toward the sun just now disappearing below the horizon. *Please don't let this film fall through. Not now.*

"Sorry to hear about your personal money issues. But—"

"No! Don't say it." I palm the air between us. "How much do you want?"

He takes a deep breath, which sounds all too victorious. "The women discussed it and think twenty thousand dollars would be fair."

Twenty thousand! I swallow hard. How would the

Mambas know to come up with such a number? I glance at Colin and have to wonder how much he influenced them, maybe raising their initial suggestion? And then increasing it again. But what does any of that really matter? The real question is: where the hell am I going to find that kind of money? I look at Matt, who certainly has a lot more cash than I do. Then again, he probably funds a much more lavish lifestyle, too. Not to mention he's directing this film for free. There's nothing else I can do but pay. "Will you take credit cards?"

He laughs. But I don't hear any joy in it. "You're telling me you've got a card with that high a limit?"

I don't answer, just turn and head toward the stairs.

"Hey, wait! Where are you going?"

"Back to my tent."

"You can't. Not in the dark. And not with all these elies here. Wait while I get my gun. I'll walk you."

"Fuck you!" I mutter under my breath once he's out of earshot.

He's back with me in a couple minutes, beckoning me away from the stairs, which I see lead directly down into the path of several huge bull elephants. "We'll walk the long way around. A lot safer. I for one don't relish being gored or trampled."

"But you want to gore me," I practically hiss.

"Not at all." He's way too quick to bark back. "What I want is for you to treat these women fairly."

"And you think I'm taking advantage of them."

"Not if I can help it." He turns away sharply.

Arms tightly crossed, I follow Colin to the tent, making sure to keep a good five feet between us. Any closer, and one of us would probably explode.

In the tent, I sink down onto my bed and empty out my back-pack, pulling out my brown leather passport and money portfolio last. But I'm so angry that my fingers fumble the zipper of the credit card sleeve. Finally, I shove the portfolio toward him. "Here! Unzip it and take them."

Resting his gun across Cate's bed, he stares at me, his green eyes hard. But there's something else I can't quite read. Then, taking a step closer, his hands steady, he deftly opens the compartment. Five plastic credit cards slide out onto my bed.

I scoop them up and slap them onto his palm. "Here, take them. Let's hope they cover the full twenty thousand. You may need to spread out the charges over the next few days so you don't exceed my cash withdrawal limits. Fill out the slips or whatever you've got to do, and I'll sign them. Let me know if the banks need me to okay the charges."

"Julia . . ."

"Whatever you're going to say, don't. You want fair treatment for these women. I heard you the first time, and I get it. I do. And actually, I agree with you—even though you probably don't believe me."

Slipping the cards into his pocket, he lifts his gun off Cate's bed and takes a step toward the front entrance of the tent, then turns back. "I hear the trucks coming back from the game drive. They'll be serving dinner soon. I'll walk you back to the lodge."

I shake my head. "No thanks. I'll pass."

"You sure?"

"Would you just go? Please."

Once outside, he zips the tent screen shut, sealing me

inside. After listening to his boots slap down the treads, I jam my stuff back into my pack, then change into my base layers and stretch out on my bed. But I don't sleep. It's impossible to shut down my swirling anger. At Colin for making me feel like I'm taking advantage of the Mambas. But mostly with myself for not having thought of some sort of compensation for these women, for even thinking they'd participate for free. Why didn't Matt or Cate say something early on? I'm not a producer. I don't know these things.

But you should!

And why the hell couldn't Colin have said something months ago when we were negotiating? To tell us now when we're ready to start tomorrow, when we can't do anything other than cough up the money.

But he did.

I'm still angry, but pretending to sleep, when Amie and Cate return much later and whisper "Thanks!" to whoever escorted them back. They giggle their way up the steps and into the tent, stumbling as they make their way through the dark to the bathroom, and finally undressing and climbing into their twin beds.

Later still, I listen to their syncopated snoring punctuated by the not-so-distant roars of a lion marking his territory. The predators are definitely on the prowl.

Fifteen

It's early yet—only 5:00 a.m.—but I give up trying to sleep. Quickly pulling on yesterday's khaki pants, I layer a long-sleeve T-shirt over a camisole. Next, my puffer jacket. I start to thread my ponytail through the back of my Milwaukee Brewers cap but remember the elephant snatching it off my head a few years back and stop. Best not. You never know when you might run into an elie. Slipping out of the tent, I zip the door closed—I hope without waking Cate and Amie. I'll come back later for my gear. It's dark yet, but I see a single light on in the lodge—probably the kitchen, where the chef is making muffins or scones or something yummy for early breakfast before the other guests head out on the morning game drive and we go to work.

Standing on the deck, I hear the rustling and munching of mopane leaves on the side of the tent. A careful scan of the water hole reveals a bunch of large gray boulders. Every once in a while, one of them moves. Elephants. Or maybe hippos. They're way too close, and I don't have an armed escort. There's no point in doing something stupid and getting Tonderai or one of the other rangers in trouble. So, I sit and do my best to get a handle on the anger that's still messing with my brain.

Get it together! There's work to be done today, and this crap will only get in the way. Another half hour and someone will come around with our wake-up call. I just hope it's not Colin.

Eventually, Tonderai appears, his flashlight illuminating the bottom of the steps. "I see you are ready to go to the lodge. Please wait for me while I wake the others."

"Of course."

He climbs the steps past me. "Wakey, wakey," he calls into the tent.

Two groans answer him. From the way they sound, I'm guessing they both enjoyed themselves at the bar last night.

After making the rounds to the other tents, Tonderai returns and offers his hand to help me to my feet. Ever the gentleman, he doesn't ask why I'm awake so early or why I skipped dinner last night. We walk the short distance to the lodge, where he leaves me at the breakfast bar. There's nothing on offer yet. Not even coffee. But based on the aromas wafting in from the kitchen, there will be soon. Instead of hanging around like a sad puppy, I go back out on the deck and lean against the railing, looking at the water hole, the animals much more recognizable in the lightening gray of dawn.

I don't hear him approaching, but I catch a faint whiff of lime. Colin.

He leans his forearms on the railing next to me. "You missed a good dinner last night."

"Not exactly what I want to hear."

"Yeah, and it wasn't what I meant to say."

I let his words sit between us for a long minute, figuring he doesn't merit a response.

He tries again. "They almost don't look real in this light, do they?"

"Kind of frozen in place. Impossible to distinguish from boulders in the dark."

"Please tell me you didn't walk up here on your own."

"Nope. I was smart and waited for Tonderai."

"Good. Look, I want to say sorry for last night. I should have made our expectations clear months ago."

If he's expecting an apology from me, it's not coming anytime soon.

"Anyway, the women and I signed the contract. I gave it to Matt."

Thank God! I heave a sigh of relief. But I also feel the financial gut punch. "So, I take it the charges went through on the credit cards."

"Haven't heard yet. We're pretty remote out here, and it can take some time. I'll let you know."

"Thanks." My voice sounds way too sarcastic.

He takes a deep breath, having clearly decided what to say. "We've got to work together. It'll be a lot easier if we can be civil to each other."

He's right. Of course he's right. But I'm not there yet. "How's this . . . I'll be the complete professional while we're on the job."

And a bloody bitch the rest of the time, I can imagine him thinking. He straightens up and slaps his hands against the railing. "I guess that will have to do."

I follow him into the dining area where most of the tables are full. Off to one end, I see Cate by herself with two mugs of coffee and a plate of muffins.

She waves me over and points to one of the chairs. "Sit!"

I pull out the chair and sink onto the hard wooden seat.

She pushes one of the mugs to me, along with a muffin. "Eat!"

"Thanks. I take it the drinking was good last night."

"My head is pounding. Thought I'd have a drink or two, then someone brought out *scuds* of homemade beer and Amie was game—beer pong. Let me tell you, that stuff is evil."

"*Scuds*?"

"Large plastic bottles—named for the missiles the US rained down on Iraq way back when. Similar shape. At least, I think someone said that. It's all a blur."

I laugh gently because I well remember the headaches after nights of drinking home-brewed beer. I look around. "Where is Amie anyway? No, don't tell me."

"If she's smart, after puking up her guts, she's gone back to bed."

"Which is probably where you should be."

"And it's exactly where I'm headed. After you tell me what the fuck happened last night between you and Colin." God, she looks green.

I take a bite of the delicious ginger muffin, then a long sip of coffee, which I'm sure is a lot better than the *scud* that flowed last night. "What've you heard?"

"I can say only so many words before my head explodes. Just tell me."

Another sip of coffee, and I tell her the short version, only to have her grimace.

"That much I know. What I want you to tell me is how the hell you're going to pay this twenty thousand."

"Credit cards."

"Don't give me that. You're too smart to max out your cards."

"Apparently, I'm not." I break off another piece of muffin.

"And how the hell are you going to pay them off?" Her voice is low, but she's hissing.

I shrug. "Don't have enough equity in my house yet, so the only thing I can do is raid my retirement account."

"The withdrawal fees and taxes will kill you."

Shoving the rest of the muffin in my mouth, I nod. "It's either that or I don't get tenure."

She holds the mug to her lips, then thinks better of it. "Girl, you better pray this film is the best documentary ever made." Pushing back her chair, she gets gingerly to her feet. "You okay on your own today?"

I reach for another muffin. "Do I have a choice?"

It's a short ten-minute drive in Colin's jeep to the thatched-roof, cinder-block Mamba headquarters at Msasa Camp. Dressed in olive camo fatigues and military-issue boots, hair cut very short, Margaret and Zinhle, Pepsi and Barbara are waiting out front when we arrive. They're smiling and seem excited, but the sideways glances they're shooting each other reveal a bit of nervousness. I guess that's to be expected from people who've never told their stories in front of a camera before. Matt doesn't seem in the least worried. As far as actors are concerned, he's dealt with everything.

"Margaret!" I climb out over the stack of Pelican cases wedging me into a small corner of the back seat.

She hurries over and wraps her arms around me. "Julia, it has been such a long time. You are well? Do you remember everyone else? No? Please, let me introduce the others."

A few minutes later, with Margaret holding one of my

hands and Pepsi the other, the ladies lead me laughing into the building, across a narrow hallway, and past what looks to be the main office to another room.

This office is smaller than the first and, with no lamps on, dark. One desk—wooden and looking to be from the 1950s— and a straight-backed chair, also old. A filing cabinet, rusting at the bottom, stands in the far corner, and attached to the wall, a locked cabinet of semi-automatic rifles—possibly AR-15s. Then, my eyes land on the over-sized map of Hwange, dotted with different-colored pushpins.

"Yes, please." Zinhle grabs my hand. "Come look at this map." She points to one pin after another. "These are the places where poachers have killed animals."

I gasp. "But there are so many!"

Barbara walks over. "We use a different color for each year. Red was for our first year, and you can see how very many there are. But in our second year, we used blue, and there are fewer. Then the other colors as you see."

I study the map more closely. "How do you mark the poachers you catch?"

"The green pins."

There are fewer green pins than I'd like to see, but arrests add up and send a definite message to the poachers. "You're making a real difference!"

"The poachers know to be scared of us," laughs Pepsi.

"It is unfortunate we do not catch all the poachers before they kill the animals. And sometimes the men get away." Margaret's fingers touch a cluster of green pins.

I look a little further afield until I find Jozibanini Camp. "This is where they killed our crew."

"Yes." Her voice is grim. "And four tuskers."

My heart tightens. "Did you ever arrest those poachers?"

"No. This was a very odd case." She notices Colin standing in the doorway, Pelican cases in each hand. Matt's right behind him with two more cases. "Perhaps we will talk more about this later."

"Where would you like these?" Colin sounds perfectly professional. If he keeps this up, maybe, just maybe, we can work together.

"Next to the filing cabinet for now. Thanks." I do my best to match my tone of voice to his.

He nods. Okay, then. But I notice his lips are pressed firmly together.

"Oh!" Pepsi grabs my arm. "We went back to the site of the plane crash afterward to see if we could find any evidence. I think we may have something of yours."

"Something of mine? Are you sure?"

Now Colin grins. A remarkable transformation. "I'd forgotten about that. Let me get it." He's back in less than a minute with a faded blue Mets cap in hand. "I do believe this is yours." He presents it to me with a flourish.

"You found it! Unbelievable! The day before ... at Jozi, a huge bull grabbed it off my head while I was filming ..." My voice fades as I realize the full implication of this cap now being back in my hand. "That tusker ... he could've killed me, but he didn't. All he wanted was the cap ... to play with ... and they killed him." I can feel tears burning at the back of my eyes. *Do not cry!*

"Hey." Colin's voice is gentle, and for a brief moment, all professionalism vanishes. He looks like he wants to put his arms around me.

I rub my eyes. My professional face is back. "Anyway. Thanks." Taking another look at my weather-battered cap,

I'm suddenly confused. "Wait, he grabbed this at the Jozi blind. And you found it at the killing field? Are you telling me he actually carried it all that way?"

He shrugs. "Maybe it got stuck on his tusk? Who knows. Strange things are known to happen out in Hwange."

This is beyond strange and also beyond my ability to sort out.

I get back to work scoping out the room. Small and intimate. The map is great. Love the desk and the chair. The lighting, though, could be a real challenge. My eyes meet Matt's. "We await your direction."

"Who works in this office?" he asks.

Margaret raises her hand. "Most of the time, it is me."

"It's pretty dark in here, but we'll set up the lighting panels. I think we can make it work."

"The light is better in my office," Colin is quick to offer.

"We'll try it here first. I think it's important to have Margaret in her space." He takes a long, considered look around the room, then nods at Margaret. "First, though, is there someplace I could meet with the four of you? I'd like to go over your lines with you, make sure you're ready to face the camera."

"The dormitory?" Barbara suggests.

"Or maybe outside?" says Zinhle.

A few minutes later, I glance out the window to see the four women and Matt at the picnic table under a large, shady camelthorn in back of the building, leaving Colin and me inside the small office. He combs his fingers through his hair, looking uncomfortable, as if he's out of place—strange, since we're in his headquarters.

"Should we be doing something?" He laughs almost awkwardly.

I'm in my element and know exactly what I need to do. "How about you give me a tour of the headquarters? This office will be good for Margaret, but I should scope out the best places to film the other women. Inside. Maybe outside. I'm sure Matt will have some ideas and the women will, too, but you know them well. Your insights could help."

He looks surprised, but pleased. "Then let's have at it."

We take a look at the dormitory first—another smallish room with one window in front and another at the back. On hot days, they could give some much-needed cross ventilation. The beds are neatly made with a sheet and a military-issue green blanket, but there are only four—two against the front wall and two on the back. That stops me. No closets. No dressers. I take note of the single suitcase squared beneath each bed and the two small tables—one between each pair of beds—big enough for a Bible or a photograph in a cheap plastic frame. I take a step closer and recognize Zinhle holding a young girl.

"Her daughter." This from Colin, his voice gentle.

"They look exactly alike."

"She is absolutely committed to her work, but it's hard on her to be separated from the girl. It's hard on all the women."

"She lives with . . ."

"Her grandmother. Zinhle lives in fear of her ex-husband taking the girl."

"How often does she get to see her?"

He sighs heavily. "The women prefer to accumulate their time off, so it's only once every forty days."

Now it's my turn to be amazed. "They work forty days straight?"

"It's their choice. Then they rotate out and another group comes in for forty days."

"You're telling me four women and you deal with the entire anti-poaching effort of the park?" No wonder there are still so many pushpins going onto the map each year.

"There are eight women in this unit. And four other units—one to the west, another in the east, the others in the north and south. This is the headquarters, but I do a lot of driving from station to station. Except for right now."

"Because of the film?"

He nods.

I look around the room again. It's small to begin with, and for four women, it's beyond cramped. Then again, they're only in here to sleep. "But there are only four beds."

"They share." He obviously senses me cringing. "Careful of any judgments. This is a poor country. Life is very different from what you're used to."

I think of my small bungalow in Shorewood—the emphasis definitely on small and modest: five rooms, one bedroom, one study. But it's so much bigger than this. I take another look at the photo of Zinhle and her daughter, Zinhle holding onto her tightly as if it would hurt to let go. The love between them is clear. I can only imagine how much they must miss each other. One final look, and I catch a glimpse of Zinhle's pride—that she's doing right by her daughter, working to give her a future. This picture really drives home Colin's argument last night—money is so important to these women. They work hard for it. And they're proud of their accomplishments. I won't be doing them any favors if I film them as anything less than the fierce, determined women they are.

"This is the place to film Zinhle." I nod to emphasize my point. "If she agrees, of course. And Matt. And you."

Again, he looks surprised. But he takes a moment to consider my idea. "I think you're right. Would you like to see the kitchen next?"

"There's a kitchen?"

He grins. "We have to eat. Actually, Pepsi said the same thing when she first arrived."

"Let me guess. She likes to cook."

"I'd say she rivals the chef at Marula, although she tends to stay with traditional foods: *sadza* and relish. Every once in a while, she'll make a stew."

Like the other rooms, the kitchen is small—a counter with a single burner and a wash basin. In the corner, a fridge like the one I had in my room at college. From the window I see a round hut in the back—smoke swirling out the front door.

He nods toward the small dwelling. "The outdoor kitchen is where Pepsi does most of her cooking—over an open fire." A few yards farther is the picnic table, where Matt is still talking with the women.

"Is that everything?"

"Except for my office."

I hold up my hand to stop him. "Unless Barbara works in there with you, I don't need to see it." Maybe my voice is a little too sharp.

He takes a step back. "No, she doesn't. But there's the gun cabinet in Margaret's office. Barbara's in charge of it. Perhaps she could stand there?"

"A good possibility."

"She also works in the garden—grows most of our veg. Given how arid everything is in these parts, it's amazing what she's able to produce."

Without thinking, I put my hand on his forearm. "Perfect.

I love the juxtaposition of guns and growing. I hope Matt can see it, too." Glancing down, I see my hand on his sweatered arm and quickly snatch it back. "Sorry."

He quirks his eyebrow. "No worries."

Sixteen

"Ignore the camera and speak naturally," says Matt as he backs out of Margaret's office and into the hall.

"Yes." Margaret nods. Already mic'd up, she turns to look at the papers we've strewn across her desk and whispers, "I am ready now."

The two tungsten panels are positioned in the corners behind me to even out the ambient light. Matt and I absolutely want the shadows at play in this footage to reinforce Margaret's story of escape from her abusive husband and her work now as one of the fiercest women in the Mambas.

With the tripod positioned to film her partly in profile, I turn on the camera.

Hands in her lap, fingers pleating the camo cloth of her pants, Margaret stares at the papers in front of her. And doesn't say a word.

Five minutes tick slowly by.

"Cut!" Matt is back in the room, bending over Margaret. "Remember, I said to have your hands on top of the desk. You're sorting through the papers, making notes with this pencil."

"Yes. Of course. I am sorry."

I smile. "It's okay. No worries. We'll just film again."

Matt steps out of the room. "Scene one. Take two."

Camera on. This time Margaret's left hand is curled into a tight fist atop the papers, her right hand wringing the life out of the pencil stub. I keep the camera running, but she doesn't say her lines.

"Cut!" Matt kneels next to Margaret. "I need you to speak the lines. You were perfect when we rehearsed. Would you like to run through them again?"

"No." Margaret's voice isn't above a whisper.

"Is there a problem?"

"No."

"Shall we try again?"

She nods.

"Scene one. Take three."

Hands in place, Margaret takes a deep breath and says her lines—rushing through the words at breakneck speed.

"Cut!"

"Margaret," Matt says from the hall, "could you please say them more slowly, more naturally, as if you're telling me about your life. And your job."

"Yes, of course."

"Scene one. Take four."

Her delivery is slower but wooden, robotic. The Margaret from earlier has completely disappeared.

"Cut!"

I turn off the camera. "Matt? Could you . . . go . . . talk to Colin or something?"

Margaret turns to me, tears flowing down her cheeks. "I did not think it would be this difficult."

I pull her off the chair and into my arms. My heart is close to breaking as I feel her muscles contracting with each sob. "You don't have to do this."

"Yes." Her voice is strong. "I must."

"Why?"

"To let the people know what we are doing to help the animals. And our children."

Suddenly the other three women crowd into the room. I take a deep breath as Barbara comes perilously close to one of the lighting panels. "For me," she says, "I want to let the people know about how I confronted my ex-husband. How I was able to escape his beatings. How this job let me get away. This job, it saved my life. My children's lives. And now I can save animals."

Okay, this is good. The women have a reason for doing this. And the film is important to them. They're not just doing it for me. So, what's holding Margaret back? "Is it the camera that's bothering you? Or me? Or Matt?"

Margaret sits down hard. "I am not sure. Maybe it is what Barbara said. 'The people.' I don't know who will see this movie. I look at the papers on my desk and see many faces of people I do not know."

Yeah, baring your soul in front of the camera, in front of strangers, is a daunting proposition—to say the least. I honestly don't know how actors do it. But at least actors are dealing with made-up stories. These women are telling the stories of their own lives.

"We do not know you either." Zinhle narrows her eyes.

I nod. Even though a couple hours ago we were laughing and chatting together like old friends, we really don't know each other. And here I've been snooping through their belongings, looking at a picture of Zinhle with her daughter. A totally uneven playing field.

Matt is back in the doorway with Colin hovering behind him. "We ready to go?"

"No!" we say in unison.

I wave them both off. "Go find some Zambezis or something. We'll let you know when we're ready." Once I see them, beers in hand, sitting at the picnic table, I sink cross-legged onto the concrete floor. "I'll go first."

One by one, the other women join me on the floor, looking a bit confused.

I'm not at all sure what I should say, where I should begin, so I just start talking. "I want to make this film—no, I *have* to make it—to keep my job."

Someone inhales her breath sharply.

"The thing is, the last time I was in Zimbabwe, I was part of a crew making a film about the elephants' migration."

"Yes." I recognize Margaret's voice. "That was when we first met you."

"Well, after the plane crash, I couldn't get work as a cinematographer anymore. No one would even hire me to operate a camera."

"But why?"

"For some reason, the people in Hollywood blamed me for the men dying in the plane crash."

"I don't understand. It wasn't your fault. The poachers shot down the plane. And they shot your friend." Margaret again. "I was there. I could tell them."

"Thanks, but it's too late. I ended up having to change jobs." I'm sure they all hear the tightness and the bitterness in my voice. "I started teaching cinematography and documentary filmmaking at a university."

"This job, do you like it?" Barbara's question.

I shrug. "It's okay." Is that really all it is? Okay? Teaching keeps me employed and pays the bills, and most of the time I'm pretty happy. "No, it's good. But now, to keep my job, I have to make this film. Then the faculty will vote on whether or not I can stay."

"You are a teacher, but you still have to do the same work as before?" Zinhle sounds incredulous.

I nod. "Yeah. Pretty crazy, huh."

Pepsi covers her mouth with her hands. "Oh! This is not right."

Tell me about it. "There's something else I want to tell you, about what else happened six years ago when we were filming. Of course, you know about the crash. But the night before . . ."

They lean forward, somehow knowing I'm finally getting to the really personal part.

I tell them about Alex and how he tried to rape me that night in camp.

They hiss sharply through their teeth, sounding for all the world like snakes in the grass.

I move on to talk about Liam. How he cheated on me. How I'd been supporting him while he made a name for himself as an actor. How he left me to make it big in Hollywood, telling me I was toxic and would hold him back. How the divorce court gave him a lot more than half of the money I'd managed to save, leaving me next-to-nothing. The court's definition of equitable. Of course, it's nothing close to what I imagine these women have gone through, and there sure weren't any children involved. But it felt abusive all the same.

"To cheat on you and then take your money, he is not a good man." Margaret puts her hand on my arm, and that's when I realize I'm crying.

I press my fingers to my eyes. "I'm sorry. This is so un-professional."

"Cheating," Barbara hisses through the gap between her two front teeth. "My husband thought it was fine to cheat on me and to possibly give me the AIDS. Men think it is their right. But when I did nothing more than smile at my neighbor, my husband punched me and broke my jaw."

It's my turn to inhale.

"Julia, what about your children?" This is from Zinhle.

My thoughts go back to the photo of her holding her daughter. I shake my head. "I don't have any. Liam wanted to wait so he could make it as an actor first. I guess it's a good thing we waited. It would've been awful to deal with custody. But . . . now . . . it may be too late . . ." Hearing myself say that stops me short. I sound like I want kids. Do I? It's not something I've thought about since Liam.

"No matter what happens between the parents, children are always a blessing." She smiles. "Blessing. That is my daughter's name." Zinhle waits a moment, head bowed, and then launches into her story. "She is twelve now and lives with my mother. They have a small farm and grow some crops. It is enough for them to eat but there is nothing extra to sell. I send everything I earn to them to pay for her schooling."

Margaret leans forward. "Zinhle is too modest. Blessing is so very smart. Top of her class. When she graduates from elementary school in December, she will go on to secondary school."

Zinhle's smile of pride lasts all of ten seconds. "Only if I can afford it. The fees are much more than I am paying now. And the boarding school is closer to me here, but also closer to where her father lives. I am afraid that he might try to take her back to get the money for himself."

My shoulders sag under the weight of her fear. So that's why she needs her share of the twenty thousand dollars. I bet each of the women has a need just as dire.

"We all have children," says Barbara. "I miss my boys so much. Their school fees are coming due again."

It's Pepsi's turn. "We all had husbands, too." She rolls back the left sleeve of her camo shirt to reveal a horrific scar covering her forearm. "He did not like the *sadza* I served him one night for dinner. He accused me of making it lumpy on purpose. Me! Make lumpy *sadza*!"

"Never!" say the three other women.

"This! You see this!" She points to her arm. "He threw the hot *sadza* at me."

I gasp. "Did you report him to the police?"

She looks surprised at the thought. "No, the police, they would not have helped me."

"So, what happened?"

"Just like always, he went to the *shebeen* and got drunk on *scud*. I got very scared, because drinking always made him even meaner."

"What happened when he got home?" I whisper in fear of what she's going to say.

She laughs. "I do not really know, because I wasn't there. My children helped me pack, quickly, quickly, and we moved to my sister's house in another village. I think he was probably very surprised."

We talk and talk and talk—through a meal of the smoothest, most delicious *sadza* ever made and topped with really spicy veg relish. Pepsi laughs when I take my first big bite only to fan my mouth, then gulp water.

"Oh God, this is good," I manage to croak out.

We keep talking about our lives and our missteps and our successes until before we know it, Matt and Colin are back in the doorway, their impatience pretty evident by their tightly crossed arms.

Smiling toward them, Margaret announces, "I think I am now ready to say my lines."

"Not today," says Matt. "Afraid it's too late to start this afternoon." He looks around the room at my camera and the lighting panels. "Let's leave all the equipment here and get an early start in the morning. Say, seven?"

"Yes." Margaret sounds confident. "In the morning, we will all do our parts. You will see."

"Great!" Matt rubs his hands together in eager anticipation, although the look in his eyes tells me he doesn't share Margaret's confidence.

Seventeen

Back at Marula Camp, I leave Matt and Colin in the lodge and head back to the tent to check on Amie and Cate. They're nowhere to be found, but their packs are gone, leading me to conclude they took off with Tonderai for a late-afternoon game drive. Feeling too crappy to work but well enough to head out onto the savanna in search of wildlife. How exactly is that fair to the rest of us who showed up to our jobs today?

There's no point taking out my frustration on an empty tent, so instead I strip off my clothes, climb into the shower, and let the warm water sluice away the dust and tension of the last couple days. I'm five minutes into a long shower, my hair lathered in shampoo, when I remember the camp is at the edge of the Kalahari Desert, where water is a precious commodity. A quick rinse, some conditioner, and I turn off the water. Pulling on clean khaki pants and a long-sleeve shirt to ward off the chill of the night to come, I comb out my hair and fluff it a bit with my fingers. As I remember from my last trip to Zimbabwe, by the time I walk the short distance to the lodge, the sun will have completely dried my hair.

I collect my gin and tonic at the bar and join the guys on the deck. They're sprawled on the same chairs they occupied last night, the one between them empty—probably waiting for me. But I'm still in no mood to make nice with Colin and so help myself to the rocker on Matt's far side. A sideways glance tells me they've both noticed. Colin is back to watching the sky burn red and orange as the sun begins to set. Matt, though, presses his lips together in annoyance. "Now that you're back, we've got to talk."

I rock gently. "About anything in particular?"

"You spent an entire day talking to the women—not filming them. We got nothing done." Matt takes a pull on his bottle of Zambezi Lager.

"I beg to differ. We accomplished a lot. As in, we got to know each other a bit better. And trust each other. Tomorrow should go a lot smoother . . . at least I hope it will." I'm a little worried, though, that when Cate and Amie join me tomorrow on cameras two and three, we could be right back at square one.

"You hope?" Matt nearly sputters. "In case you haven't noticed, we're on a bit of a time crunch. We can't afford to waste another day."

From the corner of my eye, I see Colin trying his best to hide a smile. He must think we're a bunch of idiots, running around without any idea what we're doing.

"Today wasn't a waste. We're asking Margaret and Pepsi and Zinhle and Barbara to share some things they'd really rather not talk about, especially in front of people they don't know. It's like we're asking them to strip naked—metaphorically."

Matt raises his hand in a sign of surrender. "Sorry. You're right. It's one thing to have actors play a role. It's entirely different when people have to talk about horrendous real-life experiences."

"Like Colin said last night, these women deserve our respect."

Colin leans forward. "From what Margaret told me before we left, you earned some solid points yourself today. They really appreciated you sharing your own experiences."

"You what?" Matt shoots me a look. *Since when do cinematographers talk about themselves to get the talent to relax and open up?* Oh, what he doesn't know about women.

I nearly gasp. "They told you what I said?"

"Not at all. And believe me, I asked. Margaret was adamant that what you said was confidential. Oh, and I'd take her at her word about tomorrow. They'll be ready to film." He holds a small bowl in my direction. "The chef made these especially for you. Tonderai told him you love fire-roasted cashews."

A nice peace offering, but I notice Matt isn't making a move to take the bowl to pass to me. I can practically taste those cashews. Finally, gin and tonic in hand, I shift to the empty chair between the two of them and help myself to the bowl. "Thanks."

Matt laughs. "Nuts? All I need to do is give you nuts— and you'll do what I want?"

I lick the salt off my lips. "These are very special nuts."

"You sharing?"

"Nope."

The dark of night has fallen, the moon is well above the horizon, and stars are filling the sky when we hear the land cruisers returning from the game drive. Cate leaves her fellow safari-goers at the bar, coming out onto the deck to join us. She stops next to my chair. "Sorry to abandon you for the day."

"You feeling better?" My voice is probably a bit tighter than it should be.

"Much."

"Then that's good."

"I'll return the favor, although I hope it's not so you can puke up your guts."

I smile. "I'll hold you to it."

"Tonderai took Amie and me out with the star power."

My shoulders sink. "I assume you mean Natalie and Liam."

"You assume correctly. And be forewarned: you're facing an uphill battle."

I turn to look at Cate, and sense Colin watching me. "You care to explain?"

"Amie's in raptures over both of them. And I hate to say it, but she's lovely and your ex is utterly charming."

Great. Just great. "Well, they're actors. I guess they're doing what they do best."

She claps her hand on my shoulder. "Good luck! I'm off to the bar."

I refrain from telling her to stick to iced tea.

Colin leans in close. "Will you tell me what that's all about?"

Not that I plan to tell him anything about Liam and me, but before I can say a word, we hear the clomp of feet heading our way. Matt and Colin both immediately push themselves to their feet. Taking a moment to secure my bowl of cashews on the floor, I'm a good half minute behind them.

"Matt!" Natalie literally purrs his name. No wonder he wanted her to do the narration. If someone put that much soul and sex into saying my name, I'd want him around, too.

It's not only her voice; Natalie is a stunningly beautiful woman with the glossiest blond hair and incredible facial bone structure. Then, there's her spectacular body. It's hard to tell if Colin's eyes are riveted on her face or her curves. Or maybe her bright red scarf. Whichever. She's providing definite eye candy for the male half of the crew. "We're here," Natalie continues to purr. "And what a fabulous game drive we had today." She wraps her arms around Matt's neck and kisses each cheek.

A minute later, she makes a bee-line for Colin. "How lovely to meet you. I've heard so much about the important work you're doing. It's going to be great going out in the field with you." She abandons their handshake almost immediately to drape her arms around his neck. And sure enough, his arms quickly find their way around her waist. "I know I have a lot to learn. It's important to me that I do justice to narrating this film." Again with the purring. The ways of Hollywood. Or maybe she had her gin and tonic the way Liam always liked to make them—very light on the tonic.

I've gotta hand it to Colin. He's smiling, but his eyes widen in surprise. Still, he doesn't ask what she means by going out in the field with him. Is there yet another new plan no one's mentioned to me?

Before I can ask, I find myself face-to-face with Liam Shepard—as handsome as ever and flashing a smile revealing his perfectly whitened teeth. Ever the actor.

"Julia!" Like Natalie with Matt, he purrs my name. But it sure doesn't have the same impact on me. In fact, I'd really rather he go away. Far away.

He clearly has another idea. Pulling me into his arms, he kisses me. On the lips. Warmly.

I manage to step back, putting a couple feet between us. "Liam. It's been a while."

He's not giving up easily. "So, this is what you were doing all those times you ran off to film documentaries. Here I thought you were roughing it. Boy, was I wrong. The River Lodge and this camp are downright luxurious."

For once, don't let him bait you! "I'm glad you like it here. The Ngamo Plains are beautiful. Of course, there's a poaching problem, which is why we're here making this documentary." I decide to throw a lifeline to Colin, who's still got Natalie attached to him. "Colin, perhaps you could tell us all about the increase in poaching?"

Turning toward me, he looks almost relieved, and launches into a brief speech about the rising numbers of elephant and lion deaths. When Natalie starts peppering him with questions about who's behind the poaching, it's Amie who steps up to tell about the snared elie at the last lodge. "The Zambians," she says knowingly.

"But certainly the Zambians don't come all the way down here. So, who's causing the problem in Hwange?" Okay, Natalie's done some research.

Colin fields this question. "With the high rate of unemployment throughout the country, it's likely men in the villages right outside the park. But they're just doing the dirty work—the killing and then harvesting the ivory. Who's really in charge—the cartel—we don't know."

Not quite accurate, I daresay. Colin and the Mambas must have some idea.

Before Natalie can ask any more questions, the chef appears on the deck to announce the menu for dinner: peanut butter soup, a choice of bream or steak with veggies, and chocolate mousse. Natalie links her arm through Colin's and leads us all to the long table set for eight in the center of the room.

Cate falls into step beside me. "No need to worry about Colin," she whispers. "One look at his face, and you can tell he's not falling for her."

I roll my eyes. "And what if he is? It makes no difference to me."

She raises her eyebrow. "You never were a very good liar."

By some unlucky fluke, I end up sitting directly across from Liam and next to Colin, which gives me a ringside seat to Natalie's ongoing flirtation. After an hour of her chatting nonstop with Colin and Matt, it's clear this is how she interacts with men. What's not clear is whether these same men realize quite how manipulative she is. I'm also kind of surprised at how blasé Liam is in the face of his girlfriend focusing all her attention on other men. Or maybe that's because he's concentrating on me.

"It's been a long time." His voice is low and uncomfortably intimate as he slices through his bloody steak.

I keep my eyes on my flaky bream drizzled with a creamy curry sauce. "Yes, it has."

"On the game drive today, Cate told me you've been teaching. In Milwaukee, I think she said."

Although I'm reluctant to tell him anything, I figure he could easily Google me and find out where I am. "That's right."

"She said something about you going for tenure. I take it that's the reason we're all here?" He sinks his knife into the steak.

Gee, thanks a lot, Cate. Whose friend are you, anyway? "It seems you've been busy." I close my eyes and try to savor my fish.

"Really a shame you had to leave the industry."

Is that a sneer I hear in his voice? For the first time, I wonder if Liam and his predilection for gossip maybe helped my departure along. Put in a bad word here and there for me. I shovel more food into my mouth and don't bother answering.

But he's not giving up. "Milwaukee . . ." He sounds thoughtful. I brace myself for what he might say next. "Funny, I never thought of you living in cow country."

Despite the stupidity of his comment, I feel the need to set him straight. "No cows. Milwaukee's a city."

"But don't you miss Brooklyn? Being in the center of the action?"

I shrug as I chew and wonder if maybe I should eat more slowly—to make my dinner and my excuse for not talking last longer.

He doesn't seem to notice that I haven't answered. "That was such a great apartment we had."

Oh God, where's he going with this? I tap Colin's arm and point to the bottle of Pinotage. He refills my glass and his, and I realize he's been listening with at least one ear to this bizarre conversation between exes. Not to be outdone, Liam orders another bottle of wine—a California cab with an upcharge—not one of the lodge's regular table wines. Natalie smiles her thanks while he massages the back of her neck.

A few minutes later, he turns back to me. "Look, when I went back to the apartment to get the last of my stuff, I found something of yours."

Confused, I watch as he reaches into his pocket. What

could he possibly have found? Yeah, packing to leave was most definitely a rush job, but I'm positive I took everything I wanted.

"Your locket. I remember your brother gave it to you. For your birthday, I think, right before . . . well, right before."

My hand trembles as I reach across the table. He places the locket on my palm and lets the chain fall on top of it. Nearly weightless. But to have this back means everything. "Where did you find it?"

"In one of my shoes. Don't ask. I have no idea how it got there. Anyway, I . . . uh . . . I thought you'd like to have it back." A bittersweet moment, and he lets it sit between the two of us. Then he's back to grilling me. "So, you have any idea what happened to the rest of my stuff?"

I inhale a green bean and start to cough. Finally, I manage, "Excuse me? What are you talking about?"

He lowers his voice. "Well, for one thing, the watch my father gave me. You must remember—his father gave it to him. A family heirloom?"

"With the inscription on the back."

"I'd like it back."

"Sorry. I thought you took it."

He furrows his brow while Natalie downs most of her glass of cab and pours herself another. "I didn't. Obviously, since I'm asking you for it."

Fork in hand, I stare across the table at the man I once loved. For a long moment, I think back to the night I spent stuffing his clothes and shoes in black garbage bags. Did I see the watch? I honestly don't remember. But I certainly didn't keep it for myself. "Look, I'm sorry you can't find the watch, but I don't have it."

"Julia, come on. That's the only thing I have of my grand-father's. Don't be vindictive—"

I put down my fork. "I. Don't. Have. It." Maybe I'm not whispering anymore. Damn, I don't want everyone else to have to listen to this. But they are. Taking a sneak peek at Natalie, I see her swirling the wine in her glass, a perplexed look distorting her face. I can only imagine she doesn't want to listen to me calling Liam a liar.

At the opposite end of the table, Cate takes a swig of water, then she ends my conversation with Liam before it fully erupts. "So, maybe we could hear the plan for tomorrow's shoot? Some of us would like to get to bed early tonight." She looks pointedly at me.

Next to me, Colin relaxes his shoulders. Natalie smiles gratefully. As for me, I'm happy to see both Cate and Amie sticking to water tonight. With luck, there won't be any more partying at the bar.

I look to Matt to take the lead.

"We'll leave at six-thirty. I'd like to start filming at seven. Colin, will you collect us? Or Tonderai, could you possibly drive us over to Msasa?"

"Does it have to be so early?" Natalie asks, taking a big swallow of wine. "I mean if there were a good reason to start at that time, it would be one thing, but . . ."

Mystified, I look at her closely. Does she actually think she's part of the shoot? Her work as the narrator will happen later in a sound studio back in Hollywood. She's only here to get a feel for the country.

Matt leans forward. "You can certainly sleep in. Dabs or Tonderai can leave a bit later to take you out on the morning game drive, although the earlier you get out, the better the viewing."

"Oh, no! I want to be part of the shoot." Glass back in hand, Natalie sounds emphatic. "If I'm going to do the voice-over, I really have to meet the Mambas and talk with them, get to know them. I mean, after all, I'll be speaking for them."

"No, you won't." I close my hand tightly around my fork. Damn. I should've let Matt handle this, set her straight.

Matt shoots me a look, then takes over. "I sent you the screenplay."

She smiles her million-dollar smile. "And it's wonderful. Really, it is. But you and I, we've worked together before, and I know you look at the screenplay as a suggestion, right? You always welcome ideas to flesh it out."

My stomach roils at the thought of making changes to the screenplay now. Then again, she's right. Matt is known for his willingness to work with actors, to seriously consider their suggestions. And truth be told, that's why so many people, including me, enjoy working with him.

"You have some ideas?" Matt's using his 'listening' voice, which means he might well consider making some changes.

"Well." Natalie strikes a thoughtful pose. "I'm thinking I could help out the women by speaking for them. In English. Maybe they could start saying their lines, and after a few words, you could fade out their voices for me to take over."

What the hell? *Do not say anything! Let Matt handle this!*

Next to me, Colin says with a great deal of steel in his voice, "They speak English. It's one of the official languages in this country."

"Of course they do, although it's not their first language. And their accents might be difficult for the American audience. Really, I'm only thinking of the women and trying to make things easier for them. It can be hard for untrained actors to, you know, get into character. And some of the things you're asking them to talk about, well, I know how hard it can be." Natalie looks back and forth from Colin to Matt, seemingly unsure of who's in charge. I've got to hand it to her—without being on set, she's gotten to the heart of today's problem.

"No worries." Colin eases up on the steel. "Julia did a brilliant job today getting them ready for tomorrow's filming."

She sits back in her chair. "Oh, well, I didn't realize Julia's also an acting coach." Her voice drips with sarcasm.

Big of her to finally acknowledge my existence, which is pretty crappy considering this is my film. And what's this about getting the women 'in character'? Should I say something? Or just keep quiet? While I'm debating what to do, I notice Cate and Amie and Tonderai have gone. Smart of them to take off when they had the chance. Looking out into the dark, I see a flashlight beaming a path toward our tent. Maybe I could make a mad dash after them. Matt would probably be happy to see the last of me for today. Colin would, too. Then I hear an elephant trumpet its arrival at the water hole, stopping en route to scope out the open dining area. There's no way I'm going anywhere without an armed escort.

But I absolutely cannot sit here any longer. Last night and today have finally caught up with me. I turn to Colin. "Could you possibly—"

"Would you like me to walk you to your tent?" Colin keeps his voice low.

"Please."

We stop at the gun cabinet for Colin to collect his Remington and a flashlight, then cross the lounge. Barely out of the lodge, with me a few steps ahead, he suddenly grabs my arm and jerks me back—just in time to avoid being trampled by a family of elephants on parade toward the water. We freeze in place until they're well past us.

"Stay next to me or a pace behind."

I let out my breath. "You bet. And thanks for the rescue. Just now. And back there."

"Pleasure. But I owe you thanks as well for getting me away from those Hollywood stars. I'll let Tonderai escort them and Matt to their tents."

We're almost to the tent when he says, "I take it you two were married?"

"Yeah. Before he was a 'Hollywood star.'" I make exaggerated air quotes which he probably can't see. "One of the great mistakes of my life."

"So, why did you marry him?"

"He didn't seem so bad in the beginning." We reach the steps to the tent platform. "It took me a while to discover he was an asshole."

He chuckles. "I'm sure you're not the first ex-wife to say that."

I climb to the first step, then turn to thank him again. But he's already heading back. "Hey! Thanks."

He waves the flashlight over his head. "Pleasant dreams. See you tomorrow."

Completely baffled, I watch him walk back to the lodge. What just happened here? We agreed on something. But I don't like this man. I'm still seriously pissed at having to cash out my pension to pay for something that should've been discussed and agreed on months ago—when I would've had time to write another grant or Matt could've pitched the idea to his people to get some funding. It's only been half a day since we agreed to keep things strictly professional when we have to work together, then basically go our separate ways. The only way to keep the peace. But just now, this wasn't work, and we were having a perfectly amiable conversation. Temporary allies against Liam and Natalie. Maybe. Yeah, well, we'll see how quickly things go downhill tomorrow.

Eighteen

Bundled in my puffer jacket against the early-morning chill, I'm the first out of the tent. With no hangovers today, Cate and Amie are awake and will soon be following me. The eastern horizon is a rosy pink with a deep tangerine announcing the sunrise. Light enough that we're allowed to walk to the main building unescorted—so long as we take care. I'm looking forward to a cup of coffee and a few quiet minutes to pull together my thoughts about filming the women. Sacrificing our shoot yesterday was totally worth it—as long as the women really are ready today. Although now we're behind in our schedule and will have to scramble. There's absolutely no flexibility in our timeline for Natalie to be making demands—"suggestions," as she put it. God, I hope Matt set her straight last night. With any luck, she and Liam got the message, are sleeping in, and will go out on a game drive. Maybe for the entire day.

Grabbing a mug from the sideboard, I pour myself some coffee and make my way out onto the deck. I'm almost to my chair by the railing when I see it's already occupied.

Her bright red scarf knotted elegantly around her neck, Natalie glances at me and smiles. "I was hoping you'd get here before the others."

That stops me. I help myself to Colin's usual chair, trying to figure out what I can say that won't launch her into offering more suggestions. Last night's were more than enough. Finally, I settle for, "Good morning."

"Look, I . . . uh . . . probably drank too much last night."

I keep my eyes on the elephants clustered around the near end of the water hole and slowly sip my coffee.

"It's a bad habit I've got—drinking—when I'm nervous."

Coming from one of the hottest actresses around, I find this hard to believe. Maybe it's being in Africa for the first time? "You're nervous?"

"Well, yeah. Okay, I've worked with Matt before, but this is my first voice-over, and I really want to get it right."

"Okay." Yeah, I can appreciate her wanting to do a good job.

"I don't want to just dial it in. It's important to me for people to see this as part of my brand—my commitment to women in third-world countries. And conservation of animals."

Once again, she stops me. Does she even have any experience in third-world countries? Or speaking out for endangered animals?

"Anyway, there I was last night, spouting off like I know what I'm talking about, and, well—I did do some reading—but the truth is I really don't know much. After you left, Matt talked me through a lot, and at least I think I understand better what this film is about."

"That's good."

"So, anyway, I'm sorry about the crack I made last night about you being an acting coach."

I take another sip of coffee and decide I should be gracious. "It's good you know these women aren't acting. They're living these stories."

"Believe me, Matt made that very clear."

I nod, hoping she doesn't expect me to acknowledge her new insight. Okay, so a documentary is a totally different beast from the dramas and thrillers and rom coms she's known for. But I would've thought she'd already know this film isn't make-believe.

"Yeah. Pretty dumb." She shrugs. "I also want to apologize for not acknowledging you last night. Really, that's not me. I'm all about empowering women. It's just . . . last night, maybe I . . ."

"Drank too much?"

"Sounds pretty lame, doesn't it?"

"Honestly? Yeah, pretty much." I laugh, and for the first time this morning actually look at her.

She's perfectly positioned in a ray of the rising sun, and her long blond hair absolutely gleams. Then, one deft move to toss her hair behind her shoulder reveals a small gold hoop, so rich in color it's actually glowing. I'm betting it's eighteen-karat. I'm also fairly certain I've seen this earring and its mate once before back when I was married to Liam. What? Does he have a stockpile of these earrings and gives them to his woman of the moment? Or maybe these are the very same earrings, and Liam's actually been together with Natalie all this time. That realization spins in my brain for a minute while I look away from her and toward the massive bull elephant who's moving closer to the deck, picking up speed and making a beeline toward her. And her red scarf.

I lean toward her. "Some advice?"

"Sure." She sounds happy that I'm finally talking to her instead of offering one-word responses.

"Lose the scarf. Now!"

The elephant's almost at the railing. In another moment, his trunk will lift in the air.

I'm out of my chair in a flash, pushing away her fumbling fingers. I unknot the scarf and unwind it from around her neck as fast as I can. Then, flinging it as far away from us as possible, I stare in amazement as the elie snags it midair with his trunk. He pivots toward the swimming pool, waving the scarf in triumph.

Trembling, Natalie buries her face in her hands. "Oh my God. Oh my God. He could've killed me."

From behind us, I hear the applause. I turn to see Tonderai, rifle resting across his forearm, with a broad grin and a big thumbs-up. Colin whistles. As soon as they're close enough to see Natalie, their smiles slide off their faces.

Tonderai hands his gun to Colin and kneels next to her. "You are all right. It is good Julia was here and realized what was about to happen. I do not think he was trying to hurt you. He only wanted your scarf." He points to the elie, who's still waving the scarf and attracting the attention of the other elephants. "He is playing."

Her face scary-pale, she still looks more than a little frightened. "I guess."

"Julia had a run-in with an elephant the last time she was here. Has she told you?"

"No." Natalie's voice is tiny and weak. God, she really is terrified. Tonderai telling her this story is exactly the right thing to distract her.

"A huge tusker grabbed her cap right off her head."

She looks at me. "And you were okay?"

I shrug. "I was lucky. He didn't mean any harm. But if the cap had caught on my ponytail, he could've broken my neck trying to get it off. Like Tonderai said, this guy wasn't trying to hurt you. But it's not all fun and games out here either."

Tonderai takes over. "They're wild animals, and, unlike Asian elephants, they're not at all domesticated. Those trunks can be lethal. A slap from one of them can send you flying."

"Or kill you outright." Colin presents a glass of brandy I assume he poured at the bar and carefully tucks it into Natalie's hands. "Drink this." Smart man. Although using the 'kill' word may not have been the wisest thing he could've said.

I move my chair closer until Natalie and I are knee to knee. "Another piece of advice?"

"Yeah?" Still trembling, she sips the brandy. "There's something more?"

"Don't wear red out here around animals. Or white. As you saw, bright colors can cause animals to do things we don't want. Stick to neutrals—tan and olive."

"Okay."

"You might also want to leave your earrings in the tent. They look expensive, and I don't think you want to run the risk of losing them in the bush." And I don't particularly want to look at them constantly and be reminded of that day in Brooklyn when I first became aware that my husband was cheating on me.

She runs her fingers along one of the hoops. "I guess, but I'll feel kind of naked without them. They're my absolute favorites."

What the hell can I say? So, I don't say anything at all. And hope she simply stops wearing them.

But she looks suddenly aware and very uncomfortable. "You know, don't you?"

"Now I do."

The Mambas aren't happy about having Amie and Cate and Natalie join the crew. Just as I thought, the trust I'd established with them yesterday is starting to waver. I'm grateful to Matt for picking up on that almost as quickly as I do. He sets to work clearing people out of Margaret's small office. Colin goes off somewhere, maybe to work in his own office. Professing a keen interest in gardening, Cate follows Barbara to the vegetable garden. Amie and Natalie accompany Pepsi to the kitchen to learn how to make *sadza*. Which leaves Zinhle and Margaret, Matt and me. Lucky for all of us, Liam isn't here. Apparently, last night Matt insisted he'd be in the way. So he's going on a game drive with some of the other guests and Dabs. Small victories!

Matt backs out into the hall, but Zinhle looks like she's staying put. Margaret doesn't seem to mind, and Zinhle looks eager to help me. It's darker in here than yesterday, even with the tungsten lighting panels in place, so I pull out a collapsible circular reflector and hand it to Zinhle. I position her across from the window, and the light bounces perfectly onto Margaret's face—exactly the right amount of illumination amid a wonderful play of shadows. And that alone, I decide, reveals a great deal about the Mambas' lives and work.

After mic'ing her up and doing a quick sound check, I whisper, "Okay, Margaret. When you're ready." Just for today, Matt and I decided to forego the usual 'take one' filming lingo, thinking Margaret might respond better to a personal invitation to begin.

She does. Although the first take isn't perfect—Margaret

stumbles over a couple words—her delivery is so much more natural than yesterday. Clearly, though, we need to shoot it again.

Margaret looks at me behind the camera. "It is like I am talking to the wall. Not to you."

"Forget about the camera if you can," I say. "Try talking to me."

"But you are behind the camera."

In the hall, Matt clears his throat. Obviously, I shouldn't be saying anything; that's his job.

Standing slightly to the side of the camera and tripod, I say, "Let's see if this works. Don't look at me, though. Focus on the papers on your desk—the way you were before. I love how the light falls across your profile and makes you seem like you're concentrating on your work." Glancing across at Zinhle as she lifts the reflector back to the exact position I showed her, I see she's nodding thoughtfully. She approves! I cross my fingers that I don't cast any shadow into the shot. And if this works, we'll use the same strategy with Zinhle.

Relaxed, Margaret speaks her lines—all ten of them— perfectly, as if she's saying them to me and only me. The cadence of her speech, the flow of her words, the pauses as she checks the papers in front of her and makes a few notes—it's exactly what I was hoping for.

"Cut!" says Matt softly when she finishes.

"Brava!" I smile.

"Oh, Margaret! You spoke so beautifully." Zinhle hands me the reflector, then wipes a tear off her cheek.

Margaret smiles at each of us in turn. "We are finished then?"

I hold up my index finger to stop the celebration. "First,

Matt and I need to wire the camera to the laptop and run through what I filmed—to make sure it's as perfect as I think."

Matt looks at me cross-eyed. We never look at rushes before the end of the day, but I tip my head toward the two women waiting anxiously, and he nods his agreement. A minute later, wires plugged into the laptop, Matt and I study the film. He's an old hand at this, of course, but I'm gnawing my fingernails. Margaret doesn't budge from her chair. Zinhle stands next to her, hand gently caressing her friend's shoulder. Neither woman knows where to look and keeps glancing nervously around the room. Behind me, I sense another presence—Colin, I assume.

We watch the clip a second time, studying it carefully for light and shadow, position of the camera. At least, that's what I'm assessing. Matt is putting the entire scene together—Margaret's delivery of her lines, one or two of which she ad-libbed. The quality of the sound. The lighting. The steadiness of the camera—almost as if it's locked in place. Wait! Not so static after all. I see the play of the shadows across her hands and the papers on the desk. I point it out to Matt, and he smiles.

We come to the end of the second run-through, and I know Matt is about to pronounce judgment. Even though I think it's great, I'm as nervous as Margaret and Zinhle. As director, Matt has the final say. If he wants another take, we will, even though I don't think I could replicate this exact light. And it's pretty clear to me Margaret's given us her best performance.

"Yes." That's all Matt ever says—his highest compliment.

My shoulders drop in relief.

But, looking at the others, I realize they don't know what's just happened, so I translate Matt's verdict. "It's as good as I thought. Margaret, you rocked it."

Margaret laughs, then covers her mouth with her hands. Zinhle claps her hands. It's Colin who asks, "May we see?"

Normally, we don't share dailies during the course of the shoot. We wait until the end of the day. But in this case . . .

Matt defers to me. "You mind?"

My eyes widen. This is a first. I've never had a director ask. Ever. But I smile and nod. This could be exactly what both women need. At least, I hope it's a good idea. "Let's do it." Matt and I step back so the women and Colin can get a good look, and I play the clip again.

I'm not prepared for Margaret's cascade of tears. Or for Zinhle reaching out to touch the laptop monitor. Colin's reaction is considerably more restrained: "Well done." I guess it's a compliment.

We film Zinhle sitting on her bed, the framed photograph of her with her daughter in the background, blurred out just enough. The viewers will know it's a photo of a woman and a young girl, but they won't be able to recognize them. And that's exactly what Zinhle needs to hear. With an abusive husband out there, she's adamant about keeping her daughter safe.

Matt doesn't want shadows telling Zinhle's story, so I have both Colin and Margaret with reflectors on either side of the camera, bouncing the sunlight streaming in from the windows to illuminate Zinhle's face. The tungsten panels add the right brightness, and the sound check goes off without a hitch.

The first take is a bit awkward. Zinhle has her lines memorized, but her delivery is like Margaret's was yesterday—wooden, almost robotic. Matt lets her continue for the entire three minutes before calling "cut."

Zinhle looks embarrassed. "I am very sorry. This is harder than I thought it would be. I am not sure . . ." Then, squaring her shoulders, she lifts her chin. "The problem for me is that these are not my words. This is not how I would tell my story."

Now? She's telling us now? But they all read the screenplay, and they approved it.

And what were they supposed to say to a white film crew coming from Hollywood?

Matt crosses the room and joins her on the bed, sitting at the far end, out of the frame. "How would you tell this story?"

"I . . ." She takes a deep breath, and I surreptitiously turn on the camera and step away. A single take—not something we often do with people. Zinhle hesitates on her first couple words, stumbles once, but then warms to her story. The beatings she endured. The daughter she loves more than life itself. Her determination to save the girl from the abuse her father would soon start inflicting on her. Her need for money to get away. Hearing about the possibility of a job with the Mambas. Going to the recruitment meeting. Excelling at the training—so rigorous it sent many other women home in tears. Somehow, she captures the emotional upheaval of her experience but also tells the story in a way other women facing such abuse will know what to do, how to escape.

We let her talk, much longer than the three minutes her original speech was scheduled to run. When this gets to editing, I'm sure they'll cut it down to fit, but for now we don't have to worry. I turn off the camera.

"These are the words I would like to say." Zinhle's confidence is back. "Now, you will start the camera, please?"

"Come." I wave her over, along with Margaret and Colin and Matt.

With the camera wired to the laptop, I run the clip. Zinh-le gapes as she realizes what I've done. For a moment, I worry I've abused her trust, but she quickly hugs me to her. Still watching, I find myself getting teary-eyed, and that never happens. No matter what I film, I always keep myself at a remove, completely objective. But somehow this is different.

"We're done here," Matt announces, although he shoots me a sidelong glance. Apparently, my surreptitious filming took him by surprise, too.

"How are the others doing?" Margaret looks out the window, but her view of the garden is blocked by laundry on the clothesline—a sure reminder that despite our movie-making, regular work here continues.

My camera still attached to the tripod, I follow Margaret and Zinhle and Matt down the hall to the kitchen and then out the back door. And stop dead in my tracks, Colin bumping into me from behind. Somehow, I manage to stay on my feet.

"What the hell?" Matt's whisper is barely audible. Whether or not it's a shoot he's directing, he knows better than to say anything.

And there is, indeed, a shoot happening. On the far side of the backyard—no grass, just dirt—Amie and Natalie and Tonderai are each holding circular reflectors—more to redirect the harsh late-morning sun away from the garden. Cate films, panning oh so slowly between Barbara and Pepsi. The two women are kneeling in the garden, occasionally sitting back on their heels to rest aching lower backs, while they pull weeds, harvest ripe courgettes and peppers and tomatoes. They're also talking to each other about their lives before joining the Mambas and since. The hardships and the joys.

I shoot Matt a puzzled look. This isn't how we scripted

things. Each woman was going to tell her story separately, but from what I can see, it's working. Typical Matt, he quirks an eyebrow and offers a sly half-grin at Cate's going rogue.

Another fifteen minutes, and then Barbara looks directly into the camera. "I think we are done."

Pepsi nods and giggles. "Did we do well?"

Cate turns off her camera. "Top marks, ladies!"

A moment later, Pepsi and Barbara are on their feet. Natalie, Amie, and Tonderai have tossed the reflectors to the ground, and all six of them have their arms around each other—a joyful group hug, something we neglected to do.

Finally, Natalie notices us and runs over, ending with a happy two-step in the dirt in front of us. "This has been so awesome. Even better than being in front of the camera. I loved holding the reflector!"

Not something I expected to hear from our star power, especially after last night's attempt to hijack the film. She really does seem happy, like she's doing what she's always dreamed of. I wonder what she'd say if she knew the difference in pay between the headlining actress and a lighting assistant—not even a gaffer or a best boy, neither of which we could afford. Something else about her is different. It takes me a moment to realize her hair is pulled back into a ponytail, she's not wearing a speck of make-up, and her earrings have disappeared.

She catches me inspecting her ear-lobes. "I totally forgot to take them off, but Cate read me the riot act when the camera caught them and flared. Or something."

Her camera still on her shoulder, Cate ambles over, seemingly oblivious to having gone way off script. "We saw what you were doing with Margaret and Zinhle. I figured you'd want something different from Pepsi and Barbara instead of being redundant. It came off pretty well, don't you think? Of course, we can always go back and reshoot according to your screenplay." Leave it to Cate to take the offensive. There's a reason why she's the best in the business. I seriously wish the Oscars would take notice instead of always singling out men.

Matt offers one clipped nod. "Why don't we take a break and I'll look at what you got. Colin, could we use your office? I think the light is best in there."

Pepsi hurries past us with Barbara following close behind. "The *sadza!*"

Lunch comes first, and as I expected, the *sadza* is perfectly smooth and the relish even spicier than it was yesterday. We're all chowing down, and I notice beads of sweat on Amie's and Natalie's brows. Although I warn them off the beer, they ignore me. Apparently, there's nothing better than a chilled Zambezi to cut through the heat of Pepsi's relish. I'm sticking to water because we may still have work to do this afternoon—if we've got to reshoot Barbara's and Pepsi's scenes. Given what I'm eating and the heat of the day, I'm drinking a lot of water.

The pitcher empty, I walk over to the pump to refill it—the excess splashing onto the concrete pad. I take a step back and practically collide with a small antelope—a bushbuck ewe, I think. Her front hooves placed delicately on the concrete, she's more than happy to lick up the water. A very young lamb, maybe a month old, with a sprinkling of white spots on her brown coat, snuggles against her mother's flank. Worried I could spook them if I go back to the picnic table, I don't move.

"It is all right." Pepsi waves me back. "*Mbabala* will understand. She likes to come around when I am cooking."

Moving slowly, I retreat to the table, only to discover the lamb is following me. Or so I think. When I sit, she veers away from me and heads over to Amie. Initially startled by the nuzzle of a cold, wet nose on her arm, Amie is quick to pet the curious baby.

"She will like the *sadza*," says Pepsi with a smile, "but not the relish."

In an instant, Amie is offering small, rolled balls of porridge to the lamb, who's making her way closer and closer to the plate. "What's her name?"

"*Mbabala.*" This is from Tonderai, who seems quite taken with watching Amie.

She looks at him, clearly confused. "I thought that was the mother's name."

Tonderai grins. "It's the Ndebele word for bushbuck. They don't have actual names."

Amie scratches the lamb behind her ears. "Well, I think you need a name."

The lamb looks up, her large eyes luminous.

"What about Lala?" Amie leans close to the lamb's upturned muzzle and smiles, receiving a lick across her lips in response. "I'd say that's a definite 'yes.' Lala it is."

After lunch, Matt and I retreat to Colin's office. I connect Cate's camera to the laptop, and suddenly Pepsi and Barbara are on the screen. Early on, I see the flare at the edge of the monitor—the sun glinting off Natalie's earring. But after that, it's pretty smooth. Except for occasional bursts of laughter from the two women, they do an amazing job, completely ad lib. I lean forward, enthralled. Next to me, Matt crosses his arms and studies the film.

"Let's watch it again," he says. "If we need to reshoot, I want to do it now while everyone's here."

Another half hour. It's not perfect. Far from it, but maybe that's why I like it so much. It stands in contrast to Margaret's and Zinhle's more polished work.

"What do you think?" he asks for the second time today.

I smile. "I like it. A lot. We won't use all of it, but there's more than enough for the editor to work with. Good contrast to the other spots."

"Exactly." He shoots me a grin. "I may make you into a director yet."

Back outside, we find everyone lounging with yet more beer. Their mid-day siesta—very welcome now that the sun is bearing down on us. I make a mental note to reimburse the Mambas for going through their drinks stock. Something I'm sure Colin expects.

"Well, boss?" Cate salutes Matt with her bottle of Zambezi.

"You sure let it rip." Matt salutes her in return. "Julia and I think we should run with it."

She takes a long pull. "Of course you should." Nothing modest about this woman.

"And for having nearly caught up with our schedule, I'm giving you all the rest of the afternoon off."

Tonderai pushes himself to his feet. "Perhaps a game drive in a little while? We could search for the lions we missed yesterday. Dabs told me they've spotted some cheetah, too."

"Great idea! Julia, how about you go over tomorrow's

schedule with Colin and the Mambas—make sure we're all on the same page. Colin, can you make sure she gets back to camp?" Matt doesn't wait for an answer but heads toward the vehicle with Tonderai and the rest of the crew.

In something close to disbelief, I watch them leave. Seriously? Matt's just going to take off? I get it that he wants to go on the game drive. What I don't get: he's leaving me here to do what he never ever assigns to a camera person. And apparently, the fact that I want to join the lion search doesn't matter.

Or maybe Matt and Cate are in it together—to set you up with Colin.

Oh, please! Never going to happen. Hell, we don't even like each other.

Then think of this as work. On your film. Something you've waited five long years to do.

After I hear Tonderai's vehicle growl to life, I turn toward Colin. "Sorry about this—making you drive back to Marula."

"No worries. This will give me an excuse to stay for dinner. Besides, it's Wednesday—my favorite meal of the week."

"How can you possibly know what they're serving?"

"The menu's on a weekly rota. Makes it easier on the chef. Stay long enough, and you'll see."

Nineteen

Clustered around the picnic table, we've just started reviewing our plans for tomorrow when the radio in Margaret's office crackles to life. Margaret runs inside to take the call. The rest of the women hurry into the dormitory to grab their go-packs. While Barbara unlocks the gun cabinet, I retrieve my camera and a shoulder mount.

It's impossible to make out the voice on the other end of the radio. I can't even tell whether it's a man or a woman. But Margaret can. "*Yebo.*" She repeats what sound like directions and GPS coordinates back to the other person. "We are on our way."

There's no time to do a sound check or mic up everyone. Instead, I film them collecting their AR-15s. Then I run ahead and manage to get them sprinting across the yard and climbing into the aging land cruiser. No one is giggling or even smiling. This is deadly serious work, and they're completely focused. Barbara's behind the steering wheel and revving the engine. Clearly, they're ready to go. One take.

"You coming?" yells Colin from the jeep.

Bounding into the front passenger seat of the jeep, I notice he's put one of my Pelican cases on the floor behind us.

"The speed we'll be going, we'll churn up a lot of dust. I suggest you stow the camera until we get there."

"Thanks." I lift the case onto my lap and quickly secure the camera inside. "You're okay with me coming along?"

"Bloody hell, no." He crunches his leather ranger's hat tight on his head. "This is the last thing I want to be doing with you. Promise me you'll keep your head down and do exactly as you're told."

Which could prevent me from getting anything good on film. But what can I say? "Will do."

Keying the ignition, he shoots me a wry smile. "You might want to buckle your seat belt."

"Really? On all my trips to Africa, I've never . . ."

He pulls his neck gaiter over his mouth and nose, steps on the accelerator, and we all but rocket forward into a cloud of dust.

Digging out the two ends of my seat belt, I lock them together. After positioning my own Buff to cover the lower half of my face, I drape my legs over the camera case and press it hard against the front of the seat.

The park is huge, with few, mostly unpaved roads. I'd forgotten from my last time in-country how long it takes to get anywhere. Even at the speed Colin is driving. For a good hour and a half, there's no talking. Between the engine screaming and the thundering of the jeep over the ruts and bumps in the dirt road, it's impossible. Besides which, Colin's attention is totally focused. So is mine as I pray no animal decides to dash in front of us. We're going so fast, there's no way we'd be able to stop in time. Any smaller animal would be killed instantly. But an elephant, a buffalo, or a giraffe? We crash into one of those, it would be the end of us.

Somehow the animals know to stay clear. I see the occasional antelope galloping back into the bush. And a massive herd of zebras and wildebeests thunders across the plain in the opposite direction when we roar into sight.

Eventually, though, as we're practically flying down a slope that's half washed out, Colin becomes aware of a call coming in on the radio. How he heard it, I can't imagine. As soon as we're once again on flat land, he slows the jeep until we're closer to the normal speed safari drivers observe to keep tourists safe.

He speaks into the receiver. "We're passing Makalolo Camp . . . *yebo* . . . which turnoff? Okay then, coming on."

A few minutes later, we pull up to two empty land cruisers. I quickly unpack my camera and attach it to my shoulder mount. Then, I'm out of the jeep and jogging after Colin toward the Mambas. There are no poachers to be seen. No poached animals either. But Zinhle calls us over to some acacia bushes.

I turn on the camera.

"See here." She points to some tufts of brown fur stuck onto the long, sharp thorns. "A waterbuck perhaps? Or maybe a kudu? Possibly trying to hide."

Margaret frowns. "But from a poacher or a lion?"

"Over here!" Pepsi waves us to a spot about twenty yards away.

I pan the camera across the line of Mambas running toward her. Once again, their guns are at the ready, and they're scanning the bushes and trees for any signs of poachers. Finally, I turn off the camera and join the run.

Kneeling next to the disturbed sand, Pepsi directs us to stand back, then once the camera is rolling again, she explains what we're looking at. "A kudu. You can see from the hoofprints. This is where he fell." She points to the space between Barbara and me. "There. Drops of blood." Now that she points them out, they're obvious. But I bet she's the only one who saw them.

"Poachers? Or a lion kill?" asks Barbara. "What do you think, Pepsi?"

She opens her hand so we can all see the bullet casing. "Unless lions are carrying guns, this kudu was taken by poachers. And recently. Maybe two or three hours ago?" She looks into the camera for a moment. "This is where he fell. You can see his body was here." I pan slowly to the imprint of the body in the sand. "It's still very well defined. So are the hoof marks. There's enough of a breeze that it would blow the sand back over all of this in half a day. Yes, poachers just took this animal. You can see how they dragged him to their truck right over here. Then, they used branches to cover the tire marks."

Colin kneels down. "It's unusual for poachers to work in daylight. Could it be villagers taking him for the meat?"

Margaret shrugs. "It is possible. But it is still wrong. I think we should continue our search. If this happened in the last few hours, like Pepsi says, perhaps we can catch up with them. We must stop them."

We're back on the road, heading toward where Margaret thinks village poachers might butcher the kudu. I can't stop thinking about Pepsi. "She's amazing."

Colin glances over at me. "Pepsi, you mean?"

I nod. "How could she tell it was a kudu? There wasn't any body."

"She's brilliant. Learned some from her brother, but she's honed her skills as a Mamba."

It must be close to an hour later when I ask, "How long before we catch up with the others?"

"Not sure. Barbara's driving down the central road. Another unit of Mambas is going down the west road. We're on the east side. I'll turn south in another couple minutes."

"So, we're trying to encircle the poachers and snare them."

"That's the idea." He's driving much more slowly than before, studying both sides of the road.

"Isn't it kind of strange to be poaching in the middle of the day?"

"Exactly what I'm thinking. Far too likely for there to be witnesses or to run into some hapless tourists out on a game drive. Although this isn't a well-traveled part of the park."

"You think it's a false alarm?"

He pushes his hat back on his head. "Not sure. It's most likely villagers, but it could be cartel poachers trying to out-think us. Maybe the same group that's been eluding us for months now. I'd love to catch them and put a stop to their killing. The Mambas are determined, so I figure it's only a matter of time."

"They're that fierce?"

He shoots me another grin. "I wouldn't want to run up against them."

"They're good shots?"

"I'm a good shot. Expert, in fact. These women never miss. And they shoot to kill."

That catches me. "Is that legal?"

"Technically, no. And they don't shoot the locals hunting to feed their families. But if they get caught in a firefight with poachers who are part of organized cartels, they aren't about to negotiate."

"Then, don't they run the risk of getting in trouble with the national police?"

He shrugs. "Not so far."

Another thirty minutes, and Colin eases up on the gas even more. There aren't any more ruts in the road, but we've got to be getting close to the place Margaret mentioned. He's probably hoping to keep the noise of the jeep to a minimum so we don't scare off the poachers or villagers or whoever killed the kudu.

"You mind if I take out my camera?"

"Have at it. But remember what I said before. Do exactly what I tell you, when I tell you. And be ready to dive to the ground. With or without your camera."

Ahead, I see a cloud of dust rising. Someone's driving fast. The Mambas, I'm guessing. But should we be able to see Barbara's land cruiser already? Or the other group's vehicle? From the corner of my eye, I see Colin's hands tighten on the steering wheel and feel the tension radiating off his body as he pulls to a stop.

"In answer to your question, no, we shouldn't have caught up to either group yet." His voice is low. "It could be tourists heading toward something that's been spotted. Although they're pretty far afield. Or it could be our poachers." He pulls out his binoculars and trains them on the vehicle. "Hard to say."

I scan the plains around us in search of one of the Mamba's vehicles or maybe an elephant carcass. But all I see is a mixed herd of wildebeest, zebra, and impala. Or maybe bushbuck?

Colin would probably look on me disdainfully for not being able to tell the difference. But antelope aren't my strong suit.

Suddenly, his foot is on the brake, slowing us even more. Looking ahead, I see the mystery vehicle has stopped. I take note of a white man climbing out of the driver's seat and several other white men jumping down from the seats in back. An Ndebele man exits from the front passenger seat and walks around to the rear of the truck, where he unloads a large box. A cooler.

Colin picks up the radio and notifies the Mambas. "We're at the coordinates. No sign of any poachers. Or villagers. Looks to be Gus Sinclair and his latest party of hunters. I'm not sure what they're doing this far from Buffalothorn."

A few minutes later, Colin pulls to a stop on the shady side of Gus's vehicle, then sits for a moment. Finally, he turns to me. "You mind staying here for a bit?"

"Whatever you say. Remember, I'm under orders. But a bathroom stop sometime soon would be very welcome."

"An emergency?"

"Not yet."

"I'll see what I can do." He cracks the wry grin I'm coming to like, then makes his way around the land cruiser to Gus and his guests.

A few minutes later, he's back with Gus, both of them standing at the front of the jeep. "I hear you two know each other?" His voice is flat with a healthy dose of disappointment.

"We've met." First in Jo'burg, then Vic Falls. I keep the details of our meetings to myself.

"Julia! Good to see you." Gus sounds very pleased, almost as if he'd orchestrated this rendezvous. "How's the movie coming along?"

"Making progress." I stow my camera back in its case.

Colin takes over. "We got called out about a possible poaching."

"Poachers?" Gus practically roars his laugh. "In the middle of the day? Not likely."

The same hunters I first saw in Jo'burg straggle toward the jeep just in time to hear, and they look equally astonished.

"So, what are you doing out here?" Colin doesn't laugh.

"Definitely not poaching." Gus puts a foot up on the front bumper of the jeep. I can't help noticing his well-fitting khaki shorts and muscled legs. "The guys voted to take a break with hunting and come on a game drive in the park."

Which sounds like a reasonable thing to do. I'd much rather look at wildlife than shoot it.

Colin nods then asks the man standing next to him, "Seeing much?"

"Not nearly as much as we saw at Buffalothorn. Gus did tell us there's been a lot of poaching going on in these parts. I guess the animals are scared of vehicles."

Wait a sec! Certainly, Gus knew there wouldn't be a lot of wildlife in this part of the park. So why bring his guests so far from his concession to see—nothing? Why not go to the Ngamo Plains where the savanna is teeming with every sort of animal living in Zimbabwe?

Gus ambles around to my side of the jeep and assumes a pose, backlit against the setting sun—a large tangerine fireball in a sky now blood red. I shield my eyes. The sunsets in Zimbabwe are nearly always magnificent, especially in Hwange and Vic Falls. Tonight's is no exception—absolutely stunning—except for the fact that Gus is partially blocking it.

He grins. "Sorry we couldn't give you any poachers to film

today. But I can offer you a sundowner." He looks over at the khaki-uniformed man who's setting up the bar. I can see now he's got *Buffalothorn* embroidered above his breast pocket. "Gin and tonic? Beer? Something else? What's your pleasure?"

"A Zambezi would be great," I say, climbing out of the jeep and looking toward the trees. My need to pee is quickly approaching the uncomfortable stage.

"Make that two." Colin smiles. "Much appreciated." He catches my eye and tips his head toward the acacias on the far side of Gus's vehicle.

I don't actually run to the grove, but I'm not walking either. By the time I reach the trees, I'm already unbuttoning my pants. That's when I decide it wouldn't hurt to make sure there aren't any snakes soaking up the last rays of the sun. I trust Colin checked for lions, but snakes are most definitely not my friends. In fact, they absolutely terrify me—especially the venomous ones. Please let there not be any slithering reptiles.

There aren't. Pants down around my ankles, I squat as close to the ground as possible and let loose. Oh, God, the relief!

The work of a minute and I'm back at the jeep, where the bartender is passing out frosty bottles of lager. He's back a short time later with a tall stack of aluminum tiffin boxes that he opens and spreads across the hood of the vehicle.

"Thanks, Tracker." Gus claps him on the shoulder. "What did the chef send with us?"

Assuming the military 'at ease' position, feet apart, arms behind his back, Tracker announces the menu. "Tonight with our sundowners, we have the chicken satay, spicy kudu, the pickled eggs, popcorn, and biltong."

"Oh!" My eyes lock on the last container. "Do I see roast-ed cashews?"

"Yes, madam. My apologies. These are the roasted cashews." He picks up the tin and hands it to me.

Be still my heart. I don't offer to share but do catch a glimpse of Colin's eyes—seriously amused. While I'm savoring my perfectly roasted cashews one at a time, Gus lifts his Zambezi and makes a toast to Hwange. The polished copper bracelet on his wrist clinking against his beer bottle, he salutes the park as the largest and oldest in Zimbabwe, then segues into the importance of conservation—to protect endangered species from extinction. A nice touch—probably for my benefit. We all raise our drinks, then quietly watch the sun slip below the horizon. An orange light flares for a few seconds, then follows the sun.

In the quiet of this lovely moment, I hear the churning engines of two vehicles. The Mambas, I'm sure. In another few minutes, the vehicles pull up and stop next to us. A virtual parking lot in a remote spot on the edge of the Kalahari—who would've thought. Eight camo-clad women jump out of the vehicles, and Colin walks over to them to hear what they've discovered. He's back a few minutes later. "They didn't see anyone."

"Probably because there's no one out here," Gus scoffs.

Colin ignores him and speaks to me. "They want to stay out here, check on known hiding spots once it's a bit darker."

I practically gulp. "We're out here for the night?" And me without my tungsten panels or any kind of lighting. There's no way I'll be able to film anything—if it turns out there's anything to film.

Colin shakes his head. "Nah. No point in us staying."

I breathe a sigh of relief and take another sip of beer.

Gus moves closer to me. "Hey! I've got an idea. Julia,

you've never seen Buffalothorn. How about you two join us for dinner. It's a good hour closer than Marula." He nods toward the hunters. "I'm sure they'd love the company—a bit of a change from staring at my ugly face."

The hunters chuckle and nudge each other with their elbows, clearly enjoying their time with Gus.

"You can even stay over if you'd like. Plenty of room."

Everyone's looking at me, and I don't have a clue what to say. I'm not about to hitch a ride with Gus. That would only complicate things in the morning. "What about the crew at Marula Camp? They'll be expecting us . . . well, me."

"No worries! Colin or I can radio them. It'd be nine o'clock, maybe ten, before you'd get back there anyway. You'll be doing the chef at Marula a favor by not arriving late for dinner."

Gus has a point. I think about it for all of three seconds. "Colin? You're the one driving."

He takes off his hat and runs his fingers through his hair. "Easier drive to Gus's place, and I wouldn't mind a dinner at Buffalothorn. From what I remember, the meals are pretty special, and it's been a while."

"Okay then." I smile. "Thanks, Gus. We accept." This will be a whole lot nicer than the long drive back to Marula in the dark. In an open jeep.

Twenty

It never ceases to amaze me how quickly night falls in Zimbabwe when the sun disappears. The moon is full and rising fast, but even that isn't enough to light the dirt road as it winds through the park. We pass mounds along the side of the road, but for the life of me, I can't tell whether they're elephants or *kopjes* or trees. Colin drives well, steady and sure. Ahead of us, the taillights of Gus's safari vehicle never waver. Obviously, he knows this part of the park well. Tonderai's words echo: *I worked with him some years ago . . . and he was a good guide. Honest and truly caring for the animals.*

Finally, after another long drive, we reach Buffalothorn—a massive lodge, ablaze with lights. "Wow!" I practically gasp. "Impressive."

"It's definitely a wow. Okay to visit, but I prefer Marula and Msasa. It'll be a good meal, though. Great, in fact."

As we pull up and stop, young men in what I hope are faux leopard skins spill out onto the front deck, drumming and dancing in welcome. Behind them, several women in traditional dress clap the beat, sing, and ululate—a wonderful trill of the tongue I can't manage myself but brings goose bumps to my arms.

"I'd love to record that."

"Why don't you?"

"Not tonight. I'll just soak it in."

Colin looks at me with evident amusement curling the corner of his mouth. "You mean there are times when you're not filming?"

His tease is a bit snarky for my taste. "Yes, sometimes I can actually put my work aside and exist as a human being—enjoying the moment." God, just when I start to think he could be a nice guy, he goes and opens his mouth.

The dance finished, I climb out of the jeep and reach for my Pelican case. And nearly collide with Colin, who's already got the case in hand, his rifle in the other. "I've got it. Shall we?" He nods toward the stairs leading to the deck where Gus is waiting, arms open wide in welcome.

Gus walks us into a vast, open room, brightly lit with artful chandeliers made of what look to be bleached shells. Large black-and-white photographs of big cats and wild dogs, elephants and giraffes overlook the brown leather sofas and armchairs scattered strategically throughout, designed I'm sure for private conversations. Or, at least, to give the illusion it's possible. Somehow, I bet Gus knows everything that happens in this lodge and manages to hear all that's said, no matter how private and personal. At the far end of the room, I spy a bar area unlike any I've ever seen. The bar itself runs the length of the wall and looks to be zebrawood. Behind it, shelves hold an amazing array of bottles. There's probably nothing this man can't serve up.

Colin's right, though: this is a place to enjoy for a night, but like him, I prefer Marula and Msasa. Although the lodge is absolutely luxe—over the top, in fact—it somehow leaves me a bit on edge.

"Wow!" I say again.

"Thanks." Gus beams. "It's been a labor of love. Took a few years and a lot of work to get this place exactly the way I wanted it, to attract the kind of guests I'm looking to bring here, but it's finally done."

"Impressive." I'm not sure what else I can say without actually revealing my true thoughts.

"I thought you'd like it." He takes my camera gear from Colin, and almost instantly a tall, slender woman is next to us. She's stunningly beautiful—Shona, I think. Which is odd since we're in the middle of Matabeleland. I can't help staring at her long braids swept into an elaborate updo and her brightly patterned wrap-around silk dress. "Grace, could you please take this case to room two and make sure everything is ready?"

"Of course."

"Thanks, but no." I put out my hand for my case.

The woman looks confused, and Gus flustered. "I can assure you it will be perfectly safe."

"My camera gear stays with me. Always." No one mentions that Colin's been the one toting the case.

"Whatever you want." His voice is still friendly, but his slight frown tells me I've violated some code. A moment later, his hand resting proprietarily on the small of my back, he propels me toward the bar. "Another drink? You ready for a G&T?"

"A glass of red wine, I think. Do you have a Pinotage?"

He looks at me somewhat affronted. "I can do you better than that. I have a rather nice cabernet I think you'll like."

I'm not sure what to make of a man telling me I'll prefer his choice to my own. Correction, I know exactly what to make of it. But we're guests here, and this isn't a battle I want to fight. "Okay."

"Tremblay, what about you?"

Colin offers a wry smile. "I'll have the same as the lady."

And that quite obviously catches Gus off guard. But he recovers quickly and repeats our order to the bartender. I watch as a bottle of Château Lafite Rothschild appears in front of me. 2019.

"Lovely," I say and, with my best manners, wave away the offered taste.

Gus himself pours my glass, and once again I see the copper bracelet on his wrist, glinting in the light of the chandelier. This time, though, there are some etchings in the metal—designs I've seen before but can't quite place. Not Ndebele. Shona maybe?

Presenting the large-belled crystal glass of wine to me, he watches while I take my first taste. As he probably guessed, one sip later and I'm quite literally humming. Oh God, this is the best wine ever to cross my lips. It's so smooth, so seamless, and yet so full of flavor, I almost forget to swallow. From the smug look on Gus's face, he knows I love it.

He carries the bottle to the longest table I've ever seen, made of wood so highly polished that when I touch it, I leave a fingerprint. It's set with gleaming china and sparkling crystal. If I'm not mistaken, the flatware isn't flat at all, but sterling silver. I guess this is how the wealthy live and what they expect when they go hunting in Africa. He walks to the head of the table and sets the bottle at the seat next to his. I look past Gus's five hunting guests, who've each staked out a claim along the table all the way to the opposite end where I see Colin.

Kudu is the main course tonight. How could I have forgotten Gus's predilection for dining on wild game?

"No worries," he says in a stage whisper which I'm sure

reaches all the way to the far end of the table. "I remember what you told me at River Lodge. I've ordered pork for you."

The hunter to my left leans closer. "The warthog hereabouts is real tasty, especially when it's fresh, and the chef roasts it to perfection." A Texas twang—most definitely.

"Oh, good," I manage. But kudu? Warthog? They're both wildlife not raised to be food. At least, not on my plate.

Gus leans in close, as if it's just the two of us having a private conversation. "Tell me, what's next in the movie world?" His voice cuts the length of the table, and I'm sure Colin hears him. I'm also pretty certain Gus wants him to hear.

"Not really the 'movie world.' This is just a short documentary." I seriously don't like dissing my own film, but I also don't want him thinking this is a feature-length movie.

From the other end of the table, Colin answers the question I didn't. "They'll be filming me training the Mambas."

"You?"

"Me."

Gus looks pointedly at me. "I guess it slipped Tremblay's mind that I was the primary trainer of the Mambas back in the day. In fact, I pretty much got them up and running."

Talk about awkward. I glance around me. Some of the hunters are looking back and forth from one end of the table to the other. The rest are staring at their plates.

What am I expected to say? "Well, kudos! You clearly did a great job. The women are amazing." *But why did you quit?* I want to ask. Then again, looking around at this incredible lodge, I don't have to ask. I'm sure he's making a lot more money from his hunters. And something tells me that's what he's after in life.

"Hey, Gus!" one of the guys halfway down the table calls. "With us leaving in a couple days, you could be part of the movie. Show off your training moves. You'd be great! Might end up with a starring role." The others hoot their agreement.

All except Colin, who quirks an eyebrow.

Something's going on here that I don't get. Colin didn't forget Gus helped train the Mambas. I'm beginning to realize there isn't much—if anything—Colin forgets. So, why did he announce to the table what we'd be filming next? Suddenly the answer falls into place. He knew how Gus would respond— that he'd all but demand to be part of the movie. But why would that be a good idea? And why would Colin want that? Is he trying to sabotage the documentary? Or is he goading Gus?

The ball is back in Gus's court, but he promptly passes it to me. "So, what do you say, pretty lady?"

Damn it, Colin, this is on you. "Maybe I should check with Matt. After all, he's the director. I just operate a camera." For all the arguing I've done to be part of the decision-making, these words make me cringe.

As I well know, Gus takes encouragement wherever he can find it. "We talking about Matt Monahan? The guy who was at River Lodge a few nights ago?"

I nod.

"Then I'm in. After you skipped out on dinner, we chatted for a while. I offered my services, and he was happy to accept. Good show! I'll see you at Msasa then." He does a short drumroll on the table, then lifts his glass of wine and toasts the two of us. "To working together!"

I sense my film slipping out of my control and shoot Colin a look of cross-eyed annoyance. Why in God's name did he bait Gus? And did Matt really invite Gus to be part of the film without discussing it with me? My fingers tighten around my knife until my knuckles whiten. Cutting my beautifully carved slice of warthog into teeny, tiny pieces, I fork them into my mouth, swallowing without tasting.

Finally, at midnight, the meal is done. I'm done, too, and want nothing more than to go to bed. Grace, the same woman who tried to take my Pelican case, escorts me to my room. Walking next to her, I notice her dress isn't just silk, but raw silk—designer quality. Her shoes look like something Manolo Blahnik would advertise in the Sunday magazine of *The New York Times*.

Once in my room, I somehow manage to keep from gaping at the splendor. Grace sashays around the room, pointing out all the luxuries awaiting me: rose petals floating in a tub of steaming hot water and cream silk pajamas carefully laid out on a king-sized bed. When she sweeps her hand over a bottle of champagne with two flutes and a plate of truffles, I inhale sharply. If I hadn't gotten the message from Gus constantly replenishing my every sip of the heavenly cab at dinner, I've got it now. Grace's knowing smile as she pulls a cord next to the bed and sends the mosquito net cascading protectively from the ceiling is yet more confirmation.

After she leaves, I check out what's behind the door. Not a closet. Another bedroom.

Gus's, I'm sure. Quite an assumption on his part. Okay, so I may have found him attractive. I may even have been slightly tempted in Jo'burg. But damn, I feel manipulated. Whatever he's thinking is going to happen most definitely *isn't* going to happen. Not tonight. Not ever.

I've barely locked the door when I hear footsteps in the adjoining room. Maybe he'll give me a few minutes to bathe and put on the pajamas before he tries the door. Or maybe he's thinking he'll share the bath with me. I opt to leave now.

And then what? Go in search of Colin? I have no idea where Gus has stuck him for the night, but my guess is as far away from this end of the lodge as possible.

Slipping out of my room, Pelican case in hand, I close the door behind me as softly as possible, then tiptoe along the deck, hoping to locate Colin's room. Very quickly I realize how impossible my search is. There's no way I can knock on each door. I don't like Gus's planned seduction, but it wouldn't be smart to parade his failure in front of his hunters.

I keep walking, finding my way to the other wing of the lodge before stopping to acknowledge how pointless this is. Leaning against a stretch of railing, I consider my options: return to my bedroom or hide out in the dining room until morning. Probably the two likeliest places Gus will look for me. Glancing up, I notice two burned-out lights. Odd that the staff haven't replaced these bulbs.

"Hey, are you all right?" Colin's voice. And then he's next to me, shoulder to shoulder.

I breathe a sigh of relief and set down the camera case. "I was looking for you."

"Why is that?"

"To save my virtue."

He chuckles softly. "You honestly think your virtue's safe with me?"

"I do."

"Not something a man wants to hear."

"I trust you." And I suddenly realize that I do trust him.

He's quiet for a long moment. "That's important to you."

I bet he's thinking about Liam. "Yeah, it is."

"So, what happened tonight?"

I tell him about the scene staged for my grand seduction.

He groans softly. "Bloody hell. I was afraid he might try something."

"Excuse me? Are you saying you brought me here so he could—"

"No. That's the last thing I wanted to have happen. Rumor has it, though, that there have been others."

"No surprise there. But how did you know he was planning this?"

"When we met them in Hwange this evening, it was pretty clear he was interested in you. Then there was the bottle of wine, which I happen to know ran him at least a thousand dollars US, probably more."

"It was a great wine."

"Oh, yeah." He leans closer. "Glad he actually let me have a glass. You know, for all the times he refilled your glass, you don't seem very drunk."

"Baby sips."

"Smart move." He sounds amused. Until he suddenly doesn't. Then, his index finger is pressing against my lips.

Now I hear it. A huffing sound. And something else—a sort of half growl, half hum.

It's heading this way. Getting closer. Way too close.

I squint into the darkness, hoping to see what it is. But my eyes still aren't adjusted to these deep shadows.

Then, Colin's arm is around me. "Move behind me. Slowly," he whispers.

"What is it?"

"From the sound of it, a lion."

I sense his presence—large and ferocious—a few meters in front of us. An easy leap onto the deck—if he can clear the balustrade.

"Do you have your gun?" I inch my way behind him, trying hard to keep my trembling to a minimum.

"In the room."

"Bloody hell!" Now I'm full-out terrified.

"Steady on."

Partly shielded by Colin, I look over the railing and down. And now I see him. A huge lion with what looks to be a gorgeous full mane. Old enough to have done his share of killing. Eyes gleaming. And riveted on us.

He's back on his haunches now, waiting for the right moment, and if I know anything about cats, he's about to pounce.

Except he doesn't.

He turns his massive head and looks down the deck to the other wing of the house.

Now I hear the footsteps, too. Shoe leather slapping against the wood slats.

"Reggie! There you are." As Gus passes under lights that are still working, the large hind leg he's carrying becomes visible. For some reason, I find myself impressed that he's strong enough to be lugging so much weight with seemingly very little effort. A scary thought.

"Probably from the kudu we had for dinner," Colin whispers.

My stomach churns. "I didn't need to know that."

"Here you go, old boy!" Gus heaves the leg over the railing and onto the ground.

With a snarl, Reggie bares his teeth and snags his dinner. But instead of carrying it off into the bush, he parks himself a little farther away and proceeds to gnaw the flesh off the bone.

"Likes to hang around here, don't you, Reggie." Gus walks the rest of the way to where we're standing and takes his position on the other side of me. "He wouldn't have gone for you, so long as you had something to feed him."

"And if we didn't have anything?" I choke out the words.

"Hasn't gone for anyone before." His voice sounds reassuring. But then he shrugs. "But I can't say for sure."

That shrug practically does me in. Oh my God! He didn't feed the kudu leg to the lion to save us. It's clear this cat hangs around Buffalothorn because Gus wants him here. A guard lion? It takes another couple seconds before the pieces of the puzzle fall into place: Reggie's one of the trophy animals he keeps on hand to lure in hunters. I want to hurl up my warthog dinner.

Gus puts his hand on the back of my neck, caressing gently. "You coming back to bed?"

I shrug off his hand. "I think not."

"Don't stay out here too long." Meaning, I guess, that there are other wild animals wandering the grounds. A moment later, he retraces his steps to the other wing, leaving Reggie to feast in front of us.

"*Back* to bed?" I can almost see Colin's wry grin.

"In his dreams. I locked the door between our rooms, then headed out here."

"You want to finish this night in my room?" he asks.

"Thanks. I'll feel a lot safer there." I'm desperate to get as far away as I can from Reggie before he finishes his kudu leg. But I sure hope I didn't give Colin the wrong idea.

Draping his arm across my shoulder, I can feel the laughter building inside him. "You do have a way of saying exactly what I'd rather not hear."

Still shaking—and not from the cold night air—I take another look at Reggie, who's now ripping flesh from the femur. "Could we please just go to your room!"

Twenty-One

Colin's room is nothing like mine—a fraction of the size and very rustic, with none of the amenities. The bed looks to be a double—much smaller than the king size I abandoned. We're both big people, and there's no way the two of us can sleep comfortably in a bed this small.

"I'll sleep on the floor." I'm not about to force him out of his own bed.

"We can share." He kicks off his boots, then pulls off his olive sweater and starts to unbutton his Mamba shirt.

I put my camera case on a chair and position it in front of the locked door. Not that any of this will stop Gus if he wants to get in, but at least it'll create enough noise to wake us. "No."

"I thought you trusted me." He peels off his shirt, then his pants.

"I do—to a point, which doesn't include sharing a bed." I toe off my Keens. "Besides, I don't know anything about you. Other than you're brave enough to take on a lion to save my life."

"Actually, I think that tells you quite a lot." He stands in front of me naked except for his briefs. I can't help staring at his legs and arms—all taut muscles and not an ounce of fat on him. He quirks an eyebrow. "What else do you want to know?"

I park my fists on my waist. "I don't know! Everything. Something. I don't even know your favorite color."

"Bloody hell." He pushes aside the mosquito netting and drags the duvet and a pillow off the bed, doubles it over on the hardwood floor, and lies down. "I'll sleep on the floor."

"Absolutely not." I thump down next to his feet. "Yow! This really is hard. You won't be able to sleep here."

Propping himself up on his forearms, he shoots me a look I judge to be a combination of frustration and amusement. "Believe me, I've slept on a lot worse than this."

I cross my arms, keep my eyes locked on his, and wait. But he doesn't elaborate. Finally, I try baiting him. "That's such a macho thing to say."

He doesn't take the bait. Instead, he lies back down and closes his eyes, then slows his breathing until the only thing I can hear is the slight buzz of the overhead light. I'm almost convinced he's managed to fall asleep when he speaks. "British special forces."

"Seriously?" Which is a stupid thing to say because I heard him and it actually explains a lot.

"Retired."

I open my mouth, but no words emerge.

He opens his eyes and watches me carefully. "I didn't take you for anti-military."

"I'm not." I bite my lower lip. "Well, maybe I was once, a long time ago, but . . . well . . . it's complicated."

"You care to fill me in?"

Do I want to talk about this? No, I do not. So, I tell him. "Some years ago, I marched in the protests against the US invasion of Afghanistan."

"You telling me you're pro-Taliban?"

"Not at all. I'm anti-war. And I didn't think it was helping anyone to have US or British or any soldiers dying while they tried to turn around a country no one has ever conquered. The Brits tried and failed. So did the Russians."

He holds up four fingers.

I look at him quizzically. "What's that supposed to mean?"

"Go back in history. Darius the Great, Alexander the Great, Mahmud of Ghazni, Genghis Khan. And that's only four of the conquerors."

I lean back against the bed frame. "Really? How do you happen to know this fascinating factoid?"

He props himself up on his forearms again and looks a little too self-satisfied for my taste. "I read history at university. And before you ask, the answer is Cambridge."

"Impressive."

"Anticipating your next question, the path from uni to the army wasn't that convoluted. I graduated, was at loose ends, needed a job, looked into Sandhurst, and ended up in special forces."

"Okay."

"And while you were protesting, I was finishing my third tour in Afghanistan."

Fuck. I mouth the word.

"You got that right. It was pretty fucked up. Lost too many of my men. Still is—fucked up. Only, thanks to the Taliban, it's even worse now."

"I'm sorry. Like I said . . . it's complicated." Tears welling, I bury my face in my hands. I really don't want this man to see me crying.

I can feel his eyes on me, probably trying to figure out how he tipped me over the edge of arguing to weeping.

"Who did you lose?" he asks gently, pushing himself up to sit next to me.

It takes me a minute before I can formulate a coherent response. "Everyone." I hug my knees to my chest, hoping to keep myself from exploding. Now that I've opened the rusty box where my heart used to be, explosion—or maybe implosion—is a very real possibility.

Then, I feel Colin's arm on my shoulders. He doesn't ask any more questions.

We sit in silence, welcome at first, then torturous. Finally, I take a deep breath and plunge in. "I grew up in a little town in northern New Jersey. Pretty white bread but nice. Safe. My dad worked in the city—New York. He . . . uh . . . was in his office on the ninetieth floor that day. I was thirteen." I wipe my eyes. "It hit me hard. Devastated me. I thought nothing could ever be worse. But then, my big brother, Danny, he was playing on a farm team for the majors—baseball. He enlisted and, long story short, became a SEAL. Ten years later, there was this mission in Afghanistan, and he was on a helicopter . . ."

"Hey," Colin says quietly, rubbing my back, keeping me tethered. "You don't need to do this."

My breath is coming in short gasps. Easing my legs down, I press my hand against my chest—right over my heart. "Sorry, sorry. I honestly didn't mean to dump my life history on you. But thanks for listening. You're a saint."

"Hardly a saint. But I know what it's like to lose people. I also know it can help to talk about it."

But I never talk about any of this. Not until tonight. It's been so much easier to keep it locked inside. I'm about to change the subject, move on to something safer, when I find myself saying, "You know, when the country tells you your brother died a hero, it's a lot of crap."

"I think people say things like that to make you feel better. A grateful nation and all that."

I snort a dismissive laugh. "Well, it sure didn't help my mother. She took an extended leave of absence from the university where she was teaching and retreated into her books. For a while, she was taking a lot of pills—to keep the pain at bay, to help her sleep. I kept thinking she'd get better, go back to teaching. But . . . she didn't. She's still holed up in the family house, basically letting it fall down around her." I take a deep breath. "I'm ashamed to admit I don't visit her as often as I should. In fact, I'm a terrible daughter. It just hurts so much to see her like that."

"How about you? How did you fare after your brother died?" His hand makes perfect circles on my back.

"Me?" I almost wave away his questions but find myself answering instead. "When it happened, I was in grad school, working on a PhD in comparative literature. Like mother, like daughter. I took a semester off, then couldn't find my way back to studying literature. But my father and brother would've been furious if I'd gone the recluse route." For a minute I let myself go back to those dark days after Danny died. The sheer, overwhelming grief and god-awful loneliness.

"You obviously didn't become a recluse."

I turn toward Colin. He stops rubbing my back and rests his hand on my shoulder, his eyes locked on mine, looking for all the world like he really wants to know. So, I tell him. "I changed direction and got an MFA in photography and videography. Then, right after I finished my degree, I managed to get myself on a film crew making a wildlife documentary for the BBC. My first shoot, and I worked with Cate. Thank God she took me under her wing. She's the one who really taught me cinematography. One thing led to another, and I was getting good jobs on a regular basis. Making a name for myself."

"Where did Liam come in?"

"Ah, Liam. If I could do that part of my life over again. . . . I met him right after I finished my MFA. I'd just moved to Brooklyn and was so frigging needy. In the beginning, he made me feel special, loved. In retrospect, he probably saw me as a meal ticket. But I didn't know it then—when I married him. I also didn't know what a narcissist he was, totally focused on being an actor, a star. I should have figured it out a lot sooner." I shrug. "Big mistake, marriage—it makes everything so much more complicated."

"It can do that."

"Sounds like you've had firsthand experience."

"I have. Let's just say marriage and military life don't always go well together."

"Like marriage and life as a cinematographer."

"Being away from home for long stretches, it was hard, especially on her. We tried to make it work. It didn't. We both moved on. She remarried . . . a nice guy. They've got a couple kids."

"I'm not so sure me being away was all that hard on Liam."

"I think I know what's coming." Colin's voice is incredibly gentle.

"Well, if you guessed that I came home earlier than expected to find earrings—not mine—and an open condom package, then you'd win the prize." Damn, I still sound so bitter. Clearly, I haven't moved on.

"That must've hurt."

"Oh, yeah. Only it got worse." I tell him everything. My producer trying to rape me. His payback that saved my life but ruined my career in the film industry. Liam bailing. How I ended up teaching, then needing to make a film to have any chance at tenure. I don't say anything about his demand for another twenty thousand to pay the Mambas. He can fill in that blank for himself.

We sit together for a little longer—until my butt is practically numb. I push myself to my feet and reach down to help pull him to his feet. "Come on. The bed will be a lot more comfortable."

"You trust me?"

"Yeah. Just don't . . ."

He holds up both hands in surrender. "No worries."

I climb onto the bed, and he floats the duvet down over me, then turns off the lights and slides under. Lying on our sides, we face each other, and I wait for him to go all macho—like Liam or Alex or Gus would have. Pull off my shirt, inch down my pants, kiss me, something.

But he doesn't.

Instead, he shares more of his life. "I grew up in a small village in Sussex. Idyllic. The last place in the world to prepare anyone for war. Even when I turned ten and went to boarding school, which is definitely an education in survival of the fittest."

"Sorry, I don't understand."

"You obviously don't know much about English boys' boarding schools. The bullying can be relentless and nothing short of vicious."

"Sounds . . . brutal."

He tucks a lock of my hair behind my ear. "I got through it."

"Your family, are they still there? In Sussex?" I hope there's not a trace of wistfulness or envy in my voice.

"My parents are. I've got a brother in London, a sister in Inverness. It was nice having her close by when I was training new special forces recruits in the Scottish Highlands."

I laugh. "You're kidding! The Scottish Highlands? I kind of think of *Outlander* and *Highlanders of Balforss.* Not special forces training."

"Not kidding. Have you ever been to the Highlands?"

"No."

"It's beautiful, but it can also be tough. Winters, the wind rips right through you. Summers, the midges eat you alive. Definitely not all time-travel romance. After a while, it got to be too much."

"So, you came to Zimbabwe to train the Mambas."

"I got lucky. The job came open at the right time. It seemed like the thing to do."

"That was Gus's former job?

"It was."

"You mind telling me why you told him about the shooting schedule at dinner?"

"Ah . . . that didn't go exactly as I intended. I was trying to drive home the point that I'm the trainer now, not him."

I laugh. "You're right. That didn't go according to plan."

He sighs his frustration. "My apologies."

"Oh, God, the way he acted tonight. The man's a frigging predator." I shudder. "I don't want him having anything to do with my film."

"I agree. I think the Mambas will, too."

"Good. Then we're all on the same page." I yawn—loudly—then clap a hand over my mouth. "Sorry!"

"No, I'm sorry. It's late, and I'm keeping you awake." A moment later, he whispers, "Just one more thing."

"Hmm?"

"To answer your question from earlier, my favorite color is red."

Twenty-Two

The kudu femur is still on the ground next to the deck—right where the lion left it. A few streaks of blood and a little grizzle remain, but otherwise Reggie scoured it clean. Thank God Gus was on hand with that haunch of meat, otherwise . . .

"I don't like him feeding the wildlife." Colin's voice is hard as steel and pitched low, as if he doesn't want anyone to overhear him.

"Why do you think he's doing it?"

Colin cradles his rifle. "He's either baiting animals like Reggie away from the park or keeping him here until he can parade him out for one of the hunters to kill. Whatever he's doing, he's made a wild animal dependent on humans for food."

"And last night?" I nod toward the bone.

"Last night was a display of raw power—over the lion and over us. He could've withheld the kudu haunch and unleashed Reggie on us. Or not."

My stomach churns. "That's sick."

"Let's go." He puts his free hand on the small of my back, exactly where Gus had his last night. Only this feels a whole lot less predatory—in fact, it feels kind of nice.

This morning, Grace is wearing what looks like another designer dress—only this one is solid blue. She stands waiting for us at the entrance to the dining room, ready to escort us to a small table set for two next to a picture window. "Did you enjoy your evening?" Except for the snark in her voice, I could almost take this for an innocent question. But she was the woman who likely laid the silk pajamas on the bed and drew the bath. Her query is far from innocent. Or maybe I'm still pissed off by Gus's presumption and reading her wrong.

Apparently, I don't answer quickly enough, so Colin takes over. "Thanks, we did enjoy ourselves." His hand caresses the back of my neck—just like Gus did last night. Except this time, I don't shrug Colin's hand away. With any luck, she'll report back to Gus, and maybe he'll stop hounding me.

Our play-acting doesn't fluster her, though, and she's quick to offer us breakfast and to explain Gus's absence. "He has taken the guests out to hunt. They left early this morning."

"Please thank him for his hospitality." I decide not to say anything about his attempted seduction. Or about her own part in last night's setup. A gracious move on my part, especially since I'd like nothing more than to chastise her for virtually pimping me.

To her evident surprise, we pass on breakfast, opting just to have the kitchen fill our water bottles. Then, we're on our way back to Marula. I assume Colin and I will return to our normal professional relationship. However much I appreciate him rescuing me last night, this morning I'm worried I divulged far too much about my personal life. And that could definitely compromise our working together.

"Now you've seen Buffalothorn in its full glory." Colin flashes me a grin. "What do you think?"

"You mean besides Gus trying to bed me and then that whole bizarre thing with Reggie?"

"Yeah, other than that." He laughs.

"Great food. Great wine. Amazing service. Ridiculously ostentatious." But something else was off. "Wait a sec! How do you think Grace knew to be in the dining room exactly when we walked in this morning?"

He slows the jeep as we round a bend in the road. "Hadn't thought of that. Maybe our room was bugged?"

"Seriously?" Damn, I don't like that one bit—knowing that Gus was listening in on what I told Colin.

"I'm just guessing. But look, there's no point worrying about it. They either listened in on us or they didn't."

"Yeah." I take a couple moments to tamp down my annoyance. "Okay, something else I don't understand: how can he possibly afford the place?" Not that I have any idea what kind of operating budget he'd need, but it must take a ton of money to keep it running.

"Good question. Most of us wonder the same thing. My theory? His guests pay a king's ransom to stay. He may also put a surcharge on the government permits for the hunts."

"Aha! I wonder if the hunters know?"

He exhales sharply. "They probably wouldn't care. All they want are the trophies to hang in their mansions back home."

"To feed their macho egos—"

On the dashboard, the radio buzzes. Colin is quick to answer. I tune out the back-and-forth and wait for him to finish, only he doesn't end the call. Instead, he turns to me. "It's Margaret. They just got back after a very long and cold night in the bush."

"Did they find anyone?"

"No poachers. But they did find some remains of the kudu. Clearly butchered. Margaret says they're all tired. She wants to know if you can cancel filming for today."

Another delay. My shoulders sag in defeat. Everyone's exhausted. Gus wants to be in the film. My pension will soon be depleted. This short documentary is turning into a monumental challenge. But what can I say to canceling today's shoot? Especially since it should be Matt making the decision. "Of course. Can they be ready to go with the training scenes tomorrow? So long as they're not called out again."

He nods and repeats my words into the radio. A half minute later he hangs up the receiver. "I appreciate that. The women do, too. Sometimes they push themselves to exhaustion."

"It's good you look out for them."

"Ha! They may not always agree. Sometimes I'm the one doing the pushing. Certainly when I was training them and, lest I forget, when Gus was working with them."

"Oh please, we mustn't forget him. Damn, I hope he was drinking enough last night that he's forgotten about being in the film."

Colin slows the jeep as we navigate through a series of particularly deep ruts. "Don't count on it. Where Gus's ego is concerned, he'll remember, and he's got the hunters to remind—"

Another call comes in on the radio. This time, Colin eases the jeep onto the verge. Looking ahead, I can see why. A large family of elephants is ambling slowly along the road. The last time I was in-country, I discovered elies often prefer to take the path of least resistance—a road. Especially when there are lots of mopane bushes with tender butterfly-shaped leaves on offer. The cow closest to us isn't bothering to eat.

She's breaking off sticks with lots of leaves and dragging them through the sand until she grows bored and snaps off a fresh one. The trees don't stand a chance.

Colin waves to get my attention. "This is Tonderai. He spoke with Margaret, then with Matt. Since there's no filming today, the crew would like to go into the village—Ngunyana. Natalie wants to visit the school. Matt's thinking there might be some film ops. And most important, Tonderai says his grandfather has asked to see you." He looks at me meaningfully. "Do you know who his grandfather is?"

I smile at the thought of seeing Solomon Mkhwananzi again. "Actually, I met him on the plane from Jo'burg to Vic Falls. I understand he's a *sangoma*. Get this: two of his divining bones 'jumped' out of his pocket onto the floor in front of me."

He stares at me, clearly perplexed. "Jumped? You sure about that?"

"His words, not mine. Amie and I found them on the floor in baggage claim."

"Then I think you better go see him. You do know Solomon Mkhwananzi isn't just *any sangoma*. He's probably the most powerful seer and traditional healer in this part of Zimbabwe."

Well, that explains the reactions of the men at the airport. "Good to know. And sure! I'd love to see him again."

Colin agrees to drop me off at the village school where Tonderai will meet me. In front of us, though, the extended elephant family is presenting something of a roadblock. Now, a very tiny baby covered in thick black hair has decided to take a nap in the middle of the road. Which means that everyone else waits. Including humans.

"Do me a favor?" Colin stretches his arm across the back of my seat. "Keep your eyes open in the village."

"Am I looking for anything in particular?"

He looks thoughtful, then nods. "Rumor has it some of the young men are earning money by poaching for the cartel. With jobs so scarce, it's the only way they can support their families. This is more than just taking a kudu to feed a village."

I gape. "Oh, tell me that's not true."

"I don't want you to do anything. God almighty, promise me you won't. But if you happen to notice anything odd, something that doesn't fit, let me know."

When we finally get to the sprawling village school, we park next to an empty safari land cruiser from Marula. I count three—no, four—single-story cement-block buildings, painted white and decorated with the bright flowers and geometric designs I've seen before on rural Ndebele homes. There's an open field with soccer goals at either end, then a neat row of smaller huts. A six-foot-tall chain-link fence surrounds it all.

"I think I visited this school six years ago with some of the film crew."

"Notice any changes?"

"It's gotten a lot bigger. I remember just one classroom building."

Colin points to another building next to the classes. "They've added a library."

"An entire building for a library?"

"People who come to stay at Marula Camp like to visit and bring donations. Or send them when they get home. Last I heard, they've got four sets of encyclopedias. Maybe more."

"Here I thought they'd have nothing."

"There are some schools, especially down near Jozi, that don't have nearly the same resources."

I make a mental note to do something—once I get my pension back in shape.

Colin continues our car-seat tour. "Down there, at the far end, those are homes for the teachers."

"Small."

"Believe me, with jobs as scarce as they are, the teachers are thrilled to work here and have housing as part of their remuneration."

We sit a few minutes longer while I take in the school and the kids in their maroon and gold uniforms who are charging out onto the playing field, kicking several soccer balls ahead of them. Then, I see Tonderai heading our way.

"And here comes your escort." Colin shoots me a grin. "I think you'll be in safe hands."

"Thanks for dropping me off. I hope you get some rest and maybe even some of your own work done today." Grabbing hold of my camera case and shoulder mount, I push open the jeep door and climb out. "Oh, one more thing. About those charges on my credit cards."

"Yeah?" Colin sounds wary.

"Have they gone through yet?"

"To be honest, I haven't been able to check last night or today. I will when I get back to the office."

"Good. And let me know if there's a problem. The banks may be holding back because of the big amounts being charged—even though I told them I'd probably be running up bills. Maybe I should call them."

He takes off his hat and runs his fingers through his hair—I'm guessing this is a sign of his frustration. "Tell you what. Don't worry about it. Don't do anything. I'll let you know when the charges go through. In the meantime, I've got your cards locked in my desk at headquarters."

Standing at the fence gate, Tonderai waves. I shut the passenger door and wave in response. Hat back in place, Colin keys the ignition and, with a single clipped nod, backs the jeep off the verge, coming way too close to running over my foot. Then, leaving a cloud of dust in his wake, he's gone. Sometimes the man is downright insufferable.

Twenty-Three

I kneel on the packed dirt floor in the *indumba*—a small round hut with a pleasant musky smell behind Solomon Mkhwananzi's house. Inside, it's dark and cool, and despite the day heating up outside, I'm glad I've got my puffer jacket on. At the football pitch next to the school, kids are screaming and cheering. Every once in a while, I hear Tonderai's deep voice calling a play. After dropping me off at his grandfather's, he went back to coach the kids. Solomon kneels opposite me, on the other side of the small mat he put between us.

Solomon looks at me closely. "You are nervous?"

I glance down at my hands curled into tight fists and resting on my thighs. "Maybe a little."

"The divining bones frighten you?" His voice is quiet and very gentle. "I hope *I* do not scare you."

I smile and shake my head. Solomon has been nothing but kind to me. If it weren't for him, I'd probably be sitting in some ministry in Harare, hoping for whatever permit or visa they'd insist I need. Still, Tonderai's talk of good and bad *sangomas*, witches and curses, makes my skin crawl.

"My grandson told you about *sangomas*?"

"He did." I curl my fingers even tighter. The fact that the man seems able to read my mind is a bit unsettling.

"Now, you are worried about good spirits and bad spirits, black magic and witches," he says sympathetically. "Sometimes it is not easy to explain Ndebele beliefs to outsiders. In many ways, though, what we believe is not very different from what other people believe. We have a god and powerful spirits. We honor our ancestors. We have healers to help solve problems. I use divining bones and sometimes herbs to help me." He pauses and looks at me closely. "Do you feel better now?"

"Yes. A little. Thanks for explaining."

"Now, perhaps you are wondering why I asked Tonderai to bring you to see me."

"Kind of. Yes."

"I have been thinking about our time at the airport. You found the bones that jumped out of the bag in my pocket."

"I did." Even though I know bones don't jump out of pockets, I'm still puzzled about what happened. Clearly, they were wrapped up in a bag in his pocket. How the hell did they happen to fall on the floor? Right where I'd find them?

Leaning forward, he lays his hands on top of mine. "It is the wise person who is at least a little afraid of the bones, Julia. If you believe in them, the bones are powerful. People who think they can control that power for their own selfish purposes are fools, very dangerous fools."

I sit up straight. This is all very interesting, but I don't believe in divining bones or their purported power. "How did you know you have the power to understand the bones?"

He sits back on his heels and looks at me. "I imagine in much the same way you discovered your gift for making movies. My body told me."

My stomach starts to churn. "How did your body tell you?"

"It is different for everyone. For me, it began with head-aches. Then tremors. For others, it could be an event—maybe a tragic occurrence—that makes them change direction, take a different path in life."

Despite my puffer jacket, I can feel a cold chill stalking up my spine to the back of my neck. Okay, this is getting a little too close to home.

"Ah, I see that you understand what I mean. When I first met you, I sensed your life has taken several different paths."

I take a deep breath, then tell him about my father, my brother, my mother. How losing them caused me to pursue a creative life.

He listens. That's all. Then a quiet nod. Finally, he speaks. "But then you left your creative life behind. You are a teacher now, I believe. Instead of making your own movies, you are teaching others. That is a noble calling."

"Yes." I smile but feel it wobble.

"And this is why I asked Tonderai to bring you here today."

"But I really don't have a problem. Nothing for you to heal. I mean, there are glitches with the funding, and some delays in filming, but I'll work everything out . . ."

He laughs gently. "Julia, I would never force you. When we met, I sensed a lack of resolution in your life. I thought throwing the bones for you could be my way of thanking you for returning them to me. And perhaps this could give you some help in deciding what you want to do with your life. But if you do not feel comfortable, please do not worry. You will not hurt my feelings."

Deciding what I want to do? As if I have options? I stare at the divining bones on the mat between us. Beautifully

carved, exactly as I remember them. I close my eyes and look
back on my life. My family—gone, except for my mother
who's off in la-la land, all but checked out. The crew members dead. Liam betraying me. The industry blacklisting me.
My teaching and tenure and my need to make this film. My
pension—soon to be gone, thanks to Colin. No, that's not totally fair. I should've thought about paying the Mambas. It
shouldn't have come to Colin needing to ask for the money.
Okay, so I do have some problems. In fact, my life is pretty
much a mess right now. And maybe Solomon, in his wisdom,
could give me some help.

"Okay." Damn, this feels so momentous. "Let's do it. Yeah,
I could use whatever help I can get. So, what do I do?"

He picks up the bones and puts them in my cupped
hands. "Do not be afraid. You won't feel or see or hear anything. I am not going to put you in a trance or hypnotize you."

"That's a relief!"

He closes my fingers around the bones. "Now, I want you
to think about your family and your work. Also think about
what you would like to be doing. Who you want in your life."

Closing my eyes again, I bring my palms together, letting
my body heat warm the bones, directing my thoughts into
them. The longer I think about the twists and turns of my life,
the faster they start to spin inside me until they are part of
the churning in my stomach—throbbing with an accelerating
rhythm until I feel like I could spin out of this hut. And just as
I'm about to soar, Solomon puts his hands on mine.

I let him take back the bones. He calls to my ancestors,
my father and my brother, and then he throws the bones onto
the mat.

They scatter into a pattern that makes no sense to me.

Nothing like the T the two bones formed at the airport. But Solomon leans forward and studies them from various angles. I can't imagine what he sees, what meaning he can possibly make out of them. Then again, he's the *sangoma* and has read the bones for many, many people over the years.

"You directed your thoughts well," he says. "Sometimes I ask a person to throw the bones again. But in your case, I do not need further clarification."

I'm that easy to figure out? With everything that's been going on? "Okay . . . so . . . what do the bones say?"

"They say that you need to decide what would make you happier than you are now."

That stops me. "Happier? But I am happy." Well, pretty happy. Some of the time.

"Are you? Do you wish to be teaching?"

"It's fine. I enjoy working with students, and it's good to have a reliable income. . . . It makes me feel secure." And security makes me happy.

He looks down at the bones. And now I look at them, too. They're at cross purposes to each other, almost as if they're canceling each other. Do they represent the different parts of my life? Work. Love. Aspirations. Me. A compelling image—if I'm interpreting it correctly. Then again, I have absolutely no idea what I'm looking at.

"I sense you are an excellent teacher. But what about your own stories—the stories you are meant to tell?"

"Well, sometimes it's not always possible to do exactly what we want . . ." What am I saying? That I'd rather be making films. But that ship has sailed. So, I'm not doing exactly what I want. At least I'm employed.

"Yes. I see you have a conflict. To work at a job that will give you the security you need. Or to follow the path you are meant to be on, to tell your stories and make your movies—and not be secure. Which will give you the happiness you seek?"

"I can't live without money." My voice is barely above a whisper.

"Yes, life is difficult without money. But it could hurt more to stray from the path your heart tells you to follow."

"It does. Hurt." Still, I'm whispering. It's beyond painful not to be able to do what gives me joy, to be shunned by the film industry. People think Kyle died because of me, because I was scared to fly in that tiny plane. But that wasn't true, and no one ever frigging asked. Not even Matt. He heard the stories, but he never intervened, never corrected the rumors that were running rampant. Hell, it still hurts to know the only film job I can get is when I basically hire myself.

Solomon looks at me long and hard. I think he's hoping I'll say something more definitive, agree with him. But I'm really not in a position to do that. I've got a film to make and a tenure battle to wage. Whether or not I'm meant to teach, I need the financial security.

"Julia." He gently calls my attention to the bones. "I cannot tell you what to do, what decisions to make. It is not for me to predict your future. I only read what the bones have to say today—in this moment. It is for you to decide which path you must follow."

I nod.

"There is more. Do you see how these bones run counter to each other?"

"I do."

"This one," he says, pointing to the largest of the bones, "is what we call the death bone."

I inhale sharply.

"No, do not think you are about to die. What it really signals is a change, perhaps an end to one way of living and the start of another." He takes another long look at the death bone, then glances at me.

I get the feeling he wants to say something more about the meaning of this bone, but after a quick shake of the head, he doesn't. He's seeing something—I'm sure of it. There's more to this death bone than he's telling me, and I'm guessing it may actually relate not only to change, but maybe to a real death. Mine? Someone else's? Someone I love? What isn't he telling me?

He moves on. "And this bone—"

I have no choice but to follow his lead. "The one running lengthwise between these other two?"

"Yes. It is the bone of togetherness, union. See how hard it has fallen, touching these other two bones."

"Sort of at cross purposes."

"Yes, that is one way to put it. I am seeing your happiness depends on making these other bones come into alignment."

I look up from the bones and into Solomon's kind eyes. So reassuring. And even though bone throwing in my world would be seen as nothing more than a diverting game—the Ouija board my friends and I played with as kids, or even Tarot cards—I'm beginning to see that it's not a game at all. My thoughts are weighing heavily on me, heavy enough for the bones to reflect them. And if I'm really, truly honest with myself, I'm not happy. I've been living too much in the past—an unhappy past tainted by loss. And I need to move forward.

But that confounded T from the airport keeps tugging at me. It meant something. I know it did. "A question?"

"Of course."

"At the airport, the two bones I put into your hands—they formed a T. What did that mean? You never said."

Solomon clasps my hands in both of his, a knowing smile on his lips. "I am certain you will come to understand. But please do not think too literally."

As I push myself to my feet, that's exactly what I do: think literally about the "T" problems in my life. Teaching and tenure. *Tod*—the German word for death. When I come to "Tremblay," I glance back at Solomon and realize he's looking past me to someone standing in the doorway. Tonderai. I shake my head. He is most definitely not a problem.

"Grandfather? You are ready for Amie?"

Amie?

"Why does your grandfather want to see Amie?" I ask Tonderai as he walks me back to the main gate into the schoolyard.

He looks thoughtful for a moment, then shakes his head. "I think for the same reason he wanted to see you. I assume he threw the bones for you?"

"He did."

"Did it help?"

"You know, it's kind of strange, but it did. Going in, I didn't realize that I had quite so many problems. Your grandfather helped me see them more clearly."

He laughs. "That is perhaps my grandfather's greatest skill. But you should not worry about any of this. Traditional medicine is part of our daily life. No one, not even my grandfather, expects you to believe. I suggest you take what helps you and ignore the rest."

"Good idea. So, he's going to come up with problems for Amie, too?"

"Perhaps. I'll go back in a while and rein him in."

Looking over to the football pitch, I see it's empty. Which is odd, considering how many kids were just playing there. "Where'd they all go?"

"Back to class. The children were out there for a long time."

Now I'm even more confused. "How long was I in with your grandfather?"

He checks his watch. "At least an hour and a half. Perhaps two hours."

I gape. "It felt like a few minutes."

"Another of my grandfather's great skills is making a long time go by very quickly."

"It sounds like magic."

"The only magic is that he is a very wise man." Tonderai guides me through the gate. "There are your friends," he says, pointing toward the library.

Matt and Cate, Natalie and Liam are standing in the doorway chatting with a group of men holding corrugated cardboard boxes. We're halfway there before I recognize Gus and his hunters. Oh, great, the last people I want to run into. Shouldn't they be at Buffalothorn hunting? Matt sees me first and raises his arm to wave me over. I heave a sigh loud enough that Tonderai can't help but hear me.

"You didn't enjoy your visit to Gus's lodge?" Something in his voice tells me he didn't think I would.

"Hardly." I'm tempted to tell him about Gus trying to seduce me but decide it might embarrass him. Or really piss him off. "Things got a little scary . . . with the lion he keeps there. Let's just say I'm very glad Colin was with me." Damn, I hate to think what could've happened if he hadn't been.

Tonderai presses his lips together. "This is not good."

"No. It's not."

We've almost reached the group when I hear footsteps running behind us. Turning, I see Amie.

"Hey! Wait up!" she calls.

"That was fast," I whisper to Tonderai.

He shrugs. "Perhaps she didn't need my grandfather to throw the bones."

With Amie in tow, we join the others at the library in time for one of the teachers to give us a brief tour. She smiles broadly when the hunters carry their boxes inside, opening them to reveal books. I peer over Amie's shoulder to check out the titles: *Encyclopedia Britannica.* Two complete sets. Do kids even use encyclopedias anymore? Still, it was good of the hunters to think to bring a donation. A quick glance at Gus's self-satisfied grin tells me where they got the idea.

Back outside, Natalie is all over me. "Oh, Julia, visiting this school has been wonderful. They have so little, and we have so much. I'd like to do something more—something meaningful for these kids."

Liam nods his agreement. "As soon as we get home, we can collect more books and send them over."

Before I can say a word, Gus puts his arm around my shoulder and takes over. "Great. And I'd be happy to facilitate that. Say, what if you all come to the lodge for dinner tonight? We could talk about ways you could support this school."

Natalie's eyes sparkle with excitement. Liam looks more engaged than I've seen him since he got here.

"I tell you what. We can put together a game drive this

afternoon. As for dinner, I think Julia can vouch for the food and drink." He squeezes my upper arm—a sure and unwelcome sign of possession. Everyone must be wondering what exactly happened after dinner last night. Correction: I'd be willing to bet Gus fabricated quite a fairy tale for the hunters this morning at breakfast.

Another squeeze on my arm—another cue for me to praise Buffalothorn. "It's a beautiful place, and Gus is right. The meal and the wine were truly amazing."

Finally, he lets go of me and turns his attention to the rest of the crew. "What do ya say, Matt? Maybe we could discuss my role in the film. I've got some of the best cognac you've ever had and some first-rate Cuban cigars. I might also be interested in sweetening the deal by contributing to the production costs."

It's clear Natalie and Liam are ready to go. Matt looks at each of the rest of us in turn. Cate and Amie sound eager. But I tune out as I look past him to the small one-story concrete-block building with a metal roof opposite the schoolyard. A man is waving other men in camo fatigues inside. He looks vaguely familiar, but I don't place him at first. Finally, his face clicks in place. I think it's Gus's tracker from last night. The man who passed around bottles of ice-cold Zambezi lager. It takes me a minute to sort out why this scene has captured my attention.

"It is the village *shebeen*," Tonderai whispers in my ear. "A drinking club. For members only."

So why is each man dressed like a soldier and carrying a gun? Is there some kind of weird dress code?

Suddenly, Gus's arm is back around me. "Julia? You're coming with us, aren't you? Everyone else is."

"Sorry, I was . . . lost in thought." I glance at him, and from the cold look in his eyes, I can tell he knows I was far from lost in thought. He's caught me looking at exactly what I bet he doesn't want me to see. His tracker. At the *shebeen*. With well-armed village men.

I look away from Gus and, unbidden, Colin's request to take note of anything odd, anything that doesn't fit, echoes through my mind: *Rumor has it some of the young men are earning money by poaching. With jobs so scarce, it's the only way they can support their families.*

Damn! I think I know what's going on.

"Julia?" Gus again.

Everyone has stopped talking; they're all waiting for my answer.

I smile. "You know what? You all go ahead. I'm going back to Marula to get some rest." As soon as the words are out of my mouth, I cringe, knowing I've given Gus the perfect opening.

He takes full advantage. "Your bed at the lodge is ready and waiting for you."

And damn it, I blush.

Twenty-Four

Before everyone takes off for Buffalothorn, Tonderai radios Dabs to swing by from his game drive to pick me up. Fine by me. I'll get to spend a couple hours with a few other Marula guests enjoying the wildlife and sundowners, then back to camp for dinner on my own and early to bed. At least I won't have to deal with Gus anymore today.

With everyone else in the vehicles, Matt walks me back inside the schoolyard. "We'll probably be late getting back to Marula tonight."

I roll my eyes. "Or, more likely, tomorrow."

"A possibility, I guess. Would you get in touch with Colin and tell him to have everyone ready to resume filming by noon?"

I clench my jaws. "We've already lost so much time . . ."

Matt shrugs. "Gus won't be able to get there any earlier. His hunters are leaving tomorrow."

"So now we're shooting around Gus's schedule? Damn it, Matt, we haven't even discussed having him in the film."

He puts his hand on my shoulder and walks me a bit farther from the vehicles. "Look, I think I can persuade him to cough up some money, a lot of money, which will relieve you from having to zero out your retirement account."

I gape. "How the hell do you know about my pension?" It takes me three seconds to figure it out. "Let me guess. Cate told you."

"She did. But would it be so bad? We're talking about Gus being in the film for two, maybe three minutes max. And you'll be financially secure."

Oh, God, when he puts it that way, it's tempting. Being able to keep my pension would make a huge difference in my life. But at what cost? And as soon as I ask the question, I can almost feel Gus's hand on the back of my neck, his fingers pressing hard against my carotids until I'm gasping for air.

"Why?" I practically gasp out the word.

"What do you mean why?"

"We're making a short documentary about the Mambas. Okay, I get it, he wants to appear in the film—kind of a macho ego rush. But why would he have any interest in investing? Does he think he'll get producer credit?"

Matt nods. "That's what we'll be talking about tonight."

Just then, Gus honks the horn of his vehicle, clearly impatient to get on the road.

Hand still on my shoulder, Matt pivots me toward the vehicles. "Trust me, please. This will all work out."

I lean against the schoolyard fence while I wait for Dabs to pick me up. Down the road at the *shebeen,* more men dressed in camo fatigues arrive and amble inside the little building. Then, beers in hand, they're outside again to sit on wooden chairs clustered around small, rickety-looking tables. I'm almost tempted to go over and try my luck at getting in, see what I might overhear. I could go for a cold Castle right about now. But it's members-only—that's what Tonderai said. And from the looks of it, all the members are men. I seriously doubt I'd be welcome. Not to mention that Colin would probably kill me.

Glancing down at my Pelican case and shoulder mount resting in the sand, I know exactly what I can do without angering either the camo-clad men or Colin. Slipping my camera out of the case, I mount the biggest lens I've got with me—the 100-500 mm. The 600 mm would be a lot better—easier to see the men's faces and identify them—but it's back at Msasa. No matter. This lens will be good enough. I turn on the camera.

I'm so intent on filming that it takes a few minutes before I realize the men have noticed me. They're pointing and talking among themselves.

And now several of them are standing, shoving back their chairs, crossing the dirt road and heading this way. I keep recording for as long as I dare. Okay, I've recorded some great footage to help Colin or Margaret ID these guys, but I've got to do something fast or they'll never see the film. Turning off the camera, I quickly slip out the SD card and slide in a new one. Not blank, but with the test footage I took at home to make sure each of the cards was programmed and functioning.

I'm just in time. The camera is down by my side as the men round the fenced corner of the schoolyard and close in on me. Shit! One of them has a semi-automatic pointed directly at me. Taking a deep breath, I frantically try to think of something to say, anything to explain why I'm filming the village. And them. Other than inanities that they won't believe any more than I do, I come up blank.

They're closing fast. For some reason, I focus on their camo fatigues. Not new and not real military-issue by any stretch of the imagination. Dirty, with a few tears, they look like cheap knockoffs. Is this some kind of paramilitary group? And the tracker is part of it? Does Gus know?

Enough with the questions! Put the camera in the case before things go sideways!

My fingers fumbling, I manage to detach the shoulder mount and get the camera stowed safely inside the case.

The men stop. Not another step toward me.

I peer in their direction, trying to figure out what's going on. Do they realize I'm sufficiently terrified?

One of the men is pointing down the road away from me.

Then I hear it, too. The roar of a vehicle. The driver isn't slowly tooling along the road. He's accelerating. Which is potentially dangerous because after school, lots of kids are out and about. Any one of them could dart into the road.

Thank God for Dabs. Sometimes miracles do happen.

The camo men don't discuss their plan at length. They turn and run, guns clanking against their hips.

It's not until the vehicle speeds around the corner and pulls up next to me that I realize it's not a safari land cruiser. And the driver isn't Dabs.

Colin brakes sharply, jumps out of the jeep, and is with me in an instant. His hands clamp down on my shoulders. "Are you okay?"

"Yeah, I'm good." My words sound muffled. "And very glad you showed up just now. That was getting a bit dicey. Where's Dabs?"

"On a game drive. They spotted wild dogs a good distance into the park, so he asked me to pick you up."

"Thanks for coming all this way."

He takes a step back and looks toward the *shebeen* where all is quiet. "Let's get out of here. Then perhaps you can explain why things were getting dicey."

Five minutes outside the village on the way back to Marula, Colin stops—right in the middle of the road. I look around but don't see any wildlife about to cross, no reason for him to stop. Leaning back against the driver's door, he raises his eyebrow. "Tell me."

I assume he means the men he rescued me from. I'm also guessing he's going to go all literal on me and my promise to observe and report—not to do anything. One deep breath, and I explain about the men at the drinking club. "But I didn't go over there."

He takes off his leather ranger's hat and throws it in the back seat. "Thank God for small favors. What did you do?"

"Exactly what I promised: nothing."

"Then why did I see a group of five heavily armed men marching up the road toward you?" His voice is getting way too loud.

I glance down at the camera case wedged between the seat and my legs.

He groans. "Please tell me you didn't film them."

"Will you stop yelling if I tell you what I was doing?"

Looking away from me and toward the reddening horizon, he takes a deep breath, then exhales loudly. "The truth would be preferable. Please."

I bite my lower lip, then go for the truth. "Yes, I filmed them and—"

"Bloody hell! Do you have any idea what they could've done to you? What they were about to do?"

Now it's my turn to look away. The sunset tonight is particularly beautiful. Red and pink and orange with streaks of vivid purple. And if Colin had been five minutes later . . . no, three minutes later, I might well not be seeing it right now. Or maybe they would've taken my camera and frisked me to find the SD card with all the scenes I've shot so far. Or who knows? Could be the new SD card would've satisfied them. Finally, I find my voice. "Yeah, I saw them and their guns. Big, scary guns. I've got a very good idea what could've happened." I take a deep breath. "But I'd do it again."

Looking back at him, my eyes lock on his, and I discover the strangest combination of expressions—none of them in the least professional.

"Are you going to tell me what you saw? Or do I have to guess?"

"Better than that, I could show you what I filmed."

He cracks the wry half smile that I'm loath to admit is starting to charm me. "A very good idea." Squaring himself behind the steering wheel, he keys the ignition. "Your place or mine?"

"My laptop's still at Msasa, but do you think there's any way we could stop at Marula first? I'd love to change my clothes."

"Done." He taps the heel of his hand against the dashboard. Then turns off the engine.

"What?"

"Ahead about fifty feet."

Squinting, I make out two lions. A thick-maned male sniffing the female's hind end, then grabbing the back of her neck in his mouth and going for it. There's no foreplay involved. The deed takes hardly any time at all, and then he jumps clear as she rounds on him with a vicious snarl, her front paws reaching in to slash at him.

"She doesn't seem happy."

He laughs. "Those barbs are painful for the female." Then, picking up his binocs, he whistles. "This can't be good."

"What are you talking about? Aren't new cubs always good?"

"The female—she's one of the Ponies. And the male definitely isn't part of her pride."

"So, who is he? And what happened to the Ponies' male?"

"I'm guessing he went to check on his territory and never came back. Who knows what happened to him. Could've taken over a new pride. Or died trying. This boy, though, clearly wants to take over the Ponies. There were a couple new litters a few months ago. Let's hope the lionesses managed to hide them before he moved in."

I flash on the lions we saw from the train on our trip down. "You know, I think we may have seen some of the other Ponies—over on the railroad tracks. They had cubs with them."

"Happy days!" He smiles. "All is now clear."

"You going to clue me in?"

"Lionesses are very smart and sometimes sly. I'd wager anything that this girl here is a decoy—leading the male away from the rest of the pride, especially the cubs."

"Otherwise . . ."

"Otherwise, he'd kill the cubs to bring the females into estrus."

I leave Colin on the deck at Marula Lodge, a Zambezi lager in hand, his feet propped on the railing, his eyes on the elephants drinking the clean water out of the swimming pool. Once in my tent, I decide a hot shower won't add too much time to his wait. Sluicing off the day—and last night—is exactly what I need. Afterward, I dig fresh underwear and a long-sleeved T-shirt out of my duffel, carefully rezipping it to avoid any creepy-crawlies making themselves at home among my clothes. Outside the tent, I discover the man himself, his rifle by his side, waiting for me on the small deck.

"Seriously? You didn't need to come get me. I could've walked back to the lodge."

"You know the rule. After dark, you need an escort. Besides, I'm not taking any more chances with you today."

"Thanks. I guess."

"Ready to go? Ah, the chef wants to know if we're having dinner here. If not, I'm sure Pepsi has enough. Tonight is her famous beef stew with *sadza*."

The way he says what Pepsi has on offer tells me what he's voting for. "Let's eat with the women. Besides, I want to show you this film."

Dinner is every bit as delicious as I expected and even spicier than the veg relish Pepsi served yesterday. I could seriously eat this every day. But no one lingers. They're all eager to see the footage of the men in the village. I wire my camera to the laptop, and then with the six of us crowded around, I let the film roll. All fifteen minutes of it. There's no sound except for the occasional sharp intake of breath from one or another of the women. Or Colin. I'm guessing they recognize the men. When the screen finally goes blank, no one says a word.

Now I'm questioning myself. Did I make this into more than it really was? Here I thought I was onto something. I mean really, why are men wearing uniforms and carrying guns to hang out at the village *shebeen*? Then again, maybe these men get their nuts off strutting around in fake military gear. Could be the guys are only chugging some beers. I mean, with jobs so scarce, what else do they have to occupy their time?

"So, what do you think? Do you need to see it again?"

Margaret pushes back her chair. "I cannot believe my brother is involved in this! And my brother-in-law. I know they need money to feed the children, but this is such a slap in my face."

"Could someone please tell me what 'this' is?"

"Poaching." Margaret nearly spits the word.

"Wait a minute." I look around at the women. "These guys have guns. And uniforms. How can they possibly afford them if they can't get any other jobs?"

"The way the cartel works, they provide those things and then take the money out of their pay. Very often, these men work for practically nothing." Zinhle's voice isn't offering any sympathy.

"It's clear they're planning something. When, do you think?" Colin looks at each woman. "Tonight? They all had guns, so it seems likely. Or are they still in the planning stages?"

"That is hard to say." Pepsi stands and gathers the plates from dinner. Looking at me, she adds, "You were very brave to film them. I am relieved they didn't see you." Then she heads to the kitchen to wash the dishes.

Next to me, Colin clears his throat but doesn't say anything.

For some reason, I decide that telling the truth again would be a good idea. "But they did see me."

"Oh, this is very bad!" Margaret hisses.

"I'm sorry. And I put Colin in a terrible position—he had to rescue me." Okay, maybe I should've kept that to myself. "But you guys, no one said anything about the tracker being there. What do you think it means?"

Barbara looks confused. "The tracker?"

"Which tracker?" asks Colin.

"You know, Tracker. The man who works for Gus Sinclair. We saw him last night."

Zinhle shakes her head. "I did not see him in the film."

It turns out no one did. I run the film again to check, but he's not there. I see the back of a man who could well be Tracker, but nothing more. "Damn! How could I have missed getting his face? He was definitely there, greeting each of the men who arrived. That's what first caught my attention. And I was watching him when Gus noticed."

"Gus saw you filming?" Colin's voice threatens to get louder.

"No. I'm not completely stupid. I didn't get the camera out until after they all drove away."

Zinhle cups her hands in front of her mouth. "Oh, thank the Lord!"

"Don't you see? This is what's so important. The man who works for Gus was there, acting like the ringleader for all these guys. And when Gus saw me watching, he was clearly annoyed. Which means he knows Tracker's involved and doesn't want me—us—to know."

Colin crosses his arms. "We've suspected he's baiting animals out of the park but haven't ever caught him at it. Actively poaching inside Hwange? That another story."

"Okay, maybe that's a step too far. But it would explain where he gets all his money."

"So would the astronomical fees he charges his hunters.

Don't get me wrong. Gus abuses animals with his canned hunts." Colin looks around at the three Mambas. "We'd all like to stop him. But to do that, we need solid evidence. Which we don't have."

"You're right. And honestly, poaching is way too big of a risk for him to take." I close the laptop. "Besides, I don't have any evidence his tracker was even there. I'm pretty sure I saw him. But it was at a distance, so who knows."

"What should we do?" Margaret eases her hands over the wrinkles on her camo pants.

Colin looks thoughtful. "Be aware poachers could be on the move soon. For now, without proof, we really can't do anything more."

"We've got another problem," I say unhappily.

"Are you going to tell us?" Colin's shoulders appear to sag under the weight of yet more bad news.

"The film. Gus has convinced Matt to let him be in it."

Zinhle scowls. Margaret hisses. Barbara slams her fist on the desktop.

Kind of extreme reactions for a man who used to be their trainer. Used to be—the key phrase. I wondered before why he'd quit and figured it was because he was looking to earn more money. But maybe something else happened.

Twenty-Five

It's late by the time we finish talking. Way too late for me to drag Colin out again to drive me back to Marula. With all my gear here anyway, I decide to stay the night at Msasa and be ready to start filming first thing in the morning. Then I remember Matt's parting words—about our noon start time. The Mambas have already gone to bed, so I tell Colin over another bottle of Zambezi at the picnic table in the back.

"I'm sorry," I say. "This film is turning into a first-class disaster."

Colin takes a long pull of beer. "It was clear last night that Gus wants to be in the film. What I don't follow is why it seems like he's suddenly calling the shots."

"Exactly what I said to Matt."

"And what did he say?"

I hesitate, mainly because I don't want to set him off again. But I really don't have a choice. "Apparently, Gus has talked about investing a ton of money in exchange for being a producer."

"A money man."

"Exactly."

"And in exchange for providing money, he gets to be in charge."

"More or less." We both know why the film needs money, but I'm glad we're not arguing about whether or not to pay the Mambas. Certainly I've long since come around to Colin's way of thinking.

"There's something more, I think." Colin studies me. "Why's he so set on coughing up money?"

I shrug. "I don't have a clue."

He stares at me, almost as if he knows that what he's going to say will piss me off. "He thinks it'll get him in your bed."

He's right. That does piss me off. "Gus Sinclair will never park his shoes under my bed."

He tips his beer bottle toward me and grins. "Exactly what I was hoping you'd say, but it's good to know for sure." He takes another pull. "What kind of power would he have as a producer?"

I pick at the label on my beer bottle. "I honestly don't know. This is a little film. A short documentary. I can't imagine what he thinks he'll be able to do. Unless . . ." Suddenly, I'm putting together the different parts of Gus I've discovered in the last few days. He baits animals—certainly Reggie. His tracker is possibly involved with poachers, and Gus knows about it. He wants control of my film.

Colin leans forward. "Unless?"

"This is going to sound paranoid as anything, but what if he wants to be the producer so he can deep-six the film? Make sure it never sees the light of day?"

"He'd do this because . . ."

"Because he's involved in the poaching?"

"Could be." Colin is back to looking thoughtful. "Or maybe it's because he's worried about what he did to one of the women here a few years back . . . Mercy. That it could come to light."

I stare at Colin, aghast. Mercy. She was one of the Mambas at the crash site, but she isn't here now. I assumed she was on leave or was in one of the other units or had maybe even quit. "What did he do?"

"I came on board a few months later, and the women didn't want to talk about it. Still don't. All I know is one day he was here, and then he was gone. I applied for the job opening and was hired. I also know the undisputed facts of that day."

"Are you going to tell me what happened to her?"

"She drowned."

This keeps getting worse and worse. "How could she drown? The women all know how to swim, don't they?"

"They do. It's one of the requirements for the job."

"Then what . . ."

"No one really knows—for sure. Someone must, of course, but Mercy's no longer here. Apparently, she complained to the others about Gus putting the moves on her, trying to get her in bed." He raises his eyebrow meaningfully in my direction. "What happened on that score, I don't know. What I do know: soon after Mercy talked to Margaret about it, a group of them went out on patrol. Margaret and Zinhle and Mercy. Gus was with them, partnered with Mercy. Everything was quiet, no sign of any poachers. Then suddenly, he shot off his gun and radioed Margaret, frantic. When she and Zinhle got to the water hole, he was standing on the shoreline, wet to the waist. He told them they'd stumbled across a huge, five-meter croc who'd caught Mercy by the leg and dragged her under. He was pretty certain he'd shot the croc, but neither of them surfaced."

The tears welling at the back of my eyes burn. "Colin, this is unbelievable! What happened during the investigation?"

He looks away from me, first toward the women's dorm, now dark. Then he stares into the night. "Nothing happened because they never found either Mercy or the croc. And that was all the grounds the national police needed for there not being an investigation. Somewhere along the line, the entire incident was buried."

"Are you telling me Margaret and the others just accepted that?"

"You have to remember, this is Zimbabwe. People who try to fight the system tend to disappear—even in these post-Mugabe days." He's quiet for a minute. "As Margaret has told me more than once, there will come a time."

Twenty-Six

My head is spinning. Who is the real Gus Sinclair? Tonderai said he was a good guide. But my own experience casts him as a smarmy seducer. And now this. Did he really try to save Mercy? Or did he make sure she never opened her mouth again?

What the hell is Gus trying to do? He quits a job and then puts himself forward to be in a documentary about the Mambas, one of whom was the very woman he abused? And apparently, he's willing to fork over big bucks so he can be the producer. It's all so convoluted. The only conclusion? My paranoia is well-founded. He doesn't want this film to see the light of day. I bury my face in my hands.

"Hey, you still with me?" Colin reaches across the table and places a hand gently on my shoulder.

I startle back to the present moment. We're in the backyard of Mamba headquarters, and it's got to be going on midnight. Too dark even to read my watch. I look at the night sky and am instantly mesmerized by the billions of stars—visible because out here in the middle of Hwange, there's absolutely no light pollution.

"Beautiful, isn't it?" he whispers. "I never tire of this sky.

There were parts of the Scottish Highlands where I was able to see as many stars. Northern hemisphere stars, of course."

"Lucky you. I've lived in cities for years. So many buildings and lights and trees. And smog. Sometimes I wish . . ." Nope, there's no point in wishing I could stay here. It's absolute craziness. My job and my life are back in Milwaukee.

"What do you say we finish this conversation inside? Or just go to bed? Between last night and today, I'm pretty much done in." He pushes himself to his feet and collects both our empty bottles.

"Bed?"

"Sorry, I didn't mean that the way it sounded. I asked Pepsi to put a cot in the dormitory for you."

"Perfect. Thanks." I climb over the bench and follow him through the back door into the kitchen.

Once we get to the front hallway, he turns right, beckoning me to follow him to a part of the building I haven't yet seen—his bedroom. He shoots me a reassuring glance as he closes the door behind us. "No worries. I'm not going to jump you. Let's just take a few minutes to figure out tomorrow's schedule." He pulls over a wooden ladder-back chair, turns the back toward me, and straddles it, nodding me toward the bed.

The room is military spartan. A single woolen blanket and one pillow on the narrow bed. A small metal lamp on the bedside table, alongside a book by Tony Park—*Safari*. I sit on the edge, then, toeing off my Keens, I inch myself back, gather my legs under me, and lean against the wall. My body could fit here well—this is a lot better than my bed at Marula. But it's definitely not meant to share.

"So, we start filming at noon?" Colin sounds as exhausted as I feel.

I yawn. "Whenever the rest of the crew and Gus get here."

He matches my yawn. "I'm afraid I'm about to make things even more complicated."

"Terrific! What wonderful news do you have?"

"Before they went to bed, Margaret and Zinhle told me the Mambas aren't keen to shoot scenes with Gus."

"Because of Mercy?"

He nods. "That's part of it. He didn't make any fans while he was in charge."

"I'm not about to force the women to work with him. You have any idea what we can do?"

"They did come up with a suggestion."

He's got me interested. "Do tell."

"What if, before they get here, we film some scenes the way we want them to be. The way the women want them. Zinhle thinks—and I agree—it could be something simple like the women's first day on the job."

"You mean when they arrived?"

"Exactly. They thought they could wear their regular street clothes. Then they could change into their fatigues for when you shoot the training session."

I close my eyes to conjure the scenes in front of me. Then open them again to find Colin watching me. "I like it. Do you think we could possibly shoot early while the sun is coming up?"

"Fine. They get up early anyway. But how do we explain to Matt that we went ahead on our own?"

"Good question." Again, I close my eyes, only this time it's because I'm about to fall asleep. But I'm still pondering. "We do this and tell Matt later, he'll probably be angry. So will Gus."

"Do you really care? This is your film after all." Colin's chin is now resting on the top slat of the chair.

"Nope. But Matt's the director, and although he's pretty much been giving me free rein, I shouldn't thumb my nose at him, especially in front of Gus."

"So, then . . ." His lids are drooping closed over those beautiful green eyes.

"It's probably better to beg forgiveness than to ask permission. We'll film the first couple scenes and not tell anyone. Matt will find out eventually . . . when he sees everything, but by then it'll be too late. And I'll just take the flack." I'm starting to slur my words. I hold out my hand, hoping he'll take the hint and pull me to my feet, then guide me to my cot in the dorm. Otherwise, I doubt my legs will get me there. "Sorry, but I'm pretty much brain-dead. And we're getting up early. Could we figure out how to handle Matt tomorrow?"

He doesn't take the hint.

I don't remind him about the cot.

A moment later, the light is off, and he's stretched out next to me on the bed. No matter that we're both fully dressed, we spoon well.

Twenty-Seven

We're all up early—before the sun—and crowded into Margaret's office. The Mambas don't say anything about the fact that I obviously didn't sleep on my cot last night. I don't attempt to explain, and they seem fine with it. They're all smiles when I tell them how much I like their idea about how to shoot their arrival as new recruits.

"There were more of us, of course," says Margaret. "Twelve, including Mercy."

I wonder if they heard Colin and me talking about her last night in the backyard. Their light was out, but they could easily have been awake, listening. No one says a word. I don't either, which probably confirms for them that I know.

Working as a team, we figure out the details of the scene and how it should be shot. This give-and-take feels perfect—exactly the way I was hoping Matt and Cate and I would work together.

"We think we should be carrying our suitcases," says Pepsi shyly.

"What if you film the sun rising behind us? It could be like we are starting a new life," Zinhle suggests.

"Or maybe if you stand with your back to the east?" Barbara muses. "So the sun is shining on our faces?"

"These are all great ideas! Let's do it!"

"Do you think Matt will be mad if we go ahead without him here to direct us?" Always the voice of reason, Margaret sounds worried.

Colin shoots me a wary glance.

I decide to err on the side of getting in a good shoot while we can. Afterward, I'll do my best to convince them to shoot a couple training scenes with Gus. "No worries. I'll take care of Matt—later."

While the Mambas change into their street clothes, Colin and I carry my camera gear to the dirt road out in front of headquarters. I thread on my favorite zoom lens and then attach the camera to the tripod. Unpacking my circular light reflectors, I realize there won't be anyone other than Colin available to help. Given how dark it still is, I go ahead and set up two lighting panels. Damn, this is going to be a bear of a challenge. Which is exactly why I should have had a lighting person on this shoot. God, what a shoestring of an operation.

Dressed in T-shirts, brightly patterned wrap-around skirts, and flip-flops, the four women parade out the front door, each with a well-worn suitcase in hand. They're smiling in anticipation, whispering among themselves, interrupted by an occasional excited giggle from Pepsi. I may not be giggling, but I'm as excited as they are. More than anything, I want to capture them exactly the way they are in this moment. *Please*, I pray, lifting my eyes to the rosy line of sunlight rising now on the horizon, *let this come together*.

I film the women walking single file and way too sedately down the road.

"Is this how you walked to headquarters for the first time?" I call to them.

They start over, this time nervously kicking up sand and dust.

"Really? You were scared?"

"Yes." Pepsi plants a hand on her hip. "I was very scared. I'd left my husband, and I did not know what was going to happen to me. Or to my children."

"I was so sad about leaving Blessing behind for the first time." Zinhle casts her eyes down to the sandy road. "I was trying hard not to cry."

Barbara juts out her chin. "I wasn't scared at all. I was happy to be starting a new life."

"Yes, I was also happy." Margaret swings her suitcase by her side. "And maybe a little anxious."

So many emotions on that monumental day. How do I capture all of them? "It seems to me that each one of you—and all the other women—were feeling something different. Would you be willing to imagine this morning as really that day a few years ago?"

The pink on the horizon is stretching higher in the sky now. We probably have only one take left, especially if I want to film the other two scenes I have in mind.

"Let's try it." I get behind the camera and study the women as they walk back down the road, each Mamba sashaying her hips in rhythm with the others. Were they this in tune with each other back on that day? Probably not. I'm guessing it took weeks, if not months, for them to learn to work together, to operate in sync like a well-trained unit. "Start from there," I call after them. "Be who you were on the day you first arrived here. Not who you are today."

They walk toward me. Margaret strides confidently in the lead, showing a touch of nerves when her suitcase knocks against her leg, causing her to stumble just a bit. Behind her, Barbara rolls her hips as she walks and looks thoughtfully ahead, as if ready to discover what's waiting for her. Zinhle's face is an incredible mix of emotions: relief, anticipation, and profound sadness. Then comes Pepsi. She's gnawing at her lower lip and shuffling her feet in the sand, churning up enough dust to coat her bare legs.

As they reach their marks in front of the camera, each woman turns to face the camera head-on. And then, the universe be praised, the sun crests above the horizon, streaking like a starburst across the sky behind them. I cross my fingers: *please let the lighting panels do their job and illuminate each woman's face.* Backlit against the sun isn't going to cut it. Then, I count to one hundred, leaving the women to stand still. But they're not absolutely still. Pepsi plops her suitcase down in the sand. Barbara scratches the back of her left calf with the side of her right foot. Margaret wipes perspiration from her forehead, although maybe that's to cover her shivering—it's pretty chilly this morning. And Zinhle dabs away a tear from her cheek.

"Cut!"

The women break ranks and rush over to me, all chattering at once.

"Did we do it right?"

"Can we see?"

"Is it what you wanted?"

Only Colin stays in place, but he crosses his arms over his chest and shoots me a wry grin—his best yet.

I smile. "Let's go check it out."

Back inside Margaret's office, I turn on the computer and, skipping the first few takes, play the last footage we shot, from beginning to end. Even the last one hundred seconds as the sun rose, signaling the women's initiation into the world and work of the Mambas. "Oh!" is all any of them can say, but they're smiling, all the way to their eyes.

When I finally turn off the computer, Colin claps a hand on my shoulder. "It really is perfect."

Which is absolutely the best thing he could say to me. I'm about to hug him but remember just in time that we work together a whole lot better when we keep things strictly professional. Almost reluctantly—and not a little confused about my change of heart where he's concerned—I turn back to the laptop. "Thanks to each of you. It may be a documentary, but you're all pretty good actors."

More than anything, I want all of us to luxuriate in this moment. But I have to tell them about the shoots for the rest of the day. They know there are other scenes to be filmed this afternoon. What they don't yet know for sure is that Gus will be putting them through their training paces—which is absolutely going to spoil what just happened. But I've got an idea. Fingers crossed that it works.

I take a deep breath. "How do you all feel about skipping breakfast?"

They look at me like I'm crazy. I get it; we've been awake forever, and we're all hungry.

"Here's the thing. Gus Sinclair is going to be in the scene we shoot this afternoon."

A chorus of hisses rises up around me.

I raise both hands to quiet them. "Sorry, sorry. This was definitely not my decision. Matt called this one. I'll be honest, I think Gus is angling to take over the entire film."

More hisses, louder this time.

"Believe me, I'm as angry as you are." Well, that may not be quite true. "But this is as much my film as it is Matt's and, of course, yours. I've been trying to figure out how we can keep control."

"What do you propose?" Margaret is barely able to control her fury, but at least she sounds a little curious.

"I'm thinking we'll make two movies. One of them will be secret—only we will know about it. That way, neither Gus nor Matt will have any say in it."

"But it will be a lot of work." Barbara doesn't sound pleased.

"More work—today—yes. We've already got some footage. I'll copy everything I've got on my SD cards to a flash drive that Gus and Matt won't know about. And they won't know about this morning's shoot."

"I don't understand. What about the training session?" Zinhle sounds confused.

"I think I understand!" Pepsi stops her laugh with her hands. "This is why you asked about skipping breakfast."

"Exactly."

Her eyes shining, Pepsi looks around at the other Mambas. "Our secret mission! We're going to make the training scenes now with Colin. But first, I really think we should have some bread rolls and coffee. We need to eat to train."

Sitting at the picnic table, we munch on warm rolls, slurp hot black coffee, and toss out ideas for the training part of the story and slowly sketch out how I should film it.

"No yelling!" Margaret wags her index finger at Colin sitting opposite us.

"I don't yell," Colin protests. Then, glancing at me, he adds, "Well, most of the time I don't."

She cups her mouth to my ear. "He is a good man."

Oh, good God, now the Mambas are trying to set us up.

"You should film us running," says Zinhle.

"Push-ups." This is from Barbara.

"No!" Pepsi is adamant. "I do not like push-ups."

I grin across the table at her. "They're awful, aren't they! But maybe just one or two? Remember, this is a film, not a workout." I've got a kernel of an idea starting to form: the actual training will not only show the women getting physically stronger but will also be the link showing how four individuals learned to work together. I'm betting the editor will want only a minute of the exercises and will then segue to them patrolling the savanna and the bush.

Breakfast done, the women hurry to the dorm to change into their camo fatigues. Colin pulls off his sweater, then retreats to his room to change into what many Zimbo guides prefer to wear: knee-length olive khaki shorts.

When we meet back outside, the sun is heating up the day. The golden light is gone, but I tell myself that this is good. I want to capture the women working hard, sweating. So, maybe I wasn't totally honest when I assured Pepsi they'd only need to do a couple push-ups.

Colin first leads the women on a run—in military boots. Back and forth along the road. I have to hand it to him: he starts them off slow, as if they really are fresh recruits who probably haven't done much running since they were kids. Then, he takes them through the bush directly across the road from headquarters. Slowly increasing the pace, he skirts the termite mounds and makes sharp cuts around mopane and acacia bushes. The women are right there with him. He's giving viewers a pretty nice overview of Zimbabwean flora while he's at it. And there in the distance is a small family of elephants parading past. Oh, happy days! I keep filming for nearly an hour, and they keep running farther and farther from headquarters, eventually scattering to look for possible poachers behind trees and under bushes. It's all I can do to keep up with them and film a bit here and there. Any longer and I think they'll gang up on me. They actually don't seem tired, but their skin is glistening. Exactly the look I'm going for.

Matt and Gus and the rest of the crew could be arriving soon, so I don't let anyone rest. Instead, we retreat behind headquarters, and I get them to help me move the picnic table and benches out of sight. I set the tripod with my back to the glare of the sun, which means the sun is directly on Colin and the women. Jumping jacks. Sit-ups. Push-ups. They struggle at first, especially Pepsi. Then, I pull Colin out of the scene and, taking my camera off the tripod, attach the shoulder mount. Kneeling at one end of the line of women, I film them moving through their calisthenics in perfect union. They couldn't be more in sync if they'd planned it.

Even now, the women aren't out of breath. Clearly, they're well trained, and these exercises, which would do me in, are all in a day's work.

It's going on noon, so I call a halt. I seriously don't want Matt and company catching wind of what I'm doing, what we're doing. Which means we've got to move the table and chairs back in place. In Margaret's office, I upload everything I shot this morning to my laptop and copy it to a flash drive that I slip into my pants pocket. *Might be smart to make a second copy!* Done. A second flash drive goes into my pocket.

Then I shut down the laptop and stow my camera and the rest of the gear. No need to invite any questions.

"Did you get everything?" Pepsi pops into Margaret's office to ask on her way to the outdoor kitchen where she's had lunch cooking over a slow fire.

Looking up from the Pelican case I'm closing, I hold up my crossed fingers. "I hope so. We can't risk taking a look now—"

The sound of engines roaring in the distance catches everyone's attention.

"Five minutes, max," warns Colin.

Looking out the window into the back, I see the women and Colin wiping their faces and arms—doing their best to get rid of all signs of exertion. Then, Pepsi carries a pot of leftover beef stew and another of *sadza* over to the table. I hurry outside and take my place across from Colin, just as the vehicles pull to a stop in front of the building. I'm shoveling a spoonful of stew into my mouth when I look up to see Colin's eyes widen in alarm.

"Oh my God!" I fan my mouth and reach for a can of Castle.

Pepsi can't help giggling. "Oh, Julia, I should have told you. Beef stew becomes even spicier on the second day."

"It's all the *peri peri* sauce you put in." Colin chuckles, his booted foot finding mine under the table. "African Bird's Eye chili peppers."

Almost too hot to eat. Rolling my cold beer can across my sweating forehead, I glance around at the others. They're all glistening.

Colin catches me looking. "The perfect way to conceal the fact that some of us are still sweating from the grueling training session you put us through."

"Guys! Remember, we didn't do any filming this morning."

Margaret squeezes my hand. "We are all part of this secret. You do not need to worry."

"Thanks." I take another spoonful of *sadza* with a tiny bit of beef and watch as they chow down. How are any of them going to do another training session with Gus after eating this lunch?

Twenty-Eight

Two sets of brakes squeal to a stop in front of headquarters. A few minutes later, Gus leads the guys out the kitchen door and straight over to the picnic table. Liam sniffs dramatically. "Something smells wonderful. It's been a long time since breakfast. Mind if I join you?" He looks pointedly at Margaret and Pepsi and me, as if one of us should vacate our seat.

On principle, I want to stay glued in place, but one look at Pepsi, and we both stand. She goes to get him a plate. I head to Margaret's office to retrieve my camera, where I run into Amie and Natalie and Cate, each with a Pelican case.

"So, how'd you like Buffalothorn?" I ask.

"OMG, it's amazing!" Amie nearly melts in front of me. "I mean the food was fabulous. So was the wine. And our room—I shared with Cate—was so cozy."

Cozy? My room was over-the-top ostentatious.

"Oh, plus, we got to watch Gus feed the lion who lives on the grounds. Reggie. Super cool!"

I decide to refrain from telling her my supposition that Reggie likely isn't long for this world.

Natalie puts her hands over her heart. "Really, Julia, it's incredible there's something so elegant out here. And the bed! Divine. Truly the best sleep I've had since we've been here."

I nearly cringe when she says 'bed.' Maybe I should tell them about my bedroom—adjoining Gus's. Then again, what's there to tell? Nothing happened.

"I don't understand why you didn't want to go back last night. You missed a really great dinner and breakfast." Natalie sounds sincerely perplexed.

I'm not about to tell all at this point, not with Gus sitting a mere twenty feet away and having to work with him today. So, I just shrug. "Tired, I guess."

As soon as Amie and Natalie make their way outside, Cate gives me the once-over. "They're gone. Now, tell the truth. Why didn't you go back to Gus's place last night? I've never known you to turn down a meal like that."

"Like I said, I was tired."

"And yet you didn't sleep in your bed last night." She quite literally smirks.

"How'd you know?"

"I have my sources."

I shrug. "I meant to, but we got caught up with stuff here. It got late. I slept here."

"Well, thank God. Finally—"

"We talked. That's all."

She throws her hands in the air. "Hasn't anyone ever told you that talking's overrated?"

"Fuck you!"

"Sounds fun." She laughs. "But for now, something smells delicious, and I want a bowl of it."

Just then, Liam yells. "What the hell's in this?"

Ha! Serves him right. I refrain from laughing but caution Cate. "The beef stew is pretty spicy."

"The spicier, the better!" The moment Cate leaves the room,

Colin steps into the doorway. Damn. I hope he wasn't listening to Cate and me. One look at his eyebrow quirked in amusement confirms he was. And I'm betting he heard everything.

But before he can say anything, I do. "Back to business." Holding up two flash drives, I lower my voice to a whisper. "I copied everything. Do you have anyplace safe you could keep one of these? I'll take the other."

"You made two?"

"Overkill you think?"

He shrugs. "You tell me."

"Okay, so I'm being paranoid, but then again . . . who knows what could happen. I'll feel a lot better knowing you've got my backup."

"Happy to do it." He reaches for the red one, stows it in his chest pocket, and buttons the flap.

The other returns to the deep recesses of the zippered pocket of my safari pants. "Let's hope Gus keeps his hands off me."

A moment later, Matt is standing in the doorway to Margaret's office. "Julia!"

Oh God, this feels like a conspiracy. How long was he out there?

"Oh, hi! I'm just getting my camera."

Matt helps himself to the chair, leaving me to lean against the wall. "Before you haul it out back, why don't we talk about how to film this. And where."

I smile. "Thanks for asking. I've been talking to the Mambas—and Colin—about exactly that and—"

"So, this is where you ran off to." Gus strides into the room. "Look, I've got some ideas about how we should shoot this movie."

"Julia and I were about to finalize this afternoon's scenes."

"Good. Then I'm just in time." Gus cuts in front of me and leans against the desk—looking down at Matt. A total power position.

Matt, though, doesn't let Gus's posturing get to him; he just pushes back his chair and looks past Gus to me. "Julia, you were saying?"

I actually hadn't been saying anything yet, but Gus doesn't need to know that. Off the top of my head, I suggest what I filmed Colin and the Mambas doing this morning. "What if Gus leads the women on a training run through the bush? Kind of running around the mopane trees, making sharp cuts. Maybe even carrying their guns? Then—"

Gus laughs. "The trainer doesn't exercise with the women. He tells them what to do and how to do it." He pats his stomach. "Besides, I ate too much of Pepsi's great beef stew. There's no way I could run now. I'd puke up my guts. I figure the camera could focus in on me to start—full face or maybe some profile shots. Then cut to the women running." He looks over his shoulder at me.

Jeez, the man's got an ego.

Next to me, I sense Colin quivering as he struggles not to laugh.

Gus is still talking. "You should cut back to me a few times when I'm calling out instructions. Or maybe keep one of the cameras on me. Then, we'll—"

"Then," says Matt, now on his feet, "we'll see what we've got and what else we need."

Matt has the Mambas running along the road in front of headquarters. Except they're not so much running as walking fast—and really not very fast at all. I wonder if it's because of lunch or if they're determined not to film with Gus. And for his part, Gus isn't really telling them what to do; he's standing directly in front of my camera and yelling at them.

"Faster! Faster!"

"Pick it up! Get the lard out!"

"The poachers aren't waiting for you. They're getting away."

All of which is making for lousy footage.

"Cut!" Matt waves everyone to a stop.

If Matt could get the women to run and Gus to move away from my camera, this might actually work. At least we've got three cameras filming. With her strong and steady shoulders, Cate is moving along the dirt road near the Mambas. Amie is stationary down the road a piece, filming them from the back. Natalie is by her side, and I trust she's not saying a word. With good editing, this could make a decent scene. Maybe we'll end up using some of it after all.

Matt and Gus jog over to where the women are standing in the middle of the road. Gus starts to yell again, but Matt puts a halt to that immediately. He seriously doesn't like yelling on his sets, unless he's doing it, and that almost never happens. From this distance, I can't hear what he's saying. It looks like Margaret's speaking now. Then, Gus cuts her off, the tendons in his neck straining. I should probably go over and see what I can do to help, but instead, I tap my pants pocket—checking to make sure the flash drive is secure.

Colin stands near me on the verge. "I hate how he treats the Mambas."

"I know. It's disrespectful."

"Abusive," he adds.

"Do you think they can handle it? Or should I go over there and kick in his balls?"

He gags. "Pretty tough talk. But no, these women have dealt with a whole lot worse. I just don't think they should have to tolerate this now."

"Okay, then." I step away from the camera.

He grabs my arm. "Don't even think about it."

"Hey, chill. I'm only going to be part of the conversation. As the rational one here, you should come, too." By the time we get to the small group, Gus is lecturing the women, who are clearly bored and doing their best to tune him out. As soon as she sees Colin and me, Margaret takes our presence as her signal to resume her argument. "Running in the road, this is not how we train anymore. Now we run through the bush. It is much harder, and that is why we do it. Poachers do not stand out in the open. They hide behind bushes."

Keeping a straight face, I nod my agreement. "Sounds completely reasonable to me."

"It's not how we do things," Gus scoffs.

Colin strokes the beard stubble on the side of his face. "We've changed things a bit since you were here."

"Why? I had a first-rate training regimen."

Matt doesn't let Colin answer. "Look, folks. It's already midafternoon. I want to get this scene done. Let's try one more time on the road with Gus. Then, Colin, could you put the women through their paces over there?" He points toward the bushveld, the same area where we filmed this morning.

Gus doesn't look happy, but at least he's accepting that Matt's got the final word. For now.

Margaret offers one clipped nod and leads the women back up the road toward where Amie's standing with her camera. I'm pleased to see they're jogging. Back on the verge with Colin and now Liam by my side, I take my position behind camera number one. Once again, Gus stands directly in front of the camera, partially blocking the view. But before we start, Matt uses his heel to draw an X in the sand several yards off to the side. "Your mark."

And we're on take two.

Suddenly the women are able to run. Fast. In sync. And very differently from what I filmed this morning when they showed how they ran when they first started training. Gus barely says a word, because what is there for him to say but well done.

Matt calls a brief break for Colin and the women to collect their guns, and then we're back to filming. The training run through the bush is nearly what we got from this morning's shoot, except this time there are three cameras, which gives us a lot more to work with. I make a mental note to get my hands on Cate's and Amie's SD cards after we finish and copy them onto my flash drive.

Standing next to Matt, Gus launches into a commentary of the scene we're shooting. "This is bonkers."

"Cut! No talking on the set." Matt's not yelling, but I can see the glare in his eyes from ten feet away.

"But—"

"Complain all you want after we finish shooting."

Since we don't have anyone for continuity, Matt backs up the runners all the way to the beginning. One sharp look at

Gus, who lifts his hands in surrender, and we're back to filming. Amazingly, Colin and the Mambas are moving faster, cutting around bushes more sharply this second time. Once they scatter to check out possible hiding places, they're so aggressive and fierce that I actually feel sorry for any potential poachers they find. I hate to think we've got Gus to thank for it.

When Matt calls "cut" this next time, I can hear the satisfaction in his voice. We won't know what we've got, of course, until we upload the footage to the computer, but we can all hope.

Sweaty, and their legs leaden to the point of dragging, Colin and the Mambas are clearly ready to quit for the day, although we're the only ones who know they've been filming since dawn.

I walk the ten feet over to Matt to find out if he's calling the shoot for the day. "Beers are on me!" he shouts.

Turning back, I see Liam standing way too close to my camera, an intent look on his face. "Hands off!" I yell.

He backs away. "Hey, babe, no harm done. I was just trying to help. Thought I could carry it for you."

"I carry my own gear. Always." My voice is way too strident, but I don't care. Flipping on the power switch, I hit RE-PLAY. Thirty seconds. That's all I need to make sure he hasn't screwed up anything.

There on the LCD, I see the Mambas running through the bush. All seems well. For now.

Twenty-Nine

Tonderai unloads a cooler packed full of bottles of Zambezi and cans of Castle. One quick drink, then I retreat to Margaret's office where I upload the contents of all three cameras to my laptop and the flash drive that contains the footage for the secret version of the film. Copies complete, I return each SD card to its respective camera. While I'm working, I keep an ear tuned to Matt out back briefing Colin and Gus on tomorrow's shoot: the Mambas on patrol. From what I can hear, Colin suggests a site about an hour's drive into the central area of the park. Gus, of course, has an entirely different place in mind. Matt promises to let them know his final decision tomorrow.

Gus takes off, first revving his engine, then roaring away, leaving us in a cloud of dust. We load our gear into the Marula land cruiser, and we're off. In front of me, the others are all paired off—two per row, with Tonderai driving and Matt taking the seat next to him. I'm left to squeeze into the seat at the very back in between all the gear. Directly in front of me, Amie and Cate are chatting away about what worked in this afternoon's shoot and what didn't. Cate's offering a few tips on framing the shots for greater interest. No matter that Amie's my intern and this is my film; it's like I'm not even there.

I'm looking forward to my own bed tonight—and to actually getting some rest. I'm so tired that the rocking of the vehicle is lulling me to sleep. Until we bounce over a deep rut that rockets me out of my seat. I slam the top of my head against one of the metal crossbars and, somewhat dazed, fall back onto my seat.

I must make enough noise to alert Tonderai, who slows the vehicle, then stops. "Julia, you are all right?"

"I'm . . . fine."

But Amie is already standing on her seat, pulling my hands away from the top of my head. "Oh my God, Julia! Are you okay?"

I push her hand away and rub my head. *Yow!* I can already feel a lump forming. "Really, I'm fine."

She's not having it. "Look at me! How many people do you see?"

To humor her, I start to count the people in the vehicle even though I already know there are seven of us.

Before I can say anything, Cate gently pushes Amie away, then tells me to track her index finger. "You're fine, kiddo. But would you mind holding on? Another head slam today might just do you in. As it is, I'm pretty sure you're in for the mother of all headaches." She squeezes my arm. "Might want to put an ice pack on your head when we get to camp."

I lay claim to a chair by the railing on the back deck overlooking the water hole. A bag of ice on my bruised head and a glass of iced tea—which doesn't come close to Colin's secret recipe—keep me company while I watch families of elephants arrive to drink and wallow. Everyone else retreats to their tents for showers. We leave the light panels in the back of the vehicle, but Tonderai helps Cate and Amie carry the rest of the gear to our tent.

"How are you feeling?" Natalie takes the chair next to mine.

I readjust the ice bag onto the lump. "I wish everyone would stop worrying."

"Well, you know, head injuries can be serious. And we're kind of remote out here."

"I'm good. Really."

"Okay." She definitely sounds dubious. "Anyway, I brought you one of the tartes the chef set out on the bar." She hands me a picture-perfect pastry with strawberries and raspberries. "It's fabulous. I shouldn't eat them, of course. My directors are always after me to lose weight, but I couldn't resist."

"I won't say you don't need to drop weight, even though you don't, because I know how the industry is. Anyway, thanks for this." I take a nibble. "Oh, God. Be still my heart. This is divine."

"Isn't it?" We sit for a moment in blessed silence. "Can I tell you something?"

Why not? My head is already throbbing. "Sure."

"You're so nice. Really, you're nothing like what Liam said."

"I can imagine what he told you about me."

"Believe me, you don't want to know. And now that I'm getting to know you, I'm seeing that a lot of it just isn't true." She pauses for a moment. "Well, there is one thing you should know—about his grandfather's watch."

"What's that?"

"It's not lost. It's broken. He took it to the jeweler for repairs right before we left to come here. At least, that's what he told me."

"Then why the hell . . ."

"A good question."

"Talk about vindictive. I don't get it. Why continue to plague me after all this time?"

She shrugs. "Anyway, I'm thrilled to be part of this project and glad you let me come along. You didn't have to. I know voice-over narrators hardly ever go on site. But being here, I'll be able to do a much better job. It's really opening my eyes, and I'm serious about wanting to do something to help."

"Okay, confession time. When Matt first told me about you, I agreed pretty much because of your name and reputation. But now that I'm getting to know you a little, I'm glad you're doing the narration. I think you'll be good."

"Thank you." She smiles, almost shyly it seems to me. "That means a lot."

"Do you know how long you're staying? I mean after we finish the shoot?"

She takes a deep breath. "Well, last night Gus invited us to spend a few days at his place. Liam really wants to. He loves the luxury. To be honest, he likes it a lot better than here—the tents, you know."

"Yeah, I can see that. It's luxurious—that's for sure. But to tell you the truth, I didn't know Liam was a hunter."

She looks startled. "What do you mean?"

Now I'm surprised. "Gus didn't tell you? He caters to hunters. He runs canned hunts. The lion you saw—Reggie? He's either been baited onto the property or Gus is raising him to, you know . . ."

Natalie's hands cover her gaping mouth but don't conceal the horror in her eyes. "Oh my God. No! I had no idea. I thought Reggie was . . . a pet . . . or something. This is horrible." She's rigid for a full minute. "Liam's all over me to go back and stay there for a few days." A few more moments of thinking, then she says, "I'd bet you anything he knows."

"Sorry. I shouldn't have told you."

She puts her hand on mine. "Yes, you should have. I mean how could I possibly narrate your film—a documentary about anti-poaching—if I go and stay there?"

Dinner is great—delicious chicken cutlets served with spinach cooked in peanut butter—and for once, I don't have to deal with Liam. He's sitting at the far end of the very long table. I'm doing my best to continue my conversation with Natalie.

"The first night we were here, Liam said something about you needing to make this film to get tenure?" She keeps her voice low, as if trying to prevent Liam from hearing her.

"That's right." I fork some peanut butter spinach into my mouth. God, I love this.

"You know, I've been watching you work, and I really don't get it. Why have you been blacklisted?"

I take a sip of my iced tea. "Didn't Liam tell you?"

She leans across the table and lowers her voice even more. "Yeah, but it's so preposterous I can't believe it. You're a really good cinematographer. I even went back and watched a bunch of your early documentaries. They're so great."

Keeping my voice low, I tell her the truth—Alex forcing himself on me and his payback: the last-minute switch grounding me and putting Kyle in the plane.

"Fuck."

"Exactly."

"And to think that people say you were scared of flying in that small plane." She takes a sip of her drink—sparkling water. Interesting that she's staying away from wine tonight. "Which was totally understandable. To be honest, those little Cessnas scare the bejeezus out of me." Another sip, and then she whispers, "You know, Liam really does blame you for Alex's death. He's convinced Alex would have made him a star. Pretty crazy, huh? I think he really hates being Mr. Natalie Powers."

I sit back in my chair. "But I had nothing to do with it. Alex insisted on going up. Poachers shot down the plane. Damn it all, I don't know who started the rumor, but it sounds like Liam is perpetuating it. And plenty of people still believe it. Convenient, don't you think?"

"What do you mean?"

Sitting next to me, Cate jumps in to answer. "Julia wouldn't play ball. So, when in doubt, blame the woman. And then blacklist her."

"Typical." Natalie's eyes flash her anger.

"Okay, maybe things are getting better now, but change is still slow." Cate takes a long pull on her beer. "You tell me: how many directors out there are women? Cinematographers? Camera operators on big films?" She leans across the table and whispers, "We've got Julia here, and what's she doing? Teaching for fuck's sake because she can't get a job on a film. Alex's payback has continued way after his death."

Natalie stares at me, clearly unable to respond. She finally lands on, "So, do you like teaching?"

I decide to give an honest answer. "It's been good. And it's a living. But honestly, getting out here again, making this film, it's reigniting my love for cinematography."

"Well, thank God!" Cate cheers, which causes Liam and

Matt to look our way. Once they've resumed talking, she ze-
roes in on Amie with a definite glint in her eyes. "So, tell us.
How's Julia as a teacher?"

Amie practically chokes on her food.

"Come on, that's not fair," I protest. "I'm her graduate advisor. What can she possibly say with me sitting here?"

"No, no! I feel comfortable answering because you're a
really great teacher. The best in the department. All the students—grads and undergrads—say so. It's just . . . sometimes
. . . I wish you could be out making movies. I mean . . . I kind
of think, and so do the other students, that you'd be a lot
happier."

"Really? Students think I'm not happy?" Elbow on the
table, I plant my chin in the palm of my hand and stare at
my plate. Solomon's words from yesterday swirl around my
brain. *You need to decide what would make you happier than
you are now.*

The women keep talking—at least, I hear the drone of
their voices, so much white noise—a blanket wrapping
around me. So, people think I'm unhappy. I close my eyes to
consider this idea and feel myself sinking . . .

Finally, Tonderai comes to my rescue. His hand on my
shoulder jerks me awake. "Julia?"

"I'm fine." I try to smile, but that takes too much energy.
"Just tired."

"Would you like to go to your tent?"

"Yeah. Please. Before I start snoring."

He helps me out of my chair, and we head across the dining room so he can collect his gun as well as a flashlight. As
we approach the stairs down to the ground, he offers me his
arm, which for once in my life I take. We make it across the

elephant highway without incident, and then he helps me up the stairs. He unzips the tent flap and follows me inside, probably to turn on the light and make sure I'm settled for the night.

But as soon as the light comes on, I gasp. Three Pelican cases are arrayed on my bed. Not where they should be. Each one is open, the cameras askew, and the flaps to the SD card doors open. I don't even need to look to know the cards are gone.

Thirty

"Someone doesn't want us to make this film." Cate takes a long drink of yet another beer and sets the bottle down hard on the table.

Amie looks close to tears.

Natalie is downright angry. "Who would do this?"

"When did they do it—that's the question." Matt somehow manages to sound like he's in control of the situation. Then, he looks down the table at me. "You did upload today's shoot to your laptop?"

"Of course I did." I pat the laptop resting securely on the table next to me. I also run my hand over my zippered pants pocket where now not one, but two flash drives with everything we've shot are hidden. Call me paranoid, but there can't ever be too much backup.

Scanning the length of the table, I see the surprised expression on Liam's face—as if that's the last thing he expected. Damn! Did he steal the SD cards? Could he be actively sabotaging me? Except he'd also be undermining Natalie, and somehow I don't think he'd do that. Even if he doesn't like playing second fiddle to her. But one glance at Natalie's face tells me a similar thought has occurred to her.

Amie shoots me a grin and a clipped nod. After I drilled backup, backup, backup into my film students, she'd have skewered me if I hadn't secured my own film.

"I expected nothing less." Cate holds up her beer to toast me.

Liam scrambles to recover. "So then, what's the big deal?"

"Are you kidding me?" Natalie's face is white with fury. "Suppose Julia hadn't backed up the film today. Or what if she'd planned to do it after dinner? The film would be gone. And it's too late now to reshoot everything."

Liam shrugs and waves the waiter over for more wine, leaving me to wonder if the golden couple has been arguing—possibly about Gus and Buffalothorn. Which could be the reason he's seated as far away from Natalie as he can get.

"The one thing I didn't do was make sure all the cases were locked." I cover my face with my hands.

"Wise decision!" Cate stretches her arm across my shoulders and gives me a much-needed hug.

Okay, I'm confused. "Why? I always make sure they're locked. This was a total fluke."

"Can you imagine if we'd locked them? They would've taken everything—cases, cameras, all of it. As it is, they just took the SD cards."

"Expensive SD cards," I mumble into my hands. "I've got more, but not an endless supply."

"No worries. I brought a few," Cate whispers.

"So did I," says Amie.

"Thanks, guys." I turn my attention out toward the water hole. It's way too dark to see anything except the elephants masquerading as giant gray boulders. But I do take note of the beams of light bouncing around the tents. The camp staff with their flashlights making sure everything's secure.

Sometime later, Tonderai and Dabs, rifles at their sides, are back, motioning Matt and me into the lounge. As I push back my chair, Liam takes advantage of our imminent departure to head back to the tent he shares with Natalie without even asking if she's ready to call it a night. But she seems perfectly happy to adjourn to the bar with Amie and Cate. God, I hope they drink in moderation tonight. We've got an early wake-up call tomorrow, then a long drive to wherever we're filming, and quite an arduous shoot under a hot sun.

Tonderai looks discouraged. "We couldn't find any tracks in the sand or anything caught in the vegetation. We searched all the tents as well as we could and found no SD cards for these cameras."

Dabs nods his agreement. "Tomorrow, when it is light, I will look more thoroughly, although by then it is likely any human traces will be gone—covered by animal tracks. For tonight, I would like to suggest we put the laptop in the lodge safe. You are agreeable?"

"I know I'll sleep better." Matt closes his fingers around his can of Castle.

I hand the laptop to Dabs. "Definitely."

It's a few minutes after sunrise, and we're loading our gear into the land cruiser when the Mambas pull their vehicle up next to Marula Lodge. Barbara's at the wheel, and Colin's in the passenger seat. The other three women occupy the seats behind. Gus arrives a few minutes later—alone in a Buffalothorn jeep.

We gather at the breakfast buffet in the dining area for coffee and more of those delicious ginger muffins. Off to the side, the four men confer, with Matt announcing his decision as to where we'll shoot today. Tonderai nods his agreement. Gus smirks.

With a shrug, Colin wanders over to me. "I hear you had quite an evening."

"Which part do you mean?" I do my best to sound blasé, but it's not working.

Now he looks worried. "There was more than one incident?"

"Incident? That's a bit strong."

Raising an eyebrow, he does his best to look stern but fails. "The SD cards going missing?"

"Very unfortunate." I walk him out onto the deck away from the others.

He sips his coffee. "Someone's trying to sabotage the film."

"Oh, yeah. But I can't figure out who."

"The day before yesterday, you filmed Gus's tracker at the *shebeen*. At least, it could have been him. You think he or Gus could have helped themselves to the cards? They certainly don't want anyone to see what you shot."

"Could be." I stand with my back against the railing, keeping my eyes on the crowd in the dining room. "But last night, after Tonderai and I discovered the theft and I told the crew what happened, Liam was acting downright weird."

"You think he could have stolen the cards? But why would he try to deep-six a film that will feature Natalie?"

"God only knows, but he sure jumped high up on my list of suspects."

Colin crosses his arms. "As long as we're both being honest . . . I'm worried about this."

I do my best to look nonchalant. "Hey, I'm not happy someone stole the cards, but I've backed up everything. And I've got spare cards."

"It's not the cards I'm concerned about. It's you."

"Come on. Whoever took the SD cards thinks he got what he was after."

Colin puts his hands on my shoulders, turning me so he can look me in the eye. "Until he realizes he doesn't have what he wants."

I take a breath and let it out slowly, heavily. "Yeah, there is that. If he's got a camera."

"Now, what about the other incident?"

"What do you mean?"

"You know exactly what I mean."

I avert my eyes from his, lowering them to his mouth. Damn, his lips are nice. Another breath. "It wasn't anything that doesn't happen on a game drive."

"Tell me."

"I was on the top row. We hit a deep rut, and I tapped my head on the roll bar."

This time he takes a long swallow of coffee. "A tap? You care to amend your description?"

"I bet Cate told you I slammed my head." Okay, she's a good friend, but one of these days, the woman is going to push me too far.

"You okay?"

I shrug. "It's sore. I'm fine so long as I avoid doing any headstands."

"Do me a favor?" There's that wry grin.

By concentrating hard and looking over his shoulder, I manage to keep from going weak in the knees. "Is this a professional favor?"

"It can be." He's still grinning.

"You going to tell me?"

"I'll feel a lot better having you in the vehicle with the Mambas and me."

"Oh, for heaven's—" I stop and look at him closely. *Give the man a break!* "You're serious? That'll make you feel better?"

"Much better. Five sharpshooters around you will make me feel considerably better."

"It's a deal."

Five minutes later, half my muffin still in my hand, I'm climbing into the first row at the back of the land cruiser when Liam ambles up to the lodge. He's toting a gorgeous leather duffel in one hand, a matching backpack in the other—with locks on both of them. The luggage alone must be worth a couple thousand and is totally impractical for being out in the bush. My eyes seek out Natalie, who's sitting in the Marula vehicle. She sees him and quickly turns toward Amie and starts chatting. Liam, though, seems determined to make a scene. He waves, then calls past the two land cruisers to Gus who's standing next to his jeep.

"Your invitation still open?"

"Anytime, buddy." Gus spots Liam's travel bags and does a quick scan for Natalie. It's pretty obvious what's going on, and Gus can only add, "Toss them in the back seat. You okay riding with me out to the shoot?"

"Oh, yeah." Liam's smirk makes my stomach churn. "I wouldn't miss it for the world."

Damn! What's he up to?

Once we start driving, the early-morning cold gets colder. I pull my puffer jacket tight around me. A blanket would be nice. I glance at Colin and see he's wearing shorts. Is the man immune to the cold? Okay, I'll pretend to be as tough as he is. I'm not even going to ask.

Then, Colin's hand is on the sleeve of my puffer jacket. "Would you like a blanket?"

My heart almost melts. "Yes, please." I wait for him to laugh at my wimpiness. But instead, he magically produces a cozy fleece out of the aluminum lockbox under his seat and quickly drapes it around me.

We've been on the road for at least thirty minutes, and Colin says we've probably got another hour to go. Fine with me. At least I'll be warm.

His hand rests on my blanketed arm. "Back there at Marula, Liam made quite the entrance. What was that about?"

"I'm not totally sure. Besides the fact that he's clearly on the outs with Natalie, it seems like Gus is his new best friend and he's heading over to stay at Buffalothorn."

"I noticed his bags were locked. Was anyone able to search them?"

"Good question."

We stop behind Gus's jeep and the Marula land cruiser. They're parked next to a large thicket of bushes and beyond them several towering trees—more like leafless skeletons against the bluing sky. Rifles in hand, Gus and Tonderai, both of them with belts of cartridges buckled around their hips, are hiking into the bush. Turning off the Mambas' vehicle, Barbara and the other women are on the ground in a flash, spanning out on either side, their AR-15s at the ready. Colin stays where he is, his gun across his thighs.

I shoot him an exasperated look. "I'll be fine if you want to go with them."

"It's not only you. There are the other five. We never leave civilians completely unguarded."

"So, what's going on? I don't hear anything."

"Smell."

I do, and the stench nearly knocks me flat. "Oh my God!"

"Probably an elephant. It's likely been dead a few days, maybe a week. But we're playing it safe."

"Poachers? Or a natural death?"

"We'll find out." Binoculars to his eyes, he scans the bushes to our right.

"You think someone might be hiding in there?"

"Only if they're stupid. Poachers are smart enough to stay away from buffalo thorns. They're vicious."

"How so?"

He hands me the binocs. "Take a look at one of the thorns."

I focus in on the leaves and search for a thorn. Finally, I see one and gasp. "Nasty."

"They hook down under the skin and hold you in place. Very painful—although buffalo seem to like the bushes. The bigger and more expansive, the better."

"Why?"

"Because lions hate getting caught on the thorns. So, when buffalo are cornered by lions, they'll back as far as they can into the bushes. They know the lions won't go in to get behind them."

"Pretty smart." I take another look at one of the thorns. "It's kind of ironic that Gus would name his lodge after something so wicked."

"As opposed to the marula tree? Or the msasa?"

I hand back the binocs. "As you may have guessed, botany isn't my strong suit."

He takes pity on my ignorance. "Then let me explain our camp names. Elies really like the fruit from the marula and often overindulge, which gives them the runs."

The thought of elephant diarrhea almost makes me gag.

"But they're smart, so they head on over to the msasa, which has great curative properties." He quirks a grin. "Something to keep in mind."

Tonderai and Gus are back. Rounding the buffalo thorns, they stop at the Marula land cruiser to confer with Matt, who has the good idea to call me over. "Julia, you should be part of this."

I stand up in the vehicle and swing one leg over the side. "What's up?"

"Gus and Tonderai think this could be a good place to film a couple scenes. The Mambas are securing the site, but assuming all is okay, we could focus on the poached elephant and how the women comb the area for poachers."

Colin has already climbed down and is waiting on my side of the truck, I assume to help me down. "Sounds good," I call back. "Could make for some interesting footage."

Everyone else starts unloading. I look down at Colin, who really is intent on making sure I reach the ground in one piece. One bump on the head and my reputation is ruined. I reach one foot down to the step and start to climb down, but he's got his hand on my upper arm. There's a lot of power in that hand. If I were to fall, he'd probably be able to catch me with no trouble at all.

Like he did when you first met him.

Deciding to ignore my annoying inner voice, I pull my Buff up over my mouth and nose, which doesn't do a whole lot to block the smell. My camera case in hand, I start to round the bushes and end up in Gus's hands. "Thought you might like some support. It's tough seeing an elephant like this. Especially a female."

"Thanks, I'm good. This isn't my first. But I'm sure they could use your help hauling gear."

I walk on, past the buffalo thorn bushes—which look even more wicked up close—and finally see the giant gray carcass lying on its side maybe thirty feet ahead of me. Most of the face is gone—sawed off when the poachers took the tusks. A truly horrific sight. The thick, leathery skin drapes loose over the ribs and the spine. The four things that are still intact: her feet. I stare at the toenails, then the pads—not yet worn smooth. She wasn't all that old. Tonderai or Pepsi could tell me more exactly, but I'm guessing maybe thirty-something. Prime calf-bearing age. That thought stops me. Oh, God, I hope she didn't leave a newborn or a youngster.

This elephant needs to be in the film because it's a crucial part of the story—the reason why the Mambas are out here in the first place. But I need to figure out how to include her without making viewers turn away in disgust. And above all, I need to be respectful of this once great creature. A definite conundrum.

"What're you thinking?" Colin comes up behind me, a Pelican case in one hand, his rifle in the other. True to his word, he's not about to let me go off on my own.

Matt and Gus are right on his heels, each carrying a lighting panel.

"So, here's what I'm thinking." Gus exudes enthusiasm. "Focus in on the elephant, then swing the camera off to the right, and the Mambas can come jogging across the plain, two-handing their guns in front of them."

Matt nods. He's clearly in listening mode. "Julia, how do you want to film this? It's your call."

I swallow my smirk, mostly because I know Matt has already sized up the scene and in a moment is going to take me aside to tell me his ideas. "Let's make it fast," I say. "We've still got great light, but it'll be gone soon. I'd like to start with the feet, I think." I wave Cate over. "What do you think of a quick pan around the front of the elephant?"

"It's pretty gruesome." She unpacks her camera, attaches it to the shoulder mount, then waves everyone away.

The woman's got the strongest, steadiest shoulders of anyone in the business. I never tire of watching her work. Pure artistry. She's not satisfied with her first pass, so goes for a second. Then she works her way around the other side of the animal.

As Cate finishes up, I'm still mesmerized by the animal's feet, especially her hind feet. Predators have eaten a great deal of her, although for some reason hyenas and vultures haven't yet swooped in to clean up. With the golden light of the sun streaming in from the east, I sink to my knees in the sand and film her feet.

I can almost imagine this once-beautiful female hoisting herself up and padding her way across the savanna, dragging a mopane branch in the sand. Maybe standing on her hind legs to reach her trunk into the canopy of a marula tree for some fruit. She swallows them whole, loving the sweetness. More and more fruit until she walks farther on to the msasa tree she remembers from when she was a young calf. Maybe her mother showed it to her once. From there, she leads her daughters and maybe a young son to a water hole where they frolic, throwing mud over their backs as protection against the glare of the sun. Her skin is thick, but oh so delicate and prone to burn.

Around me, the breeze whispers through the grass and the leaves. I can almost hear the deep rumble of elephants calling to each other across the miles.

Just as I'm about to stop, completely unrehearsed, the Mambas jog silently by—maybe thirty to fifty feet beyond the elephant. They look everywhere except at us because it's already clear the elie is dead. They're searching for the killers.

I film them until they disappear in the distance, then turn off the camera.

"Let me see." Cate reaches for my camera.

I shake my head. "Later. Back at the lodge."

"Now." Taking the camera, she and Matt watch what I filmed.

Still on my knees, I concentrate on the forever-silenced elephant next to me.

"Damn, girl." Cate's voice. "You put me to shame."

"Over here!" Pepsi waves at us from near a small *kopje* about a hundred yards farther away.

Oh my God! Have they actually found a poacher?

Tonderai sets off at a run with the rest of us right behind him.

Margaret, Barbara, and Zinhle stand in a half circle, looking down at some tattered white cloth hooked on a low buffalo thorn branch. Below, on the ground, several groupings of bones. Far too small to have belonged to an elephant or a buffalo or even a lion, these bones look to be human. And there are a lot of them—enough for at least three people.

Gus nods knowingly. "The poachers."

Next to him, Liam grimaces. "Good riddance." For once, he's said something I agree with.

Tonderai kneels next to one of the sets of sand-swept bones and studies them carefully. "No, I do not think these are the poachers who killed the elephant."

"Of course they are." Gus sounds seriously annoyed. "Out here late at night, lions probably attacked them, then ate them. It's happened before. What other explanation could there be?"

"These bones, they look much older. See how the sand and the wind have scoured them clean? The elephant was killed more recently." He stands and moves to another group of bones. "And see how these are partly buried." He gently brushes away the sand, digging down to unearth a skull. Definitely human.

"You don't know what you're talking about. Lions ate these men. The hyenas and vultures obviously haven't come around yet to eat the bones and finish the job. Or they would've cleaned up after the elephant, too." Disgruntled, Gus paces away from our circle, then back again. "Look, if we're done filming for the day, I'm going to take off. I've got a new group of guests coming in this afternoon."

Matt looks at him intently. "Then I guess this means goodbye. We hope to finish in the next few days—maybe a week—and it sounds like you'll be busy."

"Sorry to say, that is the case. It's been great! Looking forward to seeing the film." With a wave, Gus and Liam head back to their jeep.

Tonderai waits until he hears the engine turn over, then walks to our vehicles to get some blankets to transport the bones. While the other Mambas continue to search the area, Margaret carefully detaches the white cloth from the buffalo thorn—a slow and tedious process. Tonderai isn't gone long, and once he's back, we all help wrap the bones. "We will take these to the village for a proper burial. But first, I want to show them to my grandfather. He will know the answer."

Thirty-One

Colin and I stand just inside the doorway of the *indumba,* watching Solomon kneel reverently in front of the three blankets spread across the dirt floor. He studies the bones intently, occasionally picking one up, turning it over in his hands, letting it rest in his palms, and then returning it to the correct blanket. Who knows whether lions or leopards or hyenas dragged the bones away from the original skeleton, but Solomon takes great care to keep the sets as intact as when he first unfolded the blankets. Standing behind his grandfather, Tonderai holds the white cloth Margaret took off the buffalo thorn bush. The way it's dangling from his hand, it looks for all the world like part of a shirt. Most likely what one of these people was wearing when . . . when what? Although Tonderai is convinced these bones don't belong to the poachers who slaughtered the elephant, I can't imagine how anyone can know for sure.

Solomon takes the cloth from Tonderai and spreads it in front of him. His gnarled fingers trace the stitches in the single seam. Gently. Almost tenderly. Then he furls the cloth, letting it come to rest over a row of ribs lined up one next to the other.

Once more, he picks up the skull. "Here." He points to the hole at the back, tracing the edges as carefully as possible. "This is where they shot him. A single bullet, I think. They would not want to waste more than one on a man from Matabeleland."

"*Baba mkhulu*, what do you mean?"

Solomon's eyes glisten. "I never thought to see him again. Your father."

"How do you know these are the bones of my father?" Tonderai inches closer to his grandfather.

Leaning forward, Solomon traces the stitches in the cloth. "You see these? I would recognize the sewing of your grandmother anywhere. It is in the twist of the thread and this knot here. They were her signature."

Kneeling down next to Solomon, Tonderai takes the cloth in his hand and scrutinizes each and every stitch. "*Yebo*. As a young boy, I watched her sew. I remember asking her why she put in so many knots."

"And what did she tell you?"

"Knots hold the seams fast and make the garment stronger."

"Exactly so, my grandson. She was a wise woman."

Tonderai sits back on his heels and waits for the story we all know Solomon is about to tell.

"It was the early rain that washed away the chaff. Cleansing rains. That is what the Shona word *Gukurahundi* means." Solomon takes a deep breath, then lets it out slowly. "The massacres began two years after Mugabe became prime minister. He was a dangerous man but brave in his own way. Yet, he was always frightened of his competitor, Joshua Nkomo, and tried again and again to remove him. Finally, in 1982, he sent the Fifth Brigade—mostly Shona soldiers—to Matabeleland here in the southwestern part of the country. They came to kill anyone who spoke out against Mugabe, but they did not stop at that and killed so many more. Including my son. Your father."

"I thought *ubaba* left to find work in the mines in South Africa."

"You were too young. A baby toddling after your grand-mother. What could we possibly tell you? These soldiers came for the people in the village. They raped many of the women and girls. They chased the young men along the boundary of the park, and then into the park. Killing them. Burying their bodies. We never saw them again. The government denied this, of course. But everyone in the village knew what really happened. And now, we have three of them home again."

I put my hand on Colin's shoulder and nod toward the doorway. We should go—leave Solomon and Tonderai alone in their grief. We're halfway along the path leading to the road when Tonderai comes jogging after us.

"Julia. My grandfather would like to see you."

"But don't you two want—"

He smiles sadly and shakes his head. "My father was killed a long time ago. It is good to know he is with the ancestors. This gives both my grandfather and me peace." He gestures to Colin. "Come, let's go over to the school and find the others."

I head back into the hut. The blankets have been refolded and placed along the curved wall. "You wanted to see me?"

Solomon looks up at me and smiles. "Please, you will join me?"

Hoping he doesn't want to throw the bones for me again, I sink to my knees.

"I see you are wary. Please do not be. I do not always need to throw the bones." He laughs. "I want to know if you are pleased with this film you are making?"

"Yes, it's going well. We should finish soon."

"I am glad to hear this." He continues to study my face. "You will return here to make other films."

I'm not sure how to respond. "Are you asking a question?"

"Do you think it is a question?" He smiles. "For me, it is not a question. You must remember that I saw the bones we threw the last time you visited me."

"Believe me, I remember. I'm also pretty sure you said that I have decisions to make. And that either path I choose will likely be difficult."

"I told you then that you have more stories to tell, more films to make."

"You didn't say anything about me coming back here to make them."

"Perhaps I neglected to say that." He looks thoughtful for a moment. "Would you like to see what the bones have to say?"

I take all of three seconds to make my decision. Absolutely not. Yet, I hear myself saying, "I think that would be a good idea."

He takes the bag out of his pocket and slowly unwraps the cloth. I lean forward and cup my hands in front of him to take the four bones. Then, closing my hands over them, I let them warm to my touch and think about the many questions I suddenly have. The film. Tenure. Liam. Gus. Am I leaving anything out? I'm still not a believer, but if anything can give me some answers, I might as well try.

Letting them spill back into Solomon's hands, I listen as he calls to the ancestors and watch as he throws them down onto the mat between us. They tumble a bit differently from the last time I was here. Not as many sharp angles. Two of the bones have even aligned closely together. Earlier I was able to make out some sort of a pattern, but today nothing makes sense. I wait for him to say something. Then, growing impatient, I push. "What do you see?"

"You feel a great need to make more movies."

I snort out a laugh. "We both already know that. Do you see anything else?"

"You know the decision you must make. Or you will come to know it. Soon, I think. I am confident you will make the right decision when the time comes."

"Well, I'm not at all confident. I thought I was doing the right thing by making this documentary so I could get tenure."

"But you have other questions. These answers will become clear to you, but it will not be easy."

I feel my eyes widen. "More questions? I don't understand."

"You will. Trust me." He reaches across the mat and places his hand on mine. "But first, you must be alert and cautious. There are dangerous storms on the horizon that will try to wash away the chaff."

Thirty-Two

I find Colin waiting for me in the dappled shade of the acacia tree next to Solomon's house. One glance at his green eyes and my heart quickens, just the slightest bit—I know what one of the other questions is. But Solomon's wrong. I don't have any idea how to sort out how I feel about this man. One minute I like him—a lot. The next, I never want to see him again, which I've learned is the best way to spare myself the grief and pain my relationships always entail. And lest I forget, it's thanks to him my retirement account will soon be empty.

"What are you doing here? I thought you and Tonderai were heading over to the school to round up the rest of the crew."

He grins. "He went on ahead. I'm here as your personal bodyguard." Damn, I'll miss his smile when I go home.

"It's all of a hundred yards to the school. You don't think I can handle it on my own?"

He swings his arm across my shoulders. "What I think is that you have an uncanny ability to get in a lot of trouble in less than ten feet."

"Gee, thanks."

He tips his head toward Solomon's hut. "Everything okay?"

"Pretty much."

"You going to tell me?"

I shrug. "Solomon wanted to know how the film is going."

"What did you tell him?"

"That it's all good and I think we could be finishing soon." Should I tell him the rest? I think not. Then I hear myself repeating Solomon's words—more or less. "He says I need to make more movies. Instead of teaching."

Colin takes all of five seconds to consider that. "I think so, too."

"Really?"

"I've had a ring-side seat while you've been working. And I've seen some of what you've shot. You're good. Not to say you're not a good teacher. Amie swears you're the best. But . . ."

I wait, but he doesn't finish. "But what?"

"I think you should be out in the field with a camera."

"Even though no one wants to hire me?"

"They will."

So, what the hell does he feel about me? Anything? Or are we really sticking to a professional relationship? And he needs to keep me alive until the money transfers.

The Mambas have gone back to Msasa. That leaves the crew, Colin, and me to meet up with the kitchen staff from Marula Camp for the picnic they've planned on the hill overlooking a water hole where elephant and zebra, impala and giraffe are milling about. They've laid out an incredible lunch of beef turnovers and fried chicken, spinach quiche and lettuce salad, potato salad and coleslaw. And a line of metal and canvas camp chairs, so we can enjoy the view while we chow down.

Amie wonders aloud if the animals could catch wind of us and come looking to help themselves to our food.

"No worries," Tonderai assures her. "We're downwind."

She flashes a smile at him, and I can almost see her making a mental note of that factoid. It's her smile, though, that catches my attention. She seems to smile at Tonderai a lot. And he at her. So, that first day in Vic Falls wasn't an anomaly. To confirm my hunch, I lean close to Cate and whisper, "Do you think Tonderai and Amie . . ."

She laughs, and her voice isn't anywhere close to a whisper. "You're just now noticing?"

"Hey, when I'm in the field, I stay focused on the film. Everything else sort of goes right by me. But at least I finally noticed these two."

"Well, there's someone else you should be noticing."

I roll my eyes. "Spare me."

When Colin goes to the table for a second helping, Natalie snags his chair next to me. "I've got to tell you. We had the best time at the school."

"I didn't know you were planning a second visit."

She takes a bite of potato salad, which certainly isn't on any movie star's diet. "It wasn't planned, but since we were there, I decided to go ahead and track down the school director."

"And?"

Her legs are jiggling. "Well, I had this idea. The other day, I saw all those boxes full of encyclopedias, and then Gus's hunters brought more sets. I mean, really, how many encyclopedias does one school need?"

I work on a chicken thigh. "What did you and the director talk about?"

She's practically vibrating now. "What I could do to help—but the kind of help they really want. And need. Not just something *I* think they need. And you won't believe what she suggested."

"Tell me!"

"To start, I'm going to dig a well in the schoolyard so the children can have fresh water while they're in school. And so the teachers can have water, too—they live in huts on the grounds, you know. The people in that area, too. Then they won't have to walk so far to the other closest clean water source."

Now I'm excited. "Oh, this is a brilliant idea! And I'll bet pretty expensive, too."

She bats away my comment. "Probably about ten thousand. They'll have to drill down pretty far to reach the aquifer, but I can afford it. And the best part is that I'll get to come back to watch the installation."

We chat for a few minutes about the plans she's starting to make, then she taps my arm and nods toward Colin. "Someone's waiting for his seat. We'll talk more at dinner."

We swing by Msasa Camp to drop off Colin and to let the Mambas know to be ready for another early-morning shoot. Then we head back to Marula. Leaving her SD card with me, Cate calls dibs on the first shower, so I collect my laptop from the lodge safe to upload today's footage and review it with Matt. Over a glass of iced tea, Natalie says that she'd like to take a nap in her tent—and probably check over her belongings to make sure Liam didn't help himself to anything when he left.

Backups complete, Matt and I are ready to review today's work when someone screams.

Over and over and over.

Blood-curdling screams from someone who's fighting for their life. Screams that make my heart stop.

In less than a second, we're on our feet and out on the deck, where Amie and Natalie are trying to figure out where the screams are coming from.

Somehow, I know.

From our tent.

Cate.

I'm on the run with the others right behind me when Tonderai and Dabs rocket past us, yelling at us, "Go back and stay on the deck!"

Amie and Matt and Natalie do as they're told and retreat back onto the deck, ready to bolt into the dining area and slam the doors if necessary. But I stay on the steps, watching as, rifles at the ready, first Tonderai and then Dabs enter the tent.

A moment later, the emergency horn blares and more camp staff head to the tent.

Now, the elephants at the water hole—there must be forty of them—are jostling against each other, trumpeting their fear. They fling their heads wildly from side to side, looking for an escape route. Running through the water will be too slow. They'll never be able to escape the poachers they must sense are nearby. Finally, they decide on the pathway between the lodge and our tent and thunder past me, building speed and churning dust as they crash their way to safety.

I look back to the tent where some of the staff members are standing outside. As soon as the elephants clear out, the men run back to the lodge, each on a mission with no time to explain to me what's going on.

Cate's screams keep coming. Terrified and hoarse and full of pain.

Oh, God! What's happening? Is it a lion or a leopard that somehow got in the tent and was waiting for her when she went to take a shower?

I take a step down the staircase. My friend. My mentor. I've got to go help.

No. The worst thing I can do is get in the way, which will only make things more difficult for the guys and won't help Cate.

I brace myself for the gunshot that must be coming.

A moment later, the trainee guide, clutching what looks to be a machete, runs back to the tent and goes inside.

Now Dabs is emerging from the tent, scanning the deck until he spots me. He waves me over. I charge down the staircase and across to the tent with no care if any curious elephants might be creeping back to find out what's happening. I'm about to step inside the tent, but Dabs puts his arm out to stop me. "Not yet."

Close behind me, two guys from housekeeping carry a folding stretcher up the stairs. Dabs leads them inside. Peering after them, I see Cate sprawled on the floor, writhing and groaning, her hands over her face. They quickly lift her onto the stretcher, convince her to lie down, and carry her out of the tent and onto our small deck.

"Is Julia here?" Her hands still over her eyes, Cate sounds frantic.

I clasp hold of one of her wrists. Then, thinking better of it, move my hand to her shoulder. "I'm right here."

"It was a fucking snake."

"A Mozambican spitting cobra." Dabs looks grim as he points at his eyes, then at Cate's.

Her *eyes*! Oh God, no! No! No! No! Not her eyes. I stare at Dabs in horror.

"Tonderai and Vusa are taking care of it."

The unexpected whoosh of the machete slicing through the air and then the clunk of the metal cutting into the teak floor makes me jump. I can only imagine the blade severing the cobra in two before sinking into the wood. A moment later, Tonderai steps out of the tent and, grabbing one front corner of the stretcher, carefully guides everyone down the stairs.

I follow behind. Glancing toward the lodge, I see the others, faces strained, standing at the top of the stairs.

Back on firm ground, Cate whimpers. "Julia!" I move back into place and tighten my grip on her shoulder. "I can't see anything!"

"You will see again." Tonderai's voice is calm, comforting.

"How long?" Now Cate sounds angry.

He puts a hand on her other shoulder. "We will wait for the doctor."

"How soon will the doctor get here?" I do my best to sound hopeful.

"No," Tonderai says. "I am sorry. The doctor isn't coming here. We are medevacking Cate to the hospital in Victoria Falls. We just called, and they confirmed that they have the necessary anti-venom there. The plane is in the air now and should be here in another forty minutes. Everything is arranged. There will be an ambulance waiting at the airport."

This is going to cost a fortune. Thank God we all have trip insurance. After the last film six years ago, I wouldn't come to Africa without it.

Matt and Amie meet us halfway to the lodge, just in time to hear me tell Cate that I'll medevac with her.

She stiffens beneath my hand. "Absolutely not!"

"What do you mean? I've got to go with you."

"You listen to me! The film has to be finished, and you're the one to do it."

"No, Cate! You listen. There are more important things than this film."

She removes one of her hands from in front of her eyes and grabs my hand, holding on tight. And letting me see what that frigging snake did. Her lids are blistered and swollen. They're actually getting worse in the short time she's holding my hand. I've filmed some horrific scenes in my life, and done it without crying, without fainting, but this . . . this is bringing me to my knees.

"It's bad, isn't it?" Cate's voice has only a hint of its usual gruffness.

I'm not going to lie. "Yeah."

"So then you can see what you're up against."

I chew my lower lip, trying to figure out what she's talking about, but finally give up. "Sorry, I don't follow."

"Someone wants to kill this film. But more than that, they want you dead."

"Cate . . . it could've been any one of the three of us who took the first shower."

"You're not listening. I couldn't find my shampoo, so I raided your duffel. They put the fucking snake in your duffel."

And that's when my knees give way.

Dabs deposits me in an armchair next to Cate, who's lying on the sofa with a damp cloth draped over her eyes. The rest of the staff are back in our tent or checking for footprints in the sand. "They'll go over every inch of the grounds and all of your belongings," Tonderai assures us. "We want to make sure there are no other surprises."

Matt sits down next to me. "Obviously the snake didn't unzip Julia's duffel, slither in, and re-zip it. Which means someone put it there. Didn't anyone see anything?"

"We have questioned everyone." Dabs is back with another damp cloth for Cate. "No one saw a thing. No one sneaking into the tent. We also do not know when this happened. Maybe last night? This morning? The Mambas are on their way to help us search."

Tonderai pushes himself to his feet and walks out onto the deck. He's back a minute later. "The plane is almost here. Cate, we need to get you to the airstrip. Do you think you can sit?"

"Of course."

I stand, too. "I don't care what you say, Cate. I'm going with you."

She shoots me the middle finger. "And I say no. You're gonna stay here and finish this film. Otherwise, this"—she points to her cloth-covered face—"is all a waste."

"Cate—"

"Julia." Amie takes a step closer to Cate. "I'm going with her. I'll call when we get there, and I promise to keep everyone posted."

"Amie? Need I remind you that you hate to fly?"

She shrugs. "Yeah, well, sometimes you've just got to suck it up."

I can picture Amie's face when she sees the small Cessna and the unpaved airstrip, pock-marked with divots and ruts from this year's rains. No way will she be prepared for the takeoff.

"So then it's decided. Julia, Natalie, and I will stay on to finish the film." Matt puts his arm around my shoulders and hugs. "We'll meet you two in Vic Falls as soon as we can."

A wide-brimmed sun hat on her head and another damp towel on her eyes, Cate sits in the front seat of the Marula minivan. Amie helps load their duffels and packs, but only after Dabs swears that he's personally searched each one twice. Then, climbing into the back of the vehicle, Amie leans forward and puts her hands on Cate's shoulders.

Tonderai keys the ignition, and I squeeze Cate's hand one last time. "We'll see you soon." The second the word 'see' is out of my mouth, I cringe.

She points her finger at me. "I felt that cringe. Promise me one thing, Julia: make the best goddamned movie out there. I'll see you at Sundance."

"Deal." My voice wobbles.

"Don't you dare cry! I'm not dead yet."

"Dabs told me I'd find you here." Colin hands me a glass of his special iced tea and grabs the seat next to me on the deck—my usual place overlooking the elies at the water hole. Except I'm not watching them or even the sun that's lowering to the horizon. "You holding up okay?" he asks.

"Tell me you found something." My voice sounds flat, close to dead.

"All I found were some footprints in the sand, and they could belong to anyone. But Zinhle found a bit of cloth likely ripped off a khaki shirt. Get this, it was hanging on a buffalo thorn behind your tent."

"You think it could be important?"

"Well, Dabs and I agree it hasn't been there long. Not faded at all. And the staff here do their best to stay clear of those bushes. The last thing they want is to get caught on one of the thorns. Makes for a nasty wound that can easily go septic, especially out here."

"So, all we have to do is find someone with a ripped shirt or a body part about to rot off. No problem."

"The Mambas are on it. If there's anything out there, they'll find it. Especially with you and Cate involved." He pauses for a minute. "There's something else we need to talk about."

I take a long drink of my tea. "You know, you still haven't told me how you make this."

He props his booted feet on the railing, ankles crossed. "I believe I said it's a secret recipe."

"You're sticking with that, huh?"

"I am. And I promise to make it for you whenever you like."

Yeah, whenever you're around. "Okay, tell me what else we have to talk about."

"Matt tells me we're still filming tomorrow."

"We are. Cate is adamant we go on without her."

His nod tells me he would've done the same thing. "Matt also told me that he and Natalie will be staying in his tent tonight."

My eyes widen. "Did I miss something else?"

He laughs. "I think it's more for safety. Even though the staff searched her tent twice, she's understandably nervous."

My thoughts veer to Cate and Amie, whose plane should be landing anytime now. I heave a sigh. "I know how she feels."

"And that brings me to my question."

I turn to look at his green eyes and the curve of his lips. "Yeah?"

"Your bed or mine?"

"For safety, right?"

"Of course."

Thirty-Three

It's been hours since Cate and Amie landed in Vic Falls, and we're still waiting for an update. Tonderai reminds us that Marula Camp is fairly remote, and reception isn't always the best. Amie could be trying to call and not getting through. Which sounds reasonable since I can't reach her either. But being out of touch isn't helping my nerves. Damn it, no matter what Cate said, I should have gone with her. She's here because of me. Attacked by a cobra because of me. If she loses her sight permanently . . . or, God help me, if she dies . . .

Colin hands me a gin and tonic. "She's not going to die."

I wrap both hands around the glass to keep from dropping it. "How do you know that's what I'm worried about?"

"You've been wringing your hands. I always wondered what that phrase meant, but you've been demonstrating the perfect visual—for the last hour."

"How can you be so sure Cate will be okay? I mean, people die from cobra bites, don't they?"

He nods. "They can. But this cobra didn't bite her, and we got her to the hospital for treatment." I'm about to ask another question, but he holds up his hand. "I'm not saying she won't have a tough time because she likely will. But they've got some good doctors at the hospital in Vic Falls."

I take a long swallow of my drink—a bit stronger than is good for me, so I pour in the rest of the tonic. In the US, they give you the drink already mixed. But I prefer the way the rest of the world serves it: the gin premeasured in the glass alongside the bottle of tonic.

Settling back in my chair, I glance up to see Matt and Natalie arrive, presumably from moving her stuff into Matt's tent. But Natalie is also glowing, and her hair is wet. A shower explains the hair, but not this kind of glow. Matt stops next to my chair. "Any word?"

I shake my head. "Not yet."

"She'll call." Natalie doesn't so much sit on her chair as float down onto it. Is that what sex does for you? It's been so long, I honestly don't remember. "Julia, I know you're worried about Cate. We all are, but before they left, Amie and Dabs both told me that she's probably going to be fine."

"How would Amie know?" My voice is maybe a little too dismissive.

Natalie looks surprised. "Well, she was a biology major in college. Pre-med. I'm pretty sure that's what she said."

"*Yebo.* That is what she said." Tonderai joins our group. "We will wait to hear what the doctor says, but I agree she will be okay. Eventually. Right now, there is a great deal of pain. If any of the cobra's venom got onto her eyes, then there are some serious burns."

On her eyes? Oh God. I take another long swallow of my drink and pour in the rest of the tonic.

"The chef sent me out here to let you know dinner is ready." Tonderai sweeps his hand toward the tables behind us. "You will, please, come into the dining room?"

Looking around the table, I count five cell phones, one next to each plate. Not a single one of them has rung. I cut my steak into little pieces, then push them around on my plate. It's delicious—so everyone says—but I'm having a tough time tasting it, much less swallowing. Finally, as we're finishing the main course, Tonderai's phone rings.

He swipes his index finger across the screen. "Amie. Let me put on the speaker so we can all hear you."

"Hey, everyone! I've been trying to call for hours, but this is the first time it's gone through. So who knows how long I've got."

"Tell us how Cate is!" I ball my hands into tight fists.

"The doctor says we got here just in time. She was in so much pain, he had to use a local anesthetic so he could wash her eyes without hurting her anymore. And he gave her the anti-venom." She takes a deep breath. "I won't lie, she looks pretty bad, but he thinks she'll regain at least some of her vision."

Only some? I close my eyes in pain. There's no worse prognosis for a camera operator.

"How long will she be hospitalized?" Trust Matt to ask the pertinent question.

"Well, here's the thing. The doctor here couldn't do everything he says needs to be done. So he's transferring Cate to Johannesburg in the morning."

"Johannesburg!" I gasp. That tells me a lot. Top-notch medical care, but medevacking to another country means the doc in Vic Falls is worried.

"Yeah. The people here have been great, talking to the insurance company for me and helping arrange for the plane to medevac her in the morning. Of course I'm going with her.

Okay, guys, I'm going back in Cate's room because she wants to talk to you herself. So I'll call again when we get to South Africa."

"She can talk?"

"Of course I can talk, Julia. My eyes aren't connected to my mouth."

"Damn, you sound good."

"It helps to have the local. And the painkiller. Look, I have two things to say to you." Cate is definitely back in form.

"Shoot."

"You damn well better stay there and finish this film."

"So you told me before you left."

"Did I? I don't remember much except for the burning. Which means I also don't remember if I told you the second thing."

A quick glance around the table, and I see everyone is smiling. "Go ahead."

"You still got that phone on speaker?"

"Yeah."

"Well, turn it the fuck off—unless you want everyone there to hear."

I roll my eyes and turn it off. What can she possibly be about to say?

"Colin anywhere nearby?"

"He is."

"Then I suggest you put some space between the two of you."

My shoulders sag. Tell me she hasn't discovered something damning about him. But it's best I find out now, so, taking her advice, I push myself to my feet and walk out onto the deck. "Okay. I'm a good thirty feet away from him."

"Good. For now. I want you to promise me you'll take the man to bed."

"Cate! Give it a rest! I'm shooting a film here."

"Not twenty-four hours a day."

"Close to it."

"Listen to me. I don't want to find out that you fly home without having fucked that man."

"And how is this any of your business?"

"Because I'm your friend, and I've gotten tired of watching the two of you mooning after each other. It's so high school. Scratch that. Teenagers would've long since done something about this."

"Mooning? Seriously?" I do what I can to swallow my laugh. "There's a word I haven't heard in a long time."

"Just like you to go off on a tangent. Promise me you'll take him in hand and do the deed. You'll both be happier. And most important, I'll be happier." She snorts a noise somewhat akin to a chuckle. "Oh, and don't hang up. Amie wants to talk to Tonderai."

I probably shouldn't be surprised to turn around and see Colin and Tonderai standing in the wide doorway to the dining room. Even though we were just discussing the man, I'm a bit taken aback to see him so close. I hold out the phone to Tonderai. "Amie wants to talk to you."

Taking his cell, he retreats down the deck into the shadows.

Meanwhile, Colin doesn't move. "Mooning?"

"You heard that, huh?"

"I did."

My heart isn't quite sure what to do . . . sink, or soar. "Did you hear anything else?"

"Enough to fuel my imagination. But for now, there's chocolate mousse for dessert—quite the aphrodisiac."

I smile in lovely anticipation.

There's no way I'm going to sleep in my bed. Not even with Colin in the tent with me. Everyone assures me repeatedly the cobra is dead—cut in half—and my duffel and backpack have been searched at least three times. But I can't foresee myself ever stepping foot in that tent again. So, I opt to sleep at Mamba headquarters. In Colin's bed, which is still way too narrow for two people.

And here we are.

"I'll take the floor." He pulls off his sweater.

Standing next to him, I unzip my puffer jacket, then slip it off. "You've made this same offer before, and it never happens."

He puts his hands on my shoulders and turns me to face him. "Because you always protest."

"Yeah, well, it's your bed." My eyes meet his.

He leans in close, his lips a hair's breadth from mine. "I'm inviting you to share it. Again."

"Is your bed snake-free?"

"It is. I promise." His hands leave my shoulders and find their way to my lower back.

My arms respond by encircling his neck. Our bodies now fitted perfectly together, my lips breach the millimeter of distance between us. And, oh God, this man knows how to kiss. When he finally lets me breathe, I practically gasp for air and, taking a small step backward, I focus on his lips. Which probably isn't the best idea, given that they're making me go weak in the knees. "I . . . um . . ."

"Hey. Cate's order to stop mooning around notwithstanding, I'm not about to do anything you don't want. Despite the chocolate mousse."

"You mean . . ."

"Exactly. If you're not up for this, we can just sleep. We've done it before."

"Probably best to keep our clothes on then."

"A wise idea. Especially since you're shivering." He draws his index finger from my wrist partway along my arm, pushing up the sleeve of my shirt a few inches.

I respond by unbuttoning his shirt and unbuckling his belt.

His lips are next to my ear. "You mind if I take off your clothes?"

"I'll get colder."

"Not for long."

Later, in the dark of the room, he spoons his body against mine, keeping me warm—exactly as he promised. So do the kisses he's scattering across my neck and shoulder.

"You know, a lot of women come on safari." His voice is barely above a whisper.

"Do they?" I seriously don't want to hear what I'm sure he's about to say.

"Part of why they come, some of them at least, is to score a few nights with the guide or ranger. And many of the guides are happy to provide that extra service."

Just when I thought I was finally over Liam, my heart starting to open again, this man I trusted is about to skewer me. But what can I say? So, Cate got it wrong. I did, too. Then again, Colin and I haven't actually talked about feelings. Or plans. We fucked, and it was sensational. So, maybe I was assuming, or at least hoping, it was something more. But would my assumptions really be fair to either one of us?

Lest I forget, I'm here to make a documentary. And the filming is almost complete. As Matt said, another few days, a week. Then I'll be heading home to put together my tenure materials. And Colin will be here, eight thousand miles from Milwaukee, working with the Mambas. And bedding a whole lot of tourists—singles and probably a fair share of marrieds who manage to sneak away from their husbands for a few hours. Like Margot Macomber did in Hemingway's short story—slipping away from her husband, Francis, to enjoy time with their hunting guide Wilson in his tent. So much sex. Damn.

So, what the hell do I say? "Must be fun for those women, having such multifaceted adventures."

He wraps his arm around me, holding me tightly against him. "I want you to know I'm not one of those rangers."

Thirty-Four

I wake to sunlight streaming in the window and listen to the sounds of the Mambas and Colin moving around headquarters. This is the latest I've slept since being in Zimbabwe. I really want to stay where I am for another hour, maybe even entice Colin back to bed. But there's work to be done. And first, I've got to shower and dress.

Hold on! It's not like I can waltz my way naked to the shower, not with all these people around. Pulling on yesterday's clothes and digging something clean out of my duffel, I can't help wondering how the Mambas are going to react to me being here. I kind of doubt overnight guests are a regular thing.

I needn't have worried.

The moment I open the bedroom door, Barbara smiles and hands me a towel. "You would like a shower." It's not really a question. She tucks her arm around mine and leads me to the small bathroom next to the dormitory. "We used to bathe outside, and even now, during the rainy season, we sometimes still do. But at this time of the year, it can be very cold in the morning. Colin insisted on this indoor shower." She leans close to me. "He's a good man."

"Thanks." And knowing that water is at a premium, I take the fastest shower on record.

The moment I step back into the hall, there is Pepsi, giggling softly. "Colin, he is a good man."

"Barbara said the same thing." And I recall Margaret telling me exactly that several days ago. "It kind of feels like you all are setting us up."

"Well, we did promise Cate to do our best."

I groan out loud.

Another arm grab, and she takes me to the kitchen where she hands me two rolls and a mug of hot coffee. Then we're outside heading to the picnic table where Colin is finishing his own coffee.

"You're up."

"I am."

"You found everything you need?"

"The women have taken wonderful care of me."

Pepsi smiles and waves, then heads back inside.

Once she's out of earshot, I let him in on the refrain that's been following me. "Colin is a good man."

He laughs and takes another sip of coffee. "I've been hearing about what a good woman you are. Margaret finally admitted Cate spoke to them." He reaches across the table for my hand and starts to twine his fingers around mine. Then stops. "Sorry. Totally forgot. It's time to shift gears, isn't it."

I look at him blankly.

"To our professional relationship. As I recall, you're the one who insisted on it."

Heat climbs from my chest to my neck and onto my cheeks. I can imagine how red my face is. "You're right. Guess I really screwed that up last night."

"In a manner of speaking, but I was an equal partner." Damn the grin curling up the corner of his mouth. "And now, I have a message for you from Matt. He'd like to see you over at Marula right about now to work on the film. I think the rest of the plan is for us to join you after lunch to shoot some more scenes."

My heart pings. "It's hard to believe we're almost finished. I'm seriously not ready for this to be over."

"Neither am I." His voice sounds almost wistful. "But there's still work to be done."

When Colin pulls up in front of the lodge at Marula Camp, he reaches over to stop me. "Are you all right?"

I lean back in my seat. "Just a little worried."

"About what happened last night? With us?"

"No!" I say way too fast, like I really don't care about what we did. "Although with me leaving soon, maybe I should be worried. I mean, I'm really not the zipless fuck kind."

"The what?" He looks highly amused with maybe a touch of confusion.

"An expression Erica Jong coined decades ago in *Fear of Flying*—sort of a feminist Bible—"

"I've read the book."

"Seriously?"

"You don't need to sound so surprised. And as for zipless fucking, that's what I was trying to tell you last night. Or maybe it was this morning. I'm not into it either. Anymore. There was a time after my marriage fell apart . . ."

"Same here."

"Look, I know you're leaving. We'll figure things out."

"I'd like that." I think. Hell, I don't know what I think.

"Now, tell me what you're worried about."

"I haven't yet told Matt about the second version of the documentary."

He widens his eyes. "You did say it was a secret. But I see your point. You're going to have to tell him."

"Yeah. Like this morning. I'm sure he wants to work on blocking out the narrative arc. We've got a screenplay, but we haven't exactly followed it. In fact, the Mambas and you and I pretty much rewrote it. We'll need to give the editing guys some direction."

"Any idea how he's going to react?"

I shrug. "He's a pretty easygoing guy, but he is the director. This film's different from the other times I've worked with him, meaning I've had a lot more say. Still, the director has the final word. Honestly, I don't have a clue how he's going to react."

"Would it help if I stay? Lend some moral support? We both know you made this decision because of the Mambas."

"You know you really are a good man."

"Let's go." And good man that he is, he doesn't even offer to carry my camera gear.

We find Matt and Natalie in the dining room, lingering over coffee, my laptop in the center of the square table—open. I don't even need to ask. He knows. And he looks pretty pissed off.

"Ah, you finally decided to join us."

"Sorry, I haven't been getting a lot of sleep lately, and—" I decide my blathering won't help matters. "Coffee?" Which is more of a delaying tactic than an actual need for more caffeine.

Matt lifts his mug in a kind of salute then points toward

the sideboard. "There should still be some. Why don't you bring the pot over."

Shit. It's never a good day when Matt loads up on coffee. Caffeine can do him in, and everyone who's ever worked with him knows it. Then again, maybe he didn't get much sleep last night either, what with sharing his tent. I take another look at Natalie, who's definitely not glowing this morning, then head toward the coffee station.

I hear the slap of shoes on the plank floors and look over my shoulder to see Natalie following me. Back at the table, Colin has helped himself to one of the two free chairs—the one next to Matt, leaving me the one opposite. The perfect position to keep Matt from physically attacking me. Which he'd never do.

I collect two mugs and the little pitcher of milk, the hand-made mesh screen with beads draped across the top. No mosquitoes are getting access to this creamer. Natalie picks up the coffeepot. "I thought you could use some help," she whispers. "And by the way, you're glowing something fierce. Please don't thinking I'm prying, but I take it last night went well." It's not a question.

I'm definitely not into kiss and tell, but I've got to say something. "What? Did Cate talk to everyone?"

"Yeah. Pretty much."

"So, what about you and Matt?"

"We're tentmates. Nothing more."

"But last night you had the glow."

"Don't get me wrong, I wouldn't mind pushing our beds together, but it's not happening. What you saw was my intensive moisturizer. It's so dry out here, and I haven't been hydrating quite as much as I should."

"Tell me. How mad is he?"

She picks up the coffeepot and presses her lips together for a few seconds. "I'll be honest. When he first saw the footage you shot on your own, I thought he might erupt. But he seems to be calmer now. I hope you know what you're doing."

Yeah, so do I.

I set a mug in front of Colin and another in front of the empty chair across from Matt. Then I sit. In the line of fire. Natalie fills everyone's mug, then walks the coffeepot back across the room. From the look on her face, it's clear she wishes she were someplace else. Anyplace else. But I guess she's decided I might need her protection.

Matt turns the laptop around so I can see the monitor. The morning scene with the Mambas in street clothes, marching up the road in front of headquarters, their dilapidated suitcases in hand. It's a great still. It's also some great footage. But that's the last thing I should say.

I lift my mug but don't manage to align it with my mouth. Hot coffee splashes onto my shirt. Oh, God! What next? Rethinking my need for coffee at the moment, I set the mug back on the table. Then, taking a deep breath, I say nothing.

But Matt does. "You mind telling me what the fuck you were thinking?" So much for easygoing.

"You and the crew were at Buffalothorn. We had a free morning."

"And what, you couldn't simply wait for us to get there?" He finishes his coffee without spilling a single drop. "Or maybe, in the days since then, you could've found time to tell me you'd filmed some scenes?"

I splay my hands on the table and take a deep breath. "Let's remember you were getting in bed with Gus Sinclair.

To my way of thinking, there was no good reason for him to be in the film or to be a producer." Somehow I manage to keep my voice low, but my anger is palpable.

"Duly noted. But I did talk to you about it." Matt crosses his arms over his chest. Not yet easygoing but getting there.

"And I told you what I thought. You didn't listen."

"Not true. I listened but didn't agree with you. In fact, I thought you'd be pleased to have Gus's infusion of cash so you'd still have a pension."

Next to me, Colin stiffens. But he's smart enough to know my 403b isn't really part of this argument.

I shake my head. "I wasn't willing to sell out the Mambas for Gus's ego trip." Damn. Did I really say that? "I mean, the film."

Matt studies me for a very long thirty seconds, leaving me squirming big-time. "No, I think you meant the Mambas. And I'd very much like to hear how my decision to work with Gus is selling them out."

Colin wraps his hands around his mug. "May I?"

"By all means." Matt leans against the back of his chair.

"Some of Gus's history with the Mambas is less than stellar. There have been rumors of sexual 'favors' demanded. And one of the women died under mysterious circumstances. No one's accusing him, at least not openly, but he didn't push for an investigation."

"Oh, hell!"

"Indeed. And as I'm sure you'll understand, the Mambas weren't keen to work with him on the film. Quite honestly, if they'd known he was to be a part of it, they wouldn't have signed on in the first place."

Interesting that Colin steers clear of mentioning Gus's

possible involvement with the poachers. Or the rumors he's baiting animals for canned hunts.

Matt looks thunderstruck. "Julia? You knew this? And you didn't say?" The hurt in his voice leaves me feeling absolutely awful.

"I . . . there was . . ." I look down at my mug and wish I could dive in and disappear. *Suck it up and tell him!* "Like Colin said, there were lots of rumors about Gus. But, to be honest, we don't have any proof. Still, I didn't want to take any chances. And, well, I figured if something came to light, proved the rumors were right, I needed a backup. But I should have told you. And I'm sorry."

No one says a word, and I keep my eyes on the fly swimming in my coffee.

Finally, Matt clears his throat. "I think we both screwed up. In the future, let's both stick to what we do best. Although you've definitely got the makings of a director."

I lift my head and see his eyes smiling.

He turns toward Colin. "How sure are you about these rumors related to Gus and the woman?"

"I told you what the Mambas told me. When I came on board, I did call the deputy commissioner of the national police. He was the one who told me there was no investigation into Mercy's death. He also said that Gus hadn't asked for one."

Matt looks troubled. "I don't know Zimbabwean law, but all this seems pretty telling, if not conclusive." He glances over at Natalie. "Liam's over at Buffalothorn."

She offers a tight smile. "Liam is his own man. I've come to realize he does what he wants to do, and he's decided to join Team Gus."

"Okay, then." Matt rubs his hands together. "Are we all good?"

"Except for the bug doing the backstroke in my coffee." I wrinkle my nose.

"Well, get another cup. We've got work to do here. I say we run through the footage we've got and re-block the storyline. No point in using any of the scenes we shot with Gus. At least not if we can avoid them. Agreed?" He looks around the table at each of us in turn. "Okay then, let's get to work. Natalie, do you mind working with us? Colin, you too."

We've just finished a late lunch when Amie calls my cell with an update on Cate. Everyone crowds around as I put the phone on speaker and hold it out in front of me.

"How's the film going?" Sweet of Amie to even think about the movie.

"We should finish soon." Matt actually sounds, dare I say, happy.

"Enough with the film," I say. "How's Cate? Are you in Jo'burg?"

"Yeah, we got here late in the morning. The ambulance was waiting right outside, and the emergency people actually came right out to the plane and then helped with customs and immigration. They were so good."

"You're at the hospital now?" Jeez, I wish she'd quit with all these details, which is totally unfair, I know, because she's doing most of this singlehandedly. But cut to the chase. Please.

"We've been at the hospital for a couple hours. The doctors are with Cate now. They said they'd treat her eyes again. Apparently, they have to do it like twice a day? And it's really painful for her. Even with the meds. I'm . . . uh . . . taking a little break."

"Good." This is Natalie. "Amie, you've got to take care of yourself, too, or you won't be any help to Cate."

"Hey, Amie, it's Julia again. Do you have any idea how long they'll be keeping her?"

"The doctor in charge said he'd talk to me about everything after this first treatment. But from something one of the nurses said, I'm thinking it could be a few days to a week. Oh, sorry, I've got to go. One of the doctors needs to talk to me. I'll call you later."

No matter that the call is finished, I keep holding the phone in front of me. "I was really hoping for something more definitive. And positive. Like, she's feeling a lot better. Or she's got some of her vision back."

Natalie puts her arm around my waist and hugs. "Me, too."

Thirty-Five

After a few more days of filming, Matt and I agree that we still need some aerial footage of the Mambas scouting the savanna, but neither of us is looking forward to going up in a light-wing Cessna. For obvious reasons. Which is exactly why I brought a drone. Colin suggests a place he thinks will work, and the Mambas agree.

We load all our gear in the Mambas' land cruiser and discover there isn't enough room for all of us, so I join Colin in the jeep. We're in the lead, bouncing along the unpaved, rutted roads I've come to know pretty well. The sun is high overhead, heating up the day and bleaching the landscape. The trees and bushes are covered in reddish dust, muddying their green leaves. I've never been here in the wet season, but I can imagine how the rains must wash the savanna clean, turning the bush a vivid green.

Given the climbing temperature, there aren't many animals around. I see a few buffalo and antelope sweating it out in whatever shade they can find. Lions, of course, will wait until sundown and the nighttime chill before venturing out. Passing by a few water holes, I see they've got little to no water left. Mostly mud. Great for an elephant to wallow in. But some of the mud is caked hard. No animals will be coming here anytime soon—not until the rains return in November or maybe December.

"Where are the hippos? And the crocs?" I point toward the dried-up water hole.

"When the water gets too low, they move on. There are boreholes around the park keeping some of the pans supplied with water, like at Marula and Jozi. Animals know they'll have water year-round at those spots. Especially the elies. You can bet Gus has tapped into the aquifer, too."

"So, animals hang out at those water holes?"

"For a few days maybe. Until they eat through all the mopane leaves or whatever's on offer. Then they move on in search of food. And water." Colin glances at me, his brow furrowed. "You worked on the elephant migration documentary. I would've thought you'd know this."

"Remember, that film got cut short. But I do remember elies having to go farther and farther from water holes in search of food until they eventually have to move on to another hole closer to food."

"A real problem for them."

It's a solid hour's drive, and as soon as he pulls to a stop, I smile. "This is perfect! The way the tall grass sweeps across the land, all the way to the trees in the distance."

The land cruiser parks right behind us, and not a minute later, Matt is out of his seat, his right hand on my shoulder. "Great! Don't you think? I can see the shot. From the back, the Mambas walking through the grass toward the trees and finally into those woods." With his left hand, he points to the path he wants the women to take.

I nod. "Exactly what I was thinking."

"You've got the drone?"

"It's with the rest of the gear. To start, I'll get low behind them to shoot the scene. Then I'll use the drone for a second shot to give us a great rising view."

"A drone?" This is from Tonderai.

"Yeah." I point toward the Pelican case still in the vehicle. "Is there a problem?"

"Not if you have a license," he says. "Otherwise they are not allowed in the park. They disturb the animals."

"Lucky for us, I do have a license." I pull it out of my pocket, where it's been waiting for exactly this moment, and hand it over. "The noise bothers me, too. I'll try to limit my use."

Tonderai grins. "The animals thank you."

"Okay then. I'm seeing the opening sequence." Matt at his best. Especially now that I've stepped back to let him do his thing.

Colin leans forward. "You two work well together. That is, when you're not arguing."

"The arguing is all part of the process—the way we find our way to the best film," says Matt as he keeps staring ahead, his eyes composing what he wants to see me shoot. "I'll take practically any amount of it as long as I can work with this woman. She's the best camera in the business."

I flush. "After Cate."

"Nope. There I have to disagree." Matt pats my shoulders. "She's good, but you're better. You get into the flow and live the film."

"Matt—"

"No place for modesty. She agrees."

Even though Matt and I know exactly how we want to shoot this scene, it's still tough going. And the sun isn't doing us any favors. The women line up single file and start walking through the tall grass, purportedly on patrol. I film it, but it doesn't feel right. They do it again, this time with Zinhle in the lead. It doesn't feel any better.

I wave Margaret over. "Is this how you really do a search?"

"A regular patrol, yes, this is how we do things. But if we are searching? No. Then we have one of us on point out front." I note her use of the military term and wonder if that's from Colin. "The rest of us will walk behind." She sweeps her hand across to show me how they'd span out.

"Could you show us?" I watch from behind as Zinhle walks point, then the other three women, each about fifteen feet apart, follow her lead. Better. But it's still not quite there.

Matt steps forward. "I like Zinhle in front. What if only two women walk behind, equidistant from the midpoint." It's not a question. Matt knows what he wants. He sees it now.

And he's right.

Now I need to film it at varying heights. I shorten the legs of the tripod and kneel down on the ground. Then I capture the sequence at regular height. Finally, I set to work on the drone. The first sequence is shot from the drone rising through the air as the women walk toward the trees. The second sequence from on high.

It's a long afternoon of filming and refilming. By the time I finish, it's approaching the golden hour, and the Mambas are dripping with sweat. Everyone's ready to go back to the lodge for sundowners.

"With this light, I think a stop by the elephant cemetery is in order." Colin looks at me, then Matt.

I gulp. "Seriously?"

"It's probably my favorite place in the park."

"Oh, Julia! It is truly wonderful." Margaret smiles coyly.

"Could be worth a visit." Matt takes a step toward the land cruiser. "How far?"

Colin holds up his hands to stop everyone. "I don't think we need all of you. I was thinking Julia could film the light playing off the honeycomb. The rest of you can head back. We won't be far behind."

"Honeycomb?"

Colin's half grin makes me wonder if this little detour has nothing to do with elephants or cemeteries, but is instead a chance for an intimate moment.

Matt waves us off. "Have at it. We'll see you back at the lodge."

We park the jeep on the verge of the road, then hike around a thick patch of buffalo thorn and across the savanna. Rounding another patch of thorned bushes, we're there. One glance and I can see why this is Colin's favorite place. When he first said 'elephant cemetery,' I was picturing something horrific. But this . . . this is peaceful, almost zen-like. Scoured clean by the wind and sand, bleached white by the sun, large elephant bones are scattered across the ground. Even a few large tusks, which have somehow escaped the notice of poachers.

Rifle in his right hand, he drapes his left arm over my shoulders. "You feel it."

"I do."

"Come on. I want you to see the skulls."

I hesitate. All I can envision is bone shattered by a poacher's chainsaw.

"Trust me. I think you'll like this. In fact, I think you'll want to film it."

I take a deep breath and let him guide me to the first of the elephant skulls. Again, not at all what I expected. Skinless, of course, but otherwise the head is intact.

"Look." He points to the honeycomb taking up most of the space inside the skull.

"It really is honeycomb." I kneel down and study it. My camera is out in a flash, and with one of my smaller lenses threaded on, I'm filming. Moving with the trajectory of the lowering sun as it colors the bone gold, then pink, and finally a mellow tangerine, I can only hope I'm capturing what I see and feel. I doubt any poachers have ever been here. This isn't a place of violence, but of peace, of lives long lived. Somehow I know this is where aged elephants choose to lower themselves gently to their knees, roll onto their sides, and die, returning peacefully to the earth.

Having learned the rule of a shoot, Colin is absolutely silent, although I sense he has more to tell me. I keep filming until the sun kisses the horizon, then dips below, and the sky erupts in orange and pink and red—a glorious display.

Colin touches my shoulder. "We should go. Lions like this place, too, and will soon be on the prowl. We don't want to run across any of them."

I slip the SD card out of my camera, clutch it tight, then deposit it in my zippered pocket alongside the flash drives— a little ritual I always follow at the end of the final shoot. I'll upload today's film to the computer when we get back to the lodge. Then I pack my gear into the case. One more glance around. I don't want to leave, although I know he's right. We don't need to run into any predators tonight. Not after this.

Back at the jeep, I stow the case as usual behind my legs. Colin keys the ignition and pulls forward a few yards, only to brake. Another few yards, then he taps the brakes again.

"What's up?"

He scowls. "The brakes feel soft."

"They were okay before. Weren't they?"

"Most definitely. Otherwise I wouldn't have brought you here. I'll have Dabs check them in the morning."

We start back, Colin driving a bit more slowly than on our ride out to the cemetery. And now, of course, it's dusk. Night will be falling fast. At least the headlights are still working, which is how we see the big bull elephant blocking the road ahead as we round a bend on a fairly gentle downward slope. He doesn't move.

Colin pumps the brakes and finally jams the pedal to the floor. The jeep doesn't stop, doesn't even slow down, which agitates the elephant. Colin pulls the emergency brake. Nothing. He downshifts into second, the gears grinding loudly. Then into first, and the noise is worse.

The elie's trunk is in the air, and he's bellowing angrily, waving his head back and forth, looking for all the world like he might charge us.

Shit! Now what do we do?

Ram into the elie, or drive off the road and down the steeper slope I can just barely make out? One last attempt to stop: Colin slams the jeep into reverse, but we're too close to the edge.

"Hang on!" His hands are locked on the steering wheel.

We rocket down the slope.

Clip the edge of a boulder.

Spin in a circle. A full 360.

Somehow, Colin manages to keep the jeep from rolling over. But we do keep sliding forward until we finally come to a stop maybe ten feet from a large water hole, our front tires mired in mud.

Thanks to my death grip—one hand on the door handle, the other on the dashboard—I'm still in the jeep, although my upper arm is aching, bruised I'm sure. At least nothing's broken. And Colin's still behind the wheel. But there's no mistaking the fact that he's groaning in pain.

"Colin?"

"I may have clipped my shoulder." He turns toward me— as much as he can, which only causes him to groan again.

Unclipping my seat belt, I angle closer to check out his shoulder, but it's way too dark for me to see much. Pulling my cell out of my hip pocket, I tap on the flashlight and now can see his right arm dangling loose down at his side. I touch it gently only to have him yelp.

"Damn, Colin! This is bad. I've got to get you to the hospital."

"Could be tough. This jeep's not going anywhere. Let's see if we can get Barbara to circle back for us." He tries the radio. No reception. Not even a crackle of static. Dead. He tries again. "Something's wrong."

"No shit."

"That, too. But the radio should be operational. It's designed to withstand an accident and is the main way we get help out here. Unless someone cut the wire. Along with the brake line and the emergency brake."

Shivers of fear ripple up my arms. "Someone wants to make damn sure we don't get back to the lodge."

"Looks like it."

"But who would do that? And when?"

"Who? I've got my ideas. As to when?" He shrugs, which causes him to wince in pain. "Maybe while we were at the elephant cemetery. But I didn't try the radio until just now. So it could've been cut earlier. Same with the brake line. A slow leak."

"The only thing we really know is that we've got to get the hell out of here. What if we deflate the tires a bit? That may help us get out of the mud."

He looks impressed. "How do you know to do that?"

"My brother was a Navy SEAL."

"A good idea." Colin shakes his head. "But we still don't have any brakes." He reaches across and rubs my shoulder. "You have any reception on your cell?"

I try Tonderai's number. Nothing. "What's Margaret's number?" I tap the number as he recites it. Nothing. "Let's try yours."

One-handed, he digs his phone out of his breast pocket and passes it to me. The same result. No reception.

"So, what're we going to do?"

"I figure we've got two options. Sit here and wait for someone to find us. Eventually either Tonderai or the Mambas will realize we're missing—"

"Unless Tonderai thinks I've gone to Msasa, and the Mambas assume you're staying with me at Marula."

He takes a deep breath, which ends in a groan. "There is that."

"What's the second option?"

"Depends on how good you are with a rifle."

"Excuse me?" I stare at him. "Maybe you should know I've never even touched a gun."

He doesn't laugh. "Spend any time out in the bush, shooting a gun is the first thing you're going to have to learn how to do. Anyway, the second option is we walk."

That stops me. "Um . . . in case you haven't noticed, it's dark . . . and there are lions out there."

"And a lot of other predators. As well as elies and other animals we don't particularly want to run into. At least the snakes won't be out."

Both incredibly lousy options. I let them spin in my brain. "Lions probably won't be deterred by the jeep, will they." It's not a question.

"We'd be fine in the large safari land cruiser—they couldn't care less. The jeep, though . . ."

"Nevertheless, I vote for staying put. And you giving me a crash course with that gun of yours."

"Wise choices."

I reach for my camera case to move it into the back seat. "Shit!"

"What?"

"The camera case is gone."

"It probably went flying when we clipped the rock."

"Meaning it's back near the hill." I sigh. At least I've got some idea where to look.

Something very big splashes in front of us, and in the one headlight that's still working, I see a hippo surfacing. A moment later, he roars his displeasure at us for invading his territory. Another hippo rises out of the water and bellows. Then a third. Oh God! What else can go wrong? Hippos like to venture out of the water at night to feed on the grass. In the back of my mind, a disturbing thought rears: hippos kill more people on this continent than any other animal.

Then comes the crunch of boots on dry grass and pebbles. I whip my head around, and there behind us is Gus Sinclair. "A bit of a mishap, Tremblay?"

Thirty-Six

"Thank God you're here. We need help." Training my cell phone flashlight on Gus, I see he's got his hunting rifle in one hand and my camera case in the other. And something on his wrist that glints momentarily when the beam illuminates it. His copper bracelet.

Gus sets the camera case on the ground. "You two are damn lucky to still be alive. Bad luck, though, losing your brakes." He leans into the jeep and, before either Colin or I can react, grabs the rifle off the dashboard, then tosses it clear of the vehicle.

There's only one way Gus could know what caused the accident. He fucking cut the brake line. Or ordered one of his men to do it. And probably disabled the radio and installed some kind of GPS tracking device while he was at it.

Which means he wants us dead. But why?

It can't possibly be because I turned down his advances. More likely this has something to do with me filming Tracker at the *shebeen* in the village—even though I didn't actually get him on film. But Gus doesn't know that. I'm guessing he thinks I've got footage of him recruiting local men to help poach animals in the park. And Gus sure as shit wouldn't want anyone seeing that footage because then he'd be implicated as well. A jailing offense, I'm sure.

Damn. Colin and I are in trouble. Deep, serious trouble.

Knowing I've got one chance to play this right, I shine the flashlight onto the ground by his feet. "Oh, great! You found my camera case." Then I let the beam wander up to his left wrist. The copper bracelet glints in the light. What the hell am I doing? Colin is seriously injured and needs medical care now. So why am I mesmerized by a bit of copper?

And suddenly, I know. Six years ago, I saw a very similar gleam of light in the early morning—pyrite, I thought at the time. Mercy saw it, too, and knelt down to check it out. But when she stood up, the gleam stopped. Maybe the sun had shifted. Or, more likely, Mercy had pocketed it. Gus's bracelet. The proof that Gus had been there with the poachers who shot down the Cessna. Who executed Kyle. I'd bet anything she used that bracelet to blackmail him. And that's what got her killed.

Turning off the phone's light, I manage to scroll to what I hope is the record button and, as unobtrusively as possible, I press it. Then slowly, slowly, I slip my hand between the seats and put the cell on the floor in back of us.

Picking up my camera case, Gus slams it against the driver's door—right next to Colin—causing both of us to jump. "Julia, you really should take better care of your gear. Don't imagine you'll ever be able to use this again." Finished, he slams it to the ground, then turns back to us. "I see you're interested in my bracelet." He seems to expect me to answer.

Colin twines his fingers around mine, holding fast to my hand and keeping it low—out of Gus's sight.

"It's beautiful." I try hard to keep my voice steady, but his throwing around my camera has me freaked out. "I . . . uh . . . first noticed it when we were eating dinner at River Lodge. The carvings are exquisite. Shona, I think?"

"Very good. I'm surprised you know that. Grace gave me this."

"Grace?" From the way he says her name, it's clear they have much more than a business relationship going on.

"Grace Gwanzura. We try to keep her presence at Buffalothorn a secret. Her husband wouldn't like word getting out."

"Her husband?"

"The deputy commissioner of the national police—Simon Gwanzura. He knows, of course, what Grace is doing here. And as long as she's discreet, he doesn't put up a fuss. I'm equally sure Mr. Gwanzura likes the money she brings in." He says Gwanzura's name and title as if he knows the man has brought him immunity from any prosecution. "The name probably doesn't mean anything to you. But I bet Tremblay knows. Don't you, old chap?"

But he's wrong. I do know that name. Because Tonderai took a call from Simon Gwanzura the morning we were rushing to the crash site. He's the man who told Tonderai to stand down, to stay away from the site. We didn't, of course.

The deputy commissioner knows his wife is having some sort of relationship with Gus. Sex? Pimping women for his pleasure? Poaching for sure. And I'd bet anything that poaching—and selling the harvested ivory on the black market—is where Gus got the money to build his lodge and start running his canned hunts.

"It's really too bad you noticed the bracelet." Gus doesn't sound in the least sorry. In fact, his voice is getting harder and more threatening. "This is going to be such a waste of a beautiful woman. And I do prefer to fuck women first—before they die. Even Mercy. She found the bracelet at the crash site. Knew right away it was mine and demanded money. For her kids, she said. Her mistake."

Oh, God! This is the water hole where Gus fed Mercy to the giant croc. My stomach roils. If Colin weren't holding onto my hand, I might well turn and run into the night. And get all of three steps before this monster brought me down with a bullet in my back. But there's no way I'd leave Colin here. So, we're both going to die. That's the only possible explanation for why Gus is telling us about Grace and Mercy. Because very soon, we're going to be dead. I raise my eyes. And there, over his shoulder in the distance, the far distance, I see a pair of lights moving slowly up and down. Headlights, I'm sure. Could it possibly be the Mambas? Or more likely Tracker, coming to help Gus finish us off—the headlights on his vehicle bobbing along the rutted road.

Banking on the lights belonging to the Mambas, I do what I can to stall. "There's something I don't understand. Why did you buy me a drink at the InterCon? In fact, why were you even there?"

He laughs. "I heard you were coming back to make the documentary, and I couldn't let that happen. The last thing I wanted was more attention on the Mambas and the poaching in Hwange. And I sure as hell didn't want you digging into what happened in 2017. So, I arranged to pick up my guests in Jo'burg. I figured if I took care of everything far enough away, no one would ever suspect. I mean, people disappear all the time in South Africa. Why not you? I had it all planned: only I ended up with your little friend."

"But not in bed."

He scoffs. "She gave me everything I wanted—all the details on where you'd be and when. Then I was able to convince your idiot director to put me in the film."

Colin turns as best he can to face Gus. A huge effort on his part. "But what was the point? Why not just lay low?" His voice sounds weak—a lot weaker than I want it to be.

"Tremblay finally speaks," Gus sneers. "Why the hell do you think? I couldn't count on her and the Mambas not to uncover evidence. And then, there she was in the village when Tracker was meeting with the men. After that, all I had to do was wave some money in Matt's face. As producer, I would've been in position to scuttle the film. Or at the very least, get a hold of those SD cards."

I follow my hunch. "So, you persuaded Liam to do your dirty work and steal the SD cards?"

"It wasn't hard. A glass of cognac and a cigar. He was eager to help."

Keep him off balance! Do something unexpected! I laugh. Which really does surprise him.

"You find this amusing?"

"What you don't know about SD cards is pretty damn funny." Another glance over his shoulder, and I see the lights are definitely getting closer. If I can stall him just a little longer. *Oh please, let it be the Mambas.*

But then, they disappear. And I can't hear the engine. Oh, God. Whoever that was has turned away.

He looks perplexed for all of two seconds. "What's so goddamned funny?"

"You think all that pounding destroyed the card?" The words are out of my mouth before I realize he could well open the case and discover the SD card isn't there. Then he'll come after me. A strip search first. Then God only knows.

He doesn't totally surprise me when he loads another cartridge, cocks the gun, and swings his rifle into place, bracing it against his shoulder and pointing it at me. "You've wasted enough of my time. Out of the jeep!"

I'm not about to get out. At least not without a fight. "No."

"I told you to get out. Do it now, or I shoot Tremblay—put him out of his misery." He brings his gun way too close to Colin's head.

"Leave her out of this!" Colin squeezes my hand, then lets go and silently unsheathes a knife from his boot.

"Now, Julia." Gus's voice is scary cold.

Come on, Colin! Do your special forces thing!

"Stop stalling! Get over here now, you bitch!"

Stomach roiling, knees weakening, I lean against the jeep door and slowly climb out. Then I take a step toward the front of the jeep and stop.

"Now!" Gus yells.

"The back," Colin says at nearly the same time. Then to Gus, "Sinclair! Let her go. You want to kill someone, kill me." Opening the door, he lunges out, doing his best to swing around, slashing at Gus with the knife.

Gus looks at his slashed sleeve and laughs. "I expected more fight from you, Tremblay. But no worries. You'll be right behind her. Not in the water hole, though. Reggie will be along soon. He hasn't eaten in a few days, so he's very hungry." He steps closer to the jeep, swings his gun around, and coldcocks Colin on the side of the head.

Horrified, I stop in my tracks. "You're sick!"

"Time's up, Julia!" Gus strides around the back of the

jeep—gun in one hand, my camera case in the other. "You think your SD card is funny? Watch what I do to your documentary." He slams the case against my arm.

The pain has me gasping for breath. No way can I even think about wrestling him for the gun. Then, I watch in disbelief as he hurls the case out into the middle of the water hole. "Now, for the part that's going to really make me laugh because it's so damn funny . . . you're going to take a swim because you're desperate to rescue your camera and your precious movie. If anyone asks, that's what I'll tell them." Gus aims at my camera case floating in the middle of the water and shoots.

Clutching my bruised arm, I'm still trying to pull air into my lungs when the water hole comes alive with hippos splashing and bellowing. And off to the side, the giant bull who left the pond earlier is venting his fury. Apparently, hippos don't like the sound of gunshots, and their unearthly roars are making that clear.

Then, suddenly, they're at the water's edge, more hippos than I thought could fit in this water hole. A solid wall of hippos.

They can't be more than twenty feet away, and this close, they look god-awful huge.

Rearing back their heads, they open their mouths and bellow, their huge tusks visible even in the low moonlight.

The giant bull moves closer, his body tensing.

Gus quickly loads another cartridge and trains his gun on them.

And then, the hippos charge.

Oh my God! So frigging many animals. The ground literally trembles beneath their weight.

But it's not the hippos who get to us. As quickly as they start their charge, they stop short when they hear the loud crack of the gunshot from the far side of the water hole.

I absolutely freeze in place as Gus falls backward, his rifle skittering out of reach. Moaning, he looks up to me, reaches for me, begging for help.

A few seconds later, a croc—the biggest I've ever seen—rounds the front corner of the jeep, flipping his powerful tail wide and slashing Gus across his lower legs. Opening his mouth, the croc growls, then hisses, making sure I stand back.

An instant later, his mighty jaws clamp down on Gus's bloody legs, calling forth an unearthly scream.

Staggering, I haul myself through the open passenger door and listen to the Mambas' long, wavering ululation.

In front of us, the hippos move back, giving the croc an open path to the water.

Thirty-Seven

Another twin bed, this one in a private room at Victoria Falls Hospital where early this morning a very competent doctor was able to maneuver Colin's shoulder joint back into position and repaired some torn ligaments. That came after a pretty wild drive through the night with Dabs at the wheel. The lights I saw over Gus's shoulder turned out to be the Mambas with Tonderai and our crew along with Dabs in a second vehicle. Thank God it wasn't Tracker or any of the poachers Gus and Grace were running.

Wearing their night vision goggles, a few of the Mambas made their way around the water hole.

Margaret took the shot.

The guys were able to get Colin up the hill to one of the vehicles. Then we drove hours through the night, getting to Vic Falls sometime after midnight. The Mambas stayed behind to secure the site and search for anyone else who might've been there to help Gus. Shoot to kill being their motto. Whether or not that's legal.

Gus stayed behind, too. Whatever was left of him. Somewhere at the bottom of the water hole.

Colin's sleeping off the anesthesia now, his right arm

immobilized in a brace, an ice pack on his shoulder. I'm curled next to him, nursing my own bruised arm. My only movement—patting my zippered pants pocket to make sure I still have my SD card, my flash drives, and the cell phone with Gus's last half hour of ravings. I haven't listened to it yet and don't plan to. But something tells me there may well be an investigation this time, and I want to be prepared. Apparently, my slight hand tap is all it takes to rouse the man.

"Hey." He sounds groggy.

"You're awake," I whisper. No point alerting the nurses or anyone else out in the hall that the patient has come around. "How are you doing?"

"Me?" I nearly snort out the word. "You're the one who had surgery. How are *you* feeling?"

"It hurts like hell. Even with the painkillers."

"How's your head?"

"Not so great. But I asked about you." He presses a kiss to the side of my head. "I'm so bloody sorry about what happened last night. I should have protected you. And, on top of everything, you lost your camera."

"Hey, you're alive. And I'm fine." I snuggle against him. "And don't worry about the camera. It's insured, although proving it's at the bottom of a water hole with a giant croc could be a challenge."

"I'm your witness."

"I may need to take you up on that. I'm sure the insurance company will be in touch." I turn to look at him.

Another kiss. This one on my lips.

"Did you sleep?" He sounds dubious. As well he should.

"Not so much."

"Because..." He threads his left arm around my shoulders.

I take a deep breath. "I'm sure you can figure it out."

"He was a predator, Julia. And he wanted to kill you." His voice cracks on the last few words.

"Yeah, well . . . that's definitely part of why I can't sleep."

"What's the other part?"

Another deep breath, and with this one, I shudder all the way down to my toes. "Every time I close my eyes, all I can see is that croc chomping down on Gus's leg. Then I hear his screams. And part of me is terrified about how that was what happened to Mercy and could've happened to me."

He holds me close to his side, both of us taking care to avoid me knocking against his right arm. "I saw that old croc slither out of the water and park himself in front of the jeep. And I was pretty sure Gus didn't notice him."

"Which is why you told me to go around the back?" I push myself up onto my elbow and gently, oh so carefully press my lips against his. And despite his pain, he's able to kiss me back.

Until some part of my brain hears the door click shut, and I realize Colin and I aren't the only people in this room. The doctor who patched up Colin's shoulder, a white lab coat over his green scrubs, stands at the foot of the bed.

Cheeks flaming, I roll off the bed and retreat to the nearby chair.

"Mr. Tremblay." The doctor chuckles. "I'm glad to find you feeling better. How is your pain?"

Colin grins. "Manageable."

The doctor smiles his appreciation. "Good. I think you will heal well as long as you wear the brace, apply ice, and do not put any strain on your arm." The way he says 'any strain' makes it very clear what kind of physical pressure he means.

"I'll do my best."

"The stitches can come out in ten days. Six to eight weeks to heal completely."

Six to eight weeks. The timeline knocks me sideways. Six weeks from now, I'll be back in Milwaukee. In the classroom. Finishing my tenure documents to meet the deadline. And far away from Zimbabwe. And from Colin. My heart tightens.

The doctor brings his hands together. "So long as you understand me. And now, there is someone waiting to see you."

He leaves the room only to have the door open again. A man in a khaki dress uniform, medals emblazoned across the chest of his jacket, his hat under his arm, stands in the doorway. If I had to guess, I'd say this is Deputy Commissioner Simon Gwanzura of the national police in person. A dramatic pose. He then crosses the room and stands at the foot of the bed, exactly where the doctor just stood.

"Mr. Tremblay."

"Deputy Commissioner. Sir." Colin wriggles to the side of the bed, and despite his hospital gown, he clearly intends to stand.

"Please, sir." Gwanzura waves him back onto the bed. "There is no need for you to stand. I have been informed of your accident. I believe the lady was also involved. As was Gus Sinclair."

Although he's looking at Colin, I answer. "Yes, I was."

He clears his throat. "You must understand that this is all highly irregular. Mr. Sinclair, of course, was Zimbabwean. But Mr. Tremblay, although you are a resident of Zimbabwe, I believe you are also still a citizen of Great Britain. And the lady is from the United States. This could create quite the diplomatic snafu."

"Yes, sir." Colin may be retired military, but he's military all the same.

"It would help me a great deal if you could tell me what happened out there in Hwange. It would be even better if you have any evidence."

I blink. Seriously? We barely escaped with our lives.

Colin pauses for a very long minute, clearly thinking through everything, hoping to remember something that will stand up in court. "Other than my word as a former British army officer, I'm not sure I have the proof you would like. Of course, the guides from the lodge and the women in the Mambas saw the aftermath." Interesting that he doesn't mention Margaret having shot Gus before the croc dragged him into the water.

"I have spoken to them, and they all agree on the particulars."

Pushing myself to my feet, I unzip my pants pocket and pull out my cell phone. "Would it help to have a recording of what Gus Sinclair said to us?"

Colin manages not to gape.

But the deputy commissioner is truly surprised. "You have a recording?"

"I can't vouch for the sound quality."

"You have not listened to it?"

I meet his eyes. "It's pretty gruesome."

He takes my phone and slips it into his jacket pocket. "You will both remain in Zimbabwe until we have resolved this issue." Not waiting for us to respond, he turns on his heel and leaves the room.

Tonderai arranges a room for us at one of the sister lodges—Zambezi Sands, right on the river. We have a spacious Bedouin tent with its own plunge pool. Not that Colin can do more than dangle his legs in the water.

Matt stops by to leave my duffel and backpack and to let me know my camera case is still somewhere at the bottom of the water hole. With what remains of Gus. He offers to stay, but knows full well we want to be alone. "I've got the rest of the gear, including your laptop. Never fear, I'll ship everything back to you. Natalie says goodbye for now. She caught an earlier flight."

"With Liam?" I ask.

He laughs. "I doubt it. That ship has sailed."

"Smart move on her part."

He rubs his hands together. "Okay, I'm off to Jo'burg, then. According to Amie, Cate's chomping at the bit to head home."

"Can she?" It's beyond me how she'll manage on her own without being able to see.

"In the next few days. Lisa's due in tonight—"

"Who?" I interrupt.

"Lisa Connelly. The actress." Matt shoots me a look that tells me how out of it I am. "Cate's partner. Meanwhile, Amie and I have tickets on the Delta flight to Atlanta tomorrow night. Then I'll head on to LA."

"Cate has a partner?"

"She doesn't advertise it, but I thought she would've told you." He shrugs. "Look, I'll be in touch in a couple weeks. But rest assured, we've got something here."

"You really think so?" After everything that's happened, I honestly don't have any sense of what we've got.

"Trust me." He pats the laptop.

We don't have to wait long for another visit from the national police. Two days later, Simon Gwanzura himself stops by our breakfast table in the main lodge.

"Ms. Wilde." He hands me my cell phone. "You are very fortunate the police were able to locate your phone. Something like this is very valuable."

"You listened to the recording?"

"Excuse me?" His face is bland. "What recording?"

What is he talking about? I know I got Gus's full confession on that phone. So maybe the quality isn't great, but the commissioner should be able to hear something. Then I begin to understand. This is all about giving the commissioner and his wife deniability. I'd bet anything the recording has been wiped off the phone.

I open my mouth to respond, but under the table, Colin puts his hand on my thigh, which I take to mean *Shut the fuck up.*

I wave away my words. "Sorry. I was obviously thinking about something else."

"I trust you have enjoyed your stay in Zimbabwe. Please come again."

After he leaves, I ask Colin what I really want to know. "What about Grace?"

He laughs. "I'm bloody glad you didn't ask Gwanzura. There are some things you don't ask a man—one being whether he's going to welcome back his cheating wife."

"I wasn't thinking about that part of it."

"Then what?"

"According to Gus, Grace was an equal partner in the poaching, and I'm betting the deputy commissioner knew all about it."

His eyes light up. "You're thinking that Gwanzura has been taking a cut?"

"Gus said as much."

He processes this new idea and then, looking me in the eyes, nods. "It makes sense. It was Gwanzura who personally stopped the investigation into the plane crash that killed your crew. And even though Gus refused to ask for an investigation into Mercy's death, I'm sure the deputy commissioner knew about it. Greed is a powerful motivator."

I pick up my cell and bring up my recordings. Just as I thought. Gone.

"Well?" Colin leans closer.

"Deleted."

"An easy way to wrap up his investigation."

Although one of the lodge guides offers to take us on a game drive later in the morning, we beg off and retreat to our tent, where Colin shows me how much fun we can have despite his right arm being immobilized in a brace. Quite an array of positions he's able to manage with a clipped wing.

It's late afternoon and time for sundowners when we finally decide to talk about the inevitable. He wraps his left arm around me and pulls me close enough to kiss the side of my head. "So."

"Yeah?"

"You're free to go."

"Legally, yes."

"Could you stay longer?"

I've been thinking about this question for the last two days and haven't come up with an answer that makes me happy. But Colin deserves to know. "The semester's about to start. And I've got to get my tenure documents together."

"Tenure." The way he says the word makes it sound so permanent—and not in a good way.

"My life is in the States."

"Is it?"

Oh, please, let's not argue. Not now. "That's not really fair. I mean, this has been wonderful. Being with you. Making another film. But my job is in Milwaukee."

"Does it have to be? I've watched you come alive the last couple weeks. What if you go back to movie-making?"

"Not the most secure career—as I all too painfully found out."

"So, financial security is what's most important to you?" He actually sounds disappointed.

"Hey, come on. I've got this habit called eating." I try to lighten the growing tension, but he's clearly not buying it. So, I pause, thinking about the options in front of me. Then twine my fingers around his. "Damn it, Colin. It's not the most important thing to me, and you know it. I gave you my pension for the Mambas. And—" My chest tightens as he pushes himself off the bed and walks across the room. What's happening here?

A minute later, he's back, tossing his Mambas shirt to me. "Could you unbutton the pocket? I can't quite manage."

I do. He digs out my five credit cards and hands them to me with a dramatic flourish.

Staring at them for a moment in confusion, I finally figure it out. "The charges went through? It sure took a long time."

"Nah. I never did it. The Mambas refused."

"But why?"

"Because Margaret told me that they look on you as a kindred spirit. I meant to give them back days ago, but . . . well . . . here they are."

A bit of financial security in my hands, I close my eyes. Can I walk away from my life in Milwaukee? From everything that's familiar? I barely know this man. It's too much of a leap. "Do you?"

"Do I what?" His voice is gruff. Total military.

"Look on me as a kindred spirit?" Oh, God. I hope I haven't taken this too far.

"Julia." He puts his left hand on my cheek. "You have to ask?"

Thirty-Eight

Milwaukee, Wisconsin – September 2023

Before classes start in September, I take Amie out to dinner at my favorite place in the Third Ward. Jing's. Great Shanghainese food. And, standing inside the door, a life-size terra cotta Chinese warrior that never fails to send chills up my spine—in a good way. I first discovered the restaurant a few weeks after I moved to Milwaukee and have been a regular ever since. Amie sounded a bit reluctant to go when I invited her, which leaves me baffled. I mean, we've eaten here before, and Jack has even cooked special dishes especially for us. It's nothing to do with the food, though, I find out as soon as we sit down at my corner table.

She rips open her package of chopsticks, snaps them apart, and scrapes them one against the other to smooth away any possible splinters. But she doesn't stop—just keeps scraping and scraping. After two minutes, I call a halt. "Tell me what's bothering you."

"I don't know how to tell you."

"Try?" I keep my voice calm, even though I sense she's about to hurl a grenade onto the table.

"Okay, okay. Please don't be mad." She takes a deep breath and looks past me toward the kitchen door. "I'm dropping out of the program. I withdrew from my courses today."

All I can do is gape. "I thought you liked the program."

"I do. And I really liked working with you this summer. But the thing is, I learned I'm not a cinematographer. And I never will be."

"Whoa! You're not a cinematographer yet. That's why you're in school—learning to become one." I wonder if I've got any chance of convincing her to change her mind. Damn, I'd bet anything Cate talked to her, even though she promised to leave it to me.

She's back to polishing her chopsticks. "No, I don't think so." Her voice is firm, decided. She doesn't sound at all regretful about leaving, only nervous about having to tell me. And she could've left without letting me know. Just disappeared.

"Last spring you were really psyched about the program. What changed?"

She waves toward the kitchen door—probably at Jack or Jing herself—then forces herself to look at me. "When we were in Zimbabwe, I watched you. Day in and day out. You've got an eye, a sixth sense about what will make a great shot and how to capture it. Like a superpower. You were living and breathing cinematography. Even Cate was shaking her head at the things you were coming up with. I'm never going to be able to do that."

"Amie, it's not a competition." I bite my lower lip because I know that's not true. In this business, it absolutely is a competition. For every job. For every camera position. Especially for women.

"That's not exactly what I mean."

"What do you mean?"

"I want to do something that brings me alive—the way cinematography does for you. And while we were in Zimbabwe, I learned what I'm really good at."

I look at her expectantly. "Which is?"

"Animals. Veterinary medicine. And well . . . you know . . . I've got an undergrad degree in biology, so . . . I'm going to apply to vet school."

"Great idea. Congratulations." I smile. But damn, she makes it sound so easy to figure out what she wants to do—and then go for it. Then, the practical, professor side of me rears its head. "But you won't start vet school until next year, right? Why not finish your MFA?"

Eyes averted. More polishing. "Because it's not me. And to be honest, I don't want to be a cinematographer. I've landed a job at the zoo working with large animals. Plus, some part-time work in a vet clinic." She looks back at me, her eyes desperate for my approval.

What can I do but agree. "Both those jobs will enhance your application."

"And I'll earn some money." She looks down at her chopsticks.

"You know, it takes a lot of courage to walk away even when you know it's the right thing to do. I really think you're going to be a lot happier." I hear the echo of Solomon Mkhwananzi's words after he threw the bones for me. *You need to decide what would make you happier than you are now.* I'd bet anything he said the same thing to Amie. The only difference: she listened.

She stops rubbing her sticks together and smiles. "Really? You think so?"

"I do. You've made a good decision."

"Oh, thank you. I've been so scared to tell you, what with your tenure . . ."

"No worries whatsoever. Now, can we order? I'm thinking of soup dumplings, Singapore noodles, and steamed fish. Does that work for you?"

She nods happily.

Meanwhile, the grenade Amie tossed has landed me with a pretty serious problem. My one and only grad student has dropped out of the program. I can't imagine my tenure committee is going to look on this favorably.

Combing my fingers through my hair, I stare at the tenure documents spread across my desk—the section I'd already written about my mentoring graduate students. Obviously, I've got to revise, but how the hell can I possibly spin Amie's decision to leave in a positive light? Or maybe I should avoid it altogether. Probably not a good option.

That's the moment my cell phone rings, vibrating its way across the desktop.

Colin. Oh, God. Exactly the person I need to talk to.

"Hey. I'm so glad you called."

"Hey yourself." His warm voice wraps around me. "How are the tenure documents coming?"

I don't say anything, and the silence between us grows.

"What happened?" His voice is all compassion.

Tears are threatening—enough that my voice wobbles. "I thought I was finished. Or close to it. Then I took Amie out to dinner last night."

"Why am I thinking things went sideways?"

"Because they did. She quit the program."

He waits a few seconds. "Did she tell you why?"

I grab a handful of tissues and wipe my tears, thankful we're not video calling so I can spare him my ugly cry. "Yeah, she explained. And it's all completely reasonable."

"You going to tell me?"

"Amie decided—actually, Cate would say she finally woke up to the fact—that she's not cinematographer material."

"Then it's a good thing. For Amie, that is."

"Of course it's a good thing for her. Although she's only been at this for a year. She could've developed."

"You think she would've?"

I shrug—something else he can't see. "Yes. I don't know. Maybe?" I wait a couple seconds, trying to gain some objectivity. "Cate would say no."

"Does she have any idea what she's going to do? Wait, let me guess—something to do with animals. Veterinary medicine?"

My mouth drops open. "How the hell did you know?"

"Tonderai told me that she talked about it with him. Apparently, every time she was dealing with animals, that's when she came alive. And look how she stepped up with Cate. She's a natural. I'm kind of surprised you didn't see it."

"I did. I just didn't put it together. What can I say? When I'm in the field, I'm pretty focused. The rest of the world kind of falls away."

"Which is one of the things I love about you."

I sniffle back a few more tears. "You're incredible. Here I am totally centered on me, completely selfish, and you make it into a positive."

"Selfish? What are you talking about?"

"I kind of tried to talk her into finishing her degree. More for my sake than hers. My chairman and the dean have already told me it was my job to convince her to stay in the program. Something about needing graduate students to keep the department afloat. They pretty much said that the tenure committee could rip me apart over this."

"Seriously? Your tenure depends on Amie staying with the program?"

"Sounds pretty crazy, but getting tenure is a brutal undertaking. Especially these days. So, yeah, the committee isn't going to be happy about this." I take a deep breath. "I didn't hound her, though. It was really clear she's much happier having made this decision. So, I told her she did the right thing. And that she was brave to do it."

"Even though it could end up costing you."

"Yeah . . . well."

"Courageous."

I smile. "She really is."

"I wasn't talking about her."

Thirty-Nine

Matt calls at the end of September to let me know the editing on the film is complete. "It's only twenty-seven minutes, that's without credits, but it's solid. Better than solid. One of the best films I've worked on. I think we should consider entering it in some film festivals. Let's see if we can get it in at Sundance."

I sit down hard on the singularly uncomfortable chair in my office. "Seriously?"

"Oh, yeah. The Mambas steal the show, but it's a great story, and your camera work is phenomenal. I just sent it to your email. Take a look and get back to me as soon as you can. Natalie's free this week and next, and I want to get the voice-over done."

I spend the afternoon watching *The Women Who Stand Between*. Five times. Then, I watch it again. And I can't find a single thing I want to change. But the first person I call to tell isn't Matt. It's Colin. His phone is ringing before I remember he's seven hours later than me, which puts him close to midnight.

Three rings and he's on the line. "Julia?"

"Hey. Sorry for calling so late. How are you? Are you out of the shoulder brace yet?"

"In bed. Wishing you were here. Still wearing the brace. Probably another week or two." He pauses for a moment, as if he's trying to suss out what to ask me. "You good? Tenure documents submitted?"

"I gave them to my department chair yesterday."

"Good. When will you hear?"

"The next step is an interview with the committee sometime this winter."

"They stretch it out, don't they." He laughs, but I can hear the disbelief.

"Oh, yeah. Anything they can do to increase the tension. But look, that's not why I'm calling. I heard from Matt today."

"Ah, the film. How's it coming along?"

"Pretty close to finished. He sent me his cut. Once I approve it, Natalie will record the voice-over. I figure we'll be complete in a few weeks."

"So, what do you think? Approval granted?" His voice is relaxed now. I can picture him lying in bed, one hand behind his head. The other resting across his chest.

"I think it's good. No, it's better than good. It's great. The Mambas are fantastic."

"Are we getting closer to the reason why you called?"

"Ha! Patience, please. Look, this is totally irregular. But I'm wondering if you and the Mambas would consider watching it? I really, really want to make sure we got it right. And you're the people who can tell us."

"I'd love to. I'm sure Margaret and all of the women would, too. But it'll take forever to get here."

"Matt sent it to me on email, and it came through fine."

"Send it. Assuming all is quiet tomorrow, we'll look at it then."

Colin returns the favor of my late-night call by waking me at five in the morning. But unlike him and the Mambas, I'm not ready to leap out of bed and hit the road in search of poachers. In fact, I'm barely coherent.

"They're still crying." His first words.

"Oh, no!" My heart sinks.

"Julia, that's a good thing. You bloody nailed it."

"Really?" I push myself to sit on the edge of the bed. Now that I'm upright, I'm actually processing his words.

"It's perfect. And what's even better—as far as those of us here are concerned—is that you asked us to take a look."

"I . . . uh . . . well, of course."

"I do have one question."

"Shoot."

"What would you have done if we said the film was off?"

I don't have to consider my answer. "Pulled it."

"In spite of everything?"

By 'everything,' I think he means the financing, the loss of my camera—which, thank God, insurance is covering most of—and my tenure. "Of course. I'm not about to put something out there that isn't right. The film has to be authentic. It has to tell the real story about the Mambas."

"It does."

I let my shoulders relax. "Thank God. It means everything to hear you say that."

"I mean every word."

"Oh, I forgot to tell you. The credits aren't there yet. They will be. And the Mambas' names will be listed. And yours. Did we ever agree to that?"

He laughs. "It's in the contract."

Forty

Watching *The Women Who Stand Between* on my laptop doesn't come close to seeing it on the big screen in a packed theater. There isn't a red carpet for the documentary shorts, but I couldn't care less. Just being here and getting front-row seats with Matt and Natalie is more than I ever dreamed would happen. Our film is the last in the lineup, and the ones before us are good. Solid, as Matt would say. As ours is announced and the opening credits roll, my nerves kick into overdrive. I'm about to reach for Colin's hand when I remember I'm sitting next to Matt. I end up clutching my hands into fists so tight that my entire body trembles.

"Relax!" Matt whispers to me. "They're gonna love it."

But I can't. Although I found nothing at all to change before, now I'm worried that I'll see major gaffes as big as Hwange elephants. *Oh, God, please don't let them laugh.*

No one laughs. In fact, no one makes a sound. When I cross my legs, the noise of my slacks rubbing together quite literally seems to fill the theater.

The opening drone shot of the women walking into the

tall grass of the savanna pulls me right in, and I'm following in their footsteps.

Zinhle talks about her daughter.

Pepsi and Barbara laugh in the garden.

Margaret with her dilapidated cardboard suitcase leads the women up the road to headquarters on their first day as Mambas.

They follow Colin in military exercise drills that would've left me panting in the sand.

They zig and zag across the savanna, hunting for poachers who are killing Africa's most endangered species.

The sun sets on women who are struggling to escape abuse, support their children, and save iconic animals.

The closing credits list the names of all the women.

At the end, I'm quite literally in tears.

So is Natalie. "It's so beautiful."

It takes me a minute to realize people are applauding—and not just a polite smattering of hands clapping. On either side of me, Matt and Natalie stand, turning to face the audience. They pull me to my feet and turn me around. That's when I see that everyone in the theater is standing.

Tonight, we're back at the theater for the awards ceremony. I'm not expecting to win. I know it's a total cliché, but seriously, the prestige of getting to launch our film at Sundance is all the award I want. Plus, everyone in the audience knows as well as I do that *Under the Bridge*—the film about homelessness in the US—is going to win. And it should. It's beyond good.

The award for best short documentary is near the end

of the ceremony. Three judges walk onto the stage, and instantly, the entire theater is silent. The head judge lifts the microphone. It doesn't work.

Nervous tittering sweeps through the theater, but I am completely serene. Ready to be the most gracious loser this place has ever seen.

Finally, a festival staffer brings another mic on stage. This one works. Much to everyone's laughing relief.

"Wonderful films, all of these, which of course made our job very difficult." The head judge directs his comments to Matt. Enough said. That was our nod. I know how these award ceremonies work.

The judge reads the names of the five finalists, and we all applaud.

Then he hands the mic and a card to the woman standing next to him, introducing her as Rumbi Sibanda. It takes a moment for her name to click into place, but then it does. She's a filmmaker from Zimbabwe. An amazingly talented woman who's not looking anywhere near me when she says, "I am honored to announce the winner of the best documentary short film—a film about my homeland, Zimbabwe. Although the filmmakers are American, this film is a true collaboration between them and the women from my country who every day risk their lives to protect endangered wildlife from poachers. *The Women Who Stand Between.*" She then goes on to read a statement lauding the film, but I don't hear a word of it.

Again, Matt drags me to my feet.

"What?"

"They're waving us onto the stage."

"You and Natalie," I protest. "Not me."

"Yes, you. You're one of the producers." He grabs my hand, and I take hold of Natalie's.

A minute later, we're standing next to the judges. Looking out on the sea of upturned faces, I find myself on the savanna in Hwange, weaving through the tall grass as the midday sun beats down on me. Off in the distance, I see a maternal herd of elies gathered around a water hole. Two boisterous teenage males play in the water. Young calves lean against their mothers' legs. Newcomers are greeted with joyful trumpeting. Trunks drape over heads and into mouths. A breeze blows past, bringing dust and the musty smell of animals.

Natalie pinches me back to the theater in Park City where the entire audience is still on their feet applauding. Before I realize what's happening, Matt pushes me forward to Rumbi, who hands me the card that announces the winner of Best Short Documentary. *The Women Who Stand Between* is scrolled in the most beautiful calligraphy ever. I smile and thank her, but then—oh, God, no—she hands me the microphone. Am I supposed to have a speech or something prepared? I'm not a director or an actor. I'm a cinematographer and sometimes a camera operator. Until a few months ago, I wasn't even working a camera. I'm definitely not a public speaker.

I wrap my fingers around the mic and stare at the audience, who are rustling themselves back into their seats. What the hell can I say? *As some of you may know, I . . . uh . . . haven't worked as a cinematographer for a few years now. Not since Hal DeBeers and I lost several crew members—Kyle and Brent and Alex—*

No! Definitely not! I mean yeah, a lot of the people in the audience know what happened, and no one spoke up. Not one. If it hadn't been for Cate and Matt, I wouldn't have been able to fight back. But I did, and I'm here.

I tighten my grip on the mic and resolve to be a gracious winner. Thanking everyone I can think of, I save the Mambas for last. "Margaret. Zinhle. Pepsi. Barbara. Filming these four incredibly fierce women in Zimbabwe and telling their stories has given me back my life as a cinematographer. These women fought to regain their lives, which they risk every single day to make sure that endangered wildlife will continue to exist."

Once we're allowed off stage, I step into a whole new world where everyone, including Rumbi Sibanda, wants to talk with me. Me.

Things get even crazier at the after-party. Five glasses of champagne later, and a promise to enter *The Women Who Stand Between* in the Southern Africa Indie Film Festival, Matt and Natalie rescue me from what promises to be a horrific hangover.

Back at our hotel, we celebrate with another bottle of champagne while Matt takes call after call on his cell.

"Congrats, Matt," I say when he finally lets the calls go to voicemail.

"Me? Hell, this is all yours. And you earned every penny." He hands me an envelope.

Opening it, I pull out a bunch of papers. A contract. Glancing down at the bottom line, I try to focus my eyes. And end up blinking several times. I gulp. "Does this really say—"

"Netflix is going to stream the film!" Natalie wraps her arms around me.

"Just awaiting your signature." Matt smiles. "And before you give away all that money, I suggest you pay yourself back the expenses of making the film."

"You're serious? This is mine?" I take another look at the contract clutched in my hand. "I can finally pay the Mambas? But what about you guys?"

Matt carefully takes back the contract before I maul it. "We knew you'd want to pay the Mambas. And just so we're clear, Cate and Natalie and I have already agreed the money is all yours."

No matter that I switched to tonic water somewhere along the line, by the time I make it to my room, I am feeling no pain. And slurring my words a bit—as I discover when I call Colin.

"Festival over?" he asks cheerfully. Like me, he and the Mambas were excited as all get-out to have our film screened.

"Yeah."

"Julia?"

"Sorry, I had a few drinks. Champagne."

"So, that's how the Hollywood bigwigs roll?"

I decide his comment doesn't need an answer. "Oh my God, Colin! We won!"

"What did you say?" I can hear him thunk down onto his chair as clearly as if he were in the room with me.

"*The Women Who Stand Between* won best short documentary! Can you believe it?"

"Bloody hell!" I can see him sitting in his small office on the sandy edge of Hwange, staring at his phone in disbelief.

Then I hear them. The Mambas. Ululating their joy. I want to be there with them, wrapping my arms around them, all of us in a group hug.

"Hey, guys, get this. Netflix is going to pay us to stream the film. You've got twenty-five thousand dollars coming your way."

I hear the cheers erupting.

"Love?" Colin's voice. "How drunk are you?"

"I'll have you know I've been drinking tonic water for the last couple hours," I huff.

"Is it really twenty-five thousand?"

"Yup. Now, I've just got to figure out how to get it to you—what with the mail as dodgy as it is in Zimbabwe."

"I've got a suggestion."

"I was hoping you would."

"Look, before you get too famous and we can't afford to book you, I have a job for you."

That sobers me up completely. "Do tell!"

"I haven't told you before because I was waiting for the official offer, but it looks like I'll be starting a new job."

"What?"

"It'll be closer to Marula Camp. I'll be recruiting and training the Cobras—a group of men who will be protecting the white rhinos."

"Excuse me? There aren't any rhinos in Hwange. The last ones were poached years ago."

"Right you are. But happy days, we've been negotiating with a private reserve in the southeast to bring in a couple of boys—best buddies—to start. To do it right, we're creating a sanctuary of sorts with armed guards. It'll be on community land for the benefit of the local people. We'll hire the Cobras from the nearby villages and train them. That'll be my job."

Now it's my turn to sit down. "But what about the Mambas?"

"Margaret's taking over as supervisor." I can hear the smile in his voice. "It's about time, don't you think? That was always the plan—for one of the Mambas to be in charge, and she's a natural."

"She'll be perfect."

"Back to what I hope will be your role in this. We'll be

transporting the boys in late May and want to film their trip. Think this is something you could do?"

"Oh, Colin!" Could I? Would I? Absolutely.

"Are you saying yes?" He sounds a little nervous. Like I might actually turn him down.

"What do you think?"

Forty-One

Milwaukee, Wisconsin – March 2024

I have no way to gauge how my interview with the tenure committee goes. They're all compliments about *The Women Who Stand Between.* As well they should be. But they aren't in the least impressed that my one and only grad student quit the program.

A few stomach-churning weeks later, Shan Nielsen summons me to his office. His secretary points to the seat directly opposite his closed door. All the better for me to stare at the Department Chair sign.

After fifteen minutes, I'm toying with the idea of leaving and making another appointment when he runs in, his backpack slung over his shoulder. "Sorry to keep you waiting. The dean was long-winded today."

He swings open his door and waves me to the chair in front of his desk. I sit. This meeting doesn't feel good. The vibe is all wrong. Bad news is coming.

Shan drops onto his chair, pulls an envelope from his pack, and places it on top of his desk. I recognize the UW–Milwaukee gold-and-black logo in the upper left corner—my name centered with the words "Personal and Confidential" typed beneath. My tenure decision.

I stare at him expectantly while he draws out the suspense, until finally he pushes himself to his feet, scoops up the envelope, and hands it to me. "Congratulations on receiving tenure. And promotion." Shaking my hand, he smiles warmly. "A unanimous decision, I'm happy to say. But promise me you won't lose any more graduate students."

He had to get that zinger in? "Thanks very much. This means a lot to me." I do my best to sound happy.

Returning to my office, I gently shut the door and open the envelope. Yes, indeed, they have awarded me tenure and promotion. Exactly what I've worked toward. So why am I not feeling happier?

Leaving the building, I glance toward the western horizon. Black clouds closing fast. A spring snowstorm. Just my luck, I walked this morning. It's not more than a mile home, so I should make it before the snow arrives—if I hoof it.

I power walk along Maryland Avenue, down one hill and up the next to Capitol, where I duck into City Market to buy a celebratory treat for tonight. The universe is with me. They've got my favorite Door County cherry pie. I get a wedge to go and continue the last few blocks of Maryland to my little navy-blue bungalow with a front porch that will soon be adrift with snow.

I down the cherry pie along with a pint of vanilla ice cream but don't feel one iota happier, and I'm definitely in no mood to talk with anyone. But everyone knows I was meeting with

Shan today, so they'll be calling. There's only one person I want to talk to. Even though it's after midnight Zim time, I call.

"Colin."

"Hey, I was hoping you'd call."

"I got tenure." My voice sounds way too flat.

"Julia, that's . . . what's wrong? This is what you wanted." He sounds miserable, like he seriously hates the fact that there are eight thousand miles between us, that he can't be here to hold me. I hate it, too.

"I know."

"Talk to me." Hearing his voice helps.

I take a deep breath. "I've been working so hard for this. Everyone—you and the Mambas, Cate and Matt—helped me. And . . ."

"And what?"

"And I'm not happy."

He waits a long ten seconds. "What would make you happy?"

I can see him in his small room at headquarters. The sounds of animals rustling and growling and roaring through the night. The feel of the dust on my skin. God, I love the dust in Zimbabwe. Working on projects that mean something important. "How are things in Hwange? What're you doing?"

He laughs. "I was sleeping."

"Sorry, sorry."

"Talking to you is much better. Hwange is good. The new headquarters is almost finished. Enough so I'm living here now. Did I tell you we're right on the edge of Marula? We're working nonstop getting ready for the rhinos to arrive—the Cobras are still training and fencing in the perimeter in their down time."

"A fence?" Did I know about a fence?

"To keep the rhinos safe. Even though many of the former poachers are now Cobras—"

"Seriously?"

"Regular work and a paycheck will keep their families fed far better than poaching ever did. Gus and Grace paid them a pittance—and sometimes not even that."

"But there are still more poachers?" Damn, will these animals ever be safe?

"There are. And we're committed to keeping these two boys safe—so we can bring in more later on."

"Which explains the fence."

"And the Cobras."

"You're brilliant."

"Feeling better?"

I stare out the French doors into my little back courtyard. So dark. But then, the security light flashes on as some small creature scurries through the mounding wet snow. "Yeah, I am." And I know what will make me happy. But can I possibly walk away from everything I know? "It's hard," I whisper.

He hears me. "Sometimes that's what makes life even better."

Almost as soon as I end my call to Colin, Cate calls. Her vision's improving, but it's been slow, which pisses her off to no end. She doesn't mince words when I tell her about getting tenure but not being thrilled with it. "So, quit!"

"But Cate, you got me this job."

"As a stop-gap. I never thought you'd stay there forever."

"It's a regular income. Security. Which is kind of important since the only job I've got lined up is for Colin."

"Paying you well, is he." It's not a question.

I don't bother to answer.

"Listen to me. Nothing in this life is secure, especially when you're not doing what you really want to do. What you should be doing. You'll get work. I don't have a doubt in the world that jobs will be coming through. Paying jobs. Soon. In the meantime, take the leap. Jump off that frigging train before it runs you over. Okay, so I mixed the metaphor. Who cares."

Forty-Two

Milwaukee, Wisconsin

Despite Cate's assurances, I can't bring myself to jump off a moving train. That's one step too scary. Instead, I land on the idea of a sabbatical. Unpaid. So, if things don't work out in Zimbabwe, I have a safety net. It doesn't take long for my department chair and the dean to approve it. They like things that don't cost the university anything.

And it doesn't take me long to arrange the rest of my life.

My car. Amie is very happy to take it off my hands for the next year.

My house. Furnished. That's what sublets are for.

The final item on my to-do list I leave until the last minute: calling my mother. She's never been a fan of my far-flung travel for work, especially to southern Africa. *It's too dangerous!* I just know she'll work herself into a frenzy and try to talk me out of going. Not that it's ever worked before, but she always makes me feel guilty. Still, I do want her to know where in the world I am.

Forty-Three

Hwange National Park, Zimbabwe – July 2024

Outside on the broad concrete stoop serving as our porch, I curl up in my favorite wicker chair. It's chilly this morning—I should go back inside and get my puffer jacket. But I stay where I am, my fingers wrapped around the mug of coffee Colin just handed me. He sits on the chair next to mine, and together we watch the sun crest the treetops on the far side of the rhino sanctuary. Homer was right when he described the rosy-colored fingers of dawn. Twenty feet in front of us, two white rhino bulls stand flank to flank. Best buddies, they're never far away from each other. Everyone thought it would be good to bring the two of them together, that it would make their move easier. Transporting them here was quite the celebration, generating a lot of excitement in each of the villages our caravan passed through—all of which I captured in the short film I made. But to be honest, now that the boys are here, we're worried. Neither one is eating well. They're not playing. They're not flourishing. For a while, they didn't even want to come out of the small enclosure that's located on the other side of the trees.

This last week, though, the boys finally emerged from their shelter and have been hanging around our small cottage. Every morning, we've been waking to find new hoofprints in the sand. Now, this morning, here they are, waiting for us. Even though rhinos are very nearsighted and probably can't see us, these two boys definitely know we're here. And to prove it, the smaller boy gently pokes the larger with the tip of his horn—the keratin horn that would net poachers a lot of money. Hence the Cobras are a vital part of this whole operation. Twenty-four seven.

In front of the stand of acacias, one of the three Cobras currently on patrol, his AR-15 slung over his shoulder, waves at us. But only for a moment. Having observed the one rhino poke his buddy, he opens his notebook and jots down this new behavior. The Cobras record everything.

Colin leans close to me. "Recognize him?"

I squint into the sun. "No. Should I?"

"That's Tracker. At least that's what Gus called him. His name's Orlando. A good man. I can see him becoming the leader of the Cobras in another year or so."

"Seriously? But what about you?"

He takes a sip of coffee. "Don't get me wrong, this is a great job. But it was only ever for the short term. I was hired to recruit and train these guys—make them into Cobras. The powers that be wanted my experience from when I was in special forces. The goal has always been for one of the Cobras to take over the rhino project and run it for the benefit of the local villages."

"And you think Orlando's the man to do it? Even though he was recruiting poachers for Gus?"

"I do. Yes, he worked for Gus, but he's now absolutely

committed to protecting the rhinos. More than that, this job has transformed his life. And elevated his status in the village. Kids look up to him now. They talk about wanting to grow up to be a scout like him."

"Being a Cobra's a big deal, huh?"

"It is."

"So, if Orlando takes over the Cobras next year, what will you do? Stay in Zimbabwe?"

"Hard to say. If there's something on offer, I'll consider it. But for now . . . I'm here." He takes another sip of coffee. "Speaking of jobs, have you decided what's next?"

One-handing my mug, I pick up the contract resting on my lap. "The BBC. A documentary on big cats in Kruger. I'll be camera number two. A no-brainer, don't you think?" I'd sure like to line up a few more jobs while I'm here. Preferably as camera number one.

In front of us, the two rhinos butt heads, then turn and race across the grassy plain toward the far corner of the sanctuary. Orlando runs behind them. Another Cobra hurries fast on his heels. Thrumming with excitement, I lean forward to watch. This is the most activity we've seen from the boys since they arrived. A turning point?

Five minutes later, Orlando radios Colin. "They are at the mud patch next to the water hole, boss." Even though Colin insists the Cobras don't need to call him 'boss,' they all do anyway.

"And what are they doing?" Colin prompts. For weeks, he's been trying to train the guys to tell him the most important information first, instead of holding back.

"*Yebo!* Now they are rolling. A good wallow."

I let myself exhale. "This is huge!"

"It is." Colin shoots me a super seductive grin. "Come on!"

"We're going to the mud wallow?" I don't want to scare the boys, not on their first foray, and too many observers will do exactly that.

"Nah." He pulls me to my feet. "They can have the mud. We're using the shower."

"A good way to conserve water," I say coyly.

"A good way for me to convince you to come back after the Kruger shoot."

I smile. "You think you can? Convince me, I mean."

"I'll give it my all."

THE END

Glossary

Zimbabwe has sixteen official languages, including Shona, English, and Ndebele. I've used some Ndebele words and phrases in *The Women Who Stand Between*, and although most of the time the meaning can be gleaned from the context, I've listed below the Ndebele-English translations.

Baba mkhulu (also seen elsewhere as uBaba Umkhulu)—paternal grandfather

CITES—an anagram for the Convention on International Trade in Endangered Species of Flora and Fauna, an international agreement that regulates trade in endangered species to prevent their over-exploitation

Gukurahundi—A series of mass killings, rapes, and genocides in Zimbabwe which were committed from 1983 until the Unity Accord in 1987 in which thousands of Ndebele were killed. The name derives from a Shona language term which loosely translates to "the early rain which washes away the chaff before the spring rains"

Hamba kahle—goodbye, go well

Indumba—a small, round sacred healing hut; a hut where ancestors are believed to reside

Linjani—How are you?

Marula—a tree with fruit that elephants love to eat, especially the fermented fruit

Mbalala—bushbuck

Msasa—the leaves of this tree medicate elephants who've
    overindulged on marula tree fruit
Sadza—a traditional food made of cornmeal and often served
    with a vegetable or meat relish
Sahle kahle—goodbye, stay well
Sangoma—a healer, seer
Sawubona—hello; literally: I see you and by seeing you, bring
    you into being
Scud—a very strong, homemade beer in large plastic bottles
    resembling the scud missiles
Shebeen—a bar, often a private club
Siyabonga—we give thanks, thank you
Yebo—yes, but it's also a catchall expression meaning at
    various times: right, I agree

Book Club Questions

1. As Julia's friend, Cate Darlington plays an important role throughout the novel. Explain her relationship to Julia.
2. Graduate student and intern Amie Raffelock develops in ways that surprise Julia. Describe how Amie changes during the course of the novel.
3. After the light-wing aircraft crash, Julia, Hal, Tonderai, and the Mambas search for survivors. Julia and one of the Mambas spot something metallic and shiny in the tall grass. What is the object and why is it important to the story?
4. Who is Gus Sinclair and why does he want to stop Julia from making her film?
5. The novel opens with a scene of lions surrounding a large parade of elephants at a water hole. What is the significance of this scene and other animal scenes throughout the book?
6. Julia tells Cate that she's "off men." Why isn't she interested in a romantic relationship?
7. How would you describe the relationship between Julia and Colin Tremblay?
8. In what ways is *sangoma* Solomon Mkhwanansi important to the novel?
9. The Mambas are the women who stand between. What kind of women become Mambas? How do they "stand between"?
10. How does the making of the film *The Women Who Stand Between* parallel Julia's life?
11. What is the significance of trees in the novel?

Acknowledgements

I first visited Zimbabwe many years ago and promptly fell in love with the people, the parks, and the animals. To be sure, the country has faced challenges, one of which is the poaching of endangered wildlife. As the characters in *The Women Who Stand Between* well know, poaching is a complex problem, and solutions are complicated. Numerous Zimbabwean organizations have risen to meet this challenge. The Black Mambas empower African women to protect wildlife. Imvelo's Water4Wildlife Trust cultivates eco-tourism to strengthen communities and promote conservation. Their male COBRA scouts and now female Cheetah scouts protect endangered wildlife. I have been privileged to walk with elephants and rhinos through Hwange National Park and to photograph these magnificent animals. I have been honored to visit rural villages and schools. Thank you to Butch, Hannah, Sibs, Vusa, Eric, Dabs, Harris, John, and Lovey for guiding me through a country I love.

Every author I know talks about writing being a solitary act. True, but I couldn't create without my writer friends who listen and listen and listen, helping me find my way through the maze. Thank you to Rochelle Melander, Darlene Junker, and Valerie Biel.

My beta readers. Just when I think I've finished, these are the people who say, "Not so fast!" First and foremost, Roi Solberg read every word of *The Women Who Stand Between* more times than I care to admit and helped enormously when I wrote myself up a tree. Nancy Backes' great authorial insight alerted me to key moments needing more development. Jennifer Rupp helped with all things theatrical and the elements of romance. Amie Gronert pinpointed a major flaw in my main character and let me borrow her name and her own playlist to use for character Amie. India McCanse provided critical feedback for an important secondary character who comes close to stealing every scene she's in. Thanks to Stephanie Raffelock for letting me borrow her last name. And Hannah Tranter was the most incredible resource, giving me crucial information about Ndebele language and culture, the National Zimbabwe Police, white rhinos, rangers, scouts, guns, and so much more.

Myriad thanks to Orange Hat Publishing and Ten16 Press for creating yet another beautiful book. It is a joy to work with editor-in-chief Michael Braun, whose keen narrative eye brought this book and these characters to life. His chapter heading graphics take me immediately to southern Africa—perhaps my favorite place in the world. As always, working with editor Lauren Blue makes my heart sing; she knows exactly how to make a story soar—from commas and dashes to catching my oft-repeated words and making me dig deep. Designer Kaeley Dunteman-Stiefvater and Dana Breunig created cover art that conveys Zimbabwe in all its glory.

A special thanks to the readers who enjoyed the Annie Hawkins Series. I hope you find Julia Wilde's adventures as intriguing. Thanks also to libraries and bookstores, book clubs and bookstagrammers—rock stars all.

As always, thanks to my husband Michael Briselli for

traveling with me time and again to Zimbabwe, where we've photographed elephants and lions, wild dogs and cheetahs, rhinos and lilac-breasted rollers and bateleur eagles.

Photo © Agnieszka Tropiło

A former university professor, Jeannée Sacken is now a photo-journalist who travels to the ends of the earth, documenting the lives of women and children. She also photographs wildlife and is deeply committed to the conservation of endangered species. Described by *MKE Lifestyle* magazine as "Indiana Jones with a camera," Jeannée has summitted Mt. Kilimanjaro, canoed the Zambezi River, kayaked the North Pacific, and driven through far-western Mongolia in a blizzard. Many of her adventures have been fictionalized into her novels. Her debut novel, *Behind the Lens*, the first book in the Annie Hawkins Series, has won numerous awards, including the 2021 American Writing Awards Novel of the Year and the Hawthorne Prize. *The Rule of Thirds*, the third book in the series, won the Killer Nashville 2024 Silver Falchion Award for Best Suspense and the 2023 Literary Global Award for Novel of the year, among other prizes. Follow Jeannée at jeanneesacken.com.